The Pachinko Girl

by Vann Chow

Tokyo Faces Series

"Hell and heaven are the hearts of men."

Japanese proverb.

Hokkaido
Northern Sea Circuit
Sapporo
Honshu
Main Island
Tokyo
Shikoku
Four Kingdoms
Kyushu
Nine Provinces

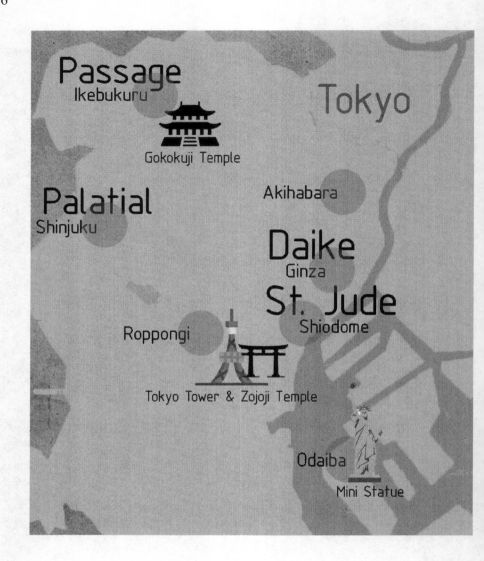

Prologue

"You know what, *Sumisu*-san, you're the first *Sumisu* I've ever met." Mr. Uchida slid his food tray next to Smith's. "Welcome to our company. Welcome to Japan!" He gave Smith a hearty slap on the back as encouragement.

"Thank you," Smith replied with a smile.   He held up his knife to cut into the *Tonkatsu* on his plate, but he decided that this was as good an opportunity as any to raise a question he'd had in the back of his mind since that morning, the first day of his external business assignment in Japan. Smith lowered his knife again. "I can't help noticing that you're all calling me *Sumisu*," Smith replied. "I"m a regular Smith. Sh-mith. It came from the German word, Schmidt, so technically, it would be fine to end it with the 't' sound. But to add a 'Sue' to it is really a misnomer."

"I know your name. *Sumisu* is one of the most popular Western names in Japan. If there's a *Gaijin* in a movie, or a play, or dialogue in a language textbook, he would be a *Sumisu*," Mr. Uchida explained as he sat himself down on the plastic chair. His eyes fixated on the whipped cream on Smith's apple strudel. "You're of German descent? Many Japanese are fascinated by German cultures. Your colleagues would be thrilled to know that," he mused.

"Well, uh, yeah. I don't know any of that," Smith contemplated the historical implications of the Japanese admiration for the Germans. He sliced into the *Tonkatsu*. Steam rose from the deep-fried pork cutlet sliced open in front of him, quickly fogging his glasses. In the time that had elapsed before his glasses regained clarity, Smith had decided that the *Tonkatsu* looked uncannily like a Viennese Schnitzel.

"It might sound a little strange, *Sumisu*-san, but I have to tell you this:

meeting a real *Sumisu* for the first time in my life excites me," Mr. Uchida had bunched the paper napkin in his hand as he spoke. "It's almost like meeting your pen pal from childhood for the first time."

"Really?" Smith squinted his eyes as he listened to his colleague's unfounded admiration for him. He decided that it was best to focus his mind on the challenging task of leaving as little crumbs on the plate as possible.

"I have always imagined what *Sumisu* looks like. I think most Japanese do, because we hear so much about him, everywhere," Mr. Uchida explained his overt interest in the simple subject of Smith's last name. "*Sumisu* could really be anyone's imagination. I'm glad mine doesn't deviate too far from the real thing," Mr. Uchida said. He had now turned his head toward Smith and was appraising him as if he were a priceless antique.

Albeit his will to fight it, the exchange had made Smith uncomfortable. The fact that Smith was such a commonly known Western surname in Japan that any foreigner was essentially a Smith to them did not sit well with him.

"God, what strange ways you lead us to question our existence," Smith thought.

***

Misa Hayami got off the metro at Ginza. Tens of taxis lined the streets when she arrived at the ground-level even at lunch time. She covered her mouth with the back of her hand as she crossed the streets towards the financial district where DaiKe was located. Hundreds of big national and international companies had set up shop in Ginza, an internationally famous business district that many considered as the Wall Street of Tokyo, the heart of the city, and perhaps even of the entire country. Most of the people whose name was on Misa's list worked in one of the headquarters of the advertising, real-estate, insurance, investment or trading companies here.

Around her, busy salarymen, as they aptly called these businessmen in Japan, were pouring out of their offices onto the streets, each hurrying to their next destinations respectively with enthusiasm. Some were heading to lunch meetings with clients. Some were heading to the noodle bar for a quick bite, and some, to reunite with their mistresses for an urban rendezvous. Men, and women too, nowadays, who worked in the offices of these incredibly tall and magnificent commercial buildings overlooking the Hibiya park in Ginza, were the elites of the countries. They were one of the most unfathomable groups of people for a country girl like Misa who grew up in the mountainous area of Northern Japan.

It was her dream to live in Tokyo, to live among these people whose dazzling, glamorous and exciting lifestyles intrigued her ever since she had visited Tokyo with her mother when she was young.

Misa touched the pendant hanging off her silver necklace from Tiffany's and thought of her mother. One of her clients had given it to her for her birthday, something that she would not be able to afford in a million years, and swapped the pendant with the one she got from her mother's leftover jewelry she inherited after her death. To use the word 'inherit' seemed inappropriate, because her mother was a very frugal woman and she had barely anything to her name when she died, except for the one big secret.

This Mr. Mura she was about to meet privately for the first time was a big shot in the metal trading company DaiKe. Even though she had looked up all the public records and pried as much as possible into his personal life from people around him, Misa still felt incredibly nervous and unprepared. A previous client had introduced them to each other, as these connections tended to happen strictly only through private introductions, and Misa could not have felt luckier, but it also meant that she had to behave and please in a certain way such that she won't offend anyone in the long chain of connections.

There were a lot of names on her list, and she had already spent three years going through them. There were just a few of them left now, and she felt the ending to be close. Perhaps today was the day when she could finally get close to the truth of what really, actually happened to her cousin and best friend Misaki, with whom she shared a nickname, sans all the bullshit that the police and the doctors told her.

Misa found a spot to sit down once she entered the lobby of the building, waiting for Mr. Mura to come down. There were hundreds of people coming in and out of the entrance every minute, and she felt no qualm to show her face there, even though she was practically a call-girl. Her age might make her look more like someone's daughter bringing forgotten lunchboxes for their fathers, though, she mused.

"Hey, Misa!" A twenty-something year old American man entered her vision. *He was…what was his name again?* They had met previously in the maid café where she worked briefly. This man was one of her 'Masters'.

"What are you doing here? I heard you quit! That's a pity. I love that place, and I love seeing you there. You don't recognize me, do you? I'm Andy."

Misa blushed. She felt caught, but she also knew the only thing she could do now was to compose herself and not make things any worse. She bowed and gave him the sweetest smile she could muster.

Instead of walking straight past her towards the exit as Misa had hoped, Andy sat next to her and whispered a question in her ear. "Who are you meeting here? Your boyfriend?" He looked curious around for young men that might be it.

"*I-eh, i-eh*, no," Misa shook her head and said, because she hadn't had a boyfriend for a very long time. In fact, not since he was, quiet unfortunately, murdered. "I'm here for something else…"

"For work?" Andy frowned. For a girl like her, there were only so many things she could do to make the money that afforded her all her fancy outfits in Tokyo, Andy observed.

"*I-eh, i-eh*, no," Misa denied that too. What she does for a living has nothing to do with this man. She might have called him 'Master' a few times, made his tea, brought him food, and kept him entertained during the meal, but everything was just an act. Everything, in fact, in Misa's life here in Tokyo, was just an act.

"Hey! Cars!" Andy spotted his buddy walking passed them coming out of the canteen with Mr. Uchida. He beckoned the man over. "Let me introduce a friend to you. This is Misa. Misa, this is Carson, but everyone calls him by his last name Smith around here."

Smith raised his eyebrows slightly, unaccustomed to how Andy's womanizing ways even showed itself in the workplace. Andy always had women to introduce to him, but never the kind that brought him business deals.

For politeness sake, Smith reached out to shake the girl's hand. Yes, she was only a girl, barely of age, he noticed. She was very beautiful, but dressed up too mature for her age.

"Nice to meet you," he said, not really giving a damn.

"Nice to meet you, too, Smith-san," Misa placed her hand in his and received a hearty squeeze. Her hand was unusually cold, and his unusually warm. The sensation of their touching hands activated something in their brains, although they hadn't quite understood what that was themselves. Their eyes locked for what felt like an eternity, and it stirred up ripples on the long-dead pools of emotions within them.

Destinies could not be avoided or altered, the Japanese says.

1. Pachinko Parlor

There was no place in Ikebukuro, Tokyo at 10 PM every night like this enormous Pachinko parlor called the *Passage*. Recently renovated, this massive gambling establishment could easily be mistaken for a ladies' department store by the unknowing eyes of the foreigners. Its blazing fluorescent white-light lit entrance and grandiose lobby were lit by two to three hundred equally as intense light bulbs all cleverly arranged on the ceiling and behind the translucent floorboards to direct all the stumbling pedestrians from the relative gloominess of the outside world to the top of the staircase where the gambling activities were concentrated. It was a living entity, convulsing with violent laughter and angry cries over a collage of noises coming from the Pachinko slot machines. As if vying for attention, the pre-recorded voices of young females, seemingly from the under-clad cartoon characters depicted on the cover of the plastic light boxes of the machine, grew ever more high-pitched and pushy when too much time had gone by in idleness after the last customer left, full-handed or empty-handed. With the shrewdness of jealous girlfriends in their choice of words to seduce their married lovers into the endless abyss of disloyalty and ensuing unhappy divorces, the internal computer of these Pachinkos would carefully select new sales pitches based on the length of its idle time and the weight of the reservoir where all the pinballs were collected. Eventually, they would be rewarded by the pinball that pushed through the plastic flaps at the inserting slots and be triggered into a frenzy activated mode consisting of even more shrill sales pitches and blinking tiny light bulbs arranged on the upright panels in a diamond or heart shape. They would greet the white-collar man who, typically, either had too much to drink or too heavy a briefcase to carry to continue on his search for the lucky machine of the night. Enticed by the comfort of the worn out leather stool before a particular machine that seemed to forebode a great conclusion to his lonesome, trying day at work, the man would try his luck.

Among these cheerless men, only occasionally stirred to irritation by the clanking sound of steel balls pouring out in an enviously large quantity into the winning buckets of their lucky yet despicable neighbors, was an American in his fifties sporting a wrinkly gray suit. It was Carson Smith. A bottle of half-empty Lipovitan, a well-known brand of energy drink that was even more well known for its aphrodisiac effects, in his hand, he inserted the 387th ball of the night into the same machine he had been playing for the past hour and a half. He habitually murmured under his breath the part of the Lord's Prayer that said 'Give us today our daily bread' multiple times in quick succession. The pinball dropped through the panel making various jingly noises as it hit the barriers on its way down. Smith dabbed his sweaty forehead nervously with the sleeves of his suit as his eyes glued painstakingly onto the ball watching it cascade downwards under the force of gravity and pure chance. He had a good feeling in his gut. "This is it. This is it!" He whispered to himself. He followed the fall of the ball so intently that he scooted off his leather stool and anchored both of his arms on the two sides of the screen to support his body weight leaning forward in anticipation for the revelation of his fate. His change of posture was so dramatic that the people surrounding him, paused their games momentarily to watch him and see how his game turned out. Even the girl who was serving drinks in the parlor had stopped dead in her tracks to watch as she passed by on her way back to the workstation. When the ball slipped through the lowest pair of flippers, a collective gasp was to be heard in the vicinity of Smith's Pachinko machine. However, in a quarter of a second, it transformed itself into a collective sigh as the ball fell into the zero bucket at the bottom making an almost inaudible, ominous ping.

"Chikuso!" Smith slapped his sweaty palm on the glass panel in frustration. Then he sighed. As far as he could remember, he had never been lucky anyway. Since there were only about 15 balls left in his coin cup from the four hundred he bought at the beginning of the night, he decided that there was no better time to leave. At least he had not lost everything. *"Knowing when is the right time to leave,"* he said to himself, *"is the true wisdom of life."*

Certainly, one would argue that he should never have gone into the parlor in the first place if he was indeed a wise man and could otherwise avoid wasting 5000 Yen in a matter of hours. However, to be honest, he had nothing else better to do on a Friday night like this when life left him on his own accord. It was a rare and peaceful night with no work to catch up, no company activities to attend, no customers to *settai* or entertain before the signing of contracts, and no late-night phone calls from the Americans to answer on the Friday before Thanksgiving weekend. He had looked forward to this empty slot in his schedule for about two months now, and he was hell bent on making use of this precious personal time to recuperate. Perhaps he would meet a nice Japanese woman and have a whirlwind love affair with her. Now that the weekend had arrived, however, he realized that he did not really have anything particularly enriching or relaxing to fill his schedule with, nor was he shameless enough to risk embarrassing himself in front of the opposite sex, whom he didn't know where to meet to begin with, and certainly not with his broken Japanese. What could he even say to them? *"Konichiwa. Watashi wa Smith desu. Hajimemashite. Ima hima?"* Good afternoon. My name is Smith. Very nice to meet you. Are you free now?

The last time he used that phrase was to a thirty something year old Japanese woman reading a *Time Magazine* in a small coffee shop by his office building about a year and a half ago. It was when he'd first transferred to Japan, and he was not even thinking of hitting on her. It was just one of those moments on a nice day when you want to make small talk with people, and it did not really matter whom it was with. Noting that she was reading an American news magazine, he thought they might be able to perhaps make a simple conversation in English after the initial introduction phase in Japanese. They didn't even go beyond that, though. In reply to his uninvited disruption, she only shot him a look of disgust and continued reading her magazine as if he was invisible, which made him extremely uncomfortable. After that, he was terrified of Japanese women, except his own secretary at work who was always courteous to him even though he suspected that it was only because he was her boss. Japanese women, in his opinion, turned out to be far more capable of inflicting pain on men due to the sheer improbability that a simple facial gesture they made could mean so much more than the abusive language of women, much better in size, in his home country.

And it wasn't like he had someone to go home to either. His family, an ex-wife and two already married kids of twenty-five and twenty-eight, were miles away in Ohio. If he was to go back home today as he secretly yearned, he doubted that anyone would welcome him in the greatly dramatized ceremonious way the 'Priceless' Visa commercials used to portray a family reunion to be — the reunion, in reality, was often much less sympathetic and much more frightening. His wife had filed divorce six months ago while he was in Japan. The possibility of his wife being dissatisfied with him after so many years of peaceful domestic life together was such a distant thought that he reserved the next flight homeward the same day he received the notice from her lawyer, thinking that it was only a misunderstanding. As it turned out, it was not. He begged, and he pleaded. He admitted to everything she accused him of and apologized in the most heartwarming fashion any living man could ever perform. *"But why don't you let me go?"* His wife said, however, *"We had stopped loving each other since years ago,"* and dispelled any notion that she might even consider withdrawing the case. She talked about their extinguished love with such conviction that Smith, usually dexterous in business negotiation, was absolutely dumbfounded. He knew it would not matter that he proved her wrong by showing how much he still loved her because she had apparently stopped loving him. And he was disinterested to know when exactly that had happened. He had always listened to his wife. He thought he could listen to her one last time. And so quietly, he left the house, suitcases completely untouched in the back of his Volkswagen and drove back to the airport the next morning while his wife was sound asleep in the bedroom, exhausted from the previous night of debate. So here he was, alone in Tokyo, the true City that Never Sleeps, located on the east side of Honshu Island, drowning in pain among twelve million Japanese people on a Friday night with nothing to do and nowhere to go.

As he had exhausted his wallet after the 387th game and was feeling kind of lethargic, he pulled his coin bucket out from the cup holder and dragged himself up to leave. His feet had grown numb from hours of sitting in the office and then the Pachinko parlor making him stagger. As he stood there trying to wait for the sensation of his two legs to come back to him, he glanced around him. The Japanese men that had once curiously turned their heads away from their own games to watch his had resumed theirs and became immediately absorbed into their own world that nobody seemed to even have time to give his bad fortune a second thought, let alone a compassionate grunt. Knowing that he would not get much sympathy out of this crowd, he took a deep breath, sucking in the bitter, invisible insults underlying the stolid atmosphere of the parlor. He regretted it, however, when the thick scent of second-hand cigarette smoke mixed with the sourness of his own sweat hit his senses. He slowly stumbled towards the staircase, pouring the rest of the steel balls into a losing fellow's coin cup on his way out.

Only when the sliding glass doors opened did he realized it was a huge mistake not to take more interest in Japanese television. It was pouring outside, and he did not bring an umbrella with him.

"What a fabulous country!" He threw his hands up in dismay and yelled sarcastically to the salarymen around as they slipped past him to leave. From his sour expression, they did not need to know English to understand what he said. The face of self-pity was universally understood.

2. St. Jude

"What's it that you want this time?" Doctor Hasegawa said to the girl without looking up from the medical report he was finishing from his previous patient. He had a lot of ad hoc appointments today at the St. Jude Hospital.

"You should have just visited me at home, instead of coming here," the doctor suggested, although he knew the girl would never visit him on her own accord if it wasn't an emergency. And his clinic, the Emergency Psychiatric Department at St. Jude was often abused by young people as an oblique but legal source to obtain non-vital recreational medications.

Misa pulled out her diary and flipped it open to the page on which she had jotted some notes about today in shorthand. "I visited the DaiKe Company today, in Ginza."

The doctor was usually uninterested in what Misa was reporting to him about her childish investigation down the lists of 'suspects' in her cousin's diary. Her cousin, also her best friend, had drowned in an accident three years ago. Convinced that her athletic swimmer of a friend was murdered by one of the men whose name was in her diary, Misa had come to Tokyo to sniff out the true identity of the perpetrator and avenge for her. The doctor knew of course what was behind the girl's death, but he had made up his mind never to share it with anyone. Nothing good could ever come out of digging up the past.

But when the doctor heard the company name DaiKe, it hit a nerve. He knew he had to thread carefully from now on, instead of dismissing Misa's theory as the baseless delirium of the vengeful that sees conspiracy everywhere, for Misa had actually come dangerously close to the people at the center of the case.

"Give me one second." The doctor shut the patient report and went out of the room to give nurse Umeko in the next room the report so she could enter everything into the computer. When he returned shortly, he locked the door behind him, not wanting to be disturbed.

"So, you were saying you went to DaiKe?"

"Yes. And I met with this Mr. Mura from the New Business Department," Misa showed Doctor Hasegawa's Mura's business card. The doctor looked at it as apathetically as he could before Misa put it away. He had already memorized the information on it, of course.

"How'd it go?"

"Good. He trusts me." Misa didn't want to have to explain exactly what happened between Mura and her after he had brought her to his spare apartment in the company's dormitory. The gist of the story was that he trusted her enough now that she knew she would eventually be awarded with the privilege to ask more question and probe around his social circle for information. "He invited me to a drinks party next week," Misa related the news to the doctor, who nodded dispassionately.

"Great. I guess that's what you want, isn't it?"

"Yes." Misa was determined to finish the path that she had started three years ago. She would find out what had really happened to her best friend very soon, as this Mr. Mura was one of the most frequently appearing name on the diary, albeit very difficult to get connected to. But she had finally made it.

"Perhaps it is true that all the names in Misaki's diary are linked in some way, that they were colluding on something sinister, but Misaki's death was an accident. She drowned in a filming set. We have looked at the death certificate the county sent over together."

"It couldn't have been so simple," Misa said. "She was an excellent swimmer. It made no sense."

"Perhaps she was under the influence of some form of hallucinogens," Hasegawa said. "It's not as if you didn't know she was living and working with the drug addict of a boyfriend at the time, making these grotesque arthouse movies together."

"Sergey…" Misa had trouble saying his name out loud after all these times. "Sergey was not a drug addict. He uses them occasionally, but he w…"

"It's okay," Hasegawa stopped her. "I know the two of you were together before Misaki stole him from you. — Think of it this way. If she hadn't done it, the person on set that day might be you."

Misa lowered her head in silence. The doctor was right. His alternative scenario was actually the original plan. She would be the girl in Sergey's movie had her cousin not visited them and stole Sergey from her. She loved her, but she hated her so much at the same time.

If she hadn't asked Misaki to come visit them in Tokyo, then she would never have met Sergey. She would surely have gone to the university by now, instead of becoming the muse in Sergey's life, like Edie Sedgwick was to Andy Warhol. She would have been his muse. Misaki wouldn't have gotten into the accident and Sergey wouldn't have killed himself out of guilt. It was all too late now.

"I know you feel guilty about her death, but it's hardly your fault."

"No," Misa retorted. "That is not it. There is something else. I just can't quite put my finger to it. Sergey liked Misaki, but to die for her? I don't believe it!"

The doctor stood up and walked behind Misa's back. She looked up curiously at what he was going to do.

"I know I can't talk you out of it. Just be careful out there, and know that you're not on your own. Let me know if you need any help," he said. Presently the doctor placed his hands on her shoulders and started to massage them.

"Sure," Misa replied the doctor curtly, so that the tremble in her voice would go undetected by the doctor whose fingers were now grabbing the muscles on her stiff and sore shoulders.

The doctor was the only 'friend' she had in the city after both Misaki and Sergey died. He was her mother's old doctor, an ex-lover, and most possibly the man who fathered her, but she didn't know for sure.

Even though Misa was ready to be touched by other men on her list in return for their trusts so she could exploit them for information, just as they had exploited her body for carnal pleasures, she was very repulsive of the idea of being touched by this particular man who could have been her father. The amorous physical contact, however innocent it might have been in the doctor's view disgusted her, knowing that he had probably likened herself to her mother, when she was just as pretty and young as she was now when they met almost twenty years ago. But she had learnt not to complain, not yet, for as long as he was useful to her. Suddenly she felt the doctor's hand slid dangerously down her back.

Not again, Misa thought. She didn't like this at all.

"I need some pills," Misa snapped and turned around to look at the doctor in the eyes, peeling herself from the doctor's wandering hands.

The doctor frowned, upset at the repulsive image that Misa's request had brought forth.

"What pills?" He asked, even though he knew what she was talking about. "Don't you already have your usual medications?"

"No, I want the same ones you let me took a year ago." Misa expression was unwavering. She had learnt to act tough and live sly, being the sheep among beasts and men worse than beasts in the big city. A simple country girl wouldn't be able to survive here, but Misa would. She was determined and unafraid.

A year ago when Misa had come to borrow some money from him, overcame by a wave of nostalgia and medication, the doctor, also an addict himself although he hid it very well, had mistaken Misa for her mother Rika, and tried to make love to her — or at least that was the doctor's sorry explanation for his atrocious behavior. Misa protested, but she was so torn by the different warring emotions — her deference for the doctor, her dependence on him financially and socially here in Tokyo, her pity for him, and her most secret, most nonsensical, irrational curiosity to know how it would feel like to make love to different men — to make up her mind in time. Before she had figured out what to do, the doctor had taken his liberty with her.

The doctor, realizing the severity of what he had done, had prescribed her a heavy dose of emergency contraceptives and told her to go home and douche herself immediately. Misa still remembered the shock and the hate she felt towards the man every time she thought of the incident. She had gulped down a bunch of these pills in his clinic, her legs and arms still shaking from the incident, and yet she had to listen to the doctor in order to save herself from further misfortune. It was the kind of insult that was so grave and so dehumanizing that had made Misa utterly impervious to emotions now. It was as if an arsonist who started a fire in your house in the middle of the night but decided to save your life in a strange twist of fate, and you couldn't help but lose your senses of right and wrong after the incident.

"You can't go on like this," the doctor hissed, angered by what Misa's demand for contraceptive meant. "You have always had a weak immune system and what you're doing now is very dangerous."

"I've told you many times," Misa said, "I don't need your approval. I only need your support." One day, Misa hoped, she wouldn't need him at all.

"You have my unrelenting support, whatever it is that you want to achieve with it. I've promised your mother to take care of you."

"I know," Misa said. Of course she knew. That was why she was here every time she was in trouble. The doctor was tired of cleaning up after her, but he could only continue, in order to protect both his daughter and his own reputation at the same time. They were both precious to him.

The doctor sighed and wrote a prescription for Progestin for Misa. Later he would have to go back to Misa's medical report and make up a list of symptoms for depression in order to get this prescription for synthetic hormone undetected by the auditors. After all, he only had access to psychiatric medications, although chemically they could do a lot more than commonly thought.

"Don't forget this," he pushed a white envelope with thousand Yen bills in it across the table. It was Misa's monthly allowance. "Quit your odd jobs and come study in the university. You know I can get you in. You only need to say yes." The doctor had asked Misa to help around at the medical laboratory before, and she had shown talents.

"Maybe someday." Misa picked up the pack of money and put them in her handbag. "*Jigan-ga-nai*, I don't have the time now," she said.

Like what Misa said, she didn't have time now nor would she would ever have time later. In fact, every minute she was alive was borrowed.

Misa was born with a genetic disease called the Williams Syndrome. It ailed the mountainous people from up North, a defect of their gene pools, so it was said. Her cousin Misaki had it, too. Many others affected with it had already passed and soon it would be her turn.

Just like them, Misa would be seized by an erratic heart and die from a sudden heart attack one day. She did not mind the prospect, because the alternative was that she would have to endure a slow grueling way to die from failure of her vital organs one by one, like some did. Different doctors had prepared her and her parents of the possibility since she was young. But by fifteen, she realized that she had enough of being scared. Instead of being paralyzed by fear and wait for her turn to die, she would do things, she wanted to see the world. That was why she was here in Tokyo in the first place. What happened afterwards was the most unfortunate, but it gave her a reason to live. She was determined to use the remaining of her time on earth to do one last thing, to avenge for her cousin, and all those she had ever loved, all those people who was wronged without them knowing why.

"Misa, listen to me," Hasegawa said. "You don't want to walk down the same path as your cousin. Things are not so simple as you think here in Tokyo. It's obvious that the list of names in your cousin's diary are names of her clients, and I think you know what kind they were. I don't want you near any of those dirty men. And especially not to sacrifice yourself under some naïve pretense of an investigation!"

"So you want me to stop investigating?" Misa questioned him. "Is it because we were destined to die anyway because of our sickness that our lives were of no importance to you?"

"That's a ridiculous statement you have just made. It's precisely because your well-being is important to me that I want you to stop."

"Then leave me alone," Misa exclaimed. "I'll find out the truth, whatever the means."

3. The Bully

The alarm did not go off as usual at 6:30 AM and Smith only realized this when the hour hand struck seven.

"Ahhh! *Saiyaku!*" He knocked his disloyal digital alarm clock off the bedside table in a rage. It rolled a couple of times on the carpeted floor before coming to a stop under the dressing table. Already late, Smith shot up from the bed trying to get dressed for work as soon as possible. As he did so, however, an unpleasant wave of woozy, dull pain struck him down with such force that he fell to his knees. Bracing his aching head with both hands, he noticed the florescent *SAT* on the alarm clock that was lying on the floor through the gap between his two forearms.

"*U-so!* No way!" It was a Saturday. A nervous-wreck as he was, naturally, he did not choose to believe it so quickly. He pulled apart the curtains of the small bedroom window and peered down at the parking lot three levels down to look for proof. To his surprise, almost all of the parking spots were still occupied, and his colleague, Nakamura-san's Honda, was still parked in its usual spot A-32. Its wheels aligned perfectly parallel to the white painted lines on the two sides of the parking spot. *"U-so!" he said* again. How could he forget! It was *the* weekend. The first weekend he had all to himself for a very long time since he started working there. In his ridiculous looking white-and-gray-striped pajamas, he jumped up and down on his mattress like a kid who just heard school was canceled for the day, with the biggest, brightest and happiest smile on his face until a migraine caught him off guard and pulled him down to the ground again as if a huge WWF fighter had crashed down on him from one corner of the fighting rink. As he lay on his bed rolling in pain, he laughed hysterically at his foolishness. It had scared his wits out of him when he thought he had overslept for work. He could not stop laughing still after a minute has gone by — the aftereffect of a self-induced panic attack.

After the panting had subdued from this early morning shock, clumsily Smith staggered into the narrow kitchen in his shoebox size apartment, provided by his company as a dormitory for single men, and started to rummage through the overhead cabinets for the can of *Gyokuro* green tea he brought back from his Kyoto business trip a couple months back. However, as soon as he found the can, the next few steps of this hangover-morning routine were relatively easy. Smith did it with the efficiency and precision of a machine designed, as if, solely for making tea. He nicked a chuck of green tea the size of a sugar cube from the compressed tea brick inside the can, crushing the tea leaves with technique between his thumb and forefinger as he went and sprinkled them inside the electric kettle with a gentle circular motion, using only his wrist. Deftly, he filled the kettle with tap water and turned the power knob to the third position that said *Medium-High.* Even with his eyes closed, for the wave of nausea had hit him again, he did not have to fumble around for the metal lid of the tea can. He had done this so many times in the one and half year in Japan that he knew exactly where the lid would be sitting already. With a quick sleight of hand, the tea can was resealed and skillfully replaced back into its original location on the cabinet where it was always hidden behind the cheaper, non-medicinal green tea he bought from the super-market downstairs for daily drinking and serving guests.

When the tea was done, Smith drank two cups of it in quick succession. By now, he was already numb to the poignant fragrance of the tea that he had stopped pausing between gulps to savor it lavishly as he used to. He used to be so careful about not wasting any of the *Gyokuro* tea, not only because of how expensive it was but also how good it tasted. Between every gulp, he would let it glide on top of his tongue and roll around his mouth until his taste buds were all fully saturated with the refreshing flavor of it. Then slowly, he would let the tea trickled down his throat, tickling it with a nice, warm sensation, which he liked so much, before swallowing everything. Now, he only saw it as a headache remedy, no more and no less. Almost immediately, his head had stopped throbbing and his vision cleared up. It happened almost instantly. It made him wonder whether the green tea was curing his hangover or his deprivation of the tea itself. Can one be addicted to tea? The rest of the world certainly was and still is, he thought to himself.

Because he did not own a television, Smith's only way to the outside world — apart from listening to occasional exchanges of news inside the company that was in English, which was minimal because of how few other English-speakers there were and that it was considered impolite to engage in a long conversation in a foreign language in the presence of others who do not understand — was for him to read the *International Herald Tribune*. *The International Herald Tribune* was the global edition of the *New York Times*. There happened to be an article on page 7 about the CEO of the American stainless steel supplier and manufacturing company, Wesley and Sons, with whom he went to school with back in the days. Apparently, Gregory H. Wesley had filed, on the day before the Thanksgiving Thursday, for a legal separation with his wife Marian Wesley after 28 years of marriage. Wesley, at 55 years old, and his wife, 52, who had two grown sons together, both agreed that their marital relationship had become incompatible, and they were reported to be living separate and apart for years already. According to the report, Wesley, the fifth generation of the Wesley family, had agreed to evenly split their properties and assets, including shares of Wesley and Sons.

Then on page 21 of the same newspaper in the Discussion section, Smith found another article concerning the Wesley's divorce, speculating the real reasons behind the split of the couple. According to it, there were rumors that Wesley was having an affair with a much younger and more attractive woman thirty years his junior. Many who sighted the couple believed the woman to be an ex-*Playboy* model who went by the name of Ashantia whose photograph was also displayed on the paper. Rumor had it that Greg had met her through a friend of a friend who invited him to a huge corporate party staffed with bunny girls as 'facilitators'.

At that point, Smith put down the paper on the table and let out a sigh. He already knew the rest of the story. This kind of things happened all the time in Japan. The only difference between having an affair here and having an affair there was that the American men would always end up losing half of his estate, while Japanese men would only earn more respect from their subordinates. Having an affair with a beautiful, younger woman was a sign of prowess and affluence. Their wives at home, as if collectively educated by rulebooks distributed nationally on 'proper' marriage etiquette, would turn a blind eye on their disloyalty quietly.

Still, seeing news like that amazed him because he and Greg were acquaintances from way back. Greg was such a pitiful wimp when they were still in *St. Luke's* together as far as he could recall. He could not imagine why anyone would be attracted to Greg at all. Everyone at school knew that he was going to inherit some kind of family business, but judging from the emaciated look on his face and his scrawny body, nobody thought that he would inherit anything more than a puny little corner pharmacy where he could have access to endless supplies of Parker's Pain Relief Cream, which he would certainly need from all abuses he took in school. Then after they graduated, Greg went to *Yale*, and Smith went to *Ohio State*. Greg moved to New York and took over his dad's fledgling material supply business and went on to take his master in business administration in *North Western*. In the years followed, he had managed to turn Wesley and Sons into a multinational company with net sales of 4 billion US dollars, while Smith got kicked out of the *Ohio State Buckeyes* football team for some dilly-dallying he refused to remember, decided that he probably need a real job from then on when he could no longer play football anymore. Smith switched from the Department of Philosophy to Department of Chemistry and became the average salaryman that he was today, working for a company that had business deals with Gregory H. Wesley's, someone he thought many years ago would be the last person in the whole wide world he would have any respect for. Even now when both of them were in the process of divorcing their wives, Greg had to show himself off by flaunting his new found girlfriend in front of the media to make sure that the insulting news would end up in a newspaper that came all the way from New York into his tiny single-man company dormitory in Ikebukuro, Japan for him to see.

Smith sighed again. He felt as if he had heard similar stories before. The wimp at school had grown to become stronger than the bully. By some devious twist of fate, he would pop back into your life years later and take his revenge in the most unimaginable ways, and make sure that you suffered as much, or more than he ever did before. "Where did I hear stories like that from?" Smith asked himself. "Was it from my father? Perhaps from grandpa?" He loathed the thought of being born into a family of losers.

4. The Emergency

It was 3 PM in the afternoon when the sudden onset of Mozart's Piano Sonata in C Minor from his cell phone shook him out of his afternoon stupor. His anxiety level always heightened whenever his cell phone rang outside of the office because he would have to risk making a fool of himself with his limited Japanese when his secretary was not around to help. Luckily, a quick glance at the front display revealed the caller to be Andy Wilkinson; an American colleague sent over from the States on a one-year assignment three years ago who still hadn't got sent back to the home office yet. The incompetent Human Resource people claimed that they were unable to locate a job opening for Andy back in the US office at his level because he had since then been promoted to a project manager during his assignment in Japan. With three years of experience living in Tokyo under his belt, Andy would help Smith get around in Tokyo while Smith would give him general advice on life in return. So Andy, a young man who was stuck in Japan indefinitely, and Smith, who was a novice in this society, had become best buddies since the first day they met at the office despite their glaring twenty years' age difference. Besides, both of them were huge Buckeye fans. When Andy was not schmoozing with off-duty bar girls, he would call Smith up for some fun pastime activities together.

Seeing the caller was him, Smith flipped his cell phone open and answered cheerfully.

"Hey! How's it going?" he said.

"—*Tatsukete kudasai. Tatsukete!*" A stranger's voice had come from the other end of the line. '*Tatsukete*' was the word for 'help' in Japanese.

Caught off guard by the plea for help, Smith found himself speechless. The voice belonged to a girl who sounded no more than twenty years old. He wanted to ask who she was and what was happening to her, but in the moment of shock, he had left all his Japanese outside the door. His mind raced to search for the right phrase in the back of the *Living in Japan for Gaijin* book he studied from time to time during the subway ride to work that might come in handy in this kind of situation. Yet his mind drew a total blank, and he could remember nothing useful. Before long the girl started to speak again. Her torrent of words was interspersed here and there with two ominous words he recognized, '*Tatsuekete kudasai*', or 'please help'. Her voice was trembling, and she sounded frightened.

"*Ano… Nan ga ata?*" He finally thought of a useful phrase and asked her what had happened.

In response to his query, Smith only heard a series of deep, heavy breathing followed by some rustling noises that indicating that she was making a lot of movements. Then he heard a gasp. The call was cut off immediately after, leaving nothing but a dreadful silence behind. Smith stood frozen in his spot not sure exactly what had happened and how he should proceed. In fact, he was not even sure what had happened. It was 3 PM on an autumn Saturday afternoon. What kind of atrocities could any woman be facing on a day like that? A day almost worthy of being glorified eternally by the brush strokes of Monet for those who come after to admire? And why was she using Andy's phone? What had happened to Andy?

Before he had time to think this through, the phone rang again. It was coming from the same number. This time, Smith did not hesitate to answer the call. He minded himself to focus and make sure he catches any useful information regarding the girl's identity, her situation and Andy's.

"*Moshi moshi. Smith-desu!*" Hello, this is Smith, he said, greeting the caller with Japanese this time.

"Hey!" In came Andy's juvenile's voice from the other end. The tone of his voice morphed into a sound of pain. *"I-tai, i-tai, i-tai...."* Smith heard him say. It didn't seem to be directed at him, though.

"Where are you? Are you okay? What's wrong with you?" Smith asked, concerned.

"What's wrong with me? I should ask you what's wrong," Andy blared into the phone. *"I-tai, i-tai, i-tai...."* He said again to the other person Smith could not see.

"What?"

"What do you mean 'what'?"

"I'm asking you! Are you hurt?"

"Well, why? My feelings are hurt because you're not here."

"Where?"

"Shibuya. The karaoke lounge in Shibuya! Did you forget?" Andy shouted into the phone over a background of cheesy Japanese pop music. Not hearing any response from Smith's side, he blared into the phone again, "It's the third station on the purple line! The PUR-PLE line! Dogen-zaka, write it down." Then a wave of girlish giggling was heard in the far distance. *"I-tai, i-tai, i-tai.... baby, stop! Kinchiru! This is forbidden! Do you understand?"*

"So you mean you are fine?"

"Why would I be? The girls here are giving me the time of my life. There are eleven of them here! Almost double that time the Korean dude was here. But this Yoshida guy will be here at 6, so you've gotta come over here ASAP. We only have the girls till 5:30!" The call ended abruptly as soon as Andy finished his sentence.

"Fuck," Smith threw his cell phone angrily on his bed. While Andy was having the time of his life singing karaoke with the bar girls, he was worrying himself about some imaginary nonsense.

"I am going to make sure that sucker gets a piece of my mind," he thought to himself, and he went into the bathroom to change.

5. Misa Hayami

The club Andy was talking about was located on Dogen-zaka, or Dogen's Hill, one of the busiest entertainment districts in Tokyo concentrated with nightclubs and love hotels. At this hour in the afternoon, Dogen-zaka looked harmless enough. Like most Tokyo streets, its two banks were lined with stores that sold the latest and greatest creations from all around the world, whether it was telecommunication devices or women's accessories, music records or healthy drinks. If it was not necessary, Smith preferred to avoid walking on streets like that where it was nearly impossible for one to stay focused on his track, because every step he took he would open up a new landscape of even more distractions. Apart from the plethora of colorful commercials he felt compelled to read, he would inevitably be tackled by some overtly enthusiastic road-side salesmen trying to talk to him about mobile services or something that was equivalent to the Japanese Scientology. And since people from all walks of life would pour into Shibuya on the weekend to shop or dine, many companies would seize the opportunity and send their staff out to conduct surveys on the streets to answer research questions like the average number of magazines Tokyo household subscribed to, the amount of time housewives spent on cleaning, or the percentage of teenagers who used one type of deodorant versus competitors'. Whenever that would happen, the pedestrian traffic would be as bad as the car traffic.

Given his appearance, Smith suspected that he was targeted less than an average 'Tokyian'. The English level of the Japanese youth was getting better and better, and it started to worry him, though. Not only would he be stopped by salesmen, sometimes he would be stopped by eager university students who wanted to practice foreign languages and would not give up any opportunity to do so when they see one. Once, he was pulled over by a pair of French literature majors in a café who thought he was French and wanted him to teach them how to order their drinks in French because of his excellent pronunciation of the tongue-curling 'r' in the word 'Grande'. Another time, a boy stopped him on his way to the subway station and asked if he would like to help him with his studies in fluent German. At least that was what it sounded like to him. Smith sometimes wondered whether his mid-western accent was really that hard to follow that he was beginning to sound like a European. While he was still in college, he had explored both French and German before he decided on Japanese. Therefore, he was able to politely reply in the language of the local, however, rusty it may be, that he was actually an American who speaks American English (to deter those students who only wanted to learn British English) and was very sorry (well, not really) that he could not help them.

When he entered the Metropol Lounge on the fifteenth floor of the Metropol Building after successfully avoiding all the obstacles on his way down Dogen-zaka Road, he was immediately taken to the biggest lounge at the back where Andy was. Andy had always hosted his clients here and had over the years brought in a lot of businesses to the lounge. Almost everyone from the lounge owner to the janitor knew him and would always take good care of any customers who came by his recommendation. He certainly never disclosed that he thought the snacks they provided stunk and their collections of English songs were pitiful. He had stayed a loyal customer because they let him reserve the lounge by the day not by the hour, which meant whenever he had a client meeting on the same evening, he could have the girls come in a couple of hours earlier before the actual guests arrive, play a few drinking games and have a couple of good Sake while sending all the charges to the company account.

Contrary to what Smith expected, he was actually glad to see Andy in his old womanizer self, flirting shamelessly with the escort-girls. As he was shoved into the center of the couch clumsily between some of the more hospitable girls, he tried to listen intently to their voices as they introduced themselves to him. None of them sounded like the mysterious caller, though. Smith was going to confront Andy if he thought making a prank call on him was very funny, but before he could say anything, Andy asked, "You sounded kinda out of it on the phone. Everything's alright?"

Still considering the possibility that Andy was the mastermind behind the call, Smith said, "Lately I am just getting a lot of weird calls to my cell. I would hear these bone-chilling breathing sounds, but nobody would talk. These weird Japanese bastards. I got one again just minutes before you called."

"Why would someone do that to a man like you? I mean this kind of harassment call only happens to attractive women or men like me," he sounded as if he was insulted that he was not targeted.

"Yeah, and I don't think I know anybody well enough to make them hate me, or be obsessed with me that much. One call came in like 4 AM, and I was so ready to break the caller's fucking neck."

"Jesus. Did you talk to him?"

"It's a her."

"Tell her to go fuck herself."

"Maybe she was at it," the two men laughed.

"I have some clues about who that might be. I stopped by the police station and reported it just before I came." At this point, Smith was pretty sure if Andy was the perpetrator, he would either call Smith out as a liar, since he never made that many phone calls to him, or he would start panicking for his foolishness and apologize. But he didn't do neither. He said calmly that going to the police was the right thing to do, and then he held out his cell phone to teach Smith how to block all unknown calls with a certain code.

"That's alright," Smith said, "the police will take care of her." There seemed to be nothing else he could do. Cell phone signals had been quite weak in one corner of his shoebox apartment. The mysterious emergency call could be routed to his number due to some odd signal transfer problems while Andy was trying to call him. Since there was no way to find out whether the call was, in fact, Andy's doing, he put it out of his mind. Warming up after a couple of sips from his drinks, Smith told Andy the news he read today about Greg Wesley's divorce. Andy decided to prod him on the topic he was too afraid to touch himself.

"Have you ever thought about remarrying and settling down here?" Andy interjected as he noticed the sour undertone in Smith's voice when he spoke of Greg's newfound romance.

"In Tokyo?" he said. "Do you know how much an apartment unit costs in here? By the time I finished paying for the flat, I would be dead."

"Well, exactly! And you'd want somebody to be by your deathbed crying when you get to that point, right?"

"Ug-hm. I am not exactly proud of the situation at home, but I did raise two great kids who'd do that for me, don't forget."

"Debra and Ethan are married. I never called my parents, and they never called me. Once you go long distance, you voluntarily gave up your right to be a part of the family. That is how it is. It's all about the few pennies they save by not making unnecessary calls."

"Don't be so morbid. I'm pretty sure if I was sent to Europe, they would call me every week, and tell me that they want to bring their kids to visit for summer vacation. Japan is just too far. Too foreign, too intimidating for them."

"What's the big deal with Europe? Americans are too close-minded. Who needs *Neuschwanstein* when we have our own castle here in the Tokyo Disney Land? Who needs the Roman Coliseum when we have the Tokyo *Keibajo* (Tokyo's Horse Racing Stadium)? I don't care if they never send me back to the States. I can stay here all my life. I don't care about those people who think I am being exiled. Look who's missing out. They treat me like a prince here. The Tokyo Tower is just as impressive as the Eiffel Tower. Even the women smell better here, which reminds me of the point I was going to make. Here, take it." Andy dug out a business card from his suit pocket and handed it over to Smith. It was in beige color with scattering pink flower petals printed on the corners. It read *Marionette Newton, Professional Matchmaker. Zwei Inc.*

"Give her a call."

Smith grumbled at his suggestion. He did not need any matchmaking.

"Just take it."

"No. It's a fucking waste of time," Smith dumped the card on the coffee table. "Besides, her name sounds fake. Marionette Newton. What kind of name is that? Next thing I know, she's gonna ask me to go have tea parties in the backyard with her puppet friends."

"As long as she speaks English, who cares?"

"Oh, so you've tried it?" Smith chuckled. Matchmaking was such an absurd idea he could not imagine Andy would give it a try.

"I was there out of sheer curiosity. She's good. She handpicked everyone in her book. She did background checks on them and interviewed them one by one to make sure they have a good lineage, good education, and good manners, you know, the whole package. Most of the women you end up meeting are the best of the best. Either an heiress to some big family business or an executive woman whom no ordinary Japanese man dares to court."

"Then why aren't you married? Instead, you are fooling around with these disease-infested whores who would suck *Miyamoto's* dick for a thousand yen?" *Miyamoto* was the ugliest man in their office who wore a comb-over. They were pretty sure he collected blow-up sex dolls and bought all sorts of custom-made outfits for them in his free time.

"Cause I'm not ready."

"Somehow I'm not surprised to hear that. And how'd you know I'm ready?"

"Cause… you look like it?"

"I'm fifty-five, and I just got a divorce."

"Exactly."

A waitress in the club's signature pink and black uniform walked in gingerly with a bowl of salted peanuts while they were speaking. Quietly she placed the snack bowl in front of the guests, tucked the platter under her arm and took out her electronic server book.

"Hi gentlemen, my name is Misa Hayami and I will be your server today. Would you like to order some drinks?" Andy smiled at Misa. He had introduced her to work here at the Metropol Lounge as a maid-hostess. It was at least a proper paying job, not the ones that could not be spoken of in the open that so many young, uneducated women engaged in nowadays such that the nation had declared the phenomenon an urgent social epidemic that needed to be solved.

Smith on the other hand was feeling queasy. He was aghast at the fact that Misa was beginning to kneel beside them on the carpeted floor, taking her role as a maid-hostess very seriously. — How could one be a maid and a hostess at the same time? And how could one convince herself to take a job so demeaning and dehumanizing? Normally, Smith would comment on it, but his mind was preoccupied with something else.

"Did you call me?" Smith snatched Misa's wrist. He was ninety percent sure that the voice of the girl in the mysterious phone call had belonged to her.

At his sudden assault, the frightened girl staggered back and knocked the decoration lamp behind her over. The platter and the order device fell out under her arm and rolled away. Andy frowned.

"What are you doing?" She shouted at Smith as she struggled to wriggle her wrist out of his grip.

"Hey! Take it easy, man." Andy had stood up from his seat too.

"No! This's the girl. It's the same voice," he let go of her wrist as he was trying to explain himself. "I'm not trying to hurt her. Far from it." Now he pointed at the girl. "She used your cell phone to call me. Did you let your cell phone out of your sight?"

"Wait. What?"

"I got a call from some girl, as I have told you, just a few minutes before your call. It displayed your numbers, too. She sounded like she was in some kind of trouble... It was not funny."

"Oh! Okay, I see what's happening now. I was showing the girls what a BlackBerry could do. All these online poker stuff. It went around. I didn't care. They are good people. Typically, it's no big deal you leave your stuff lying around. Baby–*chan*, did you try to make a call or something?" Andy asked the question in Japanese at Misa.

Misa shook her head slowly in answer to his question. Smith could not help but remain skeptical. Like a frightened animal, she had scooted to the corner of the lounge with her back against the wall.

"It's just an accident probably," Andy laughed. "Smith, you don't have to scare her. She's just a kid."

"Well, I know," Smith lowered his head, thinking hard how he should approach the situation. When he lifted up his head again, he asked the girl in a serious voice. "Are you alright? *Daijoubu desu ka, Hayami-chan?*" Andy listened to his query with a baffled look. When she did not answer, Smith said to Andy, "She gotta be. Here she is, standing right in front of me some forty-five minutes later, after asking me what I would like to drink. This is just…" Smith paused there and sighed.

Andy turned to the girl. "Misa, you can't just take people's cell phone and make prank calls like this. I'm going to have to tell Sawada-san."

At the sound of her manager's name, the girl started to sob

uncontrollably. One of the hostesses in red dress witnessed all these and went to call the manager Sawada-san anyway.

"What's going on?" Sawada–san hurried over and asked.

"Misa…" The hostess in red said, pointing at Misa, who was crying in the corner.

Smith stole a glance at the manager and saw a look of panic on his face. His facial expression changed into a look of admonishment and started to yell at Misa, "What did you do to our customers? Apologize now."

More tears rolled down her face at his yelling.

"Get your ass over here, Misa, now! If you don't want to be fired!" The manager threatened.

"It's okay," Andy stood up from the lounge couch. "Smith, can you just let it go?" Andy asked.

"I—," Before Smith could finish saying that he was not offended, but just concerned, the girl had grabbed the stems of two of the champagne flutes from the coffee table and hurled them in Smith's direction. The flutes smashed on the couch in the space right between Smith's legs, splashing the champagne all over him from his crotch up to his face. Everyone in the room made a collective gasp when the two glasses made a loud clang on the floor and shattered. Crying, Misa sprinted out of the lounge, dodging Sawada-san's attempt to stop her. For one reason or another, a surge of guilt swelled in Smith's chest. He bolted from where he was sitting and ran after the girl, his face still dripping with liquor.

"Hey!" Smith yelled after her. The girl didn't stop, beating Smith to the entrance. Smith pushed open the automatic closing doors after her and cried her name again. As he said that Misa had already pushed through the fire exit door and ran down the stairs in a fury. When Smith got there, he paused and peered down the stairwell. He could see Misa's pink uniform flashing in and out of his view as she jogged down the staircase below, leaving nothing but the sound of her sad wails in her trail. Smith went back out the stairwell and pushed the button for an elevator. They were on the fifteenth floor. Smith could not run down fifteen floors without killing his knees. So he waited impatiently for the elevator and scooted in as soon as it arrived, closing the doors on Sawada-san who had also come out to look for Misa.

"THIS WILL BE F-A-S-T-E-R!" Smith mouthed the word to Sawada-san, who looked helplessly at him through the gap of the elevator doors as they closed.

6. The Chase

Dogen-kaza Road was still as busy as earlier in the afternoon when Smith's first went into the Metropol Lounge. Smith swept his head nervously left and right trying to locate Misa but to no avail. All of a sudden, he caught a glimpse of the pink and black uniform in the reflection on the glass exterior of a road-side café across the street. *It was her*, Smith thought to himself, and he hurried across the streets to catch up, completely disregarding the traffic on the three-way intersection. Luckily, the traffic was so congested the cars were hardly moving. Most drivers were kind enough to stop for him. Many had craned their necks outside of their rolled-down windows to watch who this blundering white man in a business suit was chasing after, wondering if they had accidentally run into the sets of a Hollywood action movie in shooting. However, Smith was oblivious to his surroundings. He only thought of Misa and carefully, he weaved through the stopped cars across the streets. However, he lost sight of Misa again when he got to the opposite side. He followed his gut feeling and turned left down the streets, but Misa was nowhere to be seen. Eventually, Smith's ran out of breath, and his body started to complain, so he had to give up his mission. He sat on a fire hydrant on the side of the road to rest until his panting stopped.

"What's the point of running after her anyway? I do not know her. Why should I give a damn about what happened to her?"

At that moment, his phone rang. It was Andy.

"Hey, so, here's the story. Sawada just explained to me. He was being a little bit too friendly with the girl a little over an hour ago. He assured me nothing of the sort you'd need to worry about. At least that's what he said."

Smith was speechless, hearing what Andy just said.

"And you trust that slanty-eyed freak?"

"This is just how it is here. The men have little respect for women."

"Fuck the Japs!" Smith yelled over the phone.

"For fuck's sake, she might even like it like that. Sawada said he saw her on films. Professional adult films if you know what I mean... Get over it. Sawada said nothing happened."

Smith spent the rest of the Saturday wandering about in Shibuya. He didn't want to stay when Andy was hosting Yoshida-san, *the Shitencho,* or the Local Brand Manager of an Osaka company he was negotiating the purchase of their entire rolling mill equipment from two of their disused factories, especially not in this state. They should respect the meaning of 'weekends', the Japanese, he thought to himself. He looked down at his own clothes. The champagne that had soaked his clothes had dried out when he ran around the streets. However, the stains were visible on his white shirt, and he probably smelled like a gutter from all the sweating he did from running around. He decided to go look for some place with good air-conditioning.

***

Inside the female bathroom of the department store next to Metropol, Misa looked into her reflection from the mirror and dabbed the tears off her face carefully, trying not to ruin her makeup in the process.

Misa was trying to send herself the list of contacts in Andy's Blackberry when Sawada-san caught her. One look at her and he knew she was guilty. Misa had no other choice but to give Sawada an offer he could not refuse in exchange to keep his mouth shut. Of course, that was just a trick. As soon as he laid his hands on her, she dialed the first number on the Blackberry and cried for help. Sawada was so spooked that he scrammed off into the back office as if nothing had happened and left her to do her job. She replaced Andy's Blackberry soon after on the lounge table when no one was looking.

Misa crunched up the paper towel in her hand and smiled at her reflection, ignoring the odd look of the woman washing hands in the basin next to hers. The reason why Misa's expression was completely incongruous with the swollen teary eyes and her red, blotchy cheeks was because she knew she had played her hand well, and had averted a small crisis by conjuring up tears. With a little bit of play-acting, she had turned from guilty into guiltless.

She felt sorry for the poor Sawada, but honest people always had it worst, something that Misa had learnt in her three years in Tokyo. There was no reason why Sawada shouldn't learn the valuable life lesson himself.

Misa looked at her watch. It's still so early in the day. Normally she wouldn't be off until past midnight and she was suddenly unsure what to do with her free time. Free time costs money in the city. Every minute was a lost opportunity for her and she abhorred it. Misa made up her mind to find herself another waitressing job as soon as possible.

***

Not wanting to go back into the Metropol, Smith settled for an electronics store and tried to educate himself on the latest technology while he was taking advantage of their cooling as he window-shopped. He got really interested in a new *Sony* Netbook model when one of the salesmen was demonstrating the computer to a group of students how to use the built-in webcam to do online chats. The salesman noticed him standing at the back and beckoned him to come forward and give the product a try. Hesitantly, he pulled the earpiece and the microphone around his head. He moved around trying to position himself in front of the camera, but he still could not get all of his face on the screen. The salesman started to signal animatedly that it was because he was too tall, being over six feet and that he needed to squat down a little bit in order for him to see himself. As he was doing so, the group of students giggled behind him, and he felt slightly embarrassed at his clumsiness. The salesman who was wired to another microphone connected to another computer running the same video-conferencing software started to talk to him. As usual, he could not catch up with the guy's Japanese, so he mumbled some gibberish Japanese phrases over the microphone. However, as soon as he did that the group of students started to laugh. Some were actually clapping, applauding his heroic attempt to speak their language. Impressed, the salesman started to speak back to him in English asking him how was the weather in California, almost as if it was a sentence he memorized word for word from some English learning software. Smith replied in Japanese that Shibuya had much better weather than California. (That was if he had placed California and Shibuya in the correct order around the two conjunctions *no ho* and *yo ri*). The salesman asked him again how long would he be staying in Japan, and he replied that he loved Japan, and he wanted to live here permanently, which was a white lie. As they ping-ponged back and forth between Japanese and English, a huge crowd had gathered around them as if some kind of improvisation performance was staging. They laughed at almost everything Smith was saying to the salesman and cheered whenever he successfully completed a sentence. A few of the teenagers had taken their cell phone out and started to take pictures of them. The throng was giving the two accidental comedians so much credit that Smith found himself perspiring uncontrollably under the spell of renewed passion for dramatics. He had never been received in a more heartwarming and welcoming way as a foreigner in Japan in the past than at that moment. It might be the first time in a while that he had truly felt any confidence in himself. In fact, he was having so much fun that when the salesman asked him if he liked the computer, he answered light-headedly without thinking "*Kai tai. Todemo kai tai*," which meant I wanted to buy it, I really want to buy it. In all the glory of a well-received actor, he held up his Citibank credit card in front of the cashier for everybody to see as proudly as an Olympic champion would hold up his gold medal and the crowd gave him a big hand of applause. Shyly, he bowed his head a couple of times to his audience behind him in gratitude. As the crowd started to thin out, he shook the hands of the salesman, noting his name on the name tag on his shirt, before sambaing away with his brand new computer back home.

After showering, Smith pulled out his new toy from its casing and started to play with it. He had a computer at work too, and he was proficient in using Microsoft Office Suite. He knew how to play video and music with Real Media Player and knew how to go online to browse websites, but that was about all the experience he had with computers. Since the user manual came was bi-lingual, he spent the last couple of hours of the night before his bedtime perusing the book from the beginning to the end with the diligence of a standardized test taker. He learnt about firewall and spyware alerts, the rewritable DVD disk, the graphics card and the proper use of USB devices. However, none of them was immediately applicable to him. Just then, a speech bubble had appeared on the bottom right across the screen, letting him know that he was connected to a wireless network. It seemed like there was a free Wi-Fi connection in the employee dormitory, he did not know about previously. The Internet Explorer popped up on the screen greeting him with the latest news on Yahoo! Japan. Delighted at the free internet access from the generous neighbor who did not set an access password, he started to roam aimlessly but satisfyingly online.

Then Smith remembered the business card Andy gave him. He remembered seeing a website address on the bottom of the card, and it would not hurt to check it out. After he had retrieved the card, he started to type in the address. As soon as he hit Enter, a 3-by-4 photograph of a couple smiling happily at each other at a wedding popped up on the screen. The head of the webpage read *Zwei Matchmaking Counseling Services. Voted best in the industry by readers of AneCam magazine.* After spending the next hour devouring success stories on its webpage, Smith had become convinced of the agency's credibility and good practice. At the same time, something in those beautiful love stories listed on the site touched him and reminded him of the wonderful feeling of being in love with someone. His yearning for a life partner had grown full-fledged and by the end of the hour, he was drunk with illusions of love like a teenager. He kept tossing and turning that night and could not go to sleep. In half-consciousness, Gregory Wesley and his new wife, their backs against him, appeared in front of his eyes. They were laughing happily about something in a busy restaurant and the woman raised her wine glass to make a toast. Her voice was so familiar. Smith struggled in his hidden position to see her face, but he could not. She muttered something to Greg again and then she turned. Her face had belonged to Debbie, his ex-wife! She gave Smith a cold smile that chilled him to the bones and turned back to Greg, who said "Cheers!" as their glasses banged loudly together with such a force that they smashed into pieces just as the champagne flutes had earlier today in the karaoke box. The sharp clank woke Smith, who had broken into a sweat in his not-so-pleasant dream.

"Fuck it. I'll give her a call now," Smith bolted up from his bed and dialed his home phone number in Rosehill, Cincinnati. It took a while to connect, but eventually it started to ring. And it rang on.

"Urgh!" And down he swung the phone out of his hand in frustration. It bounced off the apartment door and made too loud a bang for 2 AM. Smith ran his palm forcefully down his face, wiping off the drips of perspiration from his forehead. His mouth hung agape, trickles of drool slipping out of the corners. And there he sat, no longer moving, for a good twenty minutes, before the attack of anguish finally subsided.

He crawled his way to the phone, cradling it in his arms as he turned around to sit with his back against the door of the apartment. Then he started to enter the number of the matchmaking service on the business card into the dial pad. At two twenty in the morning, he left a message on their answering machine asking to schedule a consultation with Marionette Newton.

No more than thirty seconds after he hung up, he started to regret having made the phone call. He thought about calling again to leave a message, saying that he had just realized that he would be out of the country in the next couple of weeks and that they could ignore his previous phone call. However, that would just make him look like a man in denial and denial itself, without the need for psychologist's opinion, was always the best proof. He didn't want to appear even more desperate than he already was, he gave up on the idea of making a fool of himself by calling a second time and went out to get some late night snacks.

7. The Test

The next day, Smith received a phone call from Zwei Matchmaking Service. They asked whether he could come for an interview this afternoon, which he duly obliged, not wanting to be the 'man in denial.' In the afternoon, Smith wore a fresh new set of clothes and went to see what matchmaking was like for the first time.

"Big tits or small tits?" That was the first thing Smith was asked when he was sitting inside the office of Marionette Newton. The lady who asked him was a blonde in her thirties with a thick British accent. At first, he thought it was a joke and waited for her to budge, but she did not.

"I'm asking you, big tits or small tits?" The lady asked again imposingly, throwing a worn-out porn magazine on the desk space in front of him. It made a loud, terrifying bang when it landed. Shocked by the unexpected interrogation, he was unable to react.

"Mr. Smith," the lady stood up from her chair and walked over to his side. She sat on the edge of the table and crossed her arm and her legs seductively. The woman was wearing a tight-fitted black sleeveless dress with a thin leather belt around her waistline and a pair of black fishnet stockings. The whole visage was so overwhelming that Smith did not know how to respond. "Let me ask you one last time. Big tits or small tits?" The woman pressed.

"What do you expect me to say?" Smith finally said, fuming. "I am looking for a lady, not a lady of the night. I am afraid I have looked in the wrong place," he said beginning to gather his belongings to leave. He realized that he was less ready than he thought he was for Japanese style matchmaking.

"Sit back down, Carson Smith Junior," she halted Smith from getting up with the porn magazine she had rolled up tightly in her palm in the way a traffic policeman did with his baton. Smith squinted his eyes skeptically, but docilely complied. The woman leaned once again on the desk behind her, scooted up and crossed her legs dramatically. Then she decided that it was not what she wanted to do, so she stood up again and waltzed over to the right-hand side of the room that was lined with rows of filing cabinets in beige. She bent down to reach for one of the drawers that was labeled miscellaneous and slid her magazine back into its place between two other issues of the same men's magazine collected in there. Smith could not help staring at her long, lean legs in black fishnet stockings as she was bending over.

Miss Newton could not seriously be applying herself for him, could she?

"You've passed the test," she said, which snapped Smith out of his trance.

"A test," Smith repeated, with a flood of understanding. "Mrs. Newton," he expressed his relief by repeating her name in honorific, who only got him a cold stare in return. Then she laid her business card on the desk before him.

"My name is Marie Newton. I am Marionette Newton's daughter and her best assistant." Marie walked over and leaned on the same side of the table again, knocking the name on her business card lying on the table twice with the tip of her forefinger. "I have heard about you from Andy. From what he said, I wasn't expecting any other answer from you to my racy question."

Queasy with the closeness between the woman and him, Smith pulled his chair backward and asked, "Is the whole sex vixen thing," he wriggled his forefinger in the air and asked, "supposed to be a test, too?" His question surprised her. She squirmed uneasily for a second and tugged the hem of her dress down.

"So," Smith said, "The two of you are dating? You and Andy," he did not need to hear the answer to know. That was the only way a testosterone man like Andy would want to be associated with a matchmaking agency.

"He found us online and did an interview with us, as you may have guessed, he failed the test miserably."

"Somehow I'm not surprised by that," Smith said. "Tell me what he said."

Marie blushed at the question and did not answer, and almost immediately a new side of her emerged, and she said to Smith in a deeper, more professional sounding tone of voice, "Let us get back to business. You are qualified to be our candidate. From now on, we, my mother, Marionette Newton, and I will represent you on *Omiai*. Our success rate is very high, and most of our past clients were able to meet their future husband or wife within a year. We do not charge a monthly fee or an annual fee, but for each individual consultation. Any calls we made to you and your prospective wife and family will be charged an hourly rate as well. For dates arrangement, there are different levels of fixed charge depending on the type of hotels or restaurants you choose to use at the time. You can stop using our dating consultation service any time you want, but you need to submit a formal written notification three months in advance. During the period indicated in the contract between us, you are not allowed to use any other dating consultation services or online dating consultant. If you successfully find a bride through us, your service would, naturally, be automatically stopped with a final commission charge. The fee will not be waived if the wedding falls through. Now do you have any question? If not, put your name here and your signature down here.*"*

Smith looked at the contract placed in front of him for a quick second and thought to himself, "Fuck you, Gregory Wesley." And he signed docilely.

8. Champagne

"Misa-*chan*, you have such a beautiful face." Mr. Mura had wrapped one of his arms around Misa's delicate bare shoulders that was exposed by the crop-top, his other hand was rubbing up and down her leg.

Misa smiled and took a sip of Dom Perignon Rose from her champagne flute. For something that looked so bubbly and exquisite, its taste was too obtrusive for her liking. Misa had to suppress a cough in her itchy throat as the scorching liquid sloshed down into her gut. Such was the nature of life in Tokyo, sparkling on the outside, prickly on the inside.

"You have no idea how much I want to throw you on a bed and ravish you right now!" Mura hissed into her ears and nibbled on her earlobe at the end of his sentence. Misa hated his bad breath more than the disgusting act. She turned her head to give the man a fake smile. Symbolically she took another gulp of the bubbly toxin and swallowed her pride. With minor impatience, she scanned for the manager, wondering when he would come over to rescue her. You couldn't learn to like a man, no matter how many times you have slept with him.

"Mura!" The older man Takeshita sitting across the table from them shouted through the noise of the crowded karaoke bar to get the man's attention. "Your girlfriend looks very familiar to me somehow," he said, staring at Misa. She squirmed uneasily, wondering if she had finally been caught.

"Misa? Impossible!" Mura shouted back. "She's new," Mura said with a look of difficult written all over his face, "but if you really want her, we could switch." He stole glances at Mr. Takeshita's female companion of the night. The average-looking escort could very well have been an old wrinkly rhinoceros when put next to Misa.

"*Nan-de so-re?!* What's that?! No, that's not what I meant at all, Mura!" The older man slapped Mura twice jokingly on the face. "You're trying too hard to please your old man!" He teased. "Don't worry. The bill will go through in the Congress very soon if you hold up your end of the deal."

Mura was not a bit embarrassed by his blatant ass-kissing. He was very pleased to hear Takeshita's reassurance about the deal. Assured, his mind was free to go back to the idle chitchat. He asked, "What then, do you mean, the honorable Mr. Takeshita?"

"I think I had a girl who looked very much like her some time ago…but it's not her, I'm sure from the lost expression on her face," Mr. Takeshita appraised Misa's for any trace of recognition.

"*Hon-dou?* Really? Tell me about it!" Mura's exaggerated facial expression showed that he had no interest in hearing Mr. Takeshita's story at all, but he had to indulge the man nonetheless. Misa though, on the other hand, had nearly stopped breathing from intense interest hearing that someone in high society Tokyo thought she looked familiar. It might just be her cousin whom he was talking about. People had always said they looked very much alike. They were two fishes from the same pond, sharing some of the same genetic makeups in their chromosomes, after all.

"Ay…I don't remember anymore. It's been a while." Takeshita explained though in an anti-climax. "I only recalled it was one of those Fat Gado's parties. I'm too old for these parties now."

The name 'Fat Gado' seemed to ring a bell. Where had Misa heard of it before?

"You are currently in your best years, my dear Representative Takeshita! I'll get us into another Fat Gado's party."

"They're getting more and more exclusive."

"Don't worry, Representative. You worry about the bill in the Congress, and I worry about everything else."

Mr. Takeshita found it amusing that Mura kept injecting the bill that would allow DaiKe a lot of competitive advantages into the conversations.

"*Mochiron*! I won't forget it even in my sleep with you nagging me constantly like my wife."

The two sly men smiled knowingly at each other and clinked their glasses.

"The game is ready, gentlemen," manager Moto finally came over and said, rounding up the esteemed guests scattered around the bar and the karaoke machine that had paid or cajoled their way on to one of the most exclusive private high-stakes poker table in Tokyo.

"Wonderful. Mr. Representative, trust me that I will play as men tonight, and you mustn't blame me for beating you at a fair game," Mura said smugly and jabbed his bourbon glass in Misa's direction, knowing that she would be smart enough to take it for him, and he stood up at the same time as Mr. Takeshita.

"It's hard to say for sure who's really winning whose money before the night's up," he said, grabbing Mura by the arm and the two men walked enthusiastically towards the poker table set up in the other room. "Don't forget that I managed to turn it all around last week with just a pair of threes. The game of poker is as unpredictable as my bowels."

Mura laughed at the old man's awful joke.

"Miss, you can't come in," a measly waiter with an audacious attitude stopped Misa from entering the poker room.

"Hey!" Mura turned around and shouted at the careless waiter. "She comes in with me." That was all he needed to say, and through the big double oak doors Misa walked into Mura's social circle.

9. Winning the Jackpot

Smith noticed her voice again, sweet like the sound of the Pied Piper. It was that hypnotic. He had wondered about the possibility of mixing up some other teenage girls' voices with hers, but the voice was impossible to forget. At the moment, the voice was conversing with another girl. Laughter boomed, the punctuating soft, feminine chatter of innocent young girls. What were they talking about? Smith wondered.

"Eh, *Oyaji!*" A boy with bleached blonde hair, atypical dark skin, and light blue Hawaiian shirt nudged him forcefully in the back with his ice cold, sweating beer bottle. The beer itself sloshed precariously up the neck of the tinted bottle. He felt the condensation on the bottle soaked into the fabric of his jacket.

"Sorry, what is the matter?" Smith eyed the apish looking boy who was looking for trouble and asked.

"Can't you speak Japanese, you turd?" he said, or so Smith guessed from his gibberish.

"*Hottoite kure.*" Smith mumbled the phrase Andy taught him when he first arrived in Tokyo, meaning, "Leave me alone, please." and tried to sidestep the boy. He wondered as he spoke those words he memorized, why Japanese people say 'please' all the time, even when they were upset.

"*Ne, nani o miteiru?* What are you looking at?" The boy asked, ignoring his request. "She's mine. Don't you dare to look at her again like that if you want to walk out of here with your eyeballs!" The menacing young boy took a swig from his bottle, the expression on his face was one of offense. Only then, Smith realized he had been ogling at Misa.

"Service," Smith lied. "I need *ser-vi-su*."   He was used to using the tourist card when he found himself in a difficult situation. "No trouble. *Onegaisumasu*. Please." He added that 'please' again, which to him really meant nothing. To explain that he did not have enough trays, he gestured at a Pachinko nearby.

"*Ser-vi-su?*" The boy repeated it skeptically and swayed, almost sloshing beer, presumably by mistake, at his face.

At the moment, Misa lifted her gaze from the girl she was talking to and saw the little drama about to unfold in her working area. She caught the eyes of Smith. The second of hesitation betrayed her. Her mouth quivered, as she began to recognize who he was.

"*Ano...*" Smith immediately said to her direction. "*Torei. Torei o... motte... dekimasu ka?* More trays. I want more trays." Jabbing his hands in the air in an attempt to show his desperation for more metal trays to hold his invisible winnings. No doubt, the boy must think he was a *Baka*, a retard. However, being regarded as an unimportant, old fool was much better than if he were to be mistaken, or perhaps more accurately speaking, caught red-handed, for ogling a teenage girl in public.

"*Ahhh. So...so...so...*" The girl scrambled to pick up a few trays from behind the counter.

Her boyfriend strolled away, mumbling harsh words, no doubt, at God.

When she looked up, Smith and her eyes met. They were the same big set of black, watery eyes that gazed up at him in distress the other day. This time, her attractive white neck and the beginning of her breasts peered through the opening of her white over-shirt, like two little halves of peeled green apples. The little package scuttled to his side with trays in her hand.

"Can we..." Smith wanted to ask if she would like to have a chat, but he was unable to do it in complete Japanese. "English? *A-e-go, Daijoubu desu ka?* Is it okay?" Ignoring the perhaps fuming young man claiming to be Misa's jealous boyfriend at the back of the store.

Misa dropped the trays at his feet in front of the Pachinko machine and stacked them nicely around him, her big eyes staring at him with an emotionless expression all the way. Then she straightened herself up again, showing off her body and her delicate sensuality, unknowingly to her, to Smith.

"*Cho to*. I come. I come later." For the next five minutes, she did not return. Smith heard, however, that Misa reprimanded the boy whom she called, as far as Smith can catch, Tatsu for harassing her clients. She seemed to have reasoned it into the boy, for the boy nodded regretfully and answered something back as if being scolded by his mother.

Smith decided to return to his seat at the Pachinko machine number 458, the one he randomly picked as his, with the ripped red leather seat. He noticed that Misa was agitated. She stroked the ruffles of her light pink uniform and readjusted her nametag carefully before she went over apologetically to a senior-looking staff at the parlor.

So she was working here now instead. Smith seemed to have made her look bad in front of her colleagues by asking directly for service, instead of waiting for her to come over like how it was dictated in the good old book of unwritten etiquette for customers in Japanese establishments that he failed to obtain a copy of. He made it all the worse by almost provoking a scene with her little boyfriend. For a country super focused on quality of service, one could not pull down his own pants to piss, so to speak, even at the urinal in Japan, he thought with distaste. Cultural blunders aside, for a second time in a few days, Smith realized that he had inadvertently messed with the girl's livelihood because of his curiosity.

Another thought crossed his mind —this was no decent place to work for a girl. This Thunderbird, a recently opened Pachinko parlor next to Passage, which he typically frequent, was set apart only by the comic book stores on the third and fourth floor of the same commercial building. It would soon be filled with the same chain-smoking gang members that passed the days here until the next deal, unemployed idiots who wanted to try their luck on Pachinko, or drunk salarymen with a penchant for molesting any unfortunate female person that came their way, like in all the other Pachinko parlors in Japan. He would not let anyone he knows work in such a place. And certainly not a girl that reminded him of his own daughter. The sight of this young, awkward Japanese girl working in a place like this upset him.

The gambling business in Japan, however, employed over 300,000 citizens a year around the country. Alone in Ikebukuro, there was at least half a dozen of them along the 1st street, which the biggest shopping and entertainment district was practically built around. One seldom witnessed any exciting police-rascal dramas as portrayed in Japanese soap operas, movies, and video games. Yet Smith has a fishy feeling about the whole gambling business. There were rumors of the Yakuza controlling all the parlors in the areas, as money laundering hubs, and occasionally, things must get out of hand here and there. Though the news never reported them, the myriads of violence in the media must have gotten their inspiration somewhere.

While minding your own business had been his motto living in a strange foreign country with a world-recognized social issue of failing morals, he could not subdue the urge to poke his head into this messy business about Misa.

What kind of place breeds what kind of personality, Smith believed that to the bones, notwithstanding his own phantom presence from one parlor to the next. By doing nothing and letting Misa work in the Thunderbird was close to hand-delivering her back to the dirty palms of men like Sawada, and this was absolutely against his English gallantry, conveniently in his blood in dire moments and good old American values.

This boyfriend of hers, one word with him revealed his dubious origin. The lack of manner, the overbearing gestures, and flouncy outfit —

he seemed to come straight out of the GTO animation that was playing on television.

In the background, the jingling and the clinking of metal balls hitting the internal gates and barriers within the active Pachinko machine around Smith continued to buzz.

Distracted by a myriad of thoughts, he slid his second last thousand-yen bill into the machine in front of him for 250 new metal balls, while keeping an eye out for Misa. Pachinko had helped him to pass the time when he was alone. He believed that if he sat long enough at the same machine, he would always be able to break even, or even win. Deep down, he knew better than this. Still, he considered that the best investment of his free time, soaking in the local stench and bad breath of other lonely Japanese people as an alternative way of blending into the colorful local scenes which he yearned to be a part of but could not. And with that excuse, he was not ashamed to just be the fly on the wall observing with pleasure the daily lives of ordinary folks playing out around him every single day. He was used to the routine of pulling the lever time after time without winning, only to be occasionally interrupted by the change of tunes when the balls fell into the center gate which activated the digital reels on the screen above. They then spun autonomously without his control, an option he typically picked after he grew out of the initial excitement of actually doing something that would cause something else to happen. As the myth-busters from a Japanese TV show had revealed, the outcome of the game was already determined the moment the ball entered the monetary fighting rink. He usually waited for a few seconds for the game to play out, telling him that either he got nothing, or small marginal wins, then repeated the same process again. Ruminating a George B. Bernard quote on game theory —

"In terms of game theory, we might say the universe is so constituted as to maximize play. The best games are not those in which all goes

smoothly and steadily toward a certain conclusion, but those in which the outcome is always in doubt. Similarly, the geometry of life is designed to keep us at the point of maximum tension between certainty and uncertainty, order and chaos."

He concluded that conventional wisdom nor scientific, mathematical proof of randomness in life could do nothing to deter human curiosity for the unknown. However small the chance of a positive outcome may be, people wanted to gamble on. And George B. Bernard was most definitely correct, because, at the moment, he was at a total loss when the elusive celebratory tune of winning the jackpot sounded above him on the overhead speakers. He kept staring at the slot machine, which was pelting one metal ball after another into the bottom tray in a frenzy, not knowing what to do when he managed to finally win the second biggest Jackpot of the house, a good 1.4 million Yen.

Yes, he had won something.

In a split second, all the philosophies were emptied out of his brain. There was only one emotion left in his rattling skull, which was busy resonating to the sound of the heavy falling balls, not of joy, but of complete embarrassment.

Why don't they start printing payouts like in Las Vegas? 1.4 million Yen, and how many clanks of balls hitting on metal trays and decibels would that mean? He felt guilty of breaking the harmony, well, the relative harmony of flashing video screens of high pitch digitalized salesladies of the sullen Pachinko parlor by piercing it with his unusual achievement.

Statistically, the odds were against him being at least one to one hundred thousand. Hence, a piece of paper would not really justify the glory of the moment.

As the sweat on his forehead dripped through his bushy brows into his eyes clouding his sight, he made out the face of Misa and her long white limbs extending across his lap to reach for the almost overflowing tray and scooping handful after handful of metal balls into trays she had brought over earlier. Smith joined in without thinking.

The trays were being filled quickly. A male colleague standing behind her quickly replaced the filled ones with empty ones. It was an amazing sight, to see so many metal balls being spat out in one go. Smith mumbled some words of amazement to himself.

Misa gave him a reassuring smile and said congratulations to him in Japanese. Smith tried to smile back, but she was already beckoning Tatsu over so he could help with carrying the filled trays to the counter. The smile on Smith's face deteriorated into nothingness.

Thump! The last of the trays hit the counter's surface. The metal balls filled up a total of 15 twelve by twenty pink plastic trays. That's how much 1.4 million Yen, or approximately fifteen thousand US dollars, weighed. It took the boy Tatsu, who proved himself to be more than a good-for-nothing, in this instance, many rounds to transfer them to the back of the store. They were laid out on the award redemption center and the manager, a skinny, shrewd-looking man in black rimmed-glassed and black suit, was nervously scooping spoonful after spoonful into the counting machine. To Smith, it was getting a bit ridiculous, this whole extended ceremony of accounting and rewarding. Smith wondered if they had ever had such a big payout since their recent opening, in what appeared to be just last spring, according to the posters and brochures Smith was given plenty of time to read during the recounting.

A lady in similar uniform was making calls with her back turned away from him. She murmured into the speaker of the beige color telephone mounted on the wall. Who was she talking to? And what was she talking about? Was it about me? Were the Yakuza coming to get him now? For looting their establishment out of sheer luck? A gambling parlor should be prepared to lose at any time if it was so readily winning from its patrons, though the current scene seemed to indicate to him a lack of a plan

B.

He walked over to the manager looking man and asked.

"Am I going to get a check?" he said. "A check," he pulled out a checkbook he happened to have as an example from the left side of his suit jacket's pocket. "Check is better. Do you get it? I don't want fifteen fucking trays of balls, or toys...no toys." He pointed at the gifts locked safely in the glass display cases behind him. "*Kore wa, shirana*i. None of these!"

"*Ie. Ie.* No, no, no." The manager waved him off. Smith looked pitifully for help in English at the rest of his staff now crowding at the front of the redemption counter. They cringed one by one at the virtual death rays that seemed to shoot out of his eyes. The responsibility finally fell on to Misa, who was on duty in the area Smith was sitting.

"Write your name here. And here...your..." Misa took the manager's instruction and started to translate what he was saying.

Her English was not bad at all. It could also just have been an illusion Smith created in his head because he had more patience with her than he had ever been with others.

"Phone number and address," Smith finished her sentence as he saw her struggling with her words.

"*Hai, hai...*" She smiled. He smiled back. "We...will call *tsu*." She continued. "when okay *a-ne... oka-ne...* okay." She made the gesture of okay with her fingers, like the gesture for number three.

"The money is okay. *Wakari mashida,*" he said in reply to encourage her. "But where do I get it?" He asked.

"Here," she turned around to ask her manager the same question in Japanese. "One moment. One moment."

And the lady who was talking suspiciously on the phone a moment ago came forward to him. He realized for the first time that they were almost at equal heights. Her chiseled face and protruding gave her an aurora of someone in powerful rank. The conspicuously long, up-curling eyelashes batted at him challengingly. As she drew up so close to him, he could almost feel the air breathed out from her small, straight pointy nose. He could now see her name, etched clearly, on the golden rectangular plate pinned to her lapel.   A Miss Katsumi Saitou. Below her name NABUO Group was written in smaller characters. She produced an envelope in her hand silently, and after showing the front side of it to him for a few seconds, she tore the plastic tape that was sealing the envelope open and begun to present the content to him. The others at the parlor, including the staff, were just as curious as he was about the contents inside, that he could almost hear them draw a collective breath. Inside the envelope, there were three plastic cards that looked much like Visa cards each inserted into the three flaps of the package. The woman then proceeded to explain in Japanese to Smith, with Misa translating for him on his side, their quite impressive names and respective usages. —The black one is a VIP card to this parlor and its sister Pachinko parlors in other parts of the country. It seemed to be a lifetime membership card that entitled him to free drinks, free snacks, and internet in any parlor he chooses to visit. Though Smith had no idea whether it was still an excellent marketing idea at his age to get a reward that only works until the end of his lifetime, he was glad. He was reminded not to forget to sign the card. The second card was a white color card. That one was obvious, for as soon as she pointed to that card, the patch of gold that signified the computer chip within a typical *V*isa card caught and reflected the light from the ceiling quartz lamp, making him blind for a second. That must be where the 1.4 million Yen was stored, he thought. He recognized the seal of Mizuho Bank on the bottom of the card, and decided that he would go visit his personal banker the next morning to get clear on any rules and tax laws he may be subjected to given his new 'source of income.' The last card, which was gray, Misa translated, was an insurance card. An insurance card? What kind of insurance? Smith asked her. She had a hard time explaining. On it, there was again the name

NABUO Group, who appeared to own also an insurance business. Misa stuttered a great deal in her translation while Miss Katsumi was on a rant. Like heavy rain, she pelted on Misa what appeared to be technical terms related to his insurance policy that Misa was translating with visibly less confidence. Young people rarely had a clue about insurance. Their youth and imprudence were their best insurance, unlike an old fart like him who could break his hip any moment now, he thought to himself.

He decided it would be best to obtain the details from the ultimate provider, instead of squeezing second-hand information from Misa, at a later time point, by asking his secretary who spoke fluent Japanese and English to call the service number on the back of the card. Whatever kind of insurance this was, it could only be a good compliment to what he had. He smiled internally for the thoughtfulness of the Japanese.

Then the whole staff congratulated him heartwarmingly once more in unison with a long Japanese phrase, as a gesture of sending him out in good spirit. Knobs on the Pachinko machine stop spinning for once and patrons of the parlor clapped when Smith walked out of the door with his digitalized winnings safe and sound in his pocket. He tapped it twice and nodded to the people watching him cheerfully as he went, thanking them for the good spirit. At the threshold, he turned and bowed, something that he rarely did, but felt compelled to do, to the good nature Japanese people who lost so much of their money here, culminating in his ultimate win. He stole another glance at Misa, she smiled weakly at him. Behind her, the boy Tatsu was mumbling some crude gibberish.

10. A Blind Date

It was less dramatic than he thought, the blind date that Marie Newton had set up for him. According to her sophisticated personality evaluation and matchmaking models advertised on the agency's website, he was 89% matching with an Australian woman called Aileen." He liked Aileen's profile. Born and raised in Sydney, University-educated, Aileen was a professional, although the profile didn't say what kind. She was five feet seven 'with a nice figure' according to the profile and was only 36 years old. More than a decade his junior.

"It has gotta beat, Wesley." He thought to himself. Of course, a second later he was also seized by the intimidating thoughts that he has to court a woman so much younger than him. What the hell was he going to say to her? Hope she's interested in international affairs, he thought sarcastically.

Sunday came around like greased lightning. He put on the same suit — a charcoal designer suit from Napolitalian made of Merino wool — and matching pants he was supposed to wear this coming Monday. It was a defying act that shifted his weekly schedule for his work outfit between Monday to Friday forward by one day. He had developed a rotation system ever since he arrived in Japan to eliminate time and effort wasted every morning to decide on an outfit ever since his divorce. As his wife was no longer there to piece together item by item a matching work-wear for him like she used to do, he had to take care of himself somehow.

He dipped his hand into the softness of his silk ties, a messy collection of around fifteen ties he owned, heaped haplessly, crisscrossing each other in one of the drawers of the white shelf, and felt at once the feeling of being at home. It had its relieving effects, the sensation of incredibly smooth, silky fabric slipping over the back of his hand, and through the insides of his fingers. When he pressed the tips of his fingers together, he felt the vigor, the energy of the fabrics and weaving patterns, and by their subtle dissimilarities, he picked a tie that best fit his mood of the day without seeing the actual tie. By this method he avoided dwelling too long on them, yet when he looped today's lucky winner, a satin tie in chocolate brown silk with peach and brown petals with a hint of rust around his neck he experienced a mixed feeling of rage and self-pity.

Debbie had bought it for his 50th birthday, he loved it and wore it only on important occasions like no other tie he owned.

Having a date with someone other than your ex-wife after being married for more than twenty-five years was an important occasion alright, but wearing a tie with such strong emotional value attached to it was a form of cowardice, a subconscious reluctance to let go.

Forcefully, he pulled the tie off his neck and stuffed it, with considerable care, back into the bottom of the drawer and grabbed the first thing he found fumbling through the pile. A light blue bow tie.

***

"No way!" Aileen Martin tossed her head back and laughed. "You're not buying me flowers, are you?" Aileen hid her face with her hands, which was all red all of a sudden. "Oh my God," Smith had called the waiter selling roses in the restaurant over, "Do you know how cliché this is?" Aileen said, and continued to laugh, rather nervously. She lifted her wine glass for another sip of red wine.

"Somehow I sensed that the beautiful lady would appreciate the gesture," Smith was talking nonsense like a well-oiled machine. He had not done it since he was twenty.

"You're one incredible man. I have never received roses on the first date, let alone," Aileen held up the rickety looking, dried up roses that Smith just bought from the waiter, "roses bought from a..."

Smith was stuffing his wallet back into his pant's pocket and could not help but chuckle at the poor state of his gift for the lady. He finished her sentence. "From a second-rate Italian restaurant where you can't order food in Italian. But one thing they did right, it's to preserve the tradition of flower hawkers. They never fail to show up, in any Italian restaurant around the world, be it Italy, Spain, Germany or Japan. You see them everywhere." Then he said in a hush, "And they are always such tackily dressed balding Italian man, with an aspiration to be an actor."

Aileen laughed. "This is mean!"

"Ask the Italians what they think about the Americans or the New Zealanders. I can guarantee you it would be the most racist thing you've ever heard."

She pressed her hand against her stomach. It was starting to hurt from laughing. Smith was imitating the waiter's dramatic pitch at the moment. "He genuinely acted like a silent movie actor. He was all theatrics with his expression and rigid movements. It's a waste for him to be selling flowers in a restaurant, don't' you think?" Aileen turned to see if the man was still around.

"Okay, okay, let's not continue to ridicule a good man for just doing his job."

"Sure," he said. "So you said you work for the...?"

"The International Human Rights Lawyers Association. The InterHRLA chapter based in Tokyo."

"Pardon, my poor memory. Acronyms are my nemesis. I never have the talent for information retention. And age, I must say, had robbed me the little of what's left." That made Aileen laughed again.

"Don't be so harsh on yourself. I have always found myself in situations where I'd wish I could forget things."

"Well, working for a non-profit organization is not the most interesting job in the world. The problem with being professionals like us is that our knowledge and experience are so highly specialized that they are not applicable to the other and thereafter difficult to share, and elicit genuine interests from one another. Humans are hunters. We are programmed to absorb and retain information that is most valuable to the improvement of our chance of survival, and in the modern world, that would be our professional careers."

"Mind if I ask, why don't you go, I don't know, to Algeria, Bangladesh, Bangalore… to one of those Arab countries where polygamy was still practiced, and young women were exchanged for cows, or to Honduras where child labor is the sole reason for their GDP growth but come to Japan instead? If I look around here, no, I am not being disrespectful. Please don't be offended. But honestly, working on human rights in Japan, in Tokyo, what sort of impact do you expect to make? What sort of unsatisfactory excuse is that for a working vacation?"

"You made me laugh all night, but nothing you said had been nearly as farcical as what you just said. Working on Human Rights issues in Japan is not as simple as it seems. Many issues are so deep-rooted many are blind to it. No one, for example, is being killed or banned flagrantly from being who he or she is by laws and that's how the Japanese government has been getting away with so much in the international arena. Japan was rarely listed in the *Human Rights Watch Journal* in the past ten years. Yet its status was not optimal. An example would be the homogeneity of the population. Less than 1.6% Japanese residents are foreign nationals, and locally born groups with non-Japanese origin are not allowed to have Japanese citizenship nor are they allowed to vote, and enjoy social benefits like the rest of them. Despite a British-like constitution drafted by the staff of the American Army, underwriting human rights and in particular called for unprecedented equality between people of different age, heritage, gender, etc. in postwar Japan, one knows a lot of work needs to be done on promoting these ideas into the minds of Japanese people when one just go take a stroll in the streets. We are facing a lot of difficulty in Japan in particular because, for one, Japanese are used to how things are, and they see no need for change. Secondly, the social protocol of not speaking about such evils openly, in case it brought you or your family shame, is keeping those dissenting voices down. But the deeper you dig, the more you find and the more you realize that Japan is significantly lagging in human rights. Women's rights, in particular. And that's what I am here for. We need more local women to speak up, to bring on the momentum."

"Okay, there is a disproportionate amount of men versus women in any management around the world, and it is not innate to Asian society. How do you propose to fix this? The French's center-right party has put forward legislation that would see to it that women make up half the figures in France's leading boardrooms in the next five years, but guess what happened? The men simply recommended prominent mogul's wives to sit on the board. They have no experience and essentially you have two persons sitting on the board representing, most of the time, the same opinion. This is not an equal distribution of power. They are simply putting up a show. And in the end, these females became the model examples of why women are, pardon my language, less capable compared to their male counterparts, because they have gotten all the wrong people to stand at the forefront, handpicked, strategically, by a group of males who wanted to hold on to their power."

"We are entirely of the same opinion, Smith. The key to any legislation is to refine it over time with experience, and slowly eliminate gray areas where companies can play around with. That's the situation over there in Europe. In Japan, we have gotten the Peace Constitution that clearly spells out Women's Rights. Its clauses are far more advanced and holistic than that portion of the Constitution of the United States, in a way. But get this, more than 50 years passed, there was not once the Constitution was amended. Life goes on in a parallel universe, and people accepted that things stayed the same way as it were, as if the constitution was never written. That's why we need an organization that is not attached to any political party to advocate for change. We work in more subtle ways, by provoking a lot of discussion in the society, appealing to the senses of the common people whose lives are restrained by the invisible chains of the biased social norm. Women's Rights covered a great deal of things. It covers, suffrage, the right to vote, right to education, equal access to information, equal access to employment opportunity, reproduction rights, abortion rights, elimination of sexual violence and enslavement against women and many, many more fronts, and it is very likely that we could only generate small, incremental change in one small part of the above areas. But the way we work is that we tried to improve the lives of women, one case at a time, one life at a time, and make sure each time we generate a lot of media coverage, not only in Japan but in Asia in general, to create pressure both in and outside of Japan. This has proven to be more effective than other more radical means. That's why I am here, as a lawyer to represent underprivileged clients, and under-informed legal advisers locally in Japan."

"You have some guts. How long ago did you move to Tokyo? And why Human Rights?"

"That was about 13 years ago. I have always had a passion for Human Rights laws. I did two internships during my studies at Amnesty International in Japan. There were just two women in a team of nine. Very naturally I looked into cases related to Women's Rights. But the turning point was when I went to Taiwan for my third internships with Amnesty. I started learning Chinese and reading up on Taiwanese Asian news related to Japanese human rights.   There were lots and lots of reports, from

Taiwan, from Hong Kong and other Chinese media reports and academic researches describing the dire situation of Women's Rights in Japan. It was the locals that were covering up their dirty businesses it seems. When I graduated, I joined InterHRLA Japan without thinking twice."

"This is mind-blowing. You can read Japanese and Chinese? I could barely remember how to spell in English. You made me wonder what I have been doing all these years."

"What have you been doing?" Aileen smiled.

"Well, it's not nearly as exciting as I thought it was before I met you. I am a Program Director of new businesses for a Japanese raw material trading company, DaiKe. You must have heard of it."

"Yes. I think about two weeks ago, your company's Director had committed to improving the number of females in upper management roles by 25% by 2013 in its annual shareholder's meeting. That's an aggressive goal to commit to."

"I am ashamed to say that I have no knowledge of that. It seems like a good cause, and hopefully it won't end up the way it did in France."

Smith felt that he had a good chat with his date, Aileen Martin, a 36-year-old, energetic, determined, intellectually sexy woman with a good sense of humor from Australia. She was surely a great catch, Smith thought to himself. Her strong feminist ideas, however, made her quite sensitive to misinterpretation of his gentlemanliness. They had debated for a good five minutes before Aileen convinced him that there was no need for him to invite her to dinner. Neither did she accept his offer to call her a taxi to take her home. She drove, he found out later.

How much does a Human Right Lawyer earn in Japan?

Instead of thinking about his date, he caught himself thinking about how much Aileen made working for a non-profit organization. He could not, for the love of God, afford to pay for parking all around Tokyo city every day. Of course, he was not completely broke himself. As a single middle age man, he had little expenses. Besides, he just won 1.4 million yen.

He did not tell anyone apart from his personal banker about his jackpot. He withheld the news from his secretary whom he originally wanted to enlist in order to get more information on his insurance policy because who knew what kind of rumors they were capable of spreading. Secretaries have full access to every detail of their managers' professional lives, and day by day encroaching their personal lives through their growing reliance on them. If his secretary were to know of his frequent late-night visits to the Pachinko parlors… he could not bear the thought of it. The gossiping powers of secretaries were not to be disregarded easily, though. Smith had heard a lot of interesting stories from them through Andy, who was the twenty-something, good-looking fellow from America that was also the secretaries' pet. They told him every nasty bit of gossips they knew.

Andy had managed quite well, only his 3rd year here, to infiltrate himself into many communities up from the tight-knitted Japanese management circle, and down to that of the window cleaning crew that came in every Friday morning. His quick wit and proficiency in Japanese and Japanese culture got him the visibility in the giant organization he craved for. Sloppiness may mark his face and he was; Smith was sure, disabled-at-birth from taking a firm stand on any matter, including the choice of a mistress, he navigated through dangerous waters on many tough situations quite well, keeping himself, while merit-free, blame-free throughout the years. He was the guy you go looking for connections, the obnoxious yet indispensable middle guy, the eunuch, whose power of introduction, association, promotion or opposition, could make or break your career if you let him.

Andy must not know about his winnings, Smith determined. Playing with Pachinko was not gambling, and even when it comes to winning a huge sum of money majestically at Pachinko that should all the more justify its harmless nature. There was no need to give the guy cards against you. Based on history, Christians were the worst kind of prosecutors.

He did not tell Andy about his date as well, though it was entirely his making that he met such an amazing young woman. Without surprise, Andy heard about it somehow and teased him one day at lunch while they were eating at the company's canteen.

"You should give her a callback."

"Who?"

"The Legally Brunette."

Smith said, "Her name is Aileen. Marie Newton told you?"

"No, the last time I saw her, she had her mouth stuffed with a ball gag. She couldn't speak."

"I am eating, Andy!" He stabbed his fork in his pasta and got up, fighting shudders from the mental picture of the S&M activity that Andy painted for him. "Coffee?"

"Yup." Such was the nature of most exchanges between these two grown men at work.

11. Television Commercial

The clock in the Design and Advertising Department on the 2nd floor stroke 10 AM. The tingling sensation on the back of Ryuuji Tanaka's hand grew into a full twitch. In the distance, a cell phone sang its ringtone. Furious, the young assistant of Tanaka, Keigo Arai answered the call.

"Where the hell are you? The team is waiting for you. The van was standing outside for almost an hour. Do you know how much... No, don't switch to your agent! I'm talking to you."

Tanaka's ear twitched as it strained to listen to the answer from the other side of the telephone.

"What do you mean he can't do it alone? We reserved your actor 2 months ago, and we've let you know today's schedule in advance. There was never any question raised. Do you have any idea how much work was involved in coordinating a day like this? "he said. "—You have to honor the contract!" The other end's reply was demonstrated by the expression on Arai's face to be dissatisfying. "No, we don't... let me ask my supervisor. One second. Okay? Don't hang up on me!"

"What is it?" Tanaka stood up from the leather couch. Towering above his assistant, he exerted an unintended effect on him. Keigo Arai started to stutter. The warm fumes from his flaring nostril clouded the glasses.

"They... y... want us to pay for... two... two. The British guy needs an extra translator."

"A hundred and twenty thousand yen later, they are asking us to pay more?" Tanaka slammed his palm on his desk. "Tell them we don't need them anymore. And we are going to report them to the Consumer Protection Agency."

"But we need someone..." Arai spoke meekly.

"I said No!" Coffee mugs and notebooks jumped as Tanaka slammed his fist on the table for the second time. "Just hang up on them!" he said. And with his trembling hand, Arai pressed the red button to end the call with a loud beeping tone. His posture was one of great disappointment.

"What are we going to do now?" Arai asked.

"Use your brain," Tanaka said. And swiftly he buttoned his suit jacket up. "There are so many foreigners in this company. Why can't we find someone internally? Arai, take the schedule, we are going up!"

"Which floor?" Arai followed Tanaka hastily into the elevator.

"I don't know," Tanaka stood there without speaking for a second. "Let's try forty-seven."

"47th floor please," Arai said to the young elevator conductor dressed in pink uniform.

No sooner than Arai's hand stopped trembling, he felt nauseated.— It must be a joke, he thought to himself. He was feeling seasick in an elevator, albeit one that was boasted to be one of the highest speed elevators in all of Tokyo's commercial buildings. To be fair, he had always taken the stairs from the lobby to his design studio on the second floor, the low-levelers both in its literal, physical sense and in the hierarchy of the company. DaiKe had 2,500 employees in Tokyo and over 13,000 employees worldwide from top management talents to operators working at the furnace. It's a massive organization in Keigo Arai's point of view. Alone in this building of 48 floors, it housed more than 2000 employees from 23 different operation units. Tanaka, his manager, and him, together with their team of bored, unambitious, middle-aged colleagues who one might mistake as patients waiting for their turns in the emergency room of a public hospital for the minor ailments they could not afford to properly care for, worked, all but on the lowest floor of the DaiKe's building located in the center of Tokyo. He should have known better when he was recruited into the company — attracted, almost blindly, into his current position by the, one could say now after the fact, blind passion and misplaced leadership of Ryuuji Tanaka and the name of DaiKe, that there would be nothing to advertise in a raw material trading company that traded metals and plastics scraps with recycling and waste management companies on essentially, *rubbish*. It had been a long time since he had designed anything other than internal company communications and someone's ten-minute PowerPoint presentations. This was his chance to shoot a three-minute television commercial that would be aired on national television during night time, the so-called 'Golden Period'. And on top of that, photos from the shoot would be turned into advertising materials for industry magazines, ads in light boxes at the bus stations, painted on the bodies of taxis and buses, big banners to be strung across the outside of buildings all over the country and beyond. The whole world would finally have the chance to see his masterpiece. This was how you make an impact in the world, to hold fast to one's assigned position in the big machine, regardless of how small, how mundane it appeared at first glance, and by hard work and unimpeded optimism he would achieve greatness in life — a romantic notion Arai was a firm believer of ever since he knew of the company's new sustainability project until today's morning. Today's morning, for once his cat did not jump on top of him as it used to do every day. It was a sure sign of something bad about to happen. The cat felt the change of luck from his body and adjusted its behaviors accordingly — something that he chose to ignore in the morning. The Japanese were fervent observers of animals' behaviors for a reason. They were a lot more sensitive than humans in detecting bad karma. What was happening to him now was a classic dream-come-true-turned-tragedy. Arai's shoulders slumped even lower at the thought of ruining the biggest opportunity of his life by listening to Tanaka-san's instruction, to hang up on the acting agency. He should have at least debated the pros and cons of accepting the acting agency's request to get a translator for the British actor they had identified for the commercial. The company was vested with money. It could pay for an extra translator or two, or fifteen. Yet that was the temper of Ryuuji Tanaka. He did not speak much, but when he did, he spoke of old traditional values, like honors, honesty, consistency as if he was stuck in the Seven Samurai's age, and he behest doing business with anyone who did not honor these secret codes. Arai stole a glance at Tanaka-san's face from his reflection on the mirror. It showed no hint of the same nauseating effect he was experiencing. However, Tanaka-san's stern countenance had a calming effect on him. He swallowed and prayed hard for the Gods' blessing.

12. The American

"What are you doing here? This floor is by appointment only." The receptionist got up from her desk immediately to stop Arai and his boss Tanaka from invading the 47th floor any further than they already did with her arms spread out in front of them, as if she was herding wandering cattle at the tip of a sharp cliff.

"Maybe we shouldn't have come here," Arai whispered nervously to his boss.

"We work here," he said to the receptionist.

"You work here?" The suspicion was higher than the national debt of Japan. "Get back down!" She ordained. Arai was about to back his way into the elevator, which was still there with its door held open by the docile elevator conductor who had by now realized her mistake. However, Tanaka stood there unmoved. Of course, no woman could give him commands. He flashed his badge at the reception, slow enough to let her see the company's logo, but fast enough not to notice his lowly status in the company's hierarchy, and proceeded to walk behind the frosted glass panel that separated the main hall and the office area, ignoring the reception's protest.

And almost immediately, he saw the guy he wanted. The face of the company. In truth, Tanaka knew he was intruding the corporate managerial floors of DaiKe, but he couldn't help feeling a bit heroic and satisfied, to have finally come up to the top, nearly the top, of the building that he had worked for, for two decades. He was himself a manager after all, why couldn't he walk this carpet and converse with the foreign talents like any other?

The man he was staring at was Smith. He was inside one of the many glass boxes built at the corners of the floor where conferences were held, pacing around the room as he spoke, in elegant professionalism and whole-hearted confidence, as Tanaka noted, to the caller at the other end of the conference call.

"Get this guy for me," Tanaka instructed Arai, who was at the moment quite busy dealing with the receptionist who threatened to call security.

"What's going on?" The voice of a man asked. Tanaka turned to look at who it belonged to.   No sooner than he did, he had to bow, and bow deeply, for it was the Chief Operational Officer of DaiKe, Mr. Ohayashi. So did everyone else around him, including the impertinent receptionist that had no respect. Tanaka was tempted to give her a nudge from the back so she would fall forward, face first. He relished on what could be and smiled to himself.

"They're intruders!" Her voice broke his pleasant reverie. Tanaka made a note to self that he should have done what was in his mind next time.

"No, no, no, sir..." Arai pulled out his own badge and presented it with both his trembling hands, stooping still, to the man. It proved to be difficult because Ohayashi was smaller than him.

Tanaka himself shot straight up and presented himself to the man.

"We are from the Commercial and Advertising Department. I am the manager of the second floor, overseeing the production of all multimedia projects."

The man grunted. Tanaka continued.

"We have a filming today, but our foreign actor could not make it due to a schedule conflict that was not known to us until last minute. I need a replacement immediately, and we know that there is no better place to find a replacement for the position of the Face of DaiKe than the managerial floors of our own company. The public will find it even more appealing if they were to know we are using real personage in our commercial, not actors."

"Really?" The man's attitude softened, as he rarely heard anything remotely as interesting as this in his time on the 47th floor and out in the sites. "Strange, I didn't hear of the project myself."

"It was all documented and approved by the marketing department, sir," Arai explained, still stooping. "For sustainability..." he added the magic word of the industry.

"Ah-ha. Yes, a wonderful effort. Your name?"

"Ryuuji Tanaka."

"Tanaka, then you must not let us down. Do you already have someone in mind as the replacement?" There was a shy smile on his face. Tanaka knew what was coming.

"We do. It's that gentleman over there."

"Surely you don't mean Smith-san?"

"Is there a problem?" Arai asked, like a good protégé of his newfound master. "We can rectify it immediately."

"Smith as the Face of DaiKe... No, no," he said, thoughtfully, without giving any explanation. "I can free up my responsibility for the afternoon. You don't want to use Smith. He's old and shriveled. Bitter. An American pig to represent our company, how is that good for us?" Ohayashi said. "We have so many other employees who would be excellent in the commercial..."

Arai's jaw dropped. Should he explain that they would like to use a foreigner in the commercial, to give the company a more international touch? Of course, he kept silent. And most reliably, his boss spoke up.

"Such as yourself," Tanaka said what was on Ohayashi's mind. "But if this company were to progress and excel as one of the top material company of the *World,* then surely a manager of his own project should be respected of his decision on matters he knows better than others. I must say

I am rarely wrong in casting actors and actresses."

Wow. Arai thought. He must be crazy to challenge Mr. Ohayashi like this. Arai and everyone else on the floor had by now stopped breathing, except Smith, who was clueless about the fuss being made over him. His muffled murmur could be heard now with ever more clarity.

"I believe we share the same vision, right?" Tanaka said.

"You go take care of it properly." Ohayashi said after a long moment of silence, and he walked off to another employee and started talking to him about his present work as if nothing had happened and nobody had been challenged, least himself. Tanaka smiled and walked over to knock on the glass door of the conference room in which Smith was just getting off the phone.

"You should ask Andy," Smith explained, for the fifth time that he had not the slightest intention of appearing on Japanese national TV, not even for his company which he had dedicated his life's work to. "No, not me, no matter what."

Tanaka, who was sitting at the end of the conference table with his back to the offices outside, crossed his arms.

"You should know that I am not leaving this room without you." He pledged adamantly. "It has now become more than a matter of face for me. It is also a matter of my professional judgment and your capability," he said.

"I have nothing to prove in the area of acting."

"You should hear what he called you..." Arai whispered under his breath and looked away, torn between wanting to challenge the man and fearing of actually being heard.

"I have heard them all," Smith replied.

"You'll be the Face of DaiKe, or at least we will try to take a few shots of you today like that. If you're any good, you will be on TV." Tanaka said, "That's as good as any revenge you can get in a civilized way from these men that jested you."

Tanaka continued, "You know, Japanese people dedicate their lives to the company. Once they go in, they don't leave. It is very difficult for them to see someone else come in at high level, and do better than them, especially when it is a foreigner who doesn't speak their language. But we want to be more than that, or at least that is my vision for the company. I am but the smallest, lowest manager of the ladder with thirty rungs. I want a foreign actor because I want to change the impression of the people of our company, and the impression of the people of the company they work for. If you cannot understand what the job means, then I will leave at your command." He stood up and slid the chair back into its place.

"To what pleasure do I owe your confidence?"

Tanaka looked Smith in the eyes and said, "You have an honest, suffering face."

His poignancy almost felt like a punch that knocked the air out of Smith.

13. Face Reader

Men often claimed that they dedicated their souls, their youths, or whatever else they could offer to their jobs as if there existed so many worthy employments around to sacrifice their lives over. What they really meant was that they had spent a lot of years on something that allowed them to pay their bills, and have a reasonable amount of domestic-problem-free time so they could dream up nonsense about all the world's would-haves, oblivious to the fact that those things they claimed to have sacrificed they would be willing to give up readily in exchange for a steady, carefree, or even boring life of a common working person when left without. Smith was old, and he had heard all tricks. He knew better.

And precisely because of that he found it the oddest that he should be in the center of attention in a trailer-turned-dressing room, parked by the Yokohama harbor where the filming of the commercial would be. All of a sudden there was glamour and show-biz in his life, pegged with a higher, greater purpose. Tanaka-san's little elevator pitch had got his head swimming with a renewed passion. Him, in a sustainability commercial, representing one of Japan's biggest heavy industry, promoting environmental-friendly policies? The higher-ups had dumped a stack of white papers on him earlier this year. Occasionally, he would skim the papers again to seek out a paragraph or two, a bullet point or two that would be an excellent sales pitch for his many account visits to the suppliers or customers. But this? An actor could always shrug his shoulders to criticism of anything he sold, as a business development manager he had to shoulder the risks of the technical writers' literary flairs, and this was too much responsibility for the little pocket change he would get out of it.

A small man flung open the trailer's door and spoke, maintaining a hunched back, to the hair stylist that was messing around with whatever little twiddle that could be done to his dirty blond short hair which, fortunately for Smith, was still considerably full and thick despite his age.

"*...tabun chushi sa rerudarou,*" *he said* as he lit a cigarette. He appeared to be one of the production workers, coming here to gossip.

The stylist lifted the comb from Smith's hair and said in visible anguish, "*Ahh...Nani no tame ni hataraku?*" Smith sensed that her momentum of his extreme makeover was lost at the news the man brought.

"*Nani ga ada?* What happened?"

"Oh..." From their reflections in the mirror, Smith could see two deers in the headlight, humanized. Then a switch seemed to have been flipped somewhere. The girl started to dance, or at least that's what appeared to Smith as if he was a child and the trailer had transformed into a kindergarten.

"*Ame, ame.*" She stretched out her fingers and wiggled them in the air. "*Futte...fu...tsuu...te.*" She dropped her body and the objects that her fingers were imitating fell like rain. So that's what they were talking about. Rain.

Learn some new Japanese words every day, Smith thought to himself. He was grateful and said thank you to the girl who danced the word for him.

Sit and wait had never been Smith's forte. He got up and walked out of the trailer, to no one's protest. It was indeed drizzling. His eyes caught sight of the stormy clouds gathered not far from where they were, below it a clear layer of bright white light, as if the sky was caught in a war between two powers. Very soon, the dark clouds would arrive at the harbor, and drench them all with her disapproval. Certainly, this was a good enough reason to call the day off, even before it begun. He took off the suit jacket that the costume lady had given him, and stood by the wooden handrail to take a good, deep breath of the fresh, crisp air, letting his lung be inflated by the beauty of nature's little wonder.

Only when he turned around did he notice that two men, one operating a huge video recorder on a tripod and the other, who was Tanaka-san in close inspection, holding an umbrella over the recorder, had been filming him from about ten feet away. Without breaking character, Smith smiled, hiding his surprise, and walked easily over to the side of the camera. Tanaka yelled cut and padded the cameraman on the back for a good take. The cameraman nodded and started packing up his equipment.

"You have been sneaky, I see," Smith said.

"Real people, real moment. That's what I wanted to capture. *Sore dake desu.* That's all." Tanaka shifted over a bit to let Smith joined him under the umbrella.

Smith gave him a smile. Tanaka looked out at the water rolling with short white waves.

"And that's it for today. We have to film another day."

"That's it?"

"Of course," Tanaka said resolutely. "Moments are better captured than recreated. It's a commercial, but to me, there is no difference between an art-house movie and a commercial. My directions are the same."

"So that's a wrap, I guess?" Smith said, hiding his slight disappointment at the lack of theatrics from the shooting team.

"Wanna go grab a beer?" Tanaka offered. Smith obliged. On this rare break from tedious office work, he thought he might take up the offer. The working day could continue endlessly afterward, he thought to himself.

Tanaka cried some Japanese over the noise of the ever-thickening rainfall, and the team replied unanimously from all corners of the landing behind them like a team of well-trained soldiers, "*Yoshi!*"

They were not nearly as uptight as the unanimous cry of enthusiasm earlier had foretold. Smith was sitting in the middle of the wood bench that went around the chef of the Teppanyaki restaurant next to Tanaka. On his right, was who seemed to be his most trusted assistant Arai. They were flanked on both sides by the rest of the team for hire of the day, all of them from outside agencies. The hair stylist girl had taken up next to the mechanic. Beside her, the driver of the trailer was pointing at something in the restaurant and getting into an excited conversation with the make-up lady that Smith had yet to have a chance to meet, but could not for the life of him missed, for she was covered in tattoos from her eyebrows to her left bared shoulders. Then there were a few more men that took care of sound, lighting, and props.

"It was a pity that the weather was not nicer," Smith remarked. "Was the shot you got okay?"

"I will have to take a more thorough look later." Tanaka took a sip of his beer and let out a '*haa*' from the depths of his throat that seemed to be a very common way of signifying appreciation in Japan, like the slurping of noodles and the teeth grinding of meat with bones. "Making a film nowadays is a lot easier than how it used to be. As long as you have some raw materials to play with, you can tell any kind of story you want."

"You are referring to all the photoshopping and editing," Smith said.

"Something like that."

"I must say, I could hardly come out a second time with you guys, despite my burning million yen-worth of passion for theater."

"*Hai, hai.*" Arai conceded in an apologetic fashion. "We have a British actor, but the acting agency, how to say, *damashu*."

"Extorted us with trickery," Tanaka said.

"No *honyakuka*, no come today."

"They wanted us to pay for a translator. This topic had never been raised before."

"*Tanaka-san wa, aego ga joju*, your boss speaks excellent English," Smith said to Arai. "*Honyakuka histsuyao wa nai.* There's no need for a translator."

"*Hai, hai.*" Arai nodded affirmatively to Smith's compliment to Tanaka. Indeed, without a common language, or a translator, it would be tough to carry on a longer conversation with them. Slowly, Arai's attention drifted to his Japanese colleagues on the right. Smith and Tanaka, a fluent English-speaker, were quickly isolated.

"Where did you manage to learn to speak such good English?"

Tanaka let out a short chuckle as if it was the funniest thing Smith had said all day. "You should hear my French. I lived in Paris in my younger years." In those obscured years, Tanaka had become obsessed with the movies from a certain French director and decided to become one himself.

"You speak French, too? I must say I am surprised at your multitudes of linguistic talents."

"Talent was not involved. It was all hard work." He explained. "When you want something, you put your nose to the grind, and you do it. There's no other way but to get your way. That's how life works."

"Does your optimism works in all situation?"

"It's optimism mixed with a bit of tragic frustration."

"Sounds familiar," Smith smiled.

"As I have said, you have a face of honest suffering."

"That's not the best compliment I have heard in the looks department," Smith said. "I would prefer a simple, handsome face anytime."

"Only the inexperienced can be simple. You..."

"I know. I am well past fifty. You probably know that already. It must be written all over my face."

"There's more to a face than wrinkles, of course." Tanaka lifted his gaze from his plate of grilled mushrooms. "I am a student of the study of faces, for many years now."

"The study of faces?"

"It's something most valuable to a man of my profession. Though the younger generations thought the art a scam."

"It's understandable to have intuitions about someone's character. But I wouldn't say it was not occasionally tarnished by prejudice."

"It's more than intuition. It is a science." Tanaka lifted his beer and jerked it in the direction of the mechanics. Smith stole a glance at the man's face. "Look at his eyes. They are protruding, like those of goldfish. He is dominating and reckless. He talks a lot, but his upper and lower lips are thin, it means he is tight-lipped about his own affairs, always taking the disguise of nonsense for hidden agendas."

"And the girl," Tanaka was now remunerating the facial features of the make-up artist sitting next to him. "She has a small forehead. Not very intelligent. Her ears, big, with earlobe, are sticking out more than the average Japanese woman — a hint of rebelliousness in her soul."

Then he shouted loudly across the table to the girl. "Yumi-chan, I can kill this man for you if he kept pestering you!"

"*Ie, ie,* No, no," she said. Smith caught the word for joking, *jodan,* from her reply.

At her reply, the mechanic got only more emboldened and started to tickle her bared shoulders, lined with mysterious oriental patterns.

"Crooked teeth and bucktooth — shy but conflicted. That made her the favorite blowjob giver in entire Japan."

Smith did not see that coming. He almost choked on his beer.

"What you can say over a set of ugly teeth, Tanaka-san!"

"Don't feign innocence. You know that already?"

"Know what?"

"Every other girl in Japanese pornography has bad teeth."

"And I thought they worked so hard because they need money for their braces."

Tanaka gave him a shrewd smile, then he said, "Before I work for DaiKe, and even a short time after, I participated in the productions of many of such movies. Forty-thousand-yen budget, twenty percent for the actress, fifteen percent to split among the actors, if there are more than one. The rest are for scenes, props, equipment, and an extra pair of hands if we need them. There was barely any money left for the director, producer, editor all-in-one." Smith guessed that Tanaka meant himself. "Often I had to borrow money from the company that commissioned the films to live another day, before at last, when the film was out, and I got paid, which would just be enough to keep me in the clear for a few weeks. Then the cycle began again. If I cast a single malapert that drove the girl too hard or didn't know how to act, I would essentially be shooting myself in the foot. There is no room for error when you have no money. You started to learn how to read people you dealt with in this environment."

"It's a fascinating story," Smith said, "but are you sure you can tell me all these? You're not afraid that I would expose your past?"

"As long as you keep it to yourself." Tanaka flashed that reassuring smile again.

Smith returned with a thoughtful stare.

"You do know that a guy from the company was fired because his wife was, before they got married, a model." Smith reminded him of the conservatism of corporate Japan.

"Snakes laid in snares everywhere. You're not one of them. My assistant is not one of them."

"I surely hope you give me no reason to use it against you." Behind the facade of politeness, in any given Japanese corporation, there were intrigues and conceits at every nook and cranny. Smith had maintained distance from office politics but nonetheless remained vigil out of necessity.

"I am an artist after all. Perhaps it was expected of me, to have a frayed end somewhere."

"Artists are forgiven anything, indeed."

"I went from making dirty movies for pennies to head of department in a big corporation. Do you think it made me a better person?"

Smith was not prepared for such a question. He hardly knew the man.

"You are taking things too seriously, Tanaka-san," he said. "I thought we were just two men drinking beers."

"If you have my time to think," Tanaka said, "You will start to take things very seriously, too."

What he said made Smith wonder if life on the second floor was really that miserable.

"Tell me what you think? I trust you will be honest."

Smith wondered what Tanaka saw in his facial features that conjured so much trust, but he was not about the crush it. To be honest, he was almost flattered by the expert face reader.

"I'm not in a position to judge anyone's character. Only God could divine that. But I hope the career change has made you happier."

Happy, a big word in just five alphabets.

Tanaka ruminated his questions for a moment, then asked Smith the same question.

"Are you happier? Here, than in America?"

"Yes," Smith answered without thinking. He hated lingering on the topic of happiness.

Another knowing smile flitted across Tanaka's face. There was more in common between a Japanese middle class and an American middle class than met the eyes.

14. The Assault

With 1.4 million yen at his disposal, he felt ever more like a coward, wanting to slip inside every single Pachinko parlor that stood brighter and warmer than usual, on his way home. He used to attribute his desire to spend the evenings at the parlors to his theory of the inevitability of luck. Now that he had proved that he could actually win money from Pachinkos, he realized that he simply had nothing better to do, plain and simple.

He could consider using some of his funds to do something meaningful. Still, 1.4 million yen was a sum of money that was a lot on the account that he won it from doing practically nothing, but too little, just barely three months of his salary at DaiKe, to do anything radical. Nonetheless, it never hurts to have extra cash on hand.

A few punks had gathered around a boy fallen on the ground in one of the many dimly lit back alleys that he passed as he was walking mindlessly towards a parlor. They were kicking at the victim, albeit already motionless, sprawling haplessly on the dirty pavement. There was a waft of smokes in front of him that smelled of noodle soup.

"Hey!" He shouted. The speed that human instinct kicked in was a subject worthy of study. In the corner of his eyes, he had spotted a barbarousness unfolding and acted according to an innate code of ethics.

The perpetrators muttered something to one another. Smith only grasped that it involved the good old word for foreigner, *Gaijin,* a couple of times.   Sizing up his potential attackers revealed that favors were on his side. He had no words for what he wanted to say in Japanese, so he blared some gibberish as loud and angry-sounding as he could. The words could have been Korean or Hindi. He hoped that regardless of his words, he had conveyed a clear message that said 'I am very angry, and you'd better run before I knock you into next week.'

"*Iko!* Let's go!" One of them hustled the others to leave, and they did.

"Run you sons of bitches!" He blared after them and chased them away with a loud, menacing growl that would make the Hulk cringed.

The alley quickly became deserted.

There was smells of blood and sour and spicy soup.

Was it Tom Yum Gong? Smith crinkled his nose.

Smith would have just walked away, now that the bad guys had been chased off. After all, the business of the alleys was better left for the justice league of Japan's underbellies. He ought to have gotten calmly, in a quickened pace, out of the way, in case the assailants come back with backups to tend to some unfinished business, such as himself.

Smith was no hero. Rescuing an underdog was not an everyday thing to him. He was a common Christian man, that believed in simple Christian value, and hence, he had a soft spot. He felt like saving this kid despite the great inconvenience should the assailants come back, or the high possibility that the boy lying here turned out to be a crook himself who had done someone such injustice that he deserved his beating.

"Are you okay? *Daijobu desuka*?" He asked. The body on the floor did nothing. Slowly, without stressing his back, he pulled up the legs of his trousers and knelt by his side. The boy was a Japanese of medium height, long, pale limbs that sported a blue Hawaiian shirt, cropped pants and sandals, though one of them were knocked off his right foot, lying astray in a puddle of dark water. He scooped the boy's head in his palms gently, trying to coax a word or two from him. Blood was trickling down his right temple, wetting Smith's sleeves. Smith rotated his hands to take a good look at the wound, and it was then that he discovered the boy was Tatsu, Misa's boyfriend. She's not gonna like what she sees. Smith carried the boy to the main street where he could get help.

Leaning Tatsu on a lamp post, Smith found the boy's cell phone on his body. The first instinct was to go to the recent calls list and ring up whoever's number that was on top. Second thought showed that to be a bad idea — who knew what kind of people had knocked the boy out, after luring him to the dark alley. It would not be a surprise if someone familiar did the trick. Smith's best solution would be to call a number that was listed as Home, OR...

" ミ サ " That's Misa in Katakana and the only Misa in the contact list.

He dialed the number. Just at that very moment, a taxi turned into the street. Smith had to scramble to the middle of the street to stop it. He outstretched his arms, for who would want to stop for a desperate foreigner whose hands were smeared with blood, gasping heavily for air from the exertion of having lunged something heavy around just recently, accompanied by possibly a dead body on the side of the street?

The call connected.

"Kon na jikan ma de, doko e itte ita nodesuka?" The distinctive voice of hers blared into the speaker. She seemed to have asked, where have you been the whole time.

Smith didn't like the idea of being the messenger of bad news. He held off speaking. He turned instead to the driver.

"Get him to the hospital! *Byoin*! And hold this!" he ordered, forcing the mobile phone into the driver's hand.

"Eh?" The taxi driver was already agitated, but when Smith had dropped the boy like a package on the back seat, shifting the boy's feet as far back as possible away from the doors and closed it without getting in the taxi himself, he almost snapped.

"Moshi moshi?" A female's voice from the other end said. *"Tatsu!"*

"Nande sore? What the hell is this?" The taxi driver barked at Smith, stunted by the huge lump of trouble hand-delivered by the big-nosed devil

of an American into his backseat. He would curse the Gods for hours after this. Smith stuffed a ten thousand yen into the man's hand to compensate his inconvenience.

"Keep the change. Now go!" Smith urged. "Go!" He slapped the trunk of the cab angrily until the driver started to make way, hopefully, to a hospital.

From the reflection of the right side-view mirror, Smith could see the cabby speaking feverishly into Tatsu's mobile phone.

"Good," he said to himself. "at least they are communicating."

Under one of the glowing lamp posts, Smith took a good look at himself. He looked like he just slaughtered a cow. This was no way to walk around Tokyo. Funny how he should worry about being stopped by the law enforcement officers in this state — where were the police when he needed them?

"Blah!" He shuddered, as he doused his dirty hands into the possibly dirtier dark water puddles and rinsed them clean. A rainy day was surely good for something. After rearranging his appearance, he hailed another cab to get off the premise.

"Andy, where are you at?" Smith consulted his Japan know-it-all.

"Home. Taking a dump? What do you want?" He asked. But instead of waiting for a reply, he continued. "You sounded flustered. Got one of these creepy callers again?"

"It's something else." And Smith explained what had happened. "Should I go to the police? I'm gonna need you to translate for me. You know my Japanese. They'd arrest me on the count of mutilating their beautiful language."

"Do you know the assailant?"

"No, of course not."

"Do you remember their faces?"

"If they come back for me now, yes." He said. "It was dark."

"C'mon, man. Don't be stupid. You know nothing's gonna come out of going to the police."

"They might still be hanging around the noodle shop or something."

"A lot of crooks are hanging around. You know that."

"So what'd you suggest I do?"

"You should probably run for your life, I'd say. You're a big shining white man, Cars."

"There is like fifty thousand people living in Ikebukuro. They won't find me."

"You don't exactly blend in."

"I live in Ikebukuro. I can't just leave."

"The Kyokuto-kan also *lives* in Ikebukuro." Kyokuto-kan, the Extreme East Yakuza, a gang famous in the Western world not for its gruesome behind-closed-doors activities and dealings, but for the elaborate, colorful body tattoos of historical warrior figures and poetry some members wore on their bodies.

"You don't even know the details."

"You didn't see shit! How'd you know the boy didn't cross somebody from the gang. I mean, to stir things up in the Kyokuto's territory? Do you think they are just a few drunks wanting to throw some punches 'cause they have self-esteem problems? The whole district is being run like a pirate ship by men tattooed with *Haiku* and *Kamons* from the tip of their noses down to the foreskins of their penises."

"Don't be so melodramatic."

"When in Rome, just walk away from pickles like the Romans do. They like to crack their whips once in a while, no big deal. He didn't die, did he? He'd tell the cops what happened if he wants to."

"Hold on. I need my hand to type the password."

And Andy's house bell rung. He almost jumped from the sofa at the sound.

"You can't be serious!" Andy turned on the video feed to the security camera by the house door, and Smith's warped forehead materialized on the screen. "Fuck me."

"Come down to meet me." Smith knew this was the only way to enlist his help, by way of friendly coercion. "No, wash your hands and come down to meet me."

"It's almost midnight. There's a 7 AM training session tomorrow. I need to sleep now."

"I will tell Cheryl we'll both be going in late, on my account." Smith knew he had the power, and his department had the budget, too, to pay for a half-day leave for somebody. "You can sleep till noon."

"Go away." Andy groaned one last time, grabbing the winter jacket laying on the couch. "I love these Proper Office Conduct training, don't you know? I need them."

"That's the most sensible thing I have heard you say all night," Smith said. "Now come down and get your Proper Conduct training directly from me."

15. Tenacity Absolutely Necessary

Headache. It creeps on us like a distant relative, readily abusing our respect for the blood-ties for their ends and reminding us that no matter how strong and independent we have grown we are still slaves to our pedigree.

Headache. Its strength underestimated like the strength of a single foot soldier, its damages paralyzing like the confidential information stolen and sent to an enemy's camp. Headache. It comes without forewarning and goes only after raiding us of our morale.

Headache, you son of a bitch.

"Yesterday you were the 'Face of the Company', and today you're already coming in late." To Smith's dismay, the news of his field day with the CAD had also spread like wildfire. The level of gossip and bitter innuendos had only added to the list of Smith's problems. With the constant lightning strikes in his head, he could care less to reciprocate the vilifying remarks.

"What have I missed?" Andy leaned forward from his swiveling chair, one of the many tightly packed around the boat-shaped rosewood table of the conference room on the 31st floor, wanting to hear Mr. Mura, the senior managing director of New Business Development, one of the many that attended the North American account calls, to explain his jest.

Before Mura had a chance to say any more, Smith pressed the call button on the Polycom SoundStation. The awfully loud dial tone cut Mura's intention to acerbate short. Andy squeezed his lips together, slightly upset about his thwarted curiosity. After all, he had spent the whole evening with the man at the police station. The topic of his afternoon excursion did not come up at all.

"Smith, did you have time to read over the analysis of the September survey?" Santo, the Assistant Product Manager, asked as soon as everyone in the call greeted each other.

Was this another jab at his TV stint? Or was this rooted from something more far-reaching? Santo was famous for his reputation as a walking lump of dissatisfaction.

"I have to go over them more thoroughly." Smith simply answered. In Japan boardrooms, one does not say outright about a colleague's mistake, so Smith damped his response that otherwise would have been 'I practically have to rewrite the whole thing, so stop bugging me.'

Sensing more should be said on the topic, Carlisse Nupp of New Business Development from the Los Angeles office chimed in. "This is Carlisse. Carson and I have been on it since last Thursday, and we have seen some inconsistency in several of the numbers, in particular between the return rates and defect levels of the..."

"Put the phone on mute," Mura commanded, cutting the woman on the line off. All hands reached for the phone as if they would be punished otherwise. He cleared his throat, preparing himself for the upcoming monologue while Carlisse on the other end of the call yapped away to a diverted audience.

"The survey results were very important to us. We have spent thousands of Yen every month to get these results and have them analyzed. If they cannot be interpreted promptly, there is no point in doing them at all, is there?" He raised his bushy eyebrows to add to the effect of his rhetorical question.

In the background, Carlisse was giving her most honest opinion about the misdoing of the Customer Relationship Management team. The manager of the CRM team, Haneda, a Japanese expat happily shipped abroad to man the CRM team in Los Angeles and now free from the shackles of the old world, was never there. No one knew where he was, but all conceded to the fact that if they were in his position, they would do the same. And so, the others had found it unfair to criticize a man who was not present, and was never present, implying that Carlisse's relentless attacks on Haneda's team lack of analytical competence were equivalent to committing office faux pas and she coming from the American office and her career too unimportant to be the concern of anyone in the Tokyo's office, meant that whatever she said on the topic should best be ignored.

It was Santo who apologized first, as always, even if it was none of his business, as if not doing so, and worse, not being the first, was going to lead him from this eternal burning inferno to another more gruesome one. One must concede that he did have the capacity of the demons from that domain. "I am sure Mr. Smith had more projects than he could manage with his demanding schedule."

The nerves of the sour man.

"It has nothing to do with my schedule. I can manage very well. This is absolutely not a concern of anyone but myself. The extra time needed was not meant for me, but for the CRM team to rectify what I have identified as chronic problem. We are trying to figure out what our customers want and how we are coping with that need with less than credible data. Whether it is the September survey or the October survey, it is the same procedure that we go through every month to collect them." Smith made a mental note not to use 'we' next time. "There is no reason why the CRM team should not have accurate and reliable data for us whenever the same group of people uses the same program to run them. I suppose what Carlisse is saying," Carlisse was indeed still saying it to the invisible audience in the realm between AT&T and Docomo, "is that these procedures that we adhere to so diligently, are fundamentally flawed." The first step to preserving the icy thin relationship with your egotistic colleagues is to blame everything but them and their kind. But this was as far as he would go along the lines of flattery, Smith thought. They could take it or leave it.

"What is the program they run?" Mr. Mura asked.

Certainly, no program was ever involved in the analysis. While highly adept at their soothsaying crafts, Mr. Haneda's team consisted of either fresh colleague graduates with psychology degrees or comfortably dressed moms who had worst mathematical and computer skills than cashiers at Walmart check-outs. Smith had been receiving data every month from Mr. Haneda's secretary, Miss Rei Taniguchi, who pulled together all the codes the representatives entered whenever they received testimonials or complaints from customers, then copied and pasted everything on the excel file, with no particular insightful addition. Still, Smith considered her the smartest individual over there.

"It's a sophisticated program that extracts the codes from all callers and compiles them." The compiling could be interpreted as analysis, perhaps. Smith had to twist the reality a little bit, like he had done, every day, for the sake of survival. "I believe it is called T-A-N," as in Taniguchi-san. It sounded believable enough.

"Who was in charge of this T-A-N?" Mr. Mura asked. Of course, everything he asked from this point on was irrelevant. It was so obvious that if you put garbage in, garbage comes out, regardless of the program. And the so-called program Smith was marshaling in was no more than a messenger of a VBA script written by someone in the ancient times, at the establishment of the CRM department, and there was no name for it. But seeing that Mr. Mura had been successfully deceived, Smith knew he could maneuver around this non-crisis crisis through this route.

"A gentleman that has retired." A man near retirement age back then had programmed it when the modern digital customer service management concept was still at its nascent period. He had contributed enough to the company to be let retired in Smith opinion. "Colin Singer. I attended his talk when I was still in Cincinnati." He made up a new name quickly. No one would notice that Colin didn't exist, except maybe Andy. But even

Andy was too young to know everyone over there.

"Smith, I want you to form a sub-team with Mr. Haneda and other important personnel and fix this."

Smith had seen this coming. Smith had witnessed so many totally useless sub-teams formed and dissolved in these weekly meetings alone that would turn his hair gray, being in a few of them himself, for every deferrable issue that popped up. "Sure, we can do that." Today he did feel like elaborating on his plans. They were always the same. The responses he got were always the same.

With that said, the predictable response showed that he had the project and Mr. Mura in his grip. He could officially do some work on staff training in Mr. Haneda's department, given that he doesn't pop back up in the least favorable moment to provide his objection. They might just be able to convince Mr. Mura to approve the budget on using external professional CRM software and technical supports, the whole nine yards, like he and Carlisse had talked about forever.

"Ok. Next topic," Mr. Mura declared, satisfied, while the world teetered on the precipice above total chaos. Andy, being adept at both languages, jotted the follow-up down into a text file in English and Japanese, to be sent up to the internal team server once the meeting was over.

"Great job, Carlisse." Santo unmuted the Polycom and said what little he could to smooth over the conversation loophole. Smith could only wonder why she hadn't hung up on them.

Another throb in the veins around his temple reminded him of the rule of T.A.N. working in Japan.

T.A.N. — Tenacity Absolutely Needed.

16. The Greatest Show On Earth

"Hondoni arigatou gozaimasu."

Misa put a glass of sparkling grape juice into his hand as he reached out to grab one from the beverage cart. He was filled with doubt whether he had done something wrong once again as if being caught stealing grape juice that he suddenly realized could only be meant for children, except children were not allowed into the parlor.

"Oh, I'm sorry." He apologized in Japanese, clearly missing the point.

"No!" Misa smiled, realizing Smith's misinterpretation. "Thank you for saving Tatsu's life."

"Oh, you're very welcome." Smith had now entered the shock phase. He was shocked that Misa knew it was him that night who called, and even more shocked to find himself being addressed by her, despite having consciously made his way here to the place she worked so that he could observe her, from a distance, and convince himself that that was all.

"In fact, thanks again, it was not the first time you helped me."

"Don't worry about it…" Smith replied. "Is your boyfriend okay?"

"My boyfriend?"

"Tatsu?"

"No…he is my younger brother!" Misa laughed at the idea that someone could mistake her brother as her boyfriend. "But yes, he is okay. He has a concussion to the head, and some broken ribs, but he will survive."

"He should watch the company he keeps," Smith advised.

Misa retracted her hand from the glass, which they had held in midair for an unusually long amount of time while they talked so that Smith could take the drink.

"I will tell him," she said.

"You as well," Smith was referring to the incident at the club earlier. There was the trace of melancholy in her eyes when she heard this. "I'm sorry."

"Is that all you know how to say in Japanese?" Misa switched to English.

"Uh, no." He tried to explain himself in Japanese, but he couldn't find the words, nor could he find the reason for his clumsiness in words. His mind was a total blank. Even the headache had stopped, leaving more idle mental capacity to self-doubt.

"Didn't you win a handsome amount of money from us last time?" she asked. "You must really love playing Pachinko."

"Uh," Smith's mind was racing to reasons beyond his cognition. "Pinball machines are different, in America, where I come from."

Misa looked around the parlor, scrutinizing the machine and their loyal patrons, checking to see if she was needed anywhere. When her gaze returned to Smith, she shrugged, showing that his affinity towards them was not mutual, having worked beside hundreds of them every day and eventually had achieved the state of sublime immunity for their visual and audial solicitations.

"A ball goes in, nothing comes out. Sometimes it hits a trigger on the way, but mostly it doesn't. That's it," Misa said. She could not have summed up the game more precisely.

"You're right," he said, reminiscing the times he passed during his childhood up until he graduated from college playing pinball. The Pinball machine's playfield was tilted at an angle, while the Pachinkos' were mostly vertical and completely up to gravity to do its work. One could score with careful maneuvering of the flippers, sling-shooters, spinners, or even tilting and nudging the pinball machine, while the Pachinkos allowed one and only one move: to fire a marble. It gave an illusion of control. One simply watched luck plays out in Pachinkos, and to some it was a completely stupid game. To Smith, and many others, however, it was *the greatest show on earth.*

"I don't know why I come here," he said. But he knew. He had been having love affairs with the naughty mistress called luck for the last six months.

"I am glad you've come," Misa said. "I really want to thank you."

"No, there's no need." Smith struggled to keep up the facade of unselfish gallantry. He sipped the grape juice from his glass to hide his nervous swallowing.

Misa darted her eyes around, thinking intently. She had taken a liking to this man. And most importantly, he worked for Mura at DaiKe. An idea formed in her head.

"Let me teach you Japanese," she decided almost instantly. "What's your name and phone number?" She pulled out a worn red cardboard address book from the pocket of her white apron and unclipped the pen from the inner page to write the information down.

"I have many other students," she added. When she saw that Smith was about to refuse her offer, she flipped her address book to the calendar, marked full with appointments in the afternoons from Monday to Sunday. "Just tell me when you're free. I can do it any day of the week. The daughter of Mr. Mura from your company's also my student."

"Great," Smith was not sure whether that was meant to be a good thing, to share a language teacher with your obnoxious boss's daughter, forming an extra link in the universe with this vulgar man, making him captive in his web of influence inside and outside of work. But Misa's infectious enthusiasm and Smith's desperate need for Japanese lessons had proven to be a winning combination. Smith was only too smitten to refuse.

17. A Second Take

"DaiKe, Smith speaking." Smith downed his last bite of the dry donut. It slid down his throat and left an unpleasant tickle in there. An eight-thirty phone call. It must be urgent.

"I have never seen a less committed man in his fifties before! I thought you would have called Aileen or me by now about the first date. You're not young anymore, and you outta work harder at what you want." It was Marie Newton, the matchmaker, whose words could pass for his mother's if she were to be alive again. A woman of early thirties acting this way screamed of hormonal imbalance. "Pardon for my honesty. Some truths just need to be heard."

"Miss Newton, I am at work." His face was flushed with red as the word 'first date' reverberated in his ear. He thought he was done with that once and for all when he got married twenty-five years ago. Back then he had moved quickly. He was deeply in love with Debbie. He knew she was the one as soon as he set his eyes on her. Aileen was great, but she was not Debbie, and could never replace her.

"That's why I am calling you now. — You know; we haven't heard from you for a long time." We? Smith was unaware that he was capable of hurting more than one woman's feeling at the same time. "I was about to set Aileen up with another man, but she thought you were so very nice and interesting on your last date that she's begged me to give you one more chance before moving on. I must tell you that we make our money through commissions, the more dates and successful matches the better. And your kind, who likes to stall, for whatever reasons even in the case of a wonderful woman who is willing to accept you as who you are is not only bogging our success rate down but is also bad for business."

"I am terribly sorry about that." The last part Smith could understand. Perhaps he had picked up the nasty habit from his portfolio of terrible clients at work. What other great weapons to use if not the most effective one to get a risk-free take at price reduction by stalling? Indecision was a customer's best friend and a sales' worst enemy. Only he did not know if one should bargain for this sort of service.

"Why, what happened? Do you not like her? Were you offended by something she said? Tell me what's on your mind."

Questions requiring self-explorations and emotional response, highly improper for business settings. *Must...get...out...of the situation*, he thought.

"No. She was great. I will schedule an appointment with her as soon as I ..."

"Don't you try to bullshit me. Let me pencil you two in for Saturday night. Seven PM. Same restaurant, and with a relationship expert."

No, I wasn't bullshitting you, and yes, Saturday was great, Smith answered, adamant to end the call right there. He hoped that it was still too early for his secretary to eavesdrop on his conversation.

As soon as he put the mouthpiece down, the phone rang again. The obnoxious and repetitive ring tone bounced off the walls of his office and strained his tolerance. He picked up the miniature rubber football with his left hand and gave it a forceful squeeze. It jumped out of his grip and disappeared under the black leather couch by the wall. — A perfect excuse not to pick up the call — Smith crouched next to the couch and slipped his hand under, sweeping for any obstruction in the thin space between the couch rails and the carpet while he let the ringtone go unanswered. Under the couch, he had found the football and extracted it out after a few attempts. And up he stood, panting, he came face to face with Mr. Tanaka, who had watched him tethered up the way old men did in amusement.

"We need a few more shots of you." He cut to the chase.

"You called?" Smith straightened his tie in the presence of the unexpected company.

"You heard it?" Tanaka crossed his arms.

They smiled at each other.

"I can't do it," Smith said. He was reluctant to allow his colleagues the pleasure of further taunts by making acting his second career. "As much as I like you and your projects, I have to turn you down. It's been, um, affecting the working atmosphere. I need to set an example for my staff instead of taking afternoon getaways with you guys." He padded Tanaka on the back and in the same gesture guided him towards the door. Tanaka turned around and planted his feet at the threshold, refusing to go away.

"That includes playing football in the office." Tanaka made it clear that he had seen the object in his hand.

Smith gave the ball a squeeze, this time making sure that it did not slip from his fingers. "It's a stress ball."

"Hmm..." Tanaka did not seem to find meaning in the words 'stress ball'. He had certainly seen them, hadn't he, Smith thought. "How about this Saturday? It's not during work hours." Tanaka suggested. Tenacious, he was.

Smith reminded himself that the man's last name was also T-A-N.

"I'm busy this Saturday." Already two appointments lined up for Saturday. He was not terribly excited for the third.

"Let us film you, follow you around as you conduct your normal Saturdays, may be interacting with the locals here and there. It will make a good story. We might be able to get a few good candid shots of you like last time."

"Using your editing magic again, huh?"

"Mr. Smith, you have a meeting on the 15th floor in two minutes." His secretary Cheryl had entered the room with an agenda for the day from the door connecting their offices. "Oh, excuse me." She said when realizing that she had intruded. Smith liked that she never said sorry, unlike the local grown Japanese who abused the word shamelessly. Thank God, there was Cheryl to keep him in his right mind. "As I have said, you have a meeting in two minutes. That's all you've gotten." and she smiled hintingly at Tanaka, who needed to go. Everything his American secretary would have said and done in the same situation. She was a Godsend.

"Don't let me down, Smith," Tanaka said, folding in multitudes of meaning into his simple words. Could Smith pretend that he did not get them?

"I have a one o'clock on Saturday. By two fifteen, I assume..." He simply could not be mean to nice people.

"I will go where you're and stay in the background. You won't even notice I am there."

"Mr. Smith. One-minute left." Cheryl said, retreating into her office, closing the connecting door behind her. She was right to be anxious. The Japanese were punctual animals.

"The cafe in Metropolitan Art Space. Punto Incotro is the name of the cafe. I am meeting my Japanese teacher there."

"*Nishi-Ikebukuro*. Will do." Tanaka raised his thumb and forefinger above his fist, and shot him with his finger handgun while winking at the same time — a strange gesture Smith had seen Japanese men do a handful of times that did not seem ill-meant — then he swiveled on his heels and disappeared.

When Smith got into the elevator with eleven seconds left to his 9 AM meeting, he found a sticky note on the button for the 15th floor.

"Smith, do wear a suit," it said, signed by Tanaka.

18. Daughter

The internet did not do him a great deal of help. If it was designed to aggravate non-Japanese speakers, then it had served its goal indisputably. First, he was unable to access the American, or any English versions of Google, Yahoo, or Bing. Something about his computer or network's address was being used to determine that he must either learn Japanese or quit. And entering the string 'Japanese language teacher rate' into the default Google Japan search bar triggered a list of websites in the nature of rating scantily clad Asian women in teacher's costumes — something he would have sacrificed a lamb in gratuity for at the age of seventeen perhaps, not fifty-five. Smith thought he had a stroke of genius when he translated the same string into Japanese with Google translator, and tried again with the translation '*Nihongo kyoshi no wariai*' in the search engine, only to be hit in the head by what seemed like an entry in a Japanese-Chinese-dictionary for robots. Apart from the bullet points, there was no signal succeeding in making heads or tails of the search results that Google had brilliantly populated the page within 0.0000028 seconds. Nevertheless, Smith clicked into the first top search result, only to be confronted with more proof of his ineffectual integration in Japan, printed in the Google-patented blue and white, not only in real life but also in the cyberspace.

How much should he pay Misa?

Too much would seem condescending. Too little would be taking advantage of her gratuity. The only reference he could draw in this regard was when he was moonlighting as a Math tutor for grade school kids when he was in junior high. That was in the sixties, and the minimum wage was still a dollar. He had asked for a dollar sixty for an hour. That amount today could hardly buy Misa a mechanical pencil from the Muji store. — He had been introduced to one of those darn things from Muji by Cheryl, his cheery secretary and compulsory portal to Japanese teenagers' lives. What was even the minimum wage in Japan? And how could he find that out without knowing Japanese when the army of search algorithms and IP address locators were turned against him? — Smith needed help.

If it wasn't for the fact that Andy had offered to teach him colloquial Japanese that involved vulgar street slangs and hip buzzwords that mismatched his age, and to induct him into his colorful and R-rated world of Japanese culture which Smith had decided earlier on was best to avoid for nothing but the sake of his health, he would have gone to Andy for help.

"Hey! Princess. How're ya?"

"Dad?" Debra answered the phone on the first ring, whispering.

"Yes, are you doing well?"

"It's eight fifteen, dad. The kids are sleeping!" she hissed. "You will wake them up."

"Oh, I am sorry." He had forgotten to check his watch again. The one tucked away in the bathroom cabinet that was never adjusted to remind him of the Central Time. To her legitimate complaint, knowing that his one and three years old grandchildren could be a bit of a handful for Debra, he felt extra guilty for calling, not to check up on them but to ask for information.

"What do you want?" Debra hissed under her breath. Her less-than-friendly attitude had made it easier for him to forgive his impertinence.

"I'm getting a Japanese teacher, and I don't know what to pay her. I just thought you might have some idea." He asked his daughter. Debra was a kindergarten teacher and was always aware of the tax rates, pay scale and raise schedules that sort of thing. She would know the answer to his question.

"What is she?" Debra asked.

Smith did not see that question coming. Does it make a difference? He wondered.

"Mm... she's, uh..." he stuttered to come up with a description of Misa that would put her in a more appropriate light for his daughter. "My neighbor introduced her to me. I think she's a student." Why did he think Misa's current identity would seem 'wrong' in his daughter's eyes? That thought scared him.

"Oh, a university student." his daughter's own conclusion saved him from overthinking. "Was Japanese education or Japanese language her major?"

"Um...no, I don't think so," Smith answered, wondering himself if Misa was old enough for tertiary education. "She can speak pretty good English, which helps."

"I would suggest seven dollars an hour. Nine tops if you really like her. No more."

"Great." Relieved now that his question had been resolved, he searched for the proper thing to say for a typical father-daughter talk.

"'kay, I've got to go," Debra said before he came up with a line.

"Thanks. Send greetings to..." Smith's last word was returned by a click followed by a succession of short blips. "...the grandchildren for me."

In his mind's eyes, he reverted to the Christmas celebration a year and nine months ago in their Rose Hill home. Everyone in the family was there, the wife, the daughter, the son-in-law, the son, the daughter-in-law, the two grandchildren, all but the now one-year-old Nathan, who had not even been conceived yet. He had not had the pleasure to meet the trooper yet, being born in the year of Tiger, destined to be a fighter and perhaps a little bit like his grandfather. Smith shut his memory down from that

Christmas celebration on, pulling the plug violently as if the thread of memory was a power cord to a plasma television. It flashed in agony before turning into a surface of dark tranquility, a realm where he chose to conduct his daily life in. He needed not to be reminded of the tragedy that happened next, not today.

***

"Arai, take off the baseball cap. You're attracting attention." Tanaka said in a hushed voice.

"*Taihen moushiwake arimasen!* My mistake, Mr. Tanaka! I thought..." Arai bowed at him in a 30-degree angle in apology.

"Shhh! *Shitsuka ni shite kudasai!*" Tanaka grunted and pulled Arai's baseball cap over his face. The boy did not see that coming but managed to catch his cap in front of his chest before it rolled off him to the ground and shoved it quickly into his Reebok backpack.

"You'd like to see paparazzi in operation, don't you? Then stop acting like an idiot. You're ruining our cover." Tanaka said under his breath. Even in an oversize Adidas tracksuit made up of too glossy a synthetic fiber, something that the renowned aristocratic dresser Ryuuji Tanaka, who was always spotted in a slim fit suit over a black turtleneck that had stayed fashionable since the nineteen-seventies, would never wear, his boss was still as stoic as he was without the monkey suit. Arai had trouble determining what was permitted and what was not on Saturdays' working hours, the gray area, the nebula of corporate hierarchies. Was he regarded as an equal on Saturdays? Should he keep the honorific after Tanaka-san's name? Was he allowed to take breaks as he pleased? Could he be making mistakes on these extracurricular assignments that would affect his career? *Just what would Confucius do?* — He mused.

"Just pretend we are father and son." Tanaka's command had solved the puzzle in Arai's head. And without forewarning, "Two Americano," he said, to the waitress passing by their table. She rolled her eyes at their impatience but quickly resolved to smile, nudged on by the dictum painted on the cafe's wall, 'We treat strangers like friends.' She smiled so hard that Arai thought her cheeks might hurt, a possibility that Arai had only considered for the first time in his life.

Arai could not get himself to drink the coffee. First, he never drank his coffee plain. And second, his hands were too shaky to raise the coffee mug without making a nervous rattle. One less move was always one good move made when one was nervous, which he definitely was. His heart was pounding as one o'clock approached. Perhaps Smith's teacher was already here right in their midst. Tanaka-san had told him, to be quiet as a *Hebi*, a snake and quick as a *Kitsune,* a fox, the two cardinal rules of being paparazzi. The image of the fox baring its shiny fangs and the slithering snakes colored this line of photography work that he admired with a darker, more sinister shade than he would like, but they also made it ever more appealing. He glanced up from his coffee at his mentor, who had now assumed the convincing appearance of being fully absorbed into the middle of Takiji Kobayashi's monumental book about Communism sitting opposite to him, with his back towards the entrance. Arai, as he was instructed, pulled out the tricked-out cell phone with high-resolution camera, and extended out the retractable keyboard to type commands into the control menu so it would start recording, when he saw the familiar Face of DaiKe, Mr. Smith appeared at the sliding glass door entrance of the Punto Incontro cafe at the Metropolitan Art Space.

"Elbows on the table," Tanaka whispered his advice, his eyes darted for a second to the lower right, before returning to his depressing book.

"Thanks." It was indeed a lot more stable and a great deal less tiresome than it would have been otherwise. Arai was thankful for his mentor.

19. Japanese Lesson

Good morning. No, good afternoon. You are very kind. Yes, you have. No, I am not. Thank you, thank you, thank you again. Shall we start? — Smith had rehearsed speaking these words in Japanese to her all night, but he was stumped immediately when the well-oiled machine of a waitress came over and asked him whether he had been here before, what would he like to drink and eat and whether he wanted to at all, or something like that. There should be a rule against bombarding customers with questions within five minutes of entering cafes as far as he was concerned. At his age, he needed his time to direct his mental capacity towards the drinks section from the small-talk section.

"*Menyu o misete kudasai.*" Misa bowed, smiled and spoke at the same time to the demanding waitress. She trotted away and came back with an insult for Smith, an English menu, a badly translated one.

"You should proof-read their spellings." Smith reverted into his comfort zone and complained to her in English. She raised her neatly plucked eyebrows to his comment, which made him aware that he had been too critical.

"Teach me Japanese." He begged, as soon as the waitress took his order. Realizing that the whole night of rehearsal did not jump-start his conversational skills in the language, he no longer felt the pressure to impress. This was the time to be humble. There was nothing to lose in front of a... child. Could he work his many personal inquiries for her into the lesson? "Teach me how to introduce myself," he asked. It was a brilliant topic.

"Let's start with the basics. But I want to know something about you first." Misa asked.

A mutual interest, Smith thought. "How long have you been in Japan?"

"Well, it's been a year. I took half a year of Japanese at the adult university before I came..." Smith cleared his throat. Misa did not seem surprised to hear that. Expectations and abilities were duly matched in her eyes, it seems. Smith relaxed a little.

"You are an American? How is America like? I have never there. I have never been anywhere, on a plane, I mean." she bit her lower lips.

"Quite different." He smiled at her in fond memories. "In general, people don't move at such breakneck pace as they do here. They conduct their lives in a more leisurely pace."

"What else is different?" Misa asked eagerly.

"And most people are quite friendly and like to ask you how you feel and how you're doing all the time. Although some people thought Americans hypocritical because of that.'"

"Why?"

"Because a lot of times, people are not really listening for the answers. They say 'How are you?' as a kind of greetings instead of a question."

Misa smiled. She found it interesting, so he continued on.

"Another difference would be that Americans rarely ask permission for, well, anything, if it's within the laws, as opposed to the Japanese. We say what's on our mind. It's in our constitution to express our opinion freely. You know what constitution is? It guarantees our freedom of speech, the freedom of expression in order to pursue — *do you know the word 'pursue'?* — happiness."

Misa thought about the difficult English words that Smith used for a moment, and then she asked, "does that mean there are laws that tell you to be happy?"

Her interpretation was not entirely wrong. Smith replied, "It's not far from it. Don't get me wrong, though. We aren't all just fat potato sacks of self-importance. It's our rights, and all of us deserve a chance to be happy. Like, like if I bought something from, say, *Isetan*, the department store, that I do not like. I might have used it already, but I'd still go back to the store and tell the manager how I'd feel and return it, and he would probably not give me a hard time. I could be getting a full refund, or a different model of the, whatever it is that I bought instead as well."

"Really?" Misa's eyes widened. She pouted her lips. "I'm always afraid if I have to return something. No, I wouldn't do it."

"Try it, next time. Then we'll see how it goes in this country." Smith said. "If everyone protects their rights, then overall as a society will get better." Despite what he said, he had not dared to return anything yet in Japan.

Misa repeatedly nodded, lost in thoughts about this faraway country she would never visit.

The song in the background of the cafe ended, and an annoying, repetitive electronic tone beat inspiration into Smith.

"And Americans don't listen to this kind of music. They like country music. Have you heard of country music? Chet Atkins, Jerry Reeds...I doubt you know them. But anyways, country music is often played with banjos, and you don't hear that in any other music anymore. And of course the fiddle, which is the violin, guitars, and harmonicas. Americans like that. Well, not all of them."

"Like Kelly Clarkson and Carrie Underwood!" Misa said.

"Ya..." He searched the country music department in his head for these names in vain. "Something like that."

"They are really amazing singers! I have their songs on my music player," Misa said enthusiastically. "The whole album from American Idol."

To avoid lingering on the subject of pop stars, he continued, "But above all, Americans are very hard working, just like the Japanese people. We can really say we created one of the best countries in the world, with creativity and bravery." He smiled, wondering if Misa understood. "My hometown, though, was not that." He snorted, which stirred her curiosity. She leaned forward and Smith began his tale. It was as his friends have always complained that once Smith started with a reverie, he was not to be stopped. And Misa's keen interest unstuck the memory dam. He took Misa by the hand and walked her through his childhood growing up in Cincinnati, in Midwest, as a Catholic, in a middle-class family, with conservative small-town values. He showed her the great landscape, the acres of land his father own where he and his brothers had played on, the birdhouse they built together, and the big Collie he owned. The story of the absurdly clever Collie that bit the postman three times got Misa grinning from ear to ear. "And my father, if he is still alive, would NEVER let me come here."

Suddenly he was pinged by a feeling of lonesomeness talking about his dead father.

"Oh well, I have talked too much." He grinned at the girl and took a sip of his coffee, feigning nonchalance. "It's your turn to tell me more about yourself. I don't even know how old you are!"

So eager was he to learn more about her, he had forgotten to keep up with his superficial motive of wanting to learn Japanese. It was just a matter of logistics. They would get around to it, he told himself and beat down the habitual urge of a businessman of sticking to the point.

"I am Misa Hayami," She said, smiling, and pulled her shoulders closer to herself as she spoke, a habit of shyness as if she was being interviewed. What charming creature she was, Smith thought. "I'm eighteen. I work as a waitress, here and there, in Ikebukuro. Hmm..." Her eyes turned into slits as she smiled nervously.

"Go on," Smith said, with an encouraging smile in return. He had already heard about the lack of public speaking or discussion training in Japanese schools and witnessed the damaging effects of it at his workplace.

"I have a younger brother," she said, "and we live together in Tokyo." Misa squirmed uncomfortably at the thought of her brother.

"Tatsu," Smith said.

She nodded.

"What kind of people does he hang out with?"

"I don't know."

"I have my theory. Would you like to know how I have found him?" Smith said.

"There's no need..."

"You know I've gone to the police afterward, and Andy — I think you remembered him, he's my colleague — gave them your name, as correspondent of the victim because we have no idea how to identify your brother, or that he is even your brother."

"The police have explained that to me already." She got up to bow at him as she said. "*Hondo ni sumimasen.* I will compensate for your trouble."

"No, don't say that. That's not why I mentioned it. I just wanted to bring that up to see if you need any help or anything."

"*Mo nani mo irimasen.* I don't need anything else...*hondo ni,* it's true."

Smith dragged her back to her seat. He felt embarrassed for making Misa bow at him. Instinctively he scanned the room hoping that no one was watching them, and there was not.

"You're not from Tokyo, are you?" Smith asked, changing the subject.

"No, no," she reverted to smiling. "I moved here after junior high ended. From near Ebetsu."

"Is that in Hokkaido?" Apart from his Japanese, his geography of

Japan could use some help.

"Yes, yes! That's right." And his wild guess had been a good one. Misa seemed sufficiently impressed that he knew which one of the four major islands she came from. "It's very small, and at the same time very big... I honestly don't know what to say about myself."

"Sure you know."

"My English is so bad."

"It's great! It's better than a lot of people I know," he said. "Just try, like I did."

"...but I don't like to talk about myself." she insisted.

That was the point he decided to drop the subject. Not everyone was an egomaniac like him. Just to imagine that there were people out there who did not want to talk about themselves, or just talk, that would have been just pure madness for him before he had arrived in Japan. Growing up in a big family, studying in a competitive university program and then getting a job at a big corporation meant you fought hard for your airtime, always. The mentality, of course, made some major adjustment recently. He had been converted, silently, one pachinko marble at a time, into an INTP of the Myers-Briggs test, an introverted thinker.

"*O-kotowari shimasu.* Sorry, I can't do that. That's the first phrase you should learn." And she drove the message home by writing it down on a napkin for him.

"*Demo nihongo ni dekiru, no?* But you can do it in Japanese, right?" Smith marshaled in all his sentence making power to create this one.

They smiled at each other.

20. The Apartment in Shiodome

A couple of days ago.

The floor rattled in the familiar dull, low hum. Tanaka untied his leather shoes at the threshold and scanned the apartment for any sign of life. Stillness — his mental filter had sieved out the background noises and vibrations that were inherent to the place. Great.

Under the street lamp that filtered into the apartment by the Shiodome train platforms, he shifted to the refrigerator under stealth, an art he had mastered by years of training in his business, and opened the door to the freezer. From his pocket, he took out his wool gloves and wriggled his hands in them. Eyes on his target, he extracted a sealed zip-loc bag from underneath the frozen TV-dinner stashed near a similar zip-loc filled with frozen cream spinach carefully, in order not to leave too many marks. The bag of old spinach had been there since the beginning, he mused. One day he would throw it away, he swore.

'2000-01', '2004-06', 'Katja M.', 'E0286XL', 'Comp' pas'...Tanaka scanned the scribbles on the side of the tapes. They were labeled, and some unlabeled, in a haphazard way, for they were not from a single collector, but from centuries of all the directors and producers that had utilized this place. A porno scrapyard, this was. It held all the footages that were too racy, too violent, too inartistic, too sloppy but too expensively produced or in strange ways too interesting to be condemned to the forgive-all fire bin. He himself had never had one that required such level of after-product care. However, the customers' tastes had changed in the time since he had retired. They had wanted more — more girls, more celebrities, more ethnicity, more gadgets, more varieties of tricks, more depths in plots, more outdoor scenes, more emotions. He felt he was not up to the job anymore.

His thoughts were interrupted by his finding. — 'Étourdir', he had spotted it. He recognized the handwriting and the no-nonsense title in French on it. Satisfied, he stashed that tape into the front pocket of his jacket and quickly replaced everything.

"One day," He whispered under his breath, his eyes staring straight through the metal freezer's door, "you all will tell such a great story." and he locked the door behind him.

***

Tanaka mounted the videotape into its cartridge and shoved it into the VHS recorder in his study at home. The raw video played automatically.

Then he settled on his usual spot on the couch, lit a freshly rolled cigarette and sucked on it.

There it was, this was how it all started, in the deserted afternoon streets of an unnamed small town.

A figure was seen trotting down the street leisurely after a quick exchange with the cameraman. He had a mop of black, unkempt long hair that cried negligence. When he walked, one got the impression that his dirty white canvas sneakers were too big for him, and any moment now he would trip. It was strange that the figure's sloppy gait should bother Tanaka as much as what he suspected would happen next. From the movie, one could see that the cameraman stayed behind and did not follow until the figure ahead of him rounded a corner. The video slowly caught up to the figure, who once again disappeared into the alleyway between two adjacent but disjointed wooden houses, right behind where the lamp post stood. The cameraman made a left towards the other side of the street swiftly. And when he settled, the view was now covered by a blurry patch of gray stones in close quarter, leaving just a small gap on the right, focused at the point where the figure had just vanished.

Twenty seconds passed, and nothing happened. The pair were waiting in a lair for something.

Tanaka took another drag from his cigarette and exhaled in a succession of small puffs. His eyes peeled to the screen of the television.

Then the camera was spun around and zoomed in on a figure crossing a busy traffic street from a small distance away. As the cameraman pressed the shutter softly, the figure's outline hardened, and the exposure was corrected. Hardly did Tanaka see her face the focus was already switched somewhere else. The cameraman swept his camera from the ground up, scanning her white feet stacked in the heeled sandals, to her pearly white calves and up her thighs. The continuum was stopped by the hem of her tightly worn mini-skirt that chaffed the contact points on her thighs pinkish red. She looked left, then right, ahead — at which point the camera swung away in a rustle of fabric rubbing against each other — then resumed slowly to position to see the girl looking right again, before completing her crossing. Three large paper bags from clothing stores dangled from her hands. They swung beside her body with inertia.

The cameraman shrunk back, as the girl turned right into the deserted street so he would not be spotted. One could hear the heartbeats of the man, throbbing violently as she strutted down the street of no return, headed towards the direction of the hidden man.

A brief moment of regrettable disappointment flitted across Tanaka's mind, as the girl clogged pass to an anticlimactic turnout. The men stayed in place, and the girl did not spot the creature hidden in his shadowy lair. Nothing happened.

Then the lens zeroed in on the girl.

Behind the lamppost, the first man lunged towards her from behind, slipped his hands under her mini-skirt and in one swift motion, yanked her underwear almost down to her knees. It was light pink with frilly lace ruffles. Her knees turned inward towards each other protectively, and she clutched the underwear before it fell. With her forward momentum curbed by the physical restraint around her thighs, the girl struggled to keep her balance.

A small yellow bird that had been perched somewhere on the branch of a nearby tree stopped its cheery chirping dived towards the man at the shock of the sudden movement below.

Excitement swelled in Tanaka's chest. He had crushed his cigarette between his fingers without noticing.

The perpetrator had sprinted away ahead. The frazzled girl's gaze followed the assailant who became smaller and smaller as he faded into the distance. Desperation on her face was chased away quickly away by helplessness — no chance of catching him.

She pulled up her underwear as fast as she could. The camera panned out. The girl looked nervously around her. — Was she searching for someone to help, or making sure that no one had witnessed her ultimate embarrassment? — She did not even have the time to yelp.

The shopping bags in her hand went crashing down her side. Her knees gave way. She squatted in the midst of the heap of clothes that had fallen out. And in this spot she stayed for a good minute, cocking her head up in despair, expressionless, shell-shocked.

Then she spotted the cameraman coming her way, who had the nerves to walk out from behind the stone wall. Her eyes looked straight into the camera. It scared Tanaka to have been spotted. He had to remind himself consciously that despite the first-person perspective the movie was filmed in, none of this was actually his misdoing.

The cameraman extended his free hand towards her. Instinctively she took his hand, without an ounce of suspicion, and struggled back on her feet with his support, completely mistaking his gesture as the gallantry that was innate to every man in Japan — so they said.

Then senses began to hit her. Her mouth fell open. Speechless. Surprised. Unsure how to act. She swallowed hard, her eyes dashing between his face and the lens. From the corner of the screen, Tanaka noticed that she had taken a step back in defense, her back coming up against the stone wall.

"What's your name?" He asked.

"Uh..." Her hesitation didn't last long. One's name was one of those things that could not be stolen from oneself, regardless of the tragedy. "I'm called Misa Hayami."

"My name is Sadao Maeda. You're very pretty." He swept his camera slowly from her head to her toes as if this was nothing but an item on an antique appraisal show.

When the camera returned to her face, Tanaka saw her blush.

"Here's your money." The cameraman waved a stack of Yens in front of her.

"Ehh?" The pitch change of her voice showed that she was genuinely surprised. "Ehh? What's this for?"

"Take it. You want them." He shoved the money closer to her body. "This is ten thousand yen."

The girl stood motionless, ogling the large amount of money in the man's hand.

"You're going to go home with this money, buy something for yourself and feel great." On he hummed his lullaby. "You did well today."

"No..." her voice trailed off. What had happened and what was happening now finally came together.

The man bent down to stuff the money into one of the paper shopping bags.

"I'm giving them to you anyway. Whether you take them or not," he said. "See? It's in there. You can use them, or throw them away. You're a beautiful and smart girl. You'll choose correctly."

Slowly, he backed away from her, his camera still pointing at her relentlessly. At a loss of what else she could do, she smoothed down the wrinkles in her mini-skirt.

"Bye now, Misa Hayami," The man said, sounding almost kind.

The screen turned dark for a second then sprung back to life as another sequence came up, in another deserted suburban Japanese street.

21. The Girl in the Tape

"Tanaka-san," Arai opened his mouth to voice his concern.

"What?" Tanaka barked.

"Did something happened?" Arai asked. "You looked terrible after you came back from the toilet."

Good observation. Tanaka was impressed.

"I was just thinking about work." Tanaka could not possibly explain everything to him without some preparations, so he chose to keep it simple. The boy was reliable and honest. He had thought about recruiting Arai into his personal projects and grooming him to become his protégé. Yet he was such a nervous wreck near persons of authority. And he had such a weak chin and a pair of sad drooping eyes. Was he able to handle it? Tanaka needed to observe him longer.

"Do you also have the impression that she was too young? In my humble opinion," Arai said, "I think this footage will not work for the commercial..." he said trailing off at the end of his sentence.

Tanaka gave Arai the death stare. "Then why didn't you say so earlier?" Tanaka had his back against their targets the whole time. He was relying completely on Arai to make the right call. The essence of paparazzi work was to be quick on your feet because circumstance changes all the time.

"I'm really sorry. I'm really sorry for not speaking up earlier." Arai looked like he was in pain.

"Shut the camera off and relax your arms. You've been holding up your cell phone for a good half an hour." Tanaka said, as quiet as he could. "Even if you're not tired, somebody will soon realize you're up to no good if you keep holding that thing in the same position."

Arai laughed nervously and flexed his arms in relief. Blood had been draining off his arms slightly after five minutes into filming. For the next twenty-five minutes that led to the ultimate numbness in his arms, he had challenged his inner demon to a fight as to whether he should utter his professional judgment or he should just do what he was told and be professional about it. One side of him was afraid that it might seem like he was making up an excuse to slack off. The other side of him was afraid that his arms might soon need to be cut off to preserve the rest of his body. Now all his emotions had seemed so unnecessary.

"The girl is very beautiful," Arai said, now rubbing his arms as inconspicuously as possible under the table. "Made me want to learn Japanese, too."

Tanaka snorted.

Yes, she was beautiful. And with such a beautiful, memorable face, Tanaka couldn't have possibly mistaken who she was. She was the real thing. The subject of his studies for the last two months. Hundreds and thousands of her frames he had studied. He had known a little bit too much about her than he was willing to admit.

Arai had noticed his uneasiness. Indeed, he felt the girl's eyes were on him as he passed en route to the men's room, which, he assured himself, was just his mind playing tricks on him. He was not being watched. Not by Mona Lisa and not by her. The girl had no idea who he was. The acquaintance was one-sided. There was no reason to be worked up, Tanaka.

"I thought his Japanese teacher would be older," Arai said, his eyes wandering off in the general direction of the pair.

"Is this how you've envisioned it?" Tanaka asked him.

"Yes, I was wondering whether we could pass this for a business meeting, with him listening carefully to what she had to say and responding in the local language. This image of a good-listener would befit DaiKe's employee. And we have the luck that they picked the seats by the window — their silhouettes against the background of cars and pedestrians passing outside. Put a blurring filter on those and boost the contrast. A close-up of their faces as they speak to each other — it would have been the kind of thing we want, or am I wrong?"

"You're quite right," Tanaka said.

"It's a pity she's a bit too young."

"Well, it doesn't always have to be business related. Imagery of the old and the young, of men and women, of a foreigner and local being in harmony together, could be quite moving. It could give the audience a new perspective on DaiKe."

"Boss, you are a genius!" Arai said. "Should we go over to talk to them?"

"No, let me talk to Smith on Monday. Let's watch them a little longer for now."

***

"What's with the suit?" Andy asked grabbing Smith on the shoulder in a forceful swoop.

"Where in the devil did you come from?" Recovering from the sudden physical assault, Smith's oratory sense was now under attack by a wave of rap music that glorifies murders and crimes in close quarters, coming out from the mp3 player that Andy had stuffed in the back pocket of his pants. Smith snatched it to turn it off.

"Let me," Andy grabbed it back and turned the volume dial down, "before we have to call technical support."

"So you're learning Japanese from Misa!" Andy said loudly in surprise, paying no heed to his surroundings. People were reading and listening to music in the museum cafe and in him came barking. Smith couldn't stand him sometimes, especially when he was wearing a hoody inside a leather jacket, with his hair made spikey by an excessive of hair gel, the look that reminded him of his daughter's favorite actor, Ryan Reynolds, whom he had never wanted to punch more in the face.

And Ryan Reynolds gave an all-too-friendly hug to his barely legal-aged Japanese teacher, without even asking whether he was intruding. This almost brought him back to the second state of shock — anger.

"Where's your leash?" He had to say it. Andy and Misa were like a drop of ketchup on Claude Monet's Water Lilies.

"Raff!" Andy barked. The man had no shame. Smith scanned the room hoping that the other patrons in the cafe would be squinting their eyes towards the agitator in unison to instill the Bushido fear and order into him, but they were as docile as he had imagined them to be.

"How'd you find us?" Smith asked. "By sniff'n?"

"Oh, don't be bitter!" Andy waved off his sarcasm with a dramatic slap on Smith's back, spitting his words of wisdom on Smith as if someone had tapped the '57' on his neck. "Misa needed someone to drive her brother home. And only one of us here drives a Honda."

Smith was tempted to stab his eyes out with his BMW keychain. Lucky for Ryan Reynolds, they were in his luggage at home that held everything from the States.

"How'd you know that?"

"Cars, I was with you when you went to the police. Remember?" Andy leaned himself against the coffee table. It sunk a quarter of an inch. "And *I* was the one who told you her name. I called her to check if she was okay yesterday and she's asked me to help pick up her brother."

"Misa, you could have asked me to accompany you." Smith decided he should appeal to Misa's common sense.

She merely smiled. How could one blame the innocent, trusting creature? However, given what had happened to her the last time in Andy's presence, maybe she should learn to stay away from men who had no regard for traditional dos-and-don'ts.

"You know what, we were just talking about you, right, Misa?" Smith said. "*O-jama-shimasu*. Just when you are walking in." — *'Jama'* meant devil. And when used as a verb, in this case, it meant 'to bother'. Either way, it fits.

"Let's go, Misa," Andy said to the girl. "You too, chop chop!" He turned to Smith. "You only paid for an hour," Andy tapped the surface of his wristwatch, which showed the time to be seven minute past two. "Or did you not?"

At Andy's vile reminder, Smith realized that he almost forgot about it.

"Misa, how shall we do it?" Smith scrambled to take out his wallet. "If you don't mind, I can pay you a little bit more than minimum..."

"Just pay for the coffee," Andy pushed the money back towards his direction. "And the cake."

"Who are you to her?" Smith questioned.

Andy pointed with his forefinger at Misa and himself and said, "Friends." Then he pointed his forefinger between Misa and Smith, and said, "Teacher-student. Hmm, not so close."

"Next Saturday again?" Misa asked as she looped the handle of her tote bag over her shoulder.

"*Ichi ji ni matte imasu.* I'll wait for you at one," Smith replied. He was proud of himself, almost.

22. Make A Wish

There were not a lot of people yet at the Zojoji Temple ground on Saturday morning. The air was crisp and fresh from any human smells. It was a sacred resting place for the bodies of many, including that of the family of the most prominent Shogun in Japanese history, Tokugawa, who effectively ruled Japan for two hundred years until the Meiji period. Its mausoleum entrance was most distinctive protected by four rows of cute baby statues that represented babies or children that had passed away. Empathetic visitors had clothed them over the years with various accessories, to keep them warm through the changes of seasons.

  The temple's solemn existence in one of the most touristic areas in Tokyo stood as a sharp contrast to the ostentatious opulence around it. Being directly next to the Tokyo Tower, wedged in an area between the old fishing harbor that housed the Tsukiji Fish Market and the newly developed high-end commercial residential area Roppongi, the temple ground where Misa stood was an expensive real estate that had remained untouched despite the relentless developments of the city.

Seeing it reminded Misa of the brief period of happiness when she had just arrived at the city full of optimism. Her French boyfriend Sergey and she had lived happily and simply together in a studio apartment not ten minutes walking from here near the Shiodome metro station that his investor had rented out for him. She would have gone to see the apartment instead today, had she not hesitated a moment too long when the metro stopped at Shiodome (Its Japanese Kanji name transliterate into 'Being stuck'). By the time she had realized, the metro was already on its way to the next station Daimon (Its Kanji name transliterate into 'Big Door'). Misa took a hint from the Gods, and decided to walk forward through the gate of new life towards the temple and did not look back.

There she found two racks hung full of *Emas*, the swinging wooden plaques carved with the temple's seal and scribbled, on the other side, with wishes of pilgrims who came before her.

'Success at the public examination!'

'I hope he will reciprocate my love.'

> *'Please give luck to my family and me for the new year!'*

> *'The promotion, don't forget about the promotion!'*

Misa read a few plaques directly in front of her as she took out her own from her bag. Sergey and she had bought a plaque here previously. 'Love and treasure each other forever', that was what the fifteen-year-old Misa wrote on the plaque in Japanese. It was a line of lyrics from a cheesy love song of her youth. On Misa's insistence, Sergey had reluctantly signed his name with a marker on the bottom of the plaque next to Misa's without knowing what he had subscribed himself to. Like most tourists, he was indefinitely more fascinated by the Tokugawa tombs than the superstitious wish-making rituals that his stubborn childish girlfriend insisted they should follow.

That year, Misa was fifteen. After her birthday, when she would be sixteen, she would have reached legal age for marriage for girls in Japan, then she would propose to Sergey, like a modern Japanese city woman who let no one but herself control her own destiny.

The monks removed the old plaques from time to time. That old one was now nowhere to be found. She wondered what the monks do to old plaques. Did they keep them? Was there a cellar under the floor of one of the temple buildings that stored the wishes of hundreds of thousands of people so that their spirits, regardless of the state of their bodies, would live on forever? Or did they burn them all, and rid the world of all frivolous, unfulfilled wishes?

The bronze bell rang not far away. It sang the hour. Misa hurried to find a free spot to hang her *Ema* and headed out.

A group of visiting primary school students brushed passed her. One of them ran in front of the *Ema* racks ignoring the teacher's instruction to stand in a circle. A swinging plaque at her eye level caught her attention.

'*Health to everyone I love,*' the small characters on the first line of the anonymous plaque read. They looked like they were written as an after-thought.

'*Let me find the killer,*' the second line that occupied most of the plaque said, '*so I could drive a knife through its heart and watch it bleed to death.*'

The girl looked nervously at the back of the woman who was just crossing the threshold of the *Sangedatsumon,* the Gate of Three Deliverance from Earthly Sins (Greed, Hatred and Foolishness). A chill ran down the little girl's spine. She wondered if this incongruous display of hatred in the wishing wall of a Buddhist temple was something peculiar enough to warrant telling her teacher about.

23. The Relationship Expert

"I'm terribly sorry I had forgotten to call back. I really meant to," Smith said apologetically to Aileen, taking her hand into his. "But know that the injustice has now been avenged. I have been sitting in a cafe for two hours waiting for someone at work to come this afternoon, but he didn't show. That's why I look like this today. Then I realized that I didn't have my apartment keys with me, and I couldn't go home to change into something proper for our date. I wandered the streets of Tokyo until now."

"Are you truly apologizing or just hinting that you would like to get an invitation to my apartment after our dinner, 'cause you can't go home?" She smiled a wickedly.

"Oh, I wouldn't dare thinking that far ahead. Don't we have a, uh, relationship expert in our midst tonight? Miss Newton, you know her, she's disruptively creative. I hope I last until the end of the ordeal with her expert to take home the beautiful mädchen." Then he corrected himself, "Well, I meant I would see to it that you are home safely, and then I would go back to mine."

"I'm just wondering what 'mädchen' meant," Aileen asked, giggling at Smith's clumsiness in expressing his feelings, as he held the door to the Italian restaurant to let her in.

"Oh, it's German for 'girl'," Smith explained. "You really can't teach an old dog new tricks. I'm learning Japanese now and the other foreign languages I learned as a kid kept popping up and messing up my sentences. It's like there's a certain area in your brain where you throw all the foreign words in, and then you realized that you've forgotten to index them!"

"Girl, you called me! You keep pretending to be confused!" She laughed, flattered at being called a girl at thirty-six.

And there, in the middle of the restaurant, sat an elderly Caucasian lady. She was wearing a white two-piece dress suit that reminded him of a mix between the Queen of England and his Oral English teacher in high school, who was always asking him to 'e-nun-ci-ate'. No doubt she was Mrs. Newton, for she was staring disapprovingly at him the same fashion he was staring at her.

"Looks like the expert is none other than Miss Newton's mother herself."

"I'm nervous," Aileen murmured to him under her breath. "Do we really need her to psycho-analyze us? I think we're getting along fine by ourselves..."

"Marriage counseling before the marriage. It makes total sense," Smith said ironically, "in Japan."

His mind perched for a few seconds on the revealing statistics he saw about the commonness of extramarital affairs in the countries where divorce was almost unheard of.

Before Smith could suggest that they sprint for the door together, a waiter came forward and took the scarf and the handbag from Aileen.

"Party of three for Mrs. Newton, I believe?" he said.

"Too late," Aileen whispered in Smith's ear. "That bag costs a fortune! And it has all my papers in it."

Smith tapped her twice on her waist to cheer her up, and then he offered to help Aileen take off her quilted coat. He was hit by the familiarity of the scene at once. This was something that he would do for Debra in a restaurant, for the last twenty-eight years. His ear twitched in reaction.

"Hello, Mrs. Newton," the two said in unison.

"Aren't you two an item already?" Marionette Newton said. Her voice was chirpier than Smith had anticipated, given the antiquity that oozed off her appearance, accentuated by the British accent that reminded him of the colonial times. To be fair, she could not have been more than ten years' senior to him, still with the working man's vigor.

After the group had ordered their drinks and food, Mrs. Newton began her session.

"Thank you for being here today. I am delighted that you two have made the commitment to come to my session together. Do we not all crave for long-lasting, trust-based and happy relationships? And that's why we usually have sessions like these for pairs that we've matched and who have shown fair interests in each other but needed a little something to jump-start the relationship. For these pairs, we would always ask them to come together and do a little exercise that will make them open up. Despite my looks, I am not a witch, and I do not make love potions. I cannot guarantee sparks, and I cannot make up feelings between two people. But what I can do, is to make the two of you consider carefully what you need and want, and about what you have as an option, as well as let me in on what other options I can offer the two of you in case we have a mismatch. The journey to finding your soulmate is not easy, and I am here to help you. So Carson Smith and Aileen Martin, let's begin."

"Wonderful," Smith remarked, liking the sound of quality. He felt a lot more comfortable with psychological assessment tests than the telling-impressive-jokes-at-a-bar competition when it came to dating.

"Good," Mrs. Newton said, taking out a stack of flashcards from her purse. "For our first exercise, I'm going to say a word, and in turns, the two of you will have to reply the first sentence that comes into your mind related to the word. The first word is ..." Mrs. Newton pulled a card randomly from her stacks of cards. "Camel. Carson, you're first."

"Um, well..."

"One sentence, remember. You can put as many pauses in it, but if your sentence ends, your turn is over. And don't be shy. You can say everything that is on your mind. This will help Aileen, and I understand you better."

"Well, then I'm going to say that I don't know how 'camel' is going to help me 'carry on' with my date," he winked at Aileen, "but I do think that Camel is a strong and intelligent animal just like me."

"Okay, my turn," Aileen took a deep breath and said.

"Oh, you've used up your sentence," Mrs. Newton said.

"No! I haven't even started!" Aileen rebutted.

"That's the rule. But okay, I'll let you have this one," Mrs. Newton conceded.

"So I think..." Aileen thought carefully, this time, not to use up her sentence too quickly before she expressed her opinion, "that camels are ugly and scary beasts because I've ridden one during my last vacation to Egypt *but,*" she stressed the 'but' in order to declare that she still hadn't finished her quota of one full stop, "with the right riders, they can be reliable transportation means for people in the desert."

Mrs. Newton had an excellent memory and quick hands. As soon as Aileen finished, she had already scribbled their answers down on two separate pieces of flashcards. She showed Smith's response to Aileen and Aileen's to Smith.

"Aileen, what do you notice about Smith's response?" she asked.

"It's different from mine," she commented jokingly. Seeing that Mrs. Newton's silently demanding a more thoughtful and sophisticated answer, Aileen said, "Well, I think Carson's comparison between himself and the camel was a bit odd."

"You wouldn't do that?" Smith said, surprised at what she picked up.

"Nope." Aileen compressed her lips into a thoughtful pout.

"And what do you think about Aileen's?" Mrs. Newton prompted Smith.

"I like her answer. Even though she failed the first time, she managed to pull off telling me something about herself and her vacation in that one short sentence. I thought that was impressive."

Aileen smiled at the compliment.

"Don't be too flattered. He was only complimenting you to avoid talking about the fact that you're not a very attentive person. First, you've gotten the question wrong. I said 'camel', not 'camels'. Second, deserts are camel's natural habitat. They don't need any training or any owner."

Smith raised his palms up to show his innocence.

"Don't be too cheery yourself either, Carson. You make a lot of assumptions. You've never seen a camel before, I believe. Otherwise, you wouldn't make that comment about their intelligence. And you are very insecure. That's why you had to compliment yourself when I said a word as neutral as a camel. But that can be good, of course, for you two, as a pair." She looked at Aileen then back at Smith, sincerely, as if she wasn't making assumptions about the unfamiliar herself. "Both of you are equally eager to show off. From this response, Smith focused more on his intellects and personality. And Aileen, you focused on appearance and experience. An interesting combination. So, you've learned so much about yourself and so much about each other already in less than five minutes. Let's do another one," She suggested, without stopping to console the distastes in the participants' mouths. "The word for this round is 'Decide'. This time, I'll ask Aileen to speak first. Mind you; it is 'Decide', present tense, not past tense."

"Wow. That's difficult," she said. "Oops! I did it again. And Oops! Again. I'll shut up until I have my sentence."

"Smith, would you let Aileen have her turn still?" Mrs. Newton asked. "She's not very attentive, is she? She likes to bend the rules, push boundaries. But I must say, this is the case for most women." She gave a satisfied smile to applaud her own keen observations.

"We're here to learn about each other, right? So I'll give Aileen another chance."

"Another chance!" Aileen blurted. "It's just a game. This hardly needs to be taken so seriously."

"What did I say?" Mrs. Newton said under her breath.

"Go on Aileen," Smith encouraged, suppressing a laugh after Mrs. Newton's jest.

"Here it comes: I decide for myself what's fair." Aileen winked at Smith, feeling triumphant.

"The Japanese for 'Decide' is Kettei and I know it because I studied a list of Japanese verbs all afternoon." Smith followed quickly with his answer.

Mrs. Newton looked up from her flashcards after she had finished jotting down their responses again. Like she did previously, she gave them the other person's card and asked what they think of them.

"I can go first," Smith volunteered. "Aileen takes her rights very seriously. She has a strong mind and a rare honesty that people here lack. I appreciate that very much in a person." He gave Aileen a smile.

"Okay," Mrs. Newton said, not imposing to them her opinion this time. "And how about Smith's?"

"*The Japanese for Decide is Kettei...*" Aileen read his response aloud. "It shows that he's a nerd. And I guess it is what you've said about him, Mrs. Newton. He likes to say smart things. I like an intelligent man. Nothing wrong with that."

Mrs. Newton nodded, then said, "He's also non-confrontational."

"I am not non-confrontational," Smith said. "See, I'm defending myself now. Right here right now."

"Then stop sweating." Mrs. Newton dabbed her napkin on his hand jokingly. "Next one. 'Separation'"

"I knew something like that was coming," Smith said. Then he picked up his glass of red wine and took a large gulp of it.

"Oh, I will get it out," Aileen said. "And don't give me a hard time about the rules. — Separation from a loved one can be a painful experience for a lot of people."

"Separation of seismic twins could be life-threatening," Smith said.

"Come off it! Stop building a wall around yourself." Aileen squinted straight at him.

"No, I am not 'building a wall around myself'," He rebuffed.

"We didn't learn anything about you in this sentence!" she argued. "The exercise is supposed to get us to know each other, right, Mrs. Newton?" Aileen looked at the old lady imploringly, rallying for her support.

"Oh, you're more attentive than I thought. Maybe you just have an intuitive understanding of how things work," Mrs. Newton mused to herself.

"This is how I talk. Exercise or not. I was being honest about the first thing on my mind when I heard the word. I like to keep conversations light, and educational. I raised two National Society scholars that way."

"Okay, let's have dinner now, kids." Just as Mrs. Newton finished her sentence, three waiters who had lined up around the table extended their arms and delivered their meals onto the table. With trained synchronization, they lifted the gold-encrusted lids of the plates and chanted, "Buon Appetito!"

24. The Boyfriend

"*Que faites-vous, Damien?*" It meant 'what are you doing' in French. Damien stood frustrated in front of the mirror next to the shower and sighed. When he saw Tanaka peeking his head into the bathroom seeing him in his dismal state, he threw his rouge brush at him.

"*Que faire, rien ne fonctionne!*" Nothing works. "*Regardez! Ici!*" Look! Here! Damien pointed with his pinky finger at the red boil on his lower lip. "*Argghh!*" He shouted, ruffling his hair in helplessness.

"*Calmez-vous, bebe!*" Calm down, baby — Tanaka said to him. He took one look at the familiar red rash on his boyfriend's lip and immediately understood what was going on. He switched to Japanese, "Are you going out tonight?"

"Of course! *Mochiron desu!*" Damien hissed back in Japanese. "Why do you think I'm fussing in front of the mirror for so long!"

"These things, they will go away in a few days." Tanaka lied. Herpes boils could last forever, especially if they scarred the skin already. But just in case it got any worse, he advised.

"Take one of the pills I have in the cabinet." He pointed to the medicine cabinet behind the mirror.

"I have a competition to judge tonight!" Damien dabbed another layer of concealer on the monstrosity, realizing that it had only made it more noticeable because the color of his skins had gotten darker after coming back from the tanning salon just last Sunday, and it was a few shades darker than the concealer. He made another loud groan at his own reflection. "*C'est ta faute!* It's all your fault! All your filthy dirty dick's fault! *Merde! Merde! Merde!*"

"What do you want me to do?" Tanaka distant himself from the crybaby. He knew the boy's temper. Any moment something could be flying in his direction. "I did not ask you to sleep with me."

"Yes, you did!" Damien shrilled, flailing his arms in the air and trailing after him like an angry zombie going after him for revenge.

"What competition is that today?" he asked him, seating himself on the couch. Tanaka noticed Damien's red carpet worthy silk gown only now.

"*Je vous l'ai dit!* I told you like a million times." Damien tumbled on the couch next to Tanaka. His brunette wig swung around the attachment points on the side of his head. "Men, men, men. They never listen. It's the Dancing Queen contest at the Decadence Bar. Abba and everything. Remember?"

"That's where we met." Tanaka pulled his right hand in between his own palms and stroked it gently. Damien was freshly shaven. The back of his hand was hairless and smooth.

"Yes, but that's not what I am talking about," Damien complained weakly, leaning against his shoulder.

"Wear a mask." Tanaka had a spark of genius. "All the fashionable teenagers do that these days."

"Oh my god, that's brilliant!" Damien scrambled off to the bathroom once again to find himself a presentable face mask. They come in all colors and designer labels. When he came out from the bathroom, he was refreshed with his hairdo fixed, his makeup retouched, and his skin so smooth it glittered — it could also have been the good deed of the glittery powder his stylist had suggested him to mix into his body spray tanning solution. "Should I pretend to be sick or should I be fashionably sick in the head?" He holstered up the facemask around his mouth and asked. His voice muffled.

"It's equally reprimandable," Tanaka replied.

"*Mon cher,* so you're gonna take good care of yourself while I'm gone?" Damien asked, adjusting the elastic strap of the face mask around the back of his head. The tangled brunette wig had made it quite difficult. "Order some Chinese food. Don't starve yourself again."

"This is not Paris anymore! I swore I would never eat that ghastly Chinese takeout again when I left, and now you're putting me through it. I can cook for myself. Japanese cooks." Tanaka asserted proudly to the French boy.

"That's right. There's no fun eating Chinese takeout by the TV when I'm not here," Damien considered as he rounded the couch to the shoe rack, holding on to the seat back to support himself sliding his right foot into the six inches' tall stiletto. "Oh, I love these shoes!"

"You designed them. I get it," Tanaka jested. "Don't worry, I'll just do some work and go to sleep."

"Work as in real work or as in your stinking boring documentary?" Damien challenged. "You're not gonna make any money from that. And you're gonna get yourself into trouble! Digging up somebody's skeletons in the closet!"

"If there are really skeletons in the closet, would you've stopped, if you were me?" Tanaka asked.

"*Oui!* Yes!" Damien said, picking up her purse to leave the apartment. "I don't want you to become another one!"

"It's not as bad as you've imagined," Tanaka said, trying to convince both of them. "You know how long I've been trying to work on something big. I know this is it."

"My ambitious *moitie*! We're exactly the same, except I pop pills." He pointed at his chest, where a resemblance of breasts had grown. He had been taking female hormones. "Don't watch too much straight porn while I'm away!"

"No!" Tanaka laughed at his boyfriend's good sense of humor. "The skeletons and I, we have both come out of the closet!"

"Good one!" Damien threw his head back in laughter. The heavy door slammed behind him as he slipped out. His fake laughs reverberated into the hallway.

As soon as Tanaka was left alone, he picked up his home phone and dialed a familiar number.

"Dr. Shinozaki. Hello, how do you do? This is Ryuuji Tanaka... *O-kage sama de!* I'm fine myself," he said. "I have important news for you. I've gotten the tape. Yes...can we review them together so I could get your analysis on it?"

Tanaka smiled. The speaker on the other side seemed to have given an affirmative answer to his suggestion. "And, and, there's something else, too." Weariness suddenly clouded his mind. For everything a person did has consequences, the Buddhist books had taught him. Was he tampering with fate? As he was wavering in indecision over whether he should tell his chanced encounter with Misa Hayami or not, he heard the sound of forks and knives clattering in the background from Dr. Shinozaki's end. There were children in the same room with him. This would not be the time for the doctor to speak about his research.

"I will not further interrupt your evening with your family, doctor. Let us speak more at our meeting. Have a great evening," Tanaka said and hung up. Misa Hayami's face appeared in his mind. He could picture the scene perfectly when a hint of internal tumult gleamed in the young woman's eyes for the first time.

25. The Reign of Love

"Ha-ha-ha!" Aileen leaned forward on her seat, suppressing her laughs. Wine sloshed around the glass in her hand forming miniature whirls. "You can't be serious!"

"Now what was the most terrible thing you've done to the opposite sex?" Mrs. Newton was able to carry on her agenda with a straight face even after Smith's shocking revelation that he had once taken off all the clothes of a girl in front of another girl. When he was in grade school, driven by curiosity, he had taken off all the clothes off of his crush's Kendra's Barbie doll to see what was hidden underneath, when Kendra had presumably gone out of the classroom to the potty. He was caught red-handed when she had returned unexpectedly. It was the first time he had felt that there were different kinds of embarrassment in life, and this humiliating kind — being absolutely hated by all the girls in class and having turned Kendra to tears — was best to avoid at all cost. While rarely admitting that he was, in some ways, traumatized by the episode, having committed something so unfathomably unforgivable at the age of ten and lost his grade school sweetheart to the condemnable male nature, he did feel a slight tremble when he finished the story. Never had the story been told to anyone but his own wife. He was surprised that a relationship expert had the power to open up the deepest secret in one's heart. Perhaps it was just that no one had ever bothered to ask him plainly, 'What was the most terrible thing you've ever done?', with a facial expression that showed he or she expected the worst, and nothing but the worst.

"The most terrible thing I have ever done..." Aileen said thoughtfully when it was her turn. "It must have been that time I've dared my brother to swim to the bottom of the dirty river that ran outside of our home. He didn't come up for a whole minute after I had already swum back to the surface. The last time I saw him conscious was when I was at the bottom. Through the murky, greenish-bluish river water, I flipped him the finger to declare triumph, thinking that he was just staring at me, wild-eyed in exhaustion. He was just floating there, and I thought he had simply given up. Oh, that was horrible. My mother was furious..."

"Was he okay?" Hearing something so unusual and cruel for the first time in all her sessions, she could not help interrupting.

"Oh, don't worry!" Aileen shrunk her neck and shoulders in, feeling guilty. "He lives. He's a diving coach now. My parents really drove it into him that he needed to face his fears for the water. He got so much training after that time that getting the diving license and then the rescue and teaching licenses were almost as easy as pie. If you ever wanted to go to that part of the world and see the amazing coral reefs, you know who to call." She winked.

"I like your story way more than mine," Smith said. "God forbid."

The time for the session had come to an end, Mrs. Newton realized. "I've heard fairly good responses from the both of you tonight," she said and turned herself slightly toward Smith. "And I have indeed enjoyed myself in your company. I think the two of you are heading in the right direction. Sometimes the connection is made not by having a lot of experience, or hobbies, or even interests in common, but by having a lot of emotions in common, and feeling sympathetic for one another. Aileen, what are the few important things that you've learnt about Smith tonight?" She didn't stop to let Aileen answer the question. "That he was a fun and intellectual person, who is also non-confrontational and does not actively share his feelings out in the open. But he is capable of opening up to the right person that knocks on the door. So, keep knocking."

Aileen nodded at the expert's analysis like a little girl sitting in mathematics class. She had discovered these qualities about the man, too. And now that she had the advantage of the information, she would keep knocking for sure until the door opened for her. She had never been known to give up anything easily.

"And what have you learnt about Aileen tonight, Carson?" Again, the question was just a lead into her speech, not a real inquiry. "That Aileen likes to indulge herself the liberation of pushing boundaries and she does not feel threatened by confrontation. She likes to share her emotions, and her experiences have a lot of impact on how she conducts her life. So what you've got to do, is to show your interests in these experiences, and be a good listener, if you choose to pursue the relationship."

"That's amazing," Aileen complimented the lady, "your analysis."

"It's time for me to go, so I'll just leave the two of you alone now. Please feel free to call my daughter if something pops up. Okay?" Mrs. Newton got up on her feet and said farewells to her clients.

"That was weird," Aileen said, gobbling down a spoonful of Crème Brulee when Mrs. Newton had left. "I have never done anything quite like this with my dates. To be counseled before there was any problem! Before the two of us have even become, 'the two of us'!" Blushing as she said that. "Maybe all couples should have a relationship expert like that on their first dates. It would have made getting to know the other person so much less awkward!"

"Ya..." Smith wiped his face with both palms, then rested them on his cheeks for a second. The feeling of recently unloaded stress on one's spring came upon him. It seemed that Mrs. Newton and even more importantly, Aileen had been deceived by his apparent composure when prodding private questions shrewdly disguised as communication exercises were being thrown at him. In any man's world, 'counseling' was as dreadful a word as Nieman Marcus. The proceeding was not exactly the way he had imagined it. It was not a multiple choice questionnaire but a full fifty-page thesis on himself. Had he not been so full of shit — there was hardly any euphemism around it — he would not have lasted through it. And now, his thoughts shifted instantly onto what had been bothering him at the back of his mind — Misa and Andy. The combination of it gave him chills he had not even perceived that night he found the fainted boy in a dark alley.

As Aileen delivered the last bite of egg custard into her mouth, Smith raised his hand in the air to signal the waiter for the check.

"Would you like to, umm, have a coffee at my place?" Aileen edged closer to the rim of her seat. Her fingers crawled seductively over the tablecloth and touched Smith's. Just at that moment, Smith lifted his hand and dived in his pocket for his wallet.

"No," Smith replied curtly. It took Aileen by surprise.

"You still don't have the keys to your apartment, right? You can come over and hang out with me until you've everything sorted out." She said, then correcting herself to solve the logistic loophole in her plan. "I have a land line. You can use it to call a locksmith. It's cheaper than calling from your cell phone." It was a desperate plan but it was worth a try, she thought.

"I just need to go see this colleague of mine. He has a spare key in his place. He is surely home by now." Smith checked the time from his wristwatch. And he glanced down at it again, as if not two seconds but hours had passed in between.

"Well, that's great!" Aileen said, exaggerating her enthusiasm to hide her disappointment. "A spare key in your colleague's place. That's smart...as everything you do." She had now gotten into her head that Carson Smith was the stupidest date she ever had. Wasn't he the one who gave her the idea to invite him home for a nightcap since he had so conveniently lost his keys and postponed doing anything against it all afternoon until their dinner? Such a perfect excuse wasted. She almost felt sorry for the man.

"Where does he live?" Aileen asked, hit by a stroke of genius. "I can drive you there. It's way faster than taking the Metro. And it's almost eleven. Taxis on Saturday night at this hour is going to cost you a fortune."

"Thank you!" Smith grabbed her hand tightly in his fist, filled with gratefulness. "He lives near the Tokyo Tower. *Minato* district."

Genius! Aileen smiled internally as she indulged herself in the warmth of the man's grip. With any luck, Aileen figured they would at least be stuck in traffic together for half an hour. And when he had retrieved the keys, she would persuade him once more to drive him back to his abode, where she would invite herself in with a clear conscience.

"Thirty-three thousand yen!" Smith looked astonished at the bill of the night. It had deviated from his calculation by almost eleven thousand yen and one heavy drinking old lady — Mrs. Newton had apparently consumed three glasses of vintage Merlot from 1991 before the two of them had arrived. The likelihood that he might even be paying for another couple's therapy session before theirs came into his mind. With reluctance, he tossed his American Express credit card in the bill holder, but soon took it back and replaced the holder with cash. "Save us the wait. And I ain't leaving no tip, so let's go before the guy comes back!" he said in a hushed tone as he stood up, reminding Aileen of a fugitive at large in movies.

"Okay..." Aileen replied, following his cue. Smith anxiousness had infected Aileen, as she realized how urgent the matter was to her date. Her heartbeat rose as she gave herself a mental push, thinking that she would earn extra points for helping her date out. By the time Aileen put her feet down on the accelerator when the traffic lights were turning yellow from green in the stretch of road ahead, she had become enslaved emotionally to Carson Smith. She would chase every whim of this man, risking traffic violations and others, in order to catch the last glimpse of green lights in his eyes. Her psychological dependency on him, often mistook as 'love' by most unsuspecting female afflicted with it, had happened without the awareness of either party.

26. A Definition of Romance

A loud sequence of muffled musical notes jotted everyone out of their lethargy. In the quiet compartment of the JR train, a black-white-and-yellow poster reprimanded the noise in bold font, 'Please do it at home. *Uchi de yarou*.'. Despite that, the short tunes borrowed from the popular anime series first aired in the seventies, *Doraemon*, about an electronic cat from the future who became friends with an introverted boy, injected a small dose of heaven into the late evening ride. Only an elderly lady gave a disapproving glance at Misa when she finally found her cell phone after a frantic rummage through her purse to turn off the sound.

'One missed call. Mr. Tsukada,' it showed on the display. Misa leaned back in her seat and looked outside so she could search for signs of where she was. Spots of indistinct lights dotted the darkness that laid outside. That made her wonder whether she had drawn the curtains closed at home. The chilly night air would be unfit for Tatsu to sleep in. He had just returned home that afternoon from the hospital, still recovering from his recent injuries. And worse, the wind might rattle the rickety windows of the old, rundown flat and wake him. And he would realize that Misa had once again slipped away while he was asleep.

"Two text messages. - Mr. Tsukada, 12:32 AM. Mr. Tsukada, 12:45 AM." The mobile device in her hand vibrated, she was once again reminded of her lateness. The text messages had arrived in her cell phone with a delay as the *Odakyu* train passed through a stretch of less well-connected suburbs on the way to *Setagaya* in southwest Tokyo.

In an attempt to soothe her anxiety, she deleted the two messages without reading, one of the few ways a person could escape temporarily from the whirlwind reality in such a highly connected city.

Before Misa had left the house, she had written a memo for her brother and stuck it to the bathroom mirror, knowing for sure that he would see it in the morning when he woke up. It lied blatantly, 'You're not awake when I have to leave for work. Morning, shift today at the Thunderbird. Love, big sister.' Lying doesn't offset caring, she thought to herself. Tatsu would get it someday. For now, she was content with her decision, for this was the only way she knew really well how to make money. Enough monetary compensation for what did not feel like work and did not fit in its description. For all the other possible occupations for a girl with no high school education, like waitressing, cleaning, office administration, security and teaching, all of which Misa had dipped her wings in, could not compete with it in the financial freedom it provided. And boy, she was good at it! Since no one, like Constanti Stanislavski, had written an 'An Actor Prepares' for her trade, no outsider should contradict her assessment of self-worth easily. And she knew she was good. She was not shy to feel the sense of pride to be knowledgeable and skilled in what she did. Sometimes, she thought the level of improvisation required in her trade could only be surpassed by the most strenuous of acting jobs. And if there were not enough reasons for her to stay in her trade, she would tell you honestly that she had grown dependent on a few of her clients. Everything they did, or merely talked about, were windows to a life-would-be, a normal life. And that's life, she would argue, she could envision easier by participating in it, even as a smallest, most trivial, most degrading of all roles, that someone like her could otherwise not attain despite her best effort. And Mr. Tsukada that she was about to meet was one of her best clients of all. His life story intrigued Misa, although he found it utterly boring.

"Misa dear, what took you so long?" Tsukada's car slid to a halt next to Misa at the guest parking area of Setagaya station near the east entrance.

His tone of voice was not one of reprimand, but of nervous anticipation. He grabbed Misa's hand as soon as she climbed in the low-set seats of his Nissan sports car, and without asking, he rubbed it against his crotch. It had sparked a violent passion in him, the passion that he had suppressed all the way in his drive over. He scooped Misa's head in his palm and forced her lips onto his. The sucking sound he made French kissing her slipped through the windows. Two equally horny teenagers a few paces away peered into the car to search for the source of it. Displeased at the unwanted attention, Tsukada switched into first gear and zipped away from the parking lot.

"The train ride took fifty minutes," only then had Misa the chance to reply him, when Tsukada shifted his focus on the road. He nodded at her explanation, while his mind was elsewhere, a dream world. A hot, steamy and wet one.

The self-heating elements of the leather seats in Tsukada's car warmed Misa thighs. It was a pleasant feeling only the rich could afford to find out to be necessary. Tsukada had it turned on again. He had once confessed to Misa that the mere thought of her lady part being warmed set him on fire. Albeit being reminded unwillingly of that fact every time she climbed into the car to find the seat heater turned on, she found nothing erotic about it, not even when she forced herself to as a thought experiment. Perhaps that was the point where men and women differ — cool gadgets and equipment always leave icy trails on a woman's mind. They quench fire, not start it. In any case, she was comfortable, and she started to relax and ease into her role. Cliché as it sounded, Mr. Tsukada liked to pretend that they were dating. But if Misa were to keep a diary, it would not describe her rendezvous with Mr. Tsukada as a matter of 'pretension'. Already at the kiss, Misa was charmed into his lover, and that loving feeling that swelled in her chest, made her feel that she could easily win a golden globe for tonight's performance.

And that winning performance was not solely on her account. Once again, Mr. Tsukada grabbed her hand and held it tightly in his grip as he drove. Only occasionally releasing it to switch gears.

Although he was not pretty — a rather tall but slender man of early forties who still had all his hair and wore, at all times, a pair of gold-rimmed glasses that reminded everyone around him of his harmlessness — his simple features made Misa let her guard down. Absurd as it might be, Tsukada was the kind of man that was sincere to himself about his need for a better sex life and felt no guilt about it. He took the whole affair seriously for that was what he wanted, and that he would treat Misa like a good partner, even in crime, sincerely.

Misa leaned closer to Tsukada and gave him a kiss on the cheek. Her face was prickled by the short stubs of beards that had grown their way out through the long working day. He raised her hand and kissed it in return.

A wave of longing for love overwhelmed Misa's sense. She did not forget about her brother, however. In the back of her mind, she was having an imaginary conversation with him — *Tatsu, I know you only want the best for me, but you've terribly misunderstood my clients, and my intention to continue. It was not only because of the money,* Misa thought. Never would she discuss her clients and her line of work with Tatsu. It would offend his sensitivity, to know that his sister was a quote-unquote prostitute. Yet she did say that last line the night before Tatsu ran out of the house in anger after their arguments and got himself into God-knows-what kind of trouble that landed him in the hospital in the end. That evening, Tatsu had caught her slipping into a stranger's car for the first time with his own eyes, after almost a year long of mocking jeers from his friends who heard rumors of his sister's self-degradation.

"Why do you sleep around with men twice your age and break up their families? What has gotten into you?"

I didn't ruin any family. Never, would I want to do that, Misa wanted to say, but her brother was on a rant.

"I know you're paying for everything here, but I can work too! I don't want your dirty money!" he said. "My sister, a *shofu*! My goodness! Is that what you want to tell Mother? What you've come to Tokyo to do? Would you like to tell grandpa this?" he said with reprehension, almost as if threatening to tell them himself if she didn't quit.

"I am not a... I am not!" Misa retorted. She despised that word, '*shoufu*', or prostitute in English. She couldn't bring herself to say it. It gave her chills just to think about it.

"I saw you! With my own eyes!" he cried, "Don't you want to live a better life, instead of sulking around, doing God-knows-what with these people?" he asked.

No, fool! Don't you see, I am living a better life already? I have never lived a better life, Misa would like to say, but she knew better than to contradict. "Would you stop lecturing me?" In the end, that was all she had the guts to say to her little brother. And her imperturbable attitude had made Tatsu snap. The apartment door banged shut after him before Misa realized the severity of the situation.

It had never been her forte to think about consequences. To live life as it came had felt right, until that very moment.

Misa turned away from the row of concrete two-story apartment buildings to look at Tsukada, as the car hurried down the narrow streets of Setagaya.

For men like Tsukada, the pleasure of making love had been denied from him since the day his wife turned into just a woman that took care of the household. If Misa was fulfilling an occasional carnal desire that was the result of days, or even years of oppression, to Misa, that was not too much to ask for.

Tsukada squeezed her hand again as he slid into the parking spot in the street outside of his empty apartment. — The wife and the baby had gone to Spain on vacation with her parents. — The little squeeze was all he needed to do, really, to set Misa's heart racing. She would gladly give her all to a man that held her hand so tight as if his dear life depended on it anytime, with or without the fringe benefit.

"You're very excited. I haven't even started..." Tsukada slipped his fore and middle finger under Misa's underwear as soon as he carried her into his bedroom. The gloomy future of his marriage hit her every time she entered this room and saw the two separate beds, set apart by a dressing table, perhaps once upon a time were pushed tightly against each other's frame. Tsukada commented again at Misa's arousal. The sliminess and wetness had been sure signs of it. "Why can't Sonja feel that way for me?" he said, and plunged himself into Misa's soft neck. He nibbled it softly between his gums as he slithered his left hand up her T-shirt. The sound of Sonja's name had once again reminded Misa of Tsukada's story of how he had met his Spanish wife during Tsukada's college days. She remembered having extra admiration for Mr. Tsukada after she heard his recollections, despite the current state of their relationship. Who could be surprised if such a rare intercultural union did not bring about one or two marital issues?

Misa's T-shirt had slid further up her body as Tsukada made his way up. When Tsukada grabbed forcefully at her breasts, the shirt gave way. It scrunched around her upper chest, revealing two plump peaches of flesh, wrapped under a white lace bra. Misa wriggled to sit herself up on the bed. Despite her enjoyment, it was clearly going too fast, and with her business in mind, she thought that would make for an undesirable precedent. As she could not afford to ever start getting requests for fifteen minutes' appointments, she asked for permission to freshen herself up. The train trip from central Tokyo at that hour had been a trying one. She pleaded, as she did before, and she further impressed the importance of the short bathroom break by dangling a piece of seductive garment in front of Tsukada. She walked, pelvis jutted back to highlight her curve, towards the bathroom. It worked every time.

"I'll light some candles," Tsukada said, scrambling to his feet to take off the suit that he was too busy to take care off when they entered.

Candles — not artificial lights — another reason why Tsukada could make her his anytime he wanted. Only a romantic would think of that. So why didn't it work between him and his wife? The question hit Misa as she twirled around the bathroom doing nothing in particular while keeping an eye on the time on her watch. Five more minutes in here, she murmured to herself.

27. Turn Into Something

Andy whistled, as Smith and an unexpected Caucasian female with a healthy figure entered his apartment.

"So this must be, uh," Andy said, his eyes peeled to the nook on Aileen's nose, for if he allowed himself to look anywhere else, he would not be able to take his eyes off. "Smith never told me your name, but you must be the lawyer." He extended his hand to Aileen, who gladly shook it.

"Don't get any idea. I've already told Aileen you're dating Miss Newton," Smith walked into the center of the living room and declared.

"I'm not dating Miss Newton," Andy clarified. "As a matter of fact, we've never dated."

"I also told her it's typical of you to deny it if anyone should ask."

Aileen pulled her hand slowly out of Andy's unrelenting grip.

"Nice apartment, huh?" Smith said to Aileen as he looked left and right inconspicuously, pretending to show interest in Andy's decor in order to scan the interiors of all the rooms.

"Come sit down." Andy guided Aileen to one of the white leather couches in the center of the living room whose tip-top condition never failed to impress Smith every time he visited. It baffled him immensely. Given the amount of frolicking that happened on this couch, the only way they could be clean was if every one of Andy's many female companions were also moonlighting as the cleaning ladies. While that thought came initially as a joke, the Japanese were obsessed with hygiene, and the chance of that being true was probably higher than his mind could fathom, on second thought.

"This place is gorgeous!" Aileen complimented the owner. "But isn't it too big for just one person? Sorry, I have assumed, from what Smith told me on the way, that you must live here alone."

The size of his apartment was five times that of Smith's and could easily be a family apartment for any Tokyians. Of course, they have different priorities in life. In fact, every younger man at Andy's age had different priorities than him — Smith thought proudly of his son who would never squander a dime on the unnecessary.

"Well, I like to have friends over," Andy explained. In case Smith would say something inappropriate that revealed his true womanizing nature in the present company, he switched theme, "and I have always loved decorating! You can buy all sorts of amazing home designs here in Japan, and it would be such a waste if I don't have anywhere to put the pieces. What do you think of the living room? I was going for minimalism with a touch of naughtiness this season." Triumphantly, he looked at the huge beige rug with a red square that laid under the couches and the TV set. Smith followed his glance and scanned the beige rug for strands of long black hair that might tell him something. Smith blamed the mixture of myopia and presbyopia when his search came up empty.

"I don't know about the decoration, but you've got your cleaning done right," Smith said, scheming in the back of his mind how he could get to the topic of concern. "Did you clean the entire afternoon?"

"No, I have a team of professionals coming in here to clean them. Three times a week during the day. D' you want an introduction? They normally only do corporate apartments. My entire building was filled with corporate rentals. I don't know if they do company dormitory," he said, earnest in his consideration to connect Smith to his janitorial service provider while underlining the fact that there was a seemingly wide gap in financial freedom between the two, with him being the bachelor of the two.

"Three times a week? That explains it," Smith murmured to himself after hearing the extravagance. Seeing that Andy could go on forever on the topic of household triviality in the presence of female company, he decided to cut straight to the chase. "So how's Misa and her brother? The boy's doing all right?"

"He survived. Two broken ribs, a broken nose and five stitches on his forehead which somebody apparently cracked open with a beer bottle." Andy recounted his injuries plainly, as if what happened to the boy was the most ordinary thing. He picked up the jug of mineral water sitting on the coffee table and offered to pour a glass for Smith, who declined.

"Who's that?" The details of the event seemed to have upset Aileen.

"My friend's..." both of the men spoke at the same time. Realizing it, Smith gave Andy the pleasure of explaining his acquaintance with Misa.

"...brother." Andy finished up the sentence. "That's a tough guy for you. He didn't want my help at all. Although that was difficult 'cause I was driving him and his sister home, as much as he didn't like it. He has to use a crutch. The broken ribs won't heal completely for another two months at least, the doctor said."

"Did he tell you why he was beaten?" Smith asked, putting his hands on his waist.

"Beaten!" Aileen exclaimed, raising her eyebrows in surprise, indicating suspicion over the kind of company they kept.

"Pskkk! He didn't even want to talk to me. Though for all it's worth, he also wasn't talking to his own sister. They probably had a fight. Siblings, they do that."

Aileen nodded approvingly, her stare fixated on the surface of the water glass in her hand as if she heard the only true statement in all of what he said tonight.

"He looked like a good-for-nothing anyway. I saw him..." Smith wanted to say Pachinko parlors, but he was not ready to share his depressing past-time with his date yet. "You know, in Ikebukuro. I've seen him around."

"It's none of my business who he is or what he does with his time. All I care about is that Misa is happy again."

"You've slept with her?" Smith was compelled to ask.

Aileen gasped. The flow of logic in men offended her some time.

"Would I have stuck around if I did?" Andy half-joked. "Pardon, my directness." He excused himself to Aileen. "We are just friends."

To that, Smith wasn't sure he should be relieved or insulted for being lied to.

"She's a little girl," Smith said protectively. "I, uh, knowing you, who could guarantee anything?" He added, with an unapologetic shrug, for having asked such an incriminating question at Andy.

"Well, I have you to thank you for our friendship," Andy said with relish and clasped his palms together in front of his chest in a gesture of expressing thankfulness in Thai culture. He rocked his closed palms back and forth as he spoke. "After we came back from the Ikebukuro precinct, I called to check how she was doing. We ended up talking for hours. I called the next few days again, and we talked some more. It just took off. I have a feeling it might, uh," Andy turned to look at Aileen, confirmed from the look in her eyes that he would never stand a chance, then returned his gaze to Smith, "turn into something."

"Turn into something?" Smith repeated after him in brooding anger. Feeling too distressed to explain his emotion and too busy to hide it, he padded his chest pocket and said, "My keys. Give them to me before I forget."

28. The Client

"Why Doctor?" Fat Gado put his legs on top of the Hasegawa's desk. The sight of his dirty soles irritated the doctor to no end, and it amused him. Fat Gado was a man amused by other people's misery. Of course, there was always one thing that amused him more, and that was making money. "Why do you look so agitated? Are you nervous to see me?"

"Mr. Gado, you cannot just come to my work place without informing me ahead of time," the doctor said in a hushed whisper, but it did not mean his tone of voice was soft.

"I'm informing you now, sensei," Fat Gado raised his eyes, as if what he said was the most self-apparent of facts.

Hasegawa looked at the needles on the wall clock then back at his unexpected visitor. "I only have two minutes, then I have to go, I'm afraid."

"Are you trying to avoid me?" His interlocutor asked with an angry undertone.

"I have a meeting with the Director of the…"

Hasegawa's sentence was cut short by the thud of a small sack of pills on the desk Fat Gado threw at him. With trained eyes, Hasegawa immediately saw that the pills were unmarked, and they had a pink haze to their appearances.

"I want these," he announced. "Make these for me."

The doctor knew such request was coming. He had been avoiding talking directly to the man for the past six months precisely because he did not want to make copy-cat drugs for the man.

"I don't know how you get these, but you better put them back into your pockets right now. We're being taped."

"Tsk!" Fat Gado waved off his comment. "Stop bluffing me, doctor. I know the thing about Psychiatrist-Patient Privilege," the looked defiantly at the security camera at the top right corner of the room, and smiled.

"Fine," Hasegawa's rubbed his face with his palm and said. He did not want to explain to the man that despite the Psychiatrist-Patient privilege, the security camera was recording his every move as per standard operating procedure as a precaution against violent patients, which there were rather plentiful in the ER. These videos would under normal circumstances not be shown to anyone for privacy reason, but it did not mean that patients could say or do anything they want in this room without consequences. For one, Hasegawa could blackmail Fat Gado with them. Not that he would dare, which was why he was now sitting here patiently listening to the man make his 'indecent proposals', but he would rather not get into that much technical details with a guy whose brains were the size of peanuts. That tiny brains of his might get the wrong ideas.

"I got them from one of the bar girls that worked for Xavier," Fat Gado started to explain. "These stuff is the hottest thing in town right now. Nine of ten clubs are paddling them in Shinjuku. I have one of my guys tried it and he said it was *the shit*, can you believe that? — He said the same thing about your H-46 last time."

"So?"

"I have the boys break his legs, of course!" Fat Gado said with a snorty laugh.

Hasegawa frowned as he picked up the bag and examine its content. He never enjoyed hearing the back story of where things come from. His clients came for his medicinal expertise, and they should just focus on the technical matter, rather than bothering him with the characteristically horrendous accounts of how things ended up on his desk.

"My boys tell me Xavier probably got them made oversea. He might even be buying from the damned Chinese scientists. We can't let that asshole make all the money, can we?"

"No, we can't," the doctor replied sarcastically, but his listener was too thick to realize it. "I could run a chemical analysis and find out what's in it," he offered proactively, wanting to be rid of the man from his sanctuary of an office as soon as possible. "But I can't promise I could replicate it exactly."

Fat Gado shook his head in feigned disappointment. "No, you don't replicate it. You improve on it. Put your magic ingredient in it. We boost its performance and sell it like a new and improved version of Xavier's. It's gonna be the star."

"That's going to take time."

"We don't have time."

"It's a delicate balance between a harmless recreational psychedelic drug and a poison. I have explained this to you before, haven't I?"

"As long as it doesn't kill anybody, nobody cares."

"See. That's the problem!"

"I want it done in two months, tops," Fat Gado said, cutting the doctor off.

"Four, I need four. At least," he begged for more time. "And you know a typical new drug takes four years to develop. I'm now quoting you four months. I can't do with less."

"We're not making cancer pills here. Just write me the approximate recipe and I will have them made elsewhere. Probably back in Indonesia. — No one will trace it back to you if anything goes wrong."

"Well they better not be. We can't get caught again like last time."

"That was almost four years ago, my dear. Get over it!"

29. Sunday

Another rare leisurely Sunday.

Smith folded the current issue of International Harold Tribute neatly and slipped it on top of the other tributes underneath the hyacinth weave coffee table. Tiny bristles of fibers had broken off here and there from wear, prickling the back of his hand. This reminded him that, while the quantity and quality of the furnishing he had for the prison of an apartment were no comparison to what Andy had so deliberately showcased to Aileen yesterday, the hyacinth weave coffee table was one of his few pride and joys in life in Japan. It was one of his few personal touches of furniture not provided for and permanently fixed to the apartment when he arrived. It cost nearly nothing and looked, completely out of place with the other unsympathetic white particleboard furniture his company's real estate management managed to squeeze in between the textured plaster walls in matching white. Yet, the purchase decision was solely his. He was for a short while ashamed that he wanted to regain his independence. By making rash consumption choices that satisfied neither of Debbie's top two criteria — branded and expensive. Since he was the higher earner of the two, in the back of his mind, he always had the notion that he was only delegating the household consumption decisions to her, as she was as opinionated about everything around the house as a theater stage manager. How could he have felt, all of a sudden, that she had been stifling his aesthetic taste and creative impulses all along from the supporting role? The more time he spent looking at the table, however, the more he was convinced that it was the right choice made in the right frame of mind. The innocent wicker table had taught him an important lesson in life.

Seeping the rest of his typical Sunday cup of green tea, Smith relished in water hyacinth's story to glory, a fascinating tale of human's ingenuity. Grew, harvested, processed and woven by hardworking fellows from Indonesia, water hyacinth that now so commonly used for weaving furniture sold all around the world was a native plant to South America. It had been introduced many years ago by the Dutch to the previous East Indies simply for their beautiful flowers that were light purple, painted in the center with a drop of yellow by God. The climate in the East Indies was so much alike that of its motherland that the floating plant started to conquer the tropical country's many lakes, bays, lagoons and even reservoirs. They grew in mats, sometimes covering miles of water, depleting oxygen for fishes and other creatures in no time, destroying not only the fishnets of local fishermen but also their livelihood altogether. The determined started to weed out the hyacinth. Meanwhile, export for rattan furniture took off, and someone had the clever idea to try weaving the roots of this dried pest of all water plants like rattan. And boy, were they successful. The alternative texture and leaner fibers gave the hyacinth products smoother, less rigid frames, and customers all over the world embraced it. Then the fishermen were no longer fishermen, and they no longer anguished over their living. A new exciting page of Indonesia's economy was hence written.

If a foreign plant that was once considered a major nuisance to Indonesia could flourish, so could he.

Between the new, happy him and the old, depressing him, there stood in the way only his lack of imagination.

Smith ran his hand along the side of the coffee table as if bewitched by the table's resilient personality.

An unbearable, tingly sensation paralyzed his legs — for the entire morning, he had been sitting cross-legged on the floor beside the table. His body finally alerted him to switch posture. He leaned against the wall right behind him for support as he tried to pry himself apart. His toes retracted in pain as if they were heads of turtles being prodded by naughty children that were his fingers. Only with the utmost valiance, he managed to straighten his legs out before him. Resting, he supported himself partially on the wall and partially with his two elbows pinned on the floor, his gaze wander aimlessly around the house, searching for something to occupy his time while his waited for his legs to come back to life.

He noticed the two set of keys lying on top of his bedside table. The lie.

Yesterday he had concocted the story of the forgotten keys in order to check on Andy that evening. Only now did he realize that in his urgency to thwart a potential breach of the age of consent, he had completely forgotten his gentlemanly manners. No thanks were said, no future date was planned, not even a polite promise of call-backs was mentioned. He must immediately make a call to his dinner date to atone for his lack of tact.

Once his legs stopped torturing him, Smith reached for the phone and called Aileen's number. Before he left the car yesterday, she insisted on typing her number directly into the directory on Smith's cell phone. That turned out to be a good call, for otherwise, he would have to admit to the fact that his initially passing interest for Aileen had gotten the piece of napkin with her contact details on it vanished into thin air.

The phone rang on, however, without being picked up.

The wait conjured from his memory another similar event. Tanaka had stood him up yesterday for their shooting appointment. Feeling obligated, he had wandered in and around the museum for some hours expecting that Tanaka would show up eventually, explaining his lateness as "habitual". That would be an excuse he was willing to accept for an artist. While the incidence had resulted in his first visit to an art exhibition in Japan and finally taking advantage of his expat assignment to explore the much coveted city of modern art that everyone else told him he should do, he was nonetheless disappointed. He wondered whether anything unpleasant had happened to Tanaka. Japanese is one of the most punctual people he had ever worked with. They could, he imagined, put the Germans to shame in their high expectation for timeliness. And for a man like Tanaka, who had pleaded him twice with his thought-provoking speeches, he would be the last person not to take a commitment to heart.

"*Masaka...* darnit. I forget about it again. Always take the contact details, Carson Smith," he reminded himself as he rolled his eyes. "Now we won't know until tomorrow."

Eleven more hours to kill with this dreadful thought in the back of his mind. He sighed internally.

What about some games of Pachinko?

30. A Beautiful Bracelet

15:30. Misa slipped into her street clothes once again and said goodbye to the other girls in the locker room. The slow Monday morning shift at Thunderbird ended uneventfully. Once again in her two-inch tall black leather clogs from *Miho Matsuda*, she dashed to the closest convenient store alone before the others could invite her to tea time and bought herself the usual salmon o*nigiri* rice triangle. It rung up two hundred forty yen. The same amount for the last 16 weeks. That was her way of tracking prices in Tokyo, and it comforted her to know that it had remained the same for another week. If only she knew economics, Misa Hayami could credit herself with the S*a-mon Onigiri* Index as a reliable inflation index across Japan much like the Big Mac Index did for international exchange rates.

Misa sauntered into the edge of Minami Ikebukuro Park and found an empty bench to sit down underneath an old Mongolian oak tree. The owner of the nearest flower stall nodded politely at her. She bowed back at a deeper angle at the kind old man from whom she had once bought a pot of pink cosmo flowers, native to Mexico, he had explained. The park was much busier than before now the Yamada electronic store had opened shop right opposite to the entrance of the park. It bothered her that the commercial activities were slowly encroaching on the park. Stalls selling beautiful imported flowers from Mexico, Australia or Netherlands she could not find fault of. Boisterous shoppers and loud hawking salesmen she could not stand.

A cold drop of rainwater fell directly on her head. Misa looked up with a smile when she saw the healthy green oak leaves soaking up the sun happily, and she wiped the wetness away with her sleeve. She noticed that the owner of the stall had put up a string of new decorative red and white lanterns with his business's name in calligraphy between two lampposts to replace the old ones that were damaged by the recent storms. Everything together gave the scene a festive mood, and it cheered Misa up greatly. She enjoyed the little moments in the park alone. The relative serenity, a rarity for one working and living in Tokyo, reminded her of her hometown.

Her stomach growled. Up until that point, Misa was running on nothing but a bowl of cold *kitsune udon* noodle soup with a slice of *aburaage* bean curd for breakfast, and her insides felt as tight as a knot. Misa drank the last drop of water from the water bottle that she brought along with her everywhere and started peeling the plastic wrapper off her rice triangle.

"Misa! That's beautiful!" Aiko had appeared from nowhere and grabbed Misa's hand in admiration. "That's the new *Anna Montague* bracelet, isn't it?"

Aiko was a girl the same age as Misa, who worked at the Thunderbird together with her. For reasons unknown to her, Aiko adored Misa's style, and she let it be known, too. It embarrassed the humble Misa greatly to be showered with compliments from one of the most fashionable people Misa had known in her life every time they met. She started avoiding being alone with Aiko all together to keep herself level-headed from all the flattery. It appeared the Aiko had sniffed out her tea time den finally. Misa managed a weak smile at Aiko for her compliment about the new bracelet.

About five centimeters taller than Misa, Aiko was a lot chubbier than Misa. But she didn't let her weight restrained her clothing choice. Her undying devotion to look exactly like models in the Can Can magazine could be spotted from a mile away. Her obsession clear with the explosion of colors in her typical clothing choice and the complex eye make-up that took an hour to do every morning and another half an hour to patch up in the afternoon during tea time and once more after dinner. She had bleached blonde hair extensions in French braids twisted into a bun in the back of her head since she watched the popular anime Mrs. Loyla set in the Victorian era, and she was a firm believer of pale skin color, unbeknownst to her after Marie Antoinette. These all together gave her an odd sort of beautiful look that one could slowly grow into liking, if one puts her mind into it, as was the case for many Hollywood-worthy looks. Misa had always found it impossible not to be in awe in appreciation of her effort to be modish whenever she looked at her.

"Where'd you get the money to pay for it, anyway?" Aiko was looking so intently at the assortments of rhinestones that her nose was almost touching Misa's arm.

"A friend bought it for me," Misa said, wriggling herself out of her grip. The truth was not far from it. Though she would change the word 'friend' into plural form. All her clients had contributed their fair shares.

"You're not..." Aiko seemed to have come to an idea. She read an article recently from Can Can about a scandal between a politician and a so-called hourly girlfriend. "you're not doing *that*, are you?" She nudged Misa on the shoulder in curiosity.

"What? What're you talking about?" Misa pretended not to understand her.

"C'mon. Don't lie to me." Aiko leaned herself against the back of the bench chair and uncapped her microwaved lunchbox. The content wafted of deliciousness. "If you tell me, I'd let you have one of the *takoyaki*."

"No, I've nothing to tell you. I teach Japanese when I'm not working in this shitty place," Misa said, rolled the seaweed paper around the rice cake. She took a bite into the finished *onigiri* and grew instantly lethargic to the taste of *takoyaki* instead. Anything was better than pre-made rice triangle sitting in the fridge for god knows how long. "Give one to me. Don't be selfish." She looked greedily at Aiko's lunch.

"It was you who's selfish!" Aiko turned away from Misa so she couldn't steal food from her. "You need to tell me how you're making all this money. I mean, the cheapest item in Anna Montague is at least twenty thousand yen! You'll have to teach 40 hours of Japanese on top of this job to make that kind of money!"

"Oh my god, you're making me so guilty!" Misa furrowed her brows. "I know I shouldn't have bought it. Should I return it? What excuse should I make up?" She pictured the dreadful saleswoman whom she checked out with, with no sense of humor at the *Shibuya 109* department store.

"No, that's not my point!" Angry that Misa was misunderstanding her intention, she turned towards her and stuffed a *takoyaki* ball into Misa's mouth, so she would shut up and hear what she had to say.

"Misa, I am begging you to tell me!" She said. "I mean, look at me! How am I supposed to keep up with the style if I work in Thunderbird? This season is ending, and the sales are on in a few weeks! If you know anything that would help me make a little extra money, I will do it. And I promise I won't tell anyone else. I'll buy you the entire Anna Montague store when I have money! I'll buy you Marc Jacobs handbags. I'll buy you Jimmy Choos. I'll even buy you pajamas from Peach John so you'd wake up every morning in style!"

"No, you'd never do that!" Misa argued.

Aiko didn't know what else she could say to lure Misa into spilling her secret. She resorted to shaking her, all the while pouting playfully. Misa's rice triangle almost fell out of her hands.

"Okay, okay. I'll tell you." Misa conceded. "But don't tell anyone and don't be shocked! You asked for it." Aiko nodded zealously in agreement and cocked her head. Misa leaned towards Aiko and whispered sweet poison into her ear.

31. Room Mate

Hisao Hasegawa was lucky, but he never attributed his life to luck. 'Be in control of one own destiny' was his motto, and hence he did not rejoice at the chance encounter with Doctor Shinozaki at the medical conference, although it had greatly convenient him.

"You have never published the findings of your magic anti-psychotic molecule at the Tokyo Medical University," Shinozaki teased his old mate at the after-party of the Medical University's annual alumni dinner. It was the first time Hasegawa had ever run into Shinozaki. The two of them had shared a dormitory as young men until Hasegawa dropped out of the program. These days, Hasegawa religiously attended all social gatherings in his professional circles, firming believing that a man's network was a man's net worth. His network was his most important asset, not his research results. This he had learnt the hard way. But now, accomplished in his own right, Hasegawa had to face the occasional harassment by people from his past who knew him as a failure and nothing more.

"I've moved on to something else since then," Hasegawa lied, not interested in elaborating further. In reality, he had never stopped studying his miracle molecule, even long after he had quit Tokyo Medical and went for a rather inconspicuous tenure at St. Jude. He had been running one of the longest and most sophisticated single-blind clinical trials in the history of Japanese medicinal psychiatric research. "What are you up to these days?" He casually asked, as custom demanded him to pay what little interest he had to his old mate, whom he was sure to never want to see again.

"Work is as interesting as work can get, but recently I have been contacted by an amateur movie-maker to look into a very peculiar case. A case of serial murders, as a matter of fact. That's filling up my leisure time quickly."

"Serial murders?" Hasegawa was surprised to hear such a topic, a topic that rarely came up in these medical conference after-parties. "I'm intrigued," he admitted.

"Several years ago, a French movie director was found dead in his studio in Tokyo. All signs pointed to it as some kind of well-thought-out hate crime. But someone in the police department— the man who hired me had found evidence — had replaced the original eye-witness and autopsy reports, claiming that the French man died of suicide instead. A simple case of drug overdose, the report said, although the unpublished photographs taken at the crime scene and other eye-witness records were obviously telling a very different story. There were sure signs of ritual killing which had been covered up, perhaps as a way to preserve the reputation of the city as the safest city in the world. It seemed that my client had stumbled into a case of obstruction of justice in the police force."

"Interesting," Hasegawa's clench on his glass tightened. He asked, "But why did the man come to you with the case? What does he want from you?"

"I was just as confused as you when I first heard of it. I told him that I was not the right person to come to for advice on how to deal with corruption in the law enforcement. I'm a psychologist."

"And what did he say?"

"He showed me the chemical analysis of the drug found in the victim's stomach. It was a jumble of a great many things — you know how these party drugs are. They are all adulterated with cheaper compounds —

but it appeared that an isomer of your miracle molecule is in it," Shinozaki said with one of his eyebrow raised.

Hasegawa could not believe what Shinozaki was implying. Did he think it would make Hasegawa lose face because his drug had been extensively used to assist killing of self and others? It was not his fault that his drug was potent, popular and easily accessible for the people with the right means. He felt his mouth went dry.

"Remember I used to edit your reports and papers for errors? I remember your molecule well," Shinozaki was relishing those memories where he was the better student. "I was absolutely intrigued. But most importantly, my client told me that there is a living suspect that he wanted me to take a look into."

"A *living* suspect?"

"Yes," Shinozaki did not wince and confirmed what he just said. "A living suspect."

"Could the suspect have been '*non-living*' instead?"

"That was the peculiar part. He wanted me to look into a young woman, a young woman who is, how shall I put it? She should have died two days prior to the death of the director. She was the director's girlfriend — the situation was very complicated. But anyway, that's what I am busy with."

Hasegawa's head nodded in the brief silence that followed, lost in thought. Then suddenly, he flicked his wrist, and his glass of wine spilled all over Shinozaki's suit. The first thing he did, as Hasegawa had expected, was to pull his cell phone out of his pocket and placed it on the tall table next to the Hors d'oeuvre.

"How clumsy of you!" Shinozaki frowned at his old mate whom he had never really liked much and now even less. Grumpily, he walked off to the restroom to clean himself up after accepting Hasegawa's half-hearted apology.

What should Hasegawa do next? Take his phone?

"Miss, is this your phone?" Randomly, he asked a woman standing by. She looked at the phone and shook her head.

"No matter! Someone else must have left it here by accident. Let me take it to the reception," he said to the woman, who couldn't care less, and pocketed the phone quickly.

32. The Mexican Unit

At 8:00 AM sharp, Smith stepped into the building of DaiKe Industry.

He felt that today was a day to try something new — the Arizona barrel cactus he bought recently at a Sunday flea market had sprouted two beautiful bright orange flowers.

Apart from the quick *"Ohayou Gozaimsu"* at the security guard at the lobby, he also skipped the rows of elevators and went directly for the stairs, after excusing himself with a series of *"sumisasen" and "gomenasai"* through the thong of DaiKe employees. It stirred a wave of curious glances from both familiar and unfamiliar faces waiting for their turns to ride the elevators. Why? For only the bottom-most caste of the company would take the stairs. And they would generally avoid being seen, coming in either earlier than everyone or much later. A *gaijin,* a foreigner, with an aura of a successful businessman befitting to be the star of the Alec Baldwin starred Glengary Glenrose, using the stairs? That was the stuff for morning coffee break gossip. —

"Who is he?"

"What is he doing?"

"He's jogging up the stairs to stay in shape."

"Americans are crazy about exercising!"

"He must be a very busy man, to have to make use of the morning minutes like that."

"That man sure has some stamina."

The intense yet whispered speculations only subsided when a loud *ding* declared the arrival of an empty elevator.

"I don't know anything. I don't know anything." Arai said

apologetically to Smith, his face proved that he was guilty of whatever he was denying. Smith had chased after Tanaka as soon as he spotted him in the corridor, but his target sneaked adeptly into his office. Smith caught Keigo Arai instead, yawning and stretching in front of the window in the coffee room at the end of the hallway, under the belief that no one was watching.

"I'm only Tanaka-san's assistant. He organized everything, and I, I don't know anything." Arai added, in his clumsy yet to-the-point English, although its level of credibility could be questioned. "But Tanaka-san had arrived. Let me show you to his office." And he led the way. Onward, Smith saw a slogan in Japanese from his original standpoint at the end of the hallway hung in the air in striking red paint against the grayish walls. It had not made sense, yet it was not extraordinary. Only until he was directly beside the first printed character, which was stretched at least three times as wide as it ought to have been on the wall to his left, did he know he was in the middle of the most amazing trick of the eye he had ever seen in his life. All the other words of the slogans were transformed like this based on the most vigorous calculations to maintain the right dimension in a so-called 'one-point perspective' by designers. Those in the middle that appeared to be hanging in the air were actually printed, in a much larger font, at the opposite end of the corridor, so that from where he was, they appeared the same size as the others on the side.

"This is interesting." He stopped to admire the print in close quarters. "What does it actually say?" Smith asked Arai, but he appeared not to have heard him nor did he slow down. Smith made a mental note that despite the very modest, and probably original office layout on this floor when it was built, as opposed to the completely renovated open offices on his floor, the artists that resided here managed to create a new dimension for themselves.

"I am terribly sorry," Tanaka said as soon as he saw Smith at the office's threshold. He stole glances at Arai and seemed to have gotten the information he wanted. Arai had kept his mouth shut, as usual. "I was caught up in some personal business and couldn't make our appointment. And it appears that we didn't get each other's contact."

"Don't worry about it. I have a part in this." Smith pulled out a business card from the inside pocket of his suit and offered it to Tanaka, who fumbled in the small, tiered document stand without finding his own. He tore a piece of yellow post-it and wrote his numbers on it.

"I am still open next Saturday. Same place same time?" Smith suggested, sticking the piece of post-it on his palm.

Tanaka stared vacantly into space for a second, then returned his gaze to Smith and asked, "Have you seen the Gokokuji Temple in Ikebukuro?"

"I don't believe so." Smith tried to locate anything he had seen that could be passed as the temple in his mind in the district but came up empty.

"It's a beautiful temple. I think it would be the perfect backdrop for the commercials."

"Sure." Smith reminded himself to look up the temple's history online in the next free moment.

"It's a very quiet place. Relatively new but survived a lot. Many young Japanese go pray there." Tanaka suggested, sowing an unsuspecting seed into Smith's head. "If you have a friend, bring him or her along."

Smith only nodded.

During lunchtime in the canteen, Smith saw Andy walking with his head down, a single apple rocked from one rim to the other on the tray he was holding. He walked like a puppet without the puppeteer, and shot straight towards the empty tables, completely forgetting to check out.

"The food's sponsored, not free," Smith called out after him next to the cashier. "I'll pay for his. I think he just has an apple. *Ringo.*" He held up his company's electronic paying card and pointed at Andy. The cashier squinted, turned around to look at who he was pointing at, then squinted back at him before she typed the new amount into her cash register, upset at Smith for repenting the sins of others. Smith swiped his card quickly to get away from the sour cashier lady and walked over to Andy, who now stood hunched over his tray, with his mouth opened. The bags under his eyes told of exhaustion.

"Cut down on the office drinking. It's showing." Smith jested, only to notice that Andy did not smile. The most unusual. As they walked towards an empty table, Smith stayed close on Andy's side, ready to prop the man up in case he should faint and fall any moment. "What's going on?" he asked.

Andy uttered some nonsense about plants, as he gazed over the artificial garden on the other side of the floor-to-ceiling windows. He picked up his apple and started to nibble on it. Only after he had gnawed the apple to its core did he become slightly more cheerful.

"Six-thirty meeting with the Americans."

"Geeze. Tell them to wake up early." Smith knew he was merely suggesting the impossible. He had fought on the other side of the battle when he was working for the American office. "What's this all about? One of those extracurricular things again?" The only international project Andy had, had belonged to his section. Whatever meeting with the Americans Smith was not invited to could only be accounted for by Andy's superior Japanese. He was summoned as a translator to seat in meetings he had no business in more often than he would like. Being the only few on DaiKe's payroll that was truly bi-lingual, he might never be released back to his natural habitat for being so indispensable, Smith thought.

"I'm not supposed to tell you. But at your level, you're gonna know soon enough. Maybe you already do."

Smith cocked his head sideways, a look that pressed Andy to skip right to the chase.

"Some people from Nomura came up with this idea," Andy leaned closer to Smith, "to do away with the Mexican unit."

"What're they gonna do about it?" Smith remembered reading about a huge personnel cut in the Mexican factories some time ago. He was under the impression that the human resource restructuring had made them leaner and more sustainable. "Sell it?"

"The Mexican unit had its third-quarter net loss doubled." Andy shook his head as he explained their financial plight. "A hundred and thirty-five million fucking dollars."

"Damn!" Smith nearly choked on the slice of fatty, stringy beef he had just put in his mouth. He took a sip of water from the glass and looked nervously around him. No one was looking back. "So what's the big idea from Nomura?" He asked quietly.

"Wesley & Sons," Andy said, not looking at him.

"How the hell do they come up with this?" Smith jerked his head back in disbelief, not for its business sense, but for the fact that his arch rivalry's company was brought into rescuing his. Andy simply shrugged. He was now playing with the seeds of his apple. "How are they gonna make this work? I mean, they're not all idiots over there." Smith asked, keeping check of his voice level.

"That's where all the contention began." Andy finally managed to crack one of the seeds open between his fingers. He looked vacantly at the space ahead and said, "There was no interest during the public offering. In the end, Nomura found Wesley and told them, look, the two of you are in equally deep shit. — They were also making a couple hundred million of losses in the third quarter. In May their shares were still trading at 14 dollars, and now they'd be happy to be worth half of it. — We'll marry the two of you so we get a handsome 20% commission from both ends. But they're smarter than that. Wesley wanted the entire Linox business."

"Everything?" Smith asked.

"Everything," Andy confirmed. "Down to the last chair."

"But not the people, obviously."

"You get the drift."

"How much are they paying?"

"I am not at liberty to tell you, am I?" Andy replied. "All I can tell you right now is that it's going be a big deal."

"Well, you and I won't have jobs to go back to when this is over!" Smith blurted. He looked directly into the mid-day sun hanging happily above them. "Of course, it's a big deal."

Linox was the general name of all the business units in North and South America. It was a combination of the word 'Linked' and 'Inox' as in 'Inox Steel', which was the trade name for Stainless Steel. While Smith was planning his next strategy for the new business unit with the Americans, the Japanese were thinking of selling them off entirely. Was this the reason why the rest of the team had been so unmotivated lately? It almost hurt him to realize that the off-hand attitude from Mr. Mura on all of his recent product ideas, including expanding the Ferro-Alloy product lines to Ferromolybdenum sheets and powder, to support the construction industry in budding South American countries whose sales performance Smith was willing to bet his own buck into, and together with the sloppy monthly survey analyses, all these might be a simple rouse to keep him from making any major long-term decision.

"How long has this been going on?" Smith asked.

"I don't know. Today was my first attendance." Andy started to clean up the mess he had made on the table playing with the apple seeds. "But I've seen proposals from Nomura from as far back as a year ago."

Smith rolled his eyes. He was after all the director of the new business unit. That used to mean something back home. He was suddenly infuriated and lost all his appetite. The feeling that he had deluded himself to be important and a controller of his own fate, as Pinocchio had been deluded to believe he was a boy, had sent his heart diving, ready to be gobbled up by any passing whale.

"Offer the Mexs to someone else," Smith suggested. "Offer it up to the public. Or make an independent spin-off out of it."

"No," Andy said curtly. "They would have done it if it could be solved like this."

"Anything you can do about it?" Smith tried, helplessly. "Anything we can do about it?"

"Like make a hundred forty million before the deal, redeem the Mexican units back and split the last five million between the two of us?" Andy pretended to think about the possibility with his arms crossed in front of his chest. "No. I don't think so."

Smith was calculating in his head how many first prizes he had to win at the Pachinko parlor to make up for the amount. He concluded that the calculation was not worth going through.

"Start loving the *Gyu-don*," Andy said as he raised from his chair to take his food tray to the collecting belt near the entrance of the kitchen. *Gyu-don,* that was the name of Smith's bowl of teriyaki beef with onions and raw eggs. "You might have to eat more of that."

Smith snorted at his remark. The issue was he might not be able to have more 'qu-dong', or whatever the atrocious bowl of unsatisfying, stringy ball of meat was called, even if he wanted. His contract belonged to the Linox Holdings, so did Andy's. The boy, however, had nothing to worry about. He would be signed back into DaiKe before one could learn to say "Donburi". But for him, he would be the last person to kneel and beg for a job at Gregory Wesley's feet. Certainly at fifty-five, one had a few more options than staying in the labour market, but one had more concerns, too, for leaving.

A million question surrounded the topic of early retirement clouded his mind for the rest of the working day. He asked Cheryl, his secretary, to look some answers up for him in an email before he left the office at eight.

33. Gift

"Misa, Misa, look at me." Mura turned her head towards him. He had his clammy fingers clasped around Misa's cheeks. Misa opened her eyes reluctantly and looked at him.

"Are you feeling good?" Though he asked, he was not waiting for a response. "I bought you something." And he released his grip to free up his hands.

Misa closed her eyes again. Her head rolled to the side in exhaustion.

"Look, Misa-chan, look." He prodded her naked waist with it. She knew the sensation. The cold, hard object Mr. Mura meant could only be one thing. Why did men think that this would be what women want? Fighting hard against the fatigue that usually washed over her after an orgasm, she propped herself up with a pillow against the bed frame behind her and took a look the gift Mura had bought her.

"Oh!" She said, seeing the object finally. "What is it?"   It was a pink paper gift box with round corners, not what she had expected. On it, a single white flower was printed on the middle flap. She reached out to grab it in her hands and examined it carefully.

Mura sat down on the bed in front of her and covered his manhood with a corner of the quilted blanket that had been draped over Misa's legs. The muscles of his arms quivered and his bulging belly rose up and down as he tried to catch his breath from the recent exertion.

"Open it." Mura nodded at Misa with a smile. It spread wrinkles around the corners of his eyes. She could count them one by one — it had made the stern man warm and genial despite his unattractive appearance.

Misa adjusted herself upright. Even though she was completely naked and, was smeared with a drying layer of body fluids that would send her running for the shower in other circumstances, she observed the customary politeness when receiving presents. Carefully, she lifted the flap with the white flower print and the other flaps spring outwards at the same time to reveal the box's content. They were a pair of beige pearl earrings dangling on a silver chain. On the chain, two intricately tied, small butterfly bows sat on top of each one of the pearls.

"Wa! *Ureshiiiii!*" Misa took out the earrings out and detached them from the cardboard that was used to hold them in place. She slid the hooks of the earrings through each of her earlobes instantly with her skillful fingers.

"You're beautiful, do you know?" Mura said, taking Misa, now completely naked with a single pair of earrings, into view. "Wear them all the time from now on," he said. Before Misa could utter a "yes", or "*hai*" in Japanese, he had started to caress her breasts again. Her "*hai*" dissolved into a soft moan.

34. I Am Your Friend

"Sumimasen," Smith said to the waitress that was passing by his seat. She didn't notice him.

"Sumimasen!" He stood up and called after her a second time. His thighs rammed directly into the bottom of the metal tray that was fitted to the bottom of his Pachinko machine and dislodged it. The metal balls in the tray clattered loudly over the unsynchronized electronic music that had been turned to the machine's loudest setting. It was the noise they made that had the waitress turning around.

"Nani ga tetsuda shimasho ka?" How can she help, she asked, sauntering back over to Smith, who was cradling the detached metal tray in his arms precariously. The balls rolled from one side to another as if they were on a wakeboard in a churning ocean.

"Misa Hayami-san wa, gogo ni, ki te imasu ka?" With his attention partially devoted not to overturn his tray, he formulated his question in Japanese with difficulty. He had meant to ask whether Misa had arrived to work yet.

"Misa wa..." the girl said hesitantly, *"kyo wa, ko nai desho."* Misa probably won't come today, she said.

"Ahh...!" The metal balls had all of a sudden rolled away from him and concentrated in the upper corner of the tray. Only by his impressive reflex was he able to jam the tray back into its position in time to prevent it from tipping over to a disastrous mess. The impressive reflex, however, was not lenient to his brittle back. He had strained it again for nothing, Smith plopped himself back on the leather stool in agony.

The waitress stood stunned beside him. Her mouth agape. In her mind, the imaginary movie of customers rolling backward on stray metal balls on the floor played automatically. At the thought of having to deal with the consequences, she crinkled her nose.

Smith gave her a weak smile to indicate that he could still make facial expressions. That jolted the girl back to the moment and with a polite bow, she walked away and vanished into the next row, happy to rid the man from her sight.

So it had been three days, Smith thought. He had gone to the Thunderbird for the last three days to catch Misa on her shift, but she did not show up at work one single time. To have the luxury of three consecutive days off in her job would be highly unlikely.

Should he be concerned? — In fact, he was already concerned. He was only retracing the mental steps that had led to his heightened uneasiness. He saw himself calling Misa and asked her if she was doing all right in his mind's eye. It would not be such an awkward thing.

A commotion had broken out at the counter. A man had swept his hands on top of the countertop and sent everything on it, including a cash register crashing down to the floor. Its drawer didn't spring open, however, in contrary to urban myth, Smith observed. That idle thought seemed to capture only him, for the rest of the customers and staff alike in Thunderbird were grabbed by the tumult that had unfolded behind the counter, for the man had jumped over to the other side to grab one of the managerial staffs who had so far been able to dodge her attacker. It didn't, however, kept her from screaming for help.

"*Yamede kudasai!* Stop it, please! I'll call the police! Tatsu-kun, you better stop now!" She ducked behind a stool when he lunged at her.

Tatsu-kun? — Smith stood up, this time, avoided ramming himself against any part of the machine, and peered at the origin of the commotion.

"Why did you fire her? What did she do wrong?" The man was but a boy. It was Tatsu, Misa's brother.

Before he could answer his own questions about whether the boy deserved to have his ass saved a second time or if it was healthy for someone with his injuries to be lunging about so violently, Smith had already leaped over to Tatsu's side and tried to pry the boy away from the woman. She was Katsumi Saitou from Nabuo Group, the woman that had given him his award money, the Head of Treasury of Thunderbird district in the Nabuo empire.

"Mr. Sumisu!" She said in a shrill voice, recognizing him. "Keep him away from me!" She said in Japanese.

"Stop it! Stop it!" Smith tried to tear the boy away from her, yet he was stubborner than Andy had described him to be. He wedged himself between the boy and Miss Saitou in desperation. Miss Saitou took the opportunity and ducked behind Smith to avoid the boy's maddening grip.

Frustrated that the boy was not slowing down, Smith shoved him back with all his might. Tatsu tumbled backward and smashed his back against the countertop.

His groans of pain made Smith feel guilty almost instantly, but he didn't show.

"Just chill! See what you've gotten yourself into?" He asked, referring not just to this event, but the one that caused him to lay in the hospital last time. Smith had forgotten that he was speaking English. That seemed to irritate the boy even more. He shoved Smith back in revenge. Smith remained in his spot unfazed as if he was merely kissed by a mosquito.

"*Nani ga kidanno ka*? What's going on?" The security finally arrived. He took Smith's place between Tatsu and Miss Saitou without excusing himself.

"*Nase ane wa kobi ni shida?* Why did you fire my sister?" Tatsu said, in between his gasps for air, "*Kanojo wa, machigai de nanimonai!* She didn't do anything wrong."

Smith strained his ears trying to understand the Japanese.

"After the way you two behaved, do you think I'll give her her job back?" Miss Saitou said. "Her *arubaito* (part-time) is against our company policy! Especially when it is something so unseemly like this...we'll not let her come back to pollute the other girl's minds."

Surprised gasps filled the background. Some of the waitresses that worked with Misa wheezed. They held each other's hands in support. Everyone who listened had understood the cause of her discharge. All, perhaps except Tatsu himself.

"That is total nonsense! Stop pretending to be so noble! She's working for someone other than Nabuo group, that's why you fired her!" Tatsu ran his hand on the counter, grabbing the first hard object he could find.

At that moment Smith had had enough with the boy. He slapped his palm hard on the boy's fist, making him drop his weapon, and he wrung his arms around the boy's shoulder to wheel him around. Naturally, Tatsu resisted.

Yet, the boy's strength was after all no match to Smith, who also had the advantage of his height. Despite Tatsu's kicking and screaming, Smith lifted him by the waist and carried him outside of the parlor. Tatsu could do nothing against it but dropped one of his own dirty sneakers in the process. The security guard furrowed at the pair and asked Miss Saitou whether he should call the police, but Miss Saitou merely shook her head sadly to everyone's relief.

The security guard picked up the stray shoe and threw them out.

Everyone returned to their business when the sliding glass doors at the entrance closed behind them.

Outside of the kitchen door in the corner, Aiko sucked in a deep breath. She had hidden herself behind the tower of used glasses. Thank goodness Miss Saitou didn't say it was she who told on Misa. She ran her fingers down her bleached blond hair and noticed that they were all tangled. Time to buy new shampoo.

"What do you want from me?" Tatsu turned around to stare at Smith after he was dropped outside of Thunderbird. "I don't know you!" He snorted, but the jerking of motion of his head had made him coughed in pain instead.

"You're not well. And unstable. I'm going to see you home," Smith explained simply. He raised a hand to hail a passing taxi, which stopped right beside them with its door slightly ajar in no time.

"Jump in!" He commanded the boy and climbed into the back of the taxi himself.

Tatsu stood beside it biting his lips. That was a sign of suppressed physical pains, Smith observed. He leaned out of the door and beckoned at Tatsu.

"*Watashiwa Misa no domotachi desu.* I'm Misa's friend. *Anata wa Misa no otosan desu.* You're Misa's brother. *Anata no men o sukuuda.* I saved your life." Smith enumerated in Japanese. "*Watashi wa Anata no domotachi desu.* I am your friend."

The simple rationale had Tatsu convinced, but he wasn't going to let on.

"*Baka.*" Tatsu cursed under his breath and crawled into the cabin. That set the taxi driver glaring at the unlikely pair of friends from the reflection in his mirror in curiosity.

35. The Pain of Reality

"The place is small. Careful not to trip on anything," Tatsu said as he opened the door to his and Misa's flat. Smith was assaulted immediately by a familiar odor. It was the smell of marijuana. He crinkled his nose. Wasn't that illegal in Japan? Maybe it was just the medical ones, he assured himself.

Tatsu threw his keychain on the uneven folding table unfazed by Smith's look of confusion and went straight for the bathroom.

Since he was left alone, Smith felt no shame pacing from one side of the wall to another of the living room, measuring its dimensions, for he was struck by how much more spacey it appeared, even though his measurements confirmed the apartment to be merely eight square meters, similar to his own living area. Without waiting for an invitation, he peered into the only room in the flat without a thread of shame in him. He persuaded himself that he was only checking it out in case he had to carry Tatsu into his bedroom for rest later, and kept a clear conscience.

There was no door to the bedroom but a sliding *shoji*, a wooden frame that had semi-transparent papers as panels. It was then that he realized it was his first time to ever see a real Japanese home, not one of those Western-styled apartments or houses that were rid of any features of traditional Japanese architecture his Japanese colleagues owned. Behind the divider, there was no bed — no bed in the traditional Western sense. A single, unmade blanket draped over a thin mat that seemed to be made out of the same material, laid near the wall on the left. Another folded set was stowed neatly in the right corner. — He had never considered sleeping on the floor. How did the Japanese do it without waking up every morning with an aching back?

After fussing about for twenty minutes in the toilet, Tatsu came out in a swathe of smokes and crashed into the bean bag on the floor. The lack of proper cushioning was hurting him, and he showed it. Smith, who had been standing by the folding table as any disciplined guest would, skidded over to his side immediately to take a look at the bandage around his chest. The boy had somehow managed to replace it by himself, no doubt with the help of some herbal 'medicinal painkiller'. Smith did not think it was his place to inquire and instead he stretched Tatsu's legs out with care and removed the boy's shoes for him.

Tatsu chuckled.

Smith followed his gaze and discovered that there was a hole in his own right sock. Smith had taken his shoes off to avoid scratching what seemed to be newly waxed floor. And a terrible looking toe was poking out of the hole.

"Where's Misa?" Smith asked, ready to shift the focus away from his feet. "I'm going to call her and ask her to come back to take care of you." With nothing better to do, Smith could keep an eye on the boy on his own for a couple of hours this evening until she returned, but his secret agenda prompted him to choose any plan that involved Misa earlier.

Tatsu decided that he should make the call himself, but she didn't pick up.

Having heard what Tatsu said earlier in Thunderbird, the possibility of where Misa could be now bothered Smith greatly. He noticed that her brother was getting equally worried. Tatsu squeezed his cell phone so hard to his face in anxiousness that the screen was completely smeared with layers of perspiration and facial oil.

With each unanswered ring, Tatsu's face turned redder. Before Tatsu could react, Smith snatched his phone over and copied Misa's number into his own cell. When he returned Tatsu's cell phone, the two of them began calling her at the same time, with even more urgency than an insurance salesman who couldn't make his quota on the last day of the month.

"Hello!" Smith got through before he could realize it. His voice echoed in his earpiece and remained unanswered for a short moment. Then the call ended with a beep. He knew he should have spoken Japanese instead.

"*Nan to iuu taka?* What did she say?" Tatsu asked even though he knew the call was too short for anything to be said. He dialed his sister's cell phone number again.

"Misa!" His call was also picked up, and this time, she didn't hang up.

She would explain everything then with a simple and logical answer, Smith thought. Before Smith's daughter turned twenty-one, he had his fair share of worries. And yet after all the heartburn, she turned out fine. Could Misa not have been out chatting with her girlfriends about whatever girls in her age chat about, and had forgotten about the time? Or perhaps she was out on a date, watching a movie? Though the thought of her and Andy left a bitter taste in his mouth. After all, she was just fired from her job. Not many girls at eighteen could say proudly that they had a job to begin with, and if she had wanted a little bit of time to herself, be a little less predictable, she could hardly be blamed for acting her age once in a while.

In any case, the brother and sister were communicating. He felt relief slowly crawling back into him.

Yet, Tatsu lowered his arm before a second had gone by. His face was pale as fresh snow. The phone rolled off his fingers and landed next to the beanbag.

Smith gritted his teeth in anticipation.

The boy's tough countenance started to crumble. His eyes, nose, and mouth, culled up like a tight fist and tears started streaming down his face. Smith reached for the phone, but Tatsu noticed despite the fact that his eyes were filled with hot tears. The two wrestled for the phone and by chance, one of them, they couldn't tell even themselves who did it, clicked the loudspeaker button.

"Ahh...ahh...ahh! Ahh!"

Misa's repeated shrills pierced through Smith's heart and set it pounding with a mixture of fear and anger.

The last gasp that was particularly lengthier and more trembly had turned even a grown man like Smith, who had in his lifetime seen enough salacious Hollywood movies and had his fair share of sex, completely red in the face. He had been subconsciously holding his breath, and that hit him with a powerful, ripping chest pain. Smith's knees buckled. He squatted next to Tatsu, whose face was white with horror.

Smith closed his eyes and focused on setting the rhythm of his breath straight again. No chance of helping the boy, and his sister, if he was going to get a heart attack now.

Tatsu hung up and avoided what further damage the sound of his own sister being violated — he did not want to think that she was a willing victim — could do to his head.

Yet Misa's voice seemed to reverberate in his eardrums long after the sound waves dissipated.

"She said... she was fine." At last, Tatsu spat out these words of hers through his trembling lips as if they disgusted him.

Smith opened his eyes and squinted compassionately at Tatsu. He was shell-shocked himself. He could only imagine how the young boy felt.

How do other people handle a situation like this?

***

The phone rang on without stopping. The Doraemon ring tone irritated Mura. He picked up Misa's call and someone said "Hello" in English back at him. Taken by surprise, he hung up before Misa could protest.

"Who the fuck was that, Misa-chan?" In fact, he was, as usual, not waiting for her answer. He had noticed the caller's name on the display. He knew distinctively that it was a man's name, and he was a *gaijin*. Through a complex yet faulty reasoning on the limited information which killed his erection almost in an instant, he had arrived at the conclusion that the caller was another one of Misa's clients. "This is my time, you're on my time, Misa-chan!"

Mura was angry.

Misa had always known that it would be difficult with Mr. Mura. Triggered by the most unexpected events, his tenderness could dissolve into murderous villainy as easy as flipping a switch on the wall. And the rising fire inside him, a self-deficiency complex that could combust readily at any moment, had cooked his head through and through this time.

"A successful man such as I am," he thought to himself, "deserves to be treated with respect."

Raged, he pulled Misa out of the bed and thrust her over to the writing desk. He turned her around, and with a light push, he pushed Misa's face and her upper torso on the surface of the desk.

The hook of Misa's left earring pressed threateningly close to her neck and pricked her skin. She struggled to roll her head around to keep it from piercing her skin. Not mindful of the signs of her resistant was unrelated to her defiance, Mura slapped his palm against her cheek to keep her down.

Misa screamed in fear as the hook scratched her neck.

During that maniacal moment, Mura's penis had grown back to its full size.

"It was just my brother calling!" Misa pleaded, willing to say anything to be released, yet she opted for the truth. "There must be something important since he called so many times!" The truth could sound so unconvincing sometimes.

Misa's cell phone rang again. It might well be Misa's brother, but Mura didn't care.

"You're hurting me. Let me go!" Misa stiffened her back to try to gain a few millimeters of space off from the surface of the table top. Mura only shifted his weight on to her himself.

"You've said it was your brother," Mura said coldly. "Okay, I'll let you talk to your brother now!"

He pressed the phone to her right ear and inserted himself at the same time inside Misa. A diabolical smile of exhilaration flitted across his face.

"Answer him." He shouted and clicked the green button with his thumb. The call connected while he pushed himself deeper into Misa's uterus.

"Misa!", Misa heard her brother call her name and felt the air go out of her —This was the most awful thing she had to do in her life, she then realized. The realization made her body tremble by itself without Mura's help. This was a psychological torturous deed Mura was doing to her. Misa could concede on anything for a good buck. She had never let any wild, impractical dream run wild in her head and poison her with virtues of dignity. The single wish she had, she spoke now to the Lord of her fate, had always been to keep Tatsu forever out of her messy, dirty world, and that seemed to be the exact opposite of Mura's intention now.

The hook on the back of her earring pricked the skin on her neck intermittently at Mura's every move. She could feel the sharp metal pin scraping against her shoulder blade, retreating, then back again.

The multitude of concerns and sensations had shot her well outside of her safety zone. Her defense system shut down and she started sobbing.

She prayed to *shin*. And she promised she would return to the shrine to pay her thanks if she could get out of here alive.

With considerable will, she blocked out all physical sensations. However strange this might sound, her body had gotten accustomed, or even numb, to the sex plays that ranged anything from gentle to potentially disfigurative. But there had always been a bottom line. She did not think that she would be in this situation where there was none.

She found it impossible to maintain a steady, logical flow of words while imagining the needle drilling into her neck and ripping her veins apart, but she had to.

An "I am fine" gushed out of her mouth between Mura's violent thrusts and that was all she could manage to say, her ultimate effort to shield the depressing nature of her work from her little brother. Then she gave way to the sharp pains she could not avoid.

It petrified Misa that Mura was larger than ever. Some men could be stimulated by the strange, shameful, erotic nature of seeing a woman in distress.

Misa clamped her mouth as tightly shut as she could and closed her eyes.

There was nothing she could do now except to wish that this would be over soon.

She squeezed her labia tighter, and that sent a wave of excitement through Mura. It rippled through the end of every single nerve fiber in him. He pulled out just before climax and stuffed the exploding device into Misa's mouth.

36. Right and Wrong

"What are you doing?" Tatsu pried the phone from Smith's hand.

"I'm calling the police." Smith typed 110 into the touchpad and was about the press on the green call button were it not for Tatsu's interference. "I'm going to call, and you're going to tell them what happened. We'll find your sister," Smith stood up so he could be out of the boy's reach. He had his cell phone clipped partially between his ears and his right shoulder so he could free up his hands to fend off Tatsu's feverish grapple.

"No, we cannot!" The boy dug his ankles deep into the bean bag so he could buttress himself higher. That compressed his wounds, and tiny red threads of blood started to seep through the layers of freshly replaced bandages around his chest. Despite that, he was bent on wrestling the phone away from Smith.

Smith's grip on the flat screen loosened under Tatsu's determined meddling. His reflex kicked in again just in time to let him swoop down to catch the falling phone with his hands, but wool socks on a waxed floor guaranteed less friction than it was needed to keep him on balance. His left foot skidded forward while the right skidded right. They twisted him in an impossible angle. He collapsed on the floor, cradling his cell phone with a paralyzing cramp on his lower back.

"Don't do it if you're Misa's friend! You're gonna get her arrested for *Enjo kosai* (subsidized dating)! They will put her in a *kankoku* (prison). She's getting paid. It's her job. — A lousy, dirty, disgusting job!" Tatsu billowed.

Getting caught — Smith hadn't thought of that, but his wits caught up with his mouth quick enough. "There are many facilities that help girls like her." Although making his point with unwavering conviction, Smith didn't really know whether they existed in Japan. He was speaking from his knowledge of American juvenile delinquency institutions. "And with some proper guidance, she can restart her life again soon enough. She's only, what, eighteen? If we don't do it now, soon it would be too late, you see?" He unlocked his phone trying to call the emergency number again.

"No! You don't understand!" Tatsu almost shouted, his hands flailing about to stop Smith. "Do you think it has never occurred to me that this might stop her? But I wish it's that simple, old man." He paused to give himself the courage to say what he had to say next.

"Just forget about what you just heard. *Zenbu wasule de kudasai!* Misa will come home when she's finished work."

"This is a civilized country. If her misconduct was misguided, there are ways to help her."

Tatsu squeezed his eyes closed, as if in pain. "It's not the first time..." His lips started trembling as he uttered these words and he could not bring himself to elaborate further.

"What first time?" Smith asked.

A long pause followed while Tatsu made up his mind about the character of the man sitting in front of him, a complete stranger, with a trustworthy face. He let down his guard.

"Her mind is all fucked up," Tatsu said. "She couldn't tell what's good and what's bad anymore."

Smith could scarcely believe the Japanese boy knew the term 'fucked up'.

"She has been *re-i-pu!*" Tatsu continued, his eyes bloodshot. He rested his right hand on the smeared bandages, bracing the pain that was deeper than the wounds that had ever been inflicted on him from any fight. "The *konyaro* (bastard) who did it was *shakuhou* (released)! The video company he worked for still makes money off of the *bi-de-o* tapes, but the police said they couldn't find grounds to stop its sales!"

Although some of the words Tatsu said were in Japanese, Smith had understood it with no effort. Smith hadn't known that he possessed the vocabulary for such a theme, and he surely did not enjoy finding out.

"You want to see it? You want to see the man's face?" Tatsu asked as if to punish Smith for doubting what he said — even for a split second, only to preserve his withering hopes that there might be fairytale-happy people out there. Why would Smith want to see something like that of Misa? Why would anyone? It was a torture itself to hear about it.

"His name is *Sa-a-ji*. One, of these damn white *gaijin* like you!" Tatsu continued.

"Sergey?" A common French name, Smith, remarked.

"*Ser-ji Le-bi-ruu,*" he said. Even in this dire time, the Japanese impossible enunciation of foreign words was getting in the way. "It was in the newspaper on *ni-sen kui nan, san-gatasu, nijuuyokka*. (March 24th of 2009)"

That was more than a couple of years ago. Misa would only have been around fifteen at the time.

On his smartphone's web browser app, Tatsu typed some keywords in Japanese on the search bar on the Yahoo! Japan page and clicked the image tab. The results loaded in a time too short for the boy to avert his eyes. Smith could see the disdain on his strained face straight away, trying to maintain composure while pushing the phone over to Smith. The results showed an array of photographs of a man at different events, taken at various media events and exhibitions.

"Who's he?" Smith asked, rhetorically. Who was this man to elope punishment for such atrocious crimes? Tatsu said there were videos of it, shouldn't that be evidence enough? He wanted to ask what was on the video, but he thought better of it.

The young boy sitting opposite to him sucked in a deep breath and said, "nothing could touch a man of this caliber, they say." There were things on this earth, over which no matter how many times you have talked or contemplated, would still leave your mind unsettled. "Just couldn't be helped. Misa and I. We were both garbage in the sewage. We'd always be the dirt on the underside of other people's shoes," he said, almost believing in these self-effacing words himself. Poor souls.

"Where are your parents?" Smith was reminded that parents usually know the best for their child. "I'm a *gaijin* as you said. I know nothing about how things work in Japan. Your parents will know what to do, huh? Give them a call."

"She couldn't help us. She's just a normal housewife — one without a husband. What's the point of troubling her?" Tatsu said, his calm voice highlighted the suppressed frustration. "Moreover, this has been going on since we've come to Tokyo." His voice trailed off. "It's all my fault."

"How's this your fault?" Smith said understanding the origin of Tatsu's self-blame, but he refused to let the boy believed that someone understood him in that regard. "Get some rest. You've stressed yourself today." He held the wounded boy by the arm to the bedroom, ignoring the numbness that was the results of straining his back — it would get worse by tomorrow, he knew —and helped the boy carefully on the bedding. "I'll wait in the living room for Misa if you don't mind, and I'll talk to her." He found the light switch of the bedroom, flipped it and wobbled out of the room, hiding his uneasy gait from the boy by sliding the room divider into place behind him immediately.

Smith sat himself down on the bean bag in the living room, feeling drained. It had been years since he had sat on one. The sensation was bittersweet.

There, old and new memories crept up on him. He pushed the involuntary visualization of what could have happened to Misa in the past three years out of his head and concentrated on what he could do and say to her when she returned. She was his responsibility now, whether he wanted the liability or not. Perhaps God had answered his prayers to integrate into Japan in his unusual, mysterious way. After all, he had gotten what he wanted —a Japanese friend, and more. Who could contradict theological speculations, and with what? None of us living would ever find proof that all of what befalls us was not part of a greater plan.

That Saturday that he would never forget, Misa didn't dial his number by accident. He was her deliverance from evil, and that was where he fit into the picture.

Despite the hour, he called Aileen Martin who was the only one in Tokyo he could trust Misa with. If this were back home, he would have asked his wife for advice. But in this strange country, and the unfamiliar status of their relationship he had yet to come to terms with, the new Debbie could hardly offer the help he sought. The new him, stripped of his sheath of support, had been groping in the dark long enough like a newly blinded man. Perhaps it was about time to get himself a walking cane, and immerse himself completely in his new identity —a single, old man.

His courage to exercise his freedom of consulting a woman other than his wife on critical issues such as this had been rewarded. Aileen, although surprised at the hour of the call and the lateness of the much-awaited call from Smith, had been kind to him. Misa and her brother's conditions in Tokyo and their dire financial need had moved Aileen. She did not need any prompt from him to get to the idea of finding Misa a more stable and suitable profession. She suggested a clerical position at the InterHRLA and gave an invitation to Smith to forward to Misa for an interview at her organization. Grateful beyond words, Smith complimented Aileen's compassion profusely over the phone. While his compliments gladly accepted, Aileen had only really been thinking about scoring more points in Smith's eyes. It was all the better if she did it by doing what she would normally do, which was to show compassion to underprivileged groups.

After he had hung up, he waited anxiously for Misa to come home. Behind the paper room divider, Tatsu laid awake.

In the well-kept Hayami's apartment, neither the boy nor the man had wanted to give way to Mister Sandman, yet sleep doused over their heads like the uninterrupted splashing of water in a Shintoism purification ritual. After an hour or less, repose fell upon them when the spirits that possessed them escaped temporarily from their bodies. They entered a pulling state of subconsciousness that was filled with remorse and sadness.

37. Evidence

Misa had earned every bit of the time she spent in Mura's house. The humiliation, the pain, she took them all in as if they were just hurdles to her in a race to win a medal and get to the podium, so she could see further and reach higher. The only thing that would make it better now was if she actually finds something, anything, that may explain what Mura, and the list of big names, such as CEOs of banks, executives of big companies and important politicians were doing in her cousin's diary.

It had taken her far too many late night 'house raids' to get to this house in particular, the grandest and largest of all. Mura was not only one of the richest men in the group, he was also a leading figure of some sort, not because of his leadership ability, but his undefeated sense of self-importance and the unarguable demonstration of seniority.

He was leading a secret circle, no doubt of it, but to what purpose? The simple explanation of patrons to the same pleasure clubs or private entertainment clique was not sufficient for her. She knew these men by now, all of them consumed with greed and self-interest. What drove them to form the coalition? What sort of gains compel them to undertake the symbiosis? And what does Misaki and Sergey had to do with it? The answer to her questions may just be in this house.

With nothing but a towel around her naked body and her cell phone in her hand, she snuck out of the bathroom on the second floor into Mura's study. That would be the logical place where anything important was stored. Mura was exhausted. Like most men, he was predictable in the way that he fell into a deep slumber after their intense physical activity. She had given him an enormously satisfying orgasm, and her experience told her that he was not going to wake up from his post-orgasmic coma anytime soon.

Misa hadn't realized it before, but she was grateful for it now that Mura was from another generation. His generation had a serious mistrust on technologies, which meant that everything was stored in physical paper form. A thorough look at all the drawers in his study desk revealed nothing of interest. That was not possible.

He must have hidden the important stuff somewhere else, like a safe.

At the risk of being caught, she snuck back into the bedroom where the naked Mura was snoring thunderously without a care in the world. In the dimmed light of the room, Misa tiptoed for the safe in the walk-in closet on the side of the room. The safe was buried under a thick swathes of clothes. It stood open to her amazement, for Mura had only moments earlier taken out her gift from it and hadn't bothered to lock it. — It should have meant that there was nothing important in there that would warrant the security, yet that was the next best place Mura could hide anything. It was dark in the unlit walk-in closet, and Misa couldn't see clearly, but she saw the dull reflection of a yellow manila envelope.

Presently, Mura made a choking noise and stirred on the bed. It scared Misa to no end. She grabbed the envelop with her eyes closed and darted out of the room into the marble-tiled bathroom once again, where there were light and she could have a moment of privacy. She locked herself in. Still panting, she leaned against the door to listen for any sound from the other side. When worse comes to worst, Misa could read whatever that was in the envelop and just flush them down the toilet. Mura might still wonder why she had been sneaking around, but he wouldn't have any incriminating evidence.

Yet after a minute of hanging by the door, Misa heard nothing. And slowly, the consistent snoring of Mr. Mura returned. She let out a sigh of relief and slowly pulled out of content of the manila envelope.

"*Muri-desu!* That's not possible!" Misa let out a hushed phrase, surprised by what she was reading. The document in her hand was Mura's will! Perhaps because Misa was still so young, just barely eighteen, her imagination did not even give her the ammunition to envision that the document in the envelop could be the older man's will.

She threw her hands down in disappointment and sighed. Then curiosity took over her. Mura had two sons, although they were both living in the United States at the moment together with their mother. Would he split his assets equally between the two? Or would he favor one of them? Misa flipped through the papers to search for the paragraphs about the beneficiary of his will.

The words on the paper jumped out at her and knocked her over figuratively. She could not believe what she was reading. The man was going to donate his entire fortune after his death to charities. There were eight different organizations in there listed as approved recipients. Misa didn't know most of them, but she recognized an organization she knew very well. An organization that was founded by a close friend of hers from her hometown who had passed away a few year ago, the William Syndrome Children Foundation of Japan, of which she was a member herself.

This despicable, self-absorbing man was going to donate his money to their specific charity? What in the world was going on?

38. Witches' Candy Mix

Donbori candy, *Nerunerunerune* witches' mix, *Ramen* gummy set, Popin' Cookin's sushi candy set, Glico's giant Caplico ice-cream candy...Misa took each one of the candy packs in the *AM-PM* convenience store and scanned their colorful descriptions carefully. She had never indulged herself with one of these, and neither did her parents. Tonight she was determined to have the '*shiawase*' experience, a satisfying feeling that was uniquely captured perhaps only by the Japanese language. It was the feeling she had when her dad had taken them for the first time to snow sledding at the Hanazono, an hour south from where they lived. It was the feeling she had when her school choir was nominated to represent the Ishikari prefecture to compete at the National Choir Competition in Tokyo.

"Give me a pack of that!" A boy with long, gray hair styled like a Mohawk, wearing a red tartan shirt and ripped jeans had entered the store and barked at the cashier for a pack of Mild Seven cigarette. A girl in a green wig and *Vocaloid Miku* cosplay costume wriggled in his arm. The back of the girl somehow looked familiar.

"I like the pink one!" She said. Misa recognized her voice and the frivolous way she dressed immediately. It was Aiko.

Just, then the boy turned his head towards the row of drink refrigerators on the right, revealing a big monotone lotus tattooed on his neck. The lotus was broken in several places, a Yakuza symbol. The image sparked intuition in Misa.

Misa took a pack of candy from the rack and walked over to greet her friend, whom she, until this moment, didn't know had a boyfriend from one of the most aggressive clans of gang in Tokyo.

That explained everything.

"Aiko-chan," Misa said. The girl turned around to meet her caller. At that moment Misa's ripped open the green sachet and splashed all its content on Aiko's face. "You deserved this and more."

Aiko could only stand there in shock, her face covered with sticky glucose powder. Some had gotten in her eyes and she was squeezing them shut in pain.

"What the hell?!" The boy next to her grunted, completely caught off guard.

"Keep the change," Misa tossed ten thousand yen on the counter. The cashier, however, was too nervous to take the money in the presence of an agitated Yakuza. His legs trembled with the pack of Mild Seven in his hands. But before the boy could do anything, Misa had already disappeared through the automatic doors into the dark park.

"Oh." Smith stepped into the convenient store a few seconds later, hoping to get something for breakfast. "Hmm..." He hummed, avoiding eye contact with the boy and his girlfriend who was covered in some sort of white powder, and walked into the snacks aisle.

Something crackled under his feet. He looked down and noticed the wrapper of *Nerunerunerune* Witches' Candy Mix. From across the rack, he saw the girl covered in white powder was now scrubbing her face feverishly while screaming at the same time. The boy next to her was laughing unsympathetically besides her. In fact, he was laughing so hard he doubled over.

"It must be good," Smith mumbled to himself and grabbed a pack of the same thing from the rack.

***

Family, she couldn't lose, yet they hurt her so much that she wished she had the power to free them from her. Friends, she longed to have, yet once again she would rather not have any.

They had betrayed her, her friends, or those that assumed the appearances of friends. It seemed that eighteen years of experience with friendship had not made her an expert on this particular relationship. Had she confused something else for friendship? Not just once, but twice, three times? Misa curled up under her favorite oak tree and thought back to the day when Aiko had asked her about what she did to make so much money besides waitressing at the Thunderbird. She scrutinized her face in her memory and yet after the third time, she still could not find a hint of mean spirit on her then innocent face. Aiko's question had come out of impulsive curiosity, she was convinced on that day. Yet the outcome of Misa's confidence made what she did appear premeditated.

Viciousness.

I could be that.

If that was the essence of survival.

Shinu kakugo de yare. Kill or be killed.

I could be vicious, too.

Kore wa machigaemashita. No, this is wrong.

The warmth of tears surged up Misa's nasal cavity and blocked her breathing intermittently, but she refused to cry.

Her eyelids were heavy, but her heart was heavier.

What was there left to do? If it weren't for Tatsu, the sheer number of times she wished she could stop living would have put suicide to the top of her priority list. Some people died of old age, some people died of sickness. She belonged to the group that died off of foolishness.

May foolishness extinct itself after her, followed by honesty, integrity, kindness, hope, love and all its poisonous derivatives that plagued those that treasured them.

Misa had trusted her secret with Aiko. No doubt now Aiko had shared it with her boyfriend, a Kyokuto-kan low-ranking minion. A gangster, nonetheless. They thrived on these gossips. Street urchins with desperate ears for anything that could place them on the good side of their bosses, who in turn needed to impress their bosses up the ranks for all the investment they put in maintaining a sizable group of men and women with no particular skills nor education on the payroll. The Kyokuto-kan dominated the market of sexual exchange in the East of Tokyo, and they would do anything to keep it this way. The leak had caused Misa her day job. It was a threat for her to stop running her own business with no agent.

"Agent," she chuckled at the thought of it. Prostitution was a business more regulated and controlled than probably everything else in the world. Yet, everyone —almost everyone —wants to take a bite of that big, multi-layered fruit cake with egg custard fillings, including the government. Misa didn't want an agent and probably would never get one, unless coerced into it, which was not an unlikely event at the rate she was going, dousing Aiko with sticky, gooey sweetener, for example.

Misa couldn't care less. She didn't really need the day job. The day job was only there to make her feel less lonely and more like a normal person, with a typical eight-hour workday, with a paycheck that could be cashed at regular intervals. It cheered up her immensely. However, it was unnecessary. She was never scared anymore either. There was nothing else men could do to her that she hadn't expected.

Nobody and nothing could get to her, she thought to herself.

In the first light of dawn, Misa could see the flower stall owner emerging from the mini-truck that doubled as the man's home from its usual parking spot not far from the park entrance. As he lifted pot after pot of flowers from the back of his truck to the roadside, someone of unusual height with a suit jacket slung over his shoulder walked over to talk to him.

The flower seller was startled. He shook his head violently and returned once again to his work.

The tall figure sauntered carelessly into the park with his head down. Then he noticed that his shadow caressed a strangely shaped shadow on the brick pavement. He raised his head to find what he was looking for in front of him, uncurling herself from the bench.

He caught the gleam in Misa's eyes. The reflection of colors from the neon signs that said *Yamada Electronics* gave the girl a wolfish look.

The protectiveness dissolved quickly away when Misa realized who he was.

There, they stared sympathetically at each other until the rising sun outlined the girl in pearly white light and they couldn't hold their gazes anymore.

Finally, Smith pulled out a piece of paper from his pocket and handed it over to her.

"She might be able to help you." It was Aileen Martin's phone number that was written on it. "This lady works for the InterHRLA. You might have heard of it. I've told her a little bit about you, that you speak a bit of English and all, and she said she might have a part-time job for you. She's a nice lady. Give her a call when you feel better."

Misa took the paper and put it away without looking. She had an idea of who this lady might be and what kind of organization she belonged to. Still, she appreciated Smith's sensitivity of not talking about the obvious.

39. Understand Me

"Let me walk you home," Smith said. "Your brother is waiting for you."

"I am an embarrassment, *ne*?" She asked.

Smith took a deep breath before answering. It gave him a moment to think of a proper response. "You're a nice girl, with so much potential."

"For what?" Misa asked. "You mean I am pretty? You *think* I am pretty, *ne*? I have no other potential, I know that."

That made Smith red in the face. Of course, Misa was a very pretty young woman, but it would just seem wrong to answer yes at the moment. "What you are doing...this is not the only thing you could do. You should know that. You're so still so young."

"I can't do what I am doing when I am old, you know?" She smiled.

"That's your sense of humor?" Smith heaved his shoulders and sat himself next to Misa.

"Your parents will be so upset to know that you are not protecting your own body. I would be if you're my child." Smith thought they didn't have to speak in riddles anymore. "I am. I am upset about what you're doing."

"*Nerunerunerune?*" Misa noticed the pack of candy in his suit's pocket.

"Oh, this." He pulled it out and brought it up to Misa's eyes. "You want it? You can have it."

"What would other people think if they see an *Ojisan* giving a pack of candy to a teenage girl in the middle of the park, and this late at night?" Misa said.

Embarrassed, he retracted his arm and cradled the pack of candy in his hands, twisting its plastic packaging.

"I just..." He couldn't find words to explain his innocent intention. "If you want me to leave you alone, I can." Smith was not very good at parenting, he now noticed. How many times do you need to be a dad to master the necessary skill?

"I know what you're trying to tell me. I really know it. And I appreciate it."

"You do?" Smith asked in disbelief. He forged on. "There's a passage in the Bible. It says your body doesn't belong to you. It belongs to your parents. And for them, you have to take good care of yourself to repay their love."

"I like you," Misa said, and she leaned her head on his shoulder. It was broad and warm. The warmth. It made her felt safe. She had always liked leaning on men's shoulders.

Smith sat there motionless, unsure how to carry himself. He mumbled on about the Bible. God was the only thing that could save him now, for Misa had grabbed his hand and wrapped his arm around her waist. He squirmed away instinctively.

"I am not trying to..." Smith pulled his head away from Misa so he could extract himself from this impossible situation. Clearly, Misa had misunderstood. "You're treating me like I am one of these men."

"Don't you want to be?"

"No! Misa." He hissed and struggled further futilely. One could argue how hard it was for a man of his strength to unwrap his arm around a tiny Japanese girl. Yet it was more difficult than he thought. She was adamant in keeping his arm right where it rested, his hand rested against her lower abdomen under her hand. He felt the ruffles of her skirt, draped over her falling and rising abdomen. A new sensation.

"I like this," she said. "Please don't move."

He tried one more time, peeling his hand off her. It only made it worse. She had dug her nails into his palm to keep his hand where it was.

"Misa, hey, Misa, no." She was now kissing him on his right cheek. He felt her breath closing in on his ear.

"Misa, I am a very old man." Smith lamented.

"I am not asking you to be my boyfriend."

"This is wrong."

"What if I want it, and you know that somewhere deep within your heart, you want it just as much as I do." Misa purred in his ears.

"I am too old for you," he repeated. And he cleared his throat. What kind of reflexive mechanism was this? That's all thousand years of evolution could offer him right now? Men are weak animals, he cursed Darwin. "I am three times your age."

"That's why you need to understand women...again." That was her reply.

It stumped Smith.

40. Documentary

Ryuuji Tanaka pulled his black corduroy pants down around his legs and sat himself on the toilet seat. The metal buckle of his leather belt swayed back and forth against the ceramic toilet bowl, making rhythmical clanging noise. Outside, white noise filled his study. He had just watched another tape to the end.

Some of the tapes did it for him. This was one of them.

Without any editing, the raw materials of a pornography production could appear to be an interrupter collection of takes and re-takes. One was constantly in tension between reality and acting. The arousal effect was, in contrast to common perception, multiples of that of the final edited release — a highly commercialized Voyager experience for the general audience that was cut to exactly two hours and fifteen minutes with minimal time to waste on subtle human emotions that flitted through the actors and actresses minds on and off set.

"Nnmmh..." A short grunt. And it was over. Tanaka sat with his bare, shivering legs motionlessly on the toilet. Waiting for the erection to subdue.

The videotape machine produced a loud click when the tape, labeled 'Étourdir', or 'Surprise' in English, hit the end. With his own panting calmed, he could hear nothing but the chirps of crickets outside the study's window that slipped through the gap between the bathroom door and its frame.

Sergey Ribery was a genius. A genius and a crook. A true artist but also a very sick man. He died a gruesome death, and perhaps he deserved to die in that way. — The Shintoism faith Tanaka subscribed to did not allow such thoughts, but who was he to uphold the ethical standard of society? Tanaka was as deeply ensnared as Sergey Ribery was in the dark world of the unspeakable.

'Étourdir' was renamed and released as 'The Beginning of an End' commercially to the wider, but less discerning public who just wanted to see some actions and a lot of tits. It turned out to be nothing like the world had ever seen before despite its commonplace title. Many men and boys alike who bought the DVD drawn by the fame of its famous French director were disappointed by the confusing storyline of the story and the obvious lack of flesh-flashing and violent intercourse.

But among fans of his work — Ribery has become a cult icon ever since his death. His works became prized possessions in the same league of Picasso to art collectors for pornography connoisseurs and everyone who worked in the industry that knew what they were doing. — 'Étourdir' satisfied a different kind of fetish, one that was there since the beginning of time that no filmmakers had ever managed to fulfill, one that, if in close inspection, Tanaka had discovered from years of observing others, everyone was a little bit into the fetish over absurdity.

When the people had finally realized that they had a strong, hidden appetite for Absurdity, everyone wanted more of it. That was the birth of a whole new genre. Ribery, a reject of the mainstream French movie-making industry, arrived to new freedom in Japan, was allowed all luxury of resources beyond what any director could imagine. And with the baggage of the common man off his shoulders, he created a masterpiece. Against conventional filming methods, he and his crew went all over Japan, looking for subjects for his extraordinary physio-psycho experiment.

He produced many films in his twenty years in Japan, but only 'Étourdir' had attained the status of one of the most discussed pornographic films in Japanese history. Third-rated movie studios, local DVD stores with a special interest section and the dark side of the internet, this were the places it shined. And the success was a result of his chanced encounter with Misa Hayami. The film they made together was his best and his last.

No one knew what exactly transpired the day he died, except Tanaka. His version of it, given that he was not present at the scene of his death was not one that the police would easily believe. And so Tanaka kept what he knew to himself until he could prove it one day in a way every man could understand.

He was, however, less interested in helping law-enforcement find the killer of Sergey Ribery, and more interested in what led to the killing, a drawn-out physio-psycho experiment that Ribery had started himself. And his death, unfortunately for her, was not the end of her story. This was where Tanaka came in. He had made it his crusade to put an end to 'The Beginning of the End'.

Tanaka heard keys jingling from behind the door to his shared apartment with Damien.

His mind cleared as fast as it was clouded. — Must stow away all evidence. He swiftly cleaned himself up and turned off the video tape player.

"Baby, I am home!" Damien said as he squeezed himself and the bags of purchases he was carrying into the hallway of their apartment so he could close the door behind him.   His spirit seemed high, undoubtedly stoked by spending a lot of money. "What mischief have you been up to while I am gone?"

And Tanaka's mind clouded as soon as it was cleared. — Caught. Must confess to something. Something trivial.

"*Je vous demande pardon.* I am sorry, baby." He grabbed the shopping bags from Damien to put them aside and sat him on the couch.

"Oh, this feels naughty!" Anxious of what Tanaka was going to say or do. Suddenly, he smelled a whiff of something rotten, of bad eggs, and his enthusiasm went out like air in a popped balloon. His boyfriend had been playing with himself while he was away. One does not need to watch videos of hidden cameras around the house to know this.

"*Non.* I lied. I promised to go with you to see my mother this weekend but I can't. Something has come up at work."

"You gave me a scare! *Pas de probleme, mon chéri!*" Damien rolled his eyes. There was always something whenever Tanaka was due to visit his mother. He cupped Tanaka's cheeks with two hands and kissed him softly on his lips. Tanaka had always imagined how they would look like from a third person's perspective whenever Damien would treat him like a fizzy, cuddly stuffed animal, with him being the older man in physique and more matured one in spirit between the two of them. This was certainly not something to be witnessed by his own faint-heated mother. But despite his mild reluctance to Damien's habitual need for expressing and receiving affections through obscure and awkward physical contact, it was a great tell-tale signal that Tanaka still had him by the balls, so to speak. Damien was eating up his fake confession like a hungry dog.

"You're too cute. Saying sorry to me for these things. True, we haven't seen her for ages since you came out." Out of the closet, he meant. Damien still remembered what an awful episode it was. To tell a Japanese mother that his son was homosexual was as big a shock as if her son had died. The intermittent contact between them did not make it appear less so. "But she's your mother, not mine. It's your call."

"I am going film the new corporate commercial." Tanaka detached Damien's palms from his unshaven face and placed them on his lap. "It's going to be seen by millions of people across Japan."

"*C'est excellent!*"

"We'll film it this Saturday at the Gokokuji Temple. Some fresh greens in the background. The stillness of the temple. Lots of sunlight. A businessman and a teenage girl..."

"Hmm...beautiful. I can imagine it already." Damien closed his eyes and let his photographer vision take over.

"Are there going to be somebody famous?"

"No," Tanaka replied curtly. "Let me cook our dinner." And he walked off to the kitchen, ending the conversation there.

Nobody famous. Just Misa Hayami, the unwilling one-time actress in the quickly-turned classic 'The Beginning of the End' in the underworld of Absurdity-Fetish pornography. A relatively 'small' genre of hundreds of thousands of devotees within Japan and more in Russia, Western, as well as Eastern Europe.

Absurdity is a difficult concept to explain. It is the quality or state of being ridiculous and unreasonable. That could be any number of things in the context of pornography, and your imagination is the limit.

He was suddenly overcome by guilt. Was it right to do what he was about to do? Was his plan, one that was drawn up the day the police announced that Ribery had died of natural cause and had never been shared with anyone, not even his boyfriend, flawed in ethical terms? The repercussions of his actions were going to be huge. Would he be able to withstand the consequences? Would Misa?

He pitied Misa.

He often did. It's almost customary to feel this way whenever he thought of this project, but it never stopped him from proceeding.

Imagery of media frenzied themselves over him, and the protagonists of his documentary overshone other ethical considerations. Fame and approval. Like any living, breathing man, he longed for them underneath the surface of doing a good deed and living complacently. No man would give up the chances that he was given.

The concept for his documentary was great, and the material was there. It was going to make a lot of noise with what he had already. And by a stroke of luck, Misa materialized herself in front of him. The project suddenly became more than just vapors in the air. The work had picked up real momentum, and nothing could stop it now, Tanaka thought.

Every man had his brighter and darker sides.

41. Breathe In, Breathe Out

Smith fell ill that evening and did two things that were unprecedented. — Called in sick and he did not feel guilty about it. He surrendered himself completely to the war between his immune system and the resilient, viral intruders.

He drifted in and out of consciousness as he lay weakly on his unmade bed for two days, his body buried under the haphazard assortment of blankets, pillows, chair cushions, and newspaper. The thought of going to the doctor, to get a piece of paper to prove his conditions if anything, a vital part of falling ill in a culture so deadly focuses on loyalty and dedication to one's employer, did not occur to him. He simply laid there, enjoying, if one could go so far as say, the ecstasy of turning off his voluntary response system and letting nature take its course.

The cellphone buzzed throughout the day, but that did not stir him. Air in, air out, air in, air out. For hours, that was all that he did. Coming down with such the terrible cold was becoming like a vacation.

Being the obsessive compulsive natural-born problem solver that he was, however, he continued to solve mathematical models and operational problems sprung at him by both the higher-ups and his subordinates in vivid life-like dreams. When he did finally wake up to clarity, he found himself drenched from head to toe in hot sweats.

He got up to get himself some water and aspirin, and without remembering how, he had collapsed on his bed once again and slept through the night.

On the third morning, the Saturday, sunlight filtered through the semi-transparent white curtain into his apartment. Part of his unshaded face heated up from the warmth of the sun so much that it woke him. He stretched himself and found that the sickness had left him without a trace. He fascinated himself over the dancing dust that surrounded the cactus near the window sill. He hadn't watered it for days, and yet it was standing there, its stems green and succulent. And the two orange flowers appeared unchanged as if they bloomed not three days but a few minutes ago. Such was the enigmatic way of Eudicots. Smith was impressed with the wonders of God's world once again.

It was a ridiculous anxiety attack that he was having, he realized. Totally out of proportion in comparison to the business meetings that he had attended throughout his career concerning hundreds of thousands of dollars for DaiKe. What was this feeling?

He doused his freshly shaven face with ice cold water from the tap and told himself to hold his horses.

A girl kissed him. And apparently infected him with the flu virus. So what?

As he wiped his face with a dry towel, he wondered whether Misa had felt the same way, not the headache and the dizziness, but the nervous tingling feeling all over his body, after kissing him, though he quickly dismissed the thought. Albeit being barely of age, she was a veteran in this arena unlike him. Despite that knowledge, he did hope he served some purpose in her life. A substitute for a fatherly figure? Too Freudian for his liking. A substitute for a boyfriend? That sounds a lot more pleasing. He decided to just go with that conclusion.

42. A Flu

The night passed uneasily for Misa. She had flashes of hotness and coldness as she lay on her bedding, twisting and turning through the night. It was perhaps for that reason that she didn't feel particularly upset about losing her day job at Thunderbird. At least she didn't have to call in sick.

A flu. She had caught the flu virus from Mr. Mura.

It happens.

There was more. As she sat on the metro on her way to her Sunday teaching appointment with Smith, she pressed her hand on her left abdomen. After that night with Mr. Mura, her uterus hurt. There were bloody spots on her panty liner, which she had to change a lot more frequently than she would like.

When is it going to heal again? She wondered. She would give it a few days of rest. That's all.

Perhaps it was nature's way of letting her feel something. She hadn't felt anything for ages. The aching sensation reminded her of the rough sexual intercourse, of those few hours. Otherwise, it would just have been another line on her schedule, nothing more. She wished it would hurt more, then maybe she would quit it all together.

But it wouldn't. It always healed, and the experience, whether it had been good or bad, would only get fussier and fussier. Then it would be out of her mind before she knew it. Humans do behave like characters in video games. One life dies, get another one and restart where you last saved. Drink some magic potion from the inventory, vital restored, ready to slash some more monsters. The only thing that changed was the number of credits. It always goes up.

"Did you get some sleep last night?" A text message from Mr. Mura flashed across the screen of her smartphone.

She only read the message in the notification page without clicking into it, for she had no intention of replying.   Some of the clients liked to keep up the appearance of being in a relationship with her. Surprisingly, Mura was one of them. They sent her text messages, which she ignored, up to a point until she sensed the frustrations had built up long enough that it might cost her the client, then she would finally reply. They always begged and whined for her attention, to see her again. She would bait them with negligence. And they would whine some more. They would call her late at night when their work days were finally over and the thought of loneliness was almost suffocating them. And finally she would concede to meet them again.

Men liked being fooled by these little tricks. They rewarded her behaviors always, with gifts or other nice gestures. Her trick had never failed.

And this time, she had resolved to make Mura feel guilty about his rough handling.

At Ikebukuro, she got off and headed towards the MAS cafe at the museum. Her whole body protested.

Not another step.

Muscles from her entire lower body ached like an orchestra of whiny violins tuning on stage before a performance. The incongruous signals of soreness were distracting. The muscle fatigue would go away eventually too, leaving nothing to the experience. Nothing lasts, but ever more credits to her avatar. — She drew the similarity between life and virtual presence again.

Or acting, she thought, as she walked towards her destination in smaller than usual steps, mindful not to make any sudden movement that would tear open any healing wounds inside her. — There are very few nerves in the uterus to warn her. She had to be careful. — Actors and actresses surely had days of moodiness, times when they felt disconnected from the parts. Yet when the show was on, they would have to stop being themselves and slip instantly into the alter ego. Good actors and actresses do, at least. The analogy hit a sweet spot for her. She likened herself to a professional actress in her mind, and it made her feel good about herself.

The mind was an easy thing to trick.

43. Lights, Camera, and Action

"What is this?" Misa asked Smith as soon as she arrived to find Smith next to a group of people setting up filming equipment — big lamps on high stands, opened silver light reflective umbrellas opposite to each of them, and people taking out professional quality filming equipment. Smith had a light layer of makeup on his face.

"What is this, Smith?" she asked again. "I thought we were just coming out for a walk together." Her hands trembled for a second until she convinced herself to relax. Taking selfies or films with friends when going out, those were no problem for her. However, whenever she saw professional cameras or other more substantial video filming equipment, something strange inside her would flutter its wings, ready to fly out of her mouth at any moment. Her stomached lurched, and she tried hard to swallow back that wretched animal of fear.

"Do you mind being the model for a TV commercial?" Smith asked, without much explanation.

"A TV commercial?" she asked unenthusiastically.

"Yes, for DaiKe. My company." Smith explained as he stamped out the cigarette he pulled from between his lips.

"Will my face be in it?"

"Why yes, you have a beautiful face. You should be everywhere, your face." Tanaka interrupted the pair as they were chatting. Unceremoniously he reached out to stroke Misa's face like she was a soft wool blanket. Misa cringed back.

"Who is he?" Misa questioned Smith. "Who are all these people?" she asked, looking around.

"My name is Ryuuji Tanaka," Tanaka said with a faint smile. "I am going to be the commercial's director today."

"Tanaka, can you explain to her in Japanese that she has nothing to worry about? Tell her the run-down. All we need to do are a few shots in front of and around the temple, right?"

"Absolutely. She can just be herself," Tanaka said.

Tanaka waved Arai over. The assistant dropped everything and scrambled over to take his manager's order.

Was it his sensitivity? Smith observed that Arai was unusually nervous when he spotted Misa. Now he was explaining something to Misa in Japanese, but he kept averting his eyes from the girl. These Otaku boys of Japan, they get butterflies in front of beautiful women, don't they? He was also young and inexperienced once.

"Misa," Smith said, "you don't have to do this if this is not what you want. It's no big deal. I didn't tell you ahead of time, my apologies." Mr. Tanaka insisted that he wanted to have an innocent, unprepared face for the commercial. "The part he has for you is perfect for you, and me."

"You and him. Two persons, from very very different places," Arai tried to explain in his sub-par English. "You young, him old. You fun and him, thinking a lot." He waved his hand around as he expressed the concept of the commercial. "DaiKe, like the old man..."

"Older man," Smith corrected him.

"Older man," Arai continued, "think ahead, protect you, protect the nice environment. Protect Japan."

Protect. Smith understood what the analogy between him and Misa would be, to the naïve Japanese consumers. But to go as far as to say that him, or DaiKe, a metal derivatives production company could protect the whole of Japan, he felt like he might want to tweet this moment and have it be kept in history forever, like when BP decided to clean up their own oil spillage in the Mexican Golf.

"We film you two, later, standing there," Arai pointed at a very old and wide tree on the other side of the garden, smiling at each other. "And you give her a hug. I need to see both of your faces."

"I think you'll have to give me directions again when we get there. I am not really following." Smith said, winking at Misa, who understood his cynicism.

"*Kono tame ni shiharawa remasu ka*? Do I get paid for this?" Misa asked matter of fact.

"You become famous. Your face all over Japan for 24 weeks at least," Arai said. "You make 500,000 yen."

As soon as Arai had finished speaking, Tanaka waved the make-up artist over. It was the same lady who had tried to pull his stray eyebrow hair with a pair of tweezers just half an hour ago. She hustled Misa to the mobile trailer where she had the make-up and wardrobe set up.

500,000 yen was not a lot, but Misa could, theoretically, skip her nighttime profession for a month. Not that she would let it happen. Client-relationships were too important to her, and she needed them for information or access to it. — Besides, she liked what she did. If she was going to live the life of Misaki, she had better like what she Misaki liked.

"Don't just stand there. Keep moving!" Arai shouted at her.

"*Hai*! Okay!" Misa picked up her pace and went along to do her makeup.

44. Gokokuji Temple

Sitting on the small stone chair in the outer court of the temple, Misa looked up at Smith and said, "Can we say whatever we want?"

"Yes," nodding towards the cameraman. "They didn't wire us up with mics right?" Smith explained.

"Are you both ready?" Arai shouted from ten meters away, holding up the action board. It was scribbled with almost illegible Japanese characters.

"Yes!" Smith raised his thumb up in the air. The suit they gave him was a bit tight. He had to be careful not to stretch his arms too much later when they were filming.

"*San! Ni! Ichi! A–Ku--Shon!*"

"What do we have to do now?" Misa moved her lips gingerly.

"You just have to chat for a few seconds." He could see the blinking signal from the corner of his eyes. An assistant was counting. And now, there's the signal for them to walk.

"And then?"

"And then you stand up," Misa rose up slowly from her stone seat, following his cue. "And we walk along this passage to the tallest pagoda in the middle of the court like I just invited you for tea, and it's gonna be all over at the pagoda."

Misa smiled.

There was no one else in the temple court today as half of it was sealed off temporarily for the filming. The court was so empty and quiet that they could hear their own feet shuffling on the thin layer of sand.

Misa seemed to have relaxed a little as they paced down the flat path, dotted with Buddha statues etched into stone plates erected on both sides of the way and a few occasional evergreens that had been grown into elegant Bonsai.

She stole a glance at Smith, who had both of his hands inside the pockets of his suit pants. Smith noticed and smiled back.

"I am so sorry."

"About?"

"About last time..." Misa said. "I didn't ask whether you wanted to kiss me."

"Anyone sane would love to kiss you," Smith said that without any inhibition because no one can hear them. There were only the two of them in this world, at this very moment, he felt. In the presence of the stone-faced Buddhas, he wanted, to be honest, even just a little.

"Am I too young for you?"

Smith didn't expect that from her. Why of course, she was too young for him. But she said it in such a way that it broke his heart. She said it as if it was something she did wrong.

"You're perfect the way you are," he said. He would love to tell her that he cared about her, but he could only care about her in a way that is acceptable to his faith, and his circumstances. "I cannot give you anything. I am an old man."

"You have already given me a lot," Misa said, pausing in her steps. "Tatsu said you left your Thunderbird credit card for us that night. There was more than a million yen in it."

"But I don't want to buy you, or your affection. I am not like that. I meant it in a good, Samaritan way."

"Like donating to the charity. You took pity on me?"

"No..." It was a hard thing to explain. "You're a wonderful girl. You deserve better. I don't know what else I can do for you and for Tatsu. He is disabled at the moment, and it's always good to have some extra money for his medicine, and household bills. For food as well. Don't you agree?"

Misa nodded in acknowledgment.

"But you have to contact Aileen. She promised to help you, and she will."

"I did call her," Misa said cheerfully. "She gave me a job!"

"Really? That's wonderful. What will you be doing?"

"Because I can read and write English, she lets me prepare all the documentation for her new case files and put them online."

"This is great."

"Thank you," Misa whispered as they paced along.

Smith decided not to say anything this time.

"You brought peace to my chaotic life."

"As you did to mine," Smith replied after a moment. He was satisfied with himself for admitting that out loud.

After being sick for so many days, he felt energized to take a walk outdoor with the girl he cared a lot about. He momentarily forgot he was in the middle of a filming and immersed completely into the serenity that the Shinto temple provided. Instead of being in a made-up setting of a commercial, he felt that he was actually living the life depicted in it. Serene, safe, protected and bright.

They were almost at the end of their route. The tall tree loomed in front of their eyes.

"Are you supposed to put your arms around me now?"

"...yes, like Arai explained."

"Facing the camera, I remember," Misa said cheekily.

The couple turned around, and Smith looped his arm around the girl.

He squeezed his arms tighter for the effect.

The view taken from the vantage point below, against the backdrop of the pagoda on the azalea-lined stone steps near the Furomon gate as the sun was about to go down — everything colluded to create the most stunning image.

Misa's body softened under the familiar warmth of a man. The build of this man was different from what she was used to, of course. He was tall, much taller than her. And she felt the contours of his strong muscles, despite the passing of years since he had been a football player, his frame was still impressive to an Asian girl. It overwhelmed Misa with physical attraction, and her cheeks started to glow. He has a good heart too, Misa thought to herself. If only, if only he was her father.

Misa smiled lightly while she stared at Smith, who was oblivious, or perhaps deliberately ignorant, of the young girl who was falling in love with him.

Tanaka had a good first-take for the commercial. Behind his professional facade, he secretly smiled to himself for reasons known only to him.

45. Something in the Air

Ever since Smith had met Misa at the temple, he found himself constantly distracted by the thought of her. It didn't help that their commercial for DaiKe was all over the company television network normally reserved for internal announcements. The wave of nostalgia would hit him in the most inappropriate timing he felt as if he was about to lose control of his mind.

And worst of all, Misa had to start working on Saturday morning as well at InterHRLA, which meant they have to temporarily suspend their short-lived Japanese lessons from now on. Secretly, he cursed at Aileen for the long working hours.

He feigned nonchalant one day and called Aileen up to ask how Misa was doing, to see if he could wiggle her out of those Saturday working hours on grounds of spending more time with her recovering sick brother. But her 'baka' brother had his own recovery schedule. He was rehabilitating himself in the midst of shady companies, alcohol, and God-knows-what. He was not in want of any attention from Misa. In the end, all Smith managed to achieve with the call was another yet-to-be-fulfilled promise of taking Aileen out. He found himself at a loss of excuse to reach Misa that would not give off a whiff of the simple, 'I am thinking about you'.

Once he was in a boardroom attending a critical meeting with the company's board of directors, he caught himself spacing out, not only once, but multiple times, during a subordinate's presentation of a project he was supervising. He had proofread the contents of the presentation a few weeks ago, but it had obviously been revised because the portions of customers from the automotive sector in the pie chart had seemed to grow larger than ever. The agricultural sector had dropped to an alarming 4.8%; there were more words on the slides in the conclusion page, and the background color of the slides had changed to an obnoxious greenish-blue obscuring the edges of the words on it making them almost impossible to read quickly. And hence at the end of the presentation where he, as an immediate manager would typically add a few ending remarks highlighting the high points of the project, was unable to perform his duty. In the end, he resorted to the inarguable statements about the amount of hard work everyone involved in the project had put in and recognized a few key people on his team before hastily passing the ball on to the next group.

Another time he was in a marketing strategies discussion with a co-worker when Cheryl had walked in to replenish the coffee for them. Without knowing why, he lost his train of thought and started to stumble on his words, only to be rescued by the cheat sheet he had on the table which he had jotted down the discussion points on a few days ago. When he regained his composure, he realized what it was that had distracted him — the sweet perfume Cheryl had worn had reminded him of Misa. He didn't know whether Misa had in fact worn the same perfume but the fragrance had somehow elicited the romantic feelings in him, and he was swept off his feet by the olfactory memory.

He had also started to go out for lunch which was very atypical of him. He tried to put himself into Misa's shoes and came up with a list of places a girl at her age would go. Once he offended Cheryl by asking a younger Japanese secretary in the department who was of around Misa's age to give him some suggestions for lunch restaurants. His logic was that she would surely have a better idea where girls eighteen of age would like to have lunch than Cheryl and him. Of course, he lied to her that he was planning for his granddaughter's visit to Japan next year. He did shudder at the mention of the word 'granddaughter'. Misa was so young she could almost be passed as his granddaughter, he would often think as he was sipping some overpriced, distasteful drinks he had ordered at the beginning of the meal in one of the many popular cafes in Ikebukuro on the list where Misa might appear. Slim chance as it was to actually running into her, he followed through with his list. It did occur to him at some point that Misa might be having takeout lunch at the InterHRLA office. Office lunch, meaning, literally sitting in front of your computer in the cuckoo clock of a cubicle to work while consuming lunch was not uncommon in most Japanese workplaces. In that case, his search would be futile. And she would most likely be eating her lunchbox with her female colleagues, chatting about boys and idols and things that he didn't understand.

Once he got sick of being disappointed, and he went to the park instead to eat his microwavable yakitori lunchbox, and he laughed at himself for being so foolish, but the sight of fallen leaves and empty chairs on the park saddened him. He knew perfectly well that a middle-aged man like him should not be longing for a girl like Misa, and he should keep his thoughts inside the safety of his own cerebrum. Yet, again and again, he would make up excuses when lunch hour arrived to walk out of the office into the streets of Ikebukuro and sit in the booth of a café closest to the window to watch the passersby pacing up and down hurriedly to their destinations. Among them, he would search for Misa's silhouette with his tireless eyes. What he had in him was an inexplicable longing to see her, a platonic feeling, a realization that his life would not mean half as much if he couldn't see her again.

But the week progressed without a word or a sign from her, his nostalgia had turned into desperation. In between meetings scheduled at floors way above his, he would always make a detour back to his office to check for any messages from Tanaka, hoping for another reshoot where Misa's attendance would be required. And he was taking more bathroom breaks and tea breaks than usual so he could have an excuse to check his cell phones for missed call or new messages. Still nothing.

At the same time, he started to run into a self-pitying phase. Every morning when he was forced to stand in front of the mirror as he brushed his teeth, he would lament how the years had not been lenient on him. He was no longer twenty-five and hopeful; he was fifty-five and divorced. His face belonged to that of an old man. His hands were veiny, his hair was gray and his hairline receding, forming the shapes of bat's ears. Already stepped into the last five years of his laborious career he was still living alone in a single's dormitory just as he was thirty years ago when he was in college. It was as if everything that had happened in the time between did not matter at all — receiving his graduation diploma from the Dean's hand, signing a mortgage for his first house, marrying the woman he loved, bring his firstborn son Ethan to the Great American Baseball Park, taking his daughter to swimming classes, being promoted to Associate Director , designing and building his second house on the four-acre land he bought in the suburbs of Cincinnati, holding his granddaughter for the first time and giving her a big kiss — they were escaping his failing memory like a dream that vanished as soon as consciousness had returned to the dreaming man. Why would anyone want to have anything to do with him? After all these years he had nothing to show for it. Not even his wife thought him worthy of keeping his last name with her.

Then it occurred to him.

"I will never be somebody in Misa's life," he mused to his reflection. "But I can be her guardian angel."

"Yes, yes, yes..." his reflection murmured back. A stray lump of hair dripped over his eyes, making his reflection looked sinister. "You're out of luck, Sergey. I'm going to make this right for Misa."

Unfortunately for Smith, his memory failed him. The surname of this monster of a movie director had escaped him. Searching for a 'Sergey, director' online had proven useless. There were hundreds of them on IMDB, and none of their profiles seemed to indicate that they had dabbled in pornography nor spent time in Japan.

Smith could hardly ask Tatsu for the tape without inflicting unnecessary pain and embarrassment on the boy. The obvious candidate to obtain any information about Sergey would be Tanaka, the TVC commercial director who had once confided in him his stint in the world of pornography. If this son-of-a-bitch Sergey person was anything as important as Tatsu had portrayed him to be, someone that the upright and efficient police of Tokyo could do nothing about, he was sure Tanaka might have heard of him.

"I have something to speak to you about. See you tomorrow in the office." Smith left a voicemail on Tanaka's cell.

46. A Scandal

"Hypocrite!", "Are DaiKe's executive paid so little?", "That's where DaiKe's money went...right into pockets of Yakuza."

The DaiKe commercial was on air since yesterday evening, on Channel 5, prime time. It was shown four times in a span of the half-hour news Smith had caught while he was smoking a cigarette at the VIP lounge of Palatial, a new pachinko parlor that popped up in Nishi-Ikebukuro. He thought the fact that no one in the lounge gave him a second look was a good indication of the amount of attention, or the lack of, he could elicit from others with the commercial, which he was glad about. Being at the center of attention was never his thing. For whatever reason, he had not needed to worry about being 'famous', or at least recognizable to the public. Not even after it was being played on repeat at the internal DaiKe TV. Not once had anybody from work come up to him to make a comment about the commercial. Not once.

He had neglected the fact that he was sitting in the corner and had hidden himself in a veil of cigarette smoke. With all the recognizable signs of 'I don't want to be disturbed', the other patrons did not dare to bother him. It was his grave mistake to think that they did not recognize him, for they did. However, they would not approach him or speak to him on the account of that. That was simply 'not done'. Only the socially awkward would fuss about a celebrity in their presence. Any good Japanese person would follow the unspoken etiquette of reserving those gossips when he was out of sight, or they would take them online altogether. And that was what happened. Someone had snapped a photograph of him in front of the pachinko machines in Palatial, feeding coins after coins into the mouth of the pachinko machine and posted it on 2Chan, the largest online forums in Japan. The caption was decidedly harmless: "Look who I saw in the new pachinko parlor? The *gaijin* in the DaiKe commercial!"

What led to the downpour of negative comments on Smith's lone visit to the parlor after business hour, was beyond Smith's wildest guess.

The netizens were reacting to the photographs like vultures circling a pile of dead bodies. It was material to exploit in an attempt to publicly denounce the company.

"Cars, you're famous." Andy snapped as soon as Smith picked up his call. Smith stubbed out his cigarette on the tray.

"Is it about the TV commercials?"

"No. Where are you? You can't be still in palatial, right?" Andy asked, hearing the tell-tale jingles and recorded coin-dropping sounds in the background bleeding into his earpiece. "I think you better go home and watch the news."

"Why? What's the matter?" Smith replied in confusion.

"Okay, just leave. And I will send the stuff to you. Stay calm." Andy urged, frustrated at the old man's cluelessness. He wouldn't know to run when the atomic bomb was dropped directly above his head.

"Email?"

"No, LINE." Then Andy realized something. Smith was a dinosaur when it came to technology. "Oh jeez, you don't have LINE, do you? I will send it to your email." And he hung up, busy forwarding a news video clip which he considered to be of utmost importance.

"I watched today's news at seven already. There was nothing special..." Smith muttered to the mouthpiece of his mobile phone. A beeping tone had already replaced Andy.

***

"Darling!" Damien almost screamed. "Darling, Oh Darling! Come here! *Ce n'est pas bien!*"

"*Nan de?* What?" Tanaka responded to his boyfriend's request with faint interest. He did not understand how two gay men could end up being so different. Damien was in a constant state of exasperation, a natural exaggerator in his response to the external world, a sensitive, delicate soul even the most dramatic of all women could not compete with him. Then there was himself, almost like his own father, a traditional Japanese man who considered composure the highest, most laudable trait of men. One who never raised his voice and exposed little of his mood, if there was any.

It was with that thought in mind that he approached Damien and joined him on the couch, who was staring wild-eyed at the midnight news on the television. The report had run almost to its full length when he started watching, but he saw what he needed to see: The corruption scandal of his company had led the star of its corporate TV commercial to become the bud of a communal joke online that gripped the entirety of Japan in a matter of hours. Memes made by netizens with Smith's photo, analogizing him to DaiKe, the eager briber, feeding the greed machine were shared at a record speed across the country's social networks.

Tanaka closed his eyes for a second to think as his heart started to swell with remorse. He had intended to use Smith to stay close to Misa, the protagonist of his private documentary. He ended up turning Smith into a public source of humiliation.

The arrival of messages flashed across the screen of his cell phone, which was lying on the coffee table in front of them. Damien picked it up and started reading, as he customarily did since day one of moving in together. There was no privacy anymore once you started sharing a life with someone as obsessive as Damien.

"You're part of a PR shit-storm, baby!" said Damien.

Tanaka grunted.

"At least now people pay attention to your work."

Damien had a point.

47. News in Your Pocket

There was not a single soul in the Design and Advertising Department at 8:30 AM. Smith decided to return later.

On his way up to the 47th floor, he checked his mobile as a front to cover his unease in the packed elevator. It appeared that almost everyone, except the two stern, expressionless managerial materials standing at either corner of the steel-box, was aghast at seeing him at work. He recalled having checked his appearance before stepping out this morning. Apart from his swelling eye bags from restless sleep last night, having spent innumerable hours scheming how he could bring up Sergey in a conversation with Tanaka without raising his suspicion, he could not think of anything else that would afford him to be greeted with such an ill set of visages.

This reminded him of Andy's agitation yesterday. The email, oh, he had forgotten about the email.

With one hand holding his phone, he thumbed to the inbox icon to check his email. There it was, Andy's email titled *My Famous White Friend*, still unopened. Smith crinkled his nose at the tasteless title that was very typical of Andy and clicked into it. A blast of Japanese by an excited female newscaster filled the elevator.

"Damn auto-play videos..." Smith said apologetically to everyone and no one in particular in the elevator as he hurried to turn off the sound.

"I like the commercial," the man standing next to Smith said. Smith noticed that the man was giving him a more-than-kind smile. "Don't worry about it."

With the video still running, his hand dropped to the level of his hip as he steered himself to look at the man who spoke. The man smiled again. He recognized a trace of apology in the man's grin.

Smith felt confusion rising inside. What was there to worry about?

"This can happen to anyone," he supplemented again as if Smith had not heard his consolation right the first time.

Before Smith could come up with a courteous reply to the man's seemingly genuine comments, someone else behind them decided to add his opinion. "Well, I think he ought to be ashamed of himself."

Just then, the elevator door opened on the 20th floor. The person who had voiced the dissenting comment squeezed past Smith and the first man to get out, leaving behind him a trail of disgruntlement that lingered in the air of the elevator.

The short exchanges bothered Smith. He hardly knew any of these people. He did not recognize the man who was rooting for him even after scanning the name on his work badge, dangling freely in front of his chest for anyone who wished to read it. *Ito Tadao, Brand Manager. Marine Logistics.*

Never worked with him.

By the 43rd floor, everybody had left the elevator, leaving the space to himself and the security camera. He glanced at the video still playing on his mobile phone on silent and found the source of confusion.

DaiKe's Mura, the senior managing director of New Business Development, had been arrested yesterday by a team of anti-corruption force from the National Police Agency in the middle of an incriminating meeting at the Prince Hotel with Member of Parliament Shoichi Takeshita. 41 million yen was exchanged as they lavishly enjoyed companies of young scantily clad women over bottles of French Romanee-Conti the price of a junior clerk's full year's salary.

The footage showed the two men and their entourage of bodyguards and escorts being handcuffed and led into a police van with dark tinted windows.

Mura, albeit ineffective and incompetent, would never have the guts or the brains to bribe a government official. The news agency's speculations of Mura's plan on financially motivating Takeshita to support the motion to revoke the Voluntary Export Restraint of white goods exporting to Europe which would lift DaiKe's sales when its customers order more materials for production to catch up with the increased demand subsequently, was all too grand to be thought out by one single person, let alone someone who spent most of his time barking irrelevant orders to others under the banner of exploring new business opportunities.

His Japanese boss was arrested. That would certainly be a reason of concern for him. Obviously, he had no part in whatever Mura was up to. But the police could have a different view. — Was there police on the 47th floor waiting for him to step out and arrest him, too? Wouldn't they first need to find evidence of his connection of which there was none? He adjusted his tie to allow himself to breathe a little better. — It was not that he had never imagined the scenario happening, for the amount of underdealings that were rumored to have happened in a corporation as big as DaiKe had sort of prepared him mentally for something like that. He knew DaiKe's business strategy was a mess, and its intricate hierarchy made clear decision making an impossible black box, even for someone who sat almost at the core of all the activities at nearly the top of the corporate ladder of its US branch. But being 'near the core' was not the same as being 'in the core'. He would never be permitted to meddle with affairs at the executive level of the central office, which ran closed-door conferences every month with people whose interests were self-promotion and preservation. New initiatives and demands were regularities that came back after these meetings, dreamt up by ancient executives who had either lost touch with the markets or were promoting opinions of whoever the lucky recipients of their favoritism were lately, and sons and daughters of wealthy executives that had inherited the posts from their parents, a common practice in Japan.

He thought back to the scene when Mura called him 'the Face of DaiKe' just a few days ago. Both of them knew this could not be farther from the truth.

Nonetheless, he had become, to the less discerning public, 'the Face of DaiKe'. Just when he had made the connection, the real news materialized in front of his eyes on the screen. The news report pulled up a screenshot of a popular forum post on 2Chan, the forum, and it had a picture of him squandering his money at the Palatial just hours after the bribery scandal broke. The collective intelligence of the crowd had determined that they should make a full mockery of him, expressing their abhorrence for corruptions in the government and big corporations one character at a time, with twenty thousand and growing commentators making a jab at his previously very private hobby of watching steel balls falling from one end to the other end of the vertical pinball machine in a raging storm of endless randomness.

"Andy," Smith was relieved to see Andy was the one welcoming him as his elevator doors swept open. Andy had been tracking the feed of the security cameras on his desktop as soon as he arrived.

"Come with me." They skipped to the closest conference room, and Andy closed the door behind him.

"Internal memo, we are invited to watch a press conference at the Hall of Thousand at eleven."

"We? The entire company?" Smith gasped.

"Don't worry, you're just the scapegoat. Being on TV and all that."

"You don't point out that someone is the scapegoat and comfort them at the same time," Smith snorted. "My public appearance at the Pachinko parlor at the most inopportune time aside, we are working in Mura's team. Did anyone say anything to you this morning? Haneda? Tanoguchi? Did they say anything? Are we gonna be invited for coffee at the station?" Smith said.

"Oh, that you don't have to worry about either," Andy said. "The business crime police were here at 7 AM, and they took almost everything with them. Computers and all. Must have been over a hundred boxes. I had to go borrow a spare laptop from the storage to watch the news, but no, they didn't take anyone with them. Just the files."

"The incriminating evidence," Smith said ironically. To be honest, he had no clue what the police would find on their computers. Could it link them to Mura's bribe in some way? Where was the fund pulled from? Was it from one of the projects he oversaw? Just when he thought he could not have been bombarded with more questions, Andy threw him one.

"Were you let in on this?" Andy asked, squinting his eyes.

"Rest assured I would have taken the retirement package if I was."

"Make sense."

Outside, Smith caught the shadow of Cheryl walk pass. She knocked twice and shoved the door open. The glasses standing in the middle of the metal tray on the conference table rattled on her entry. She had never been the graceful kind of secretary.

"What's the matter, Cheryl?" Smith asked with composure.

"What's the matter?" Cheryl could not believe her ears. "Mr. Smith I told you to install a television at home! You oughta be the first one to know about what's the matter! They took everything this morning, the police. We have nothing to work with. I don't know what your next appointment is, and I don't have my contact list with me. Neither do any of the other secretaries I know! I don't know what to do!"

"Calm down," Smith offered her his hand. She took it and was led to a chair by the long wooden conference table. She sat down opposite to Andy, who offered a glass of sparkling water from the carafe standing on the table to calm her nerves. She sipped unusually loudly.

"We must not panic," Smith said.

"*We muust knot pand-nic,*" Andy repeated with Smith's midwestern accent.

"The big guys will want you to apologize. This is how it's done in Japan. You see it all the time on TV and stuff. Men in suits bowing in public at 90-degree angle and cry. Then all crimes are forgiven."

Smith was about to ask what crime had he committed, apart from the possibility of somehow being entangled into the dirty affair between Mura and Takeshita simply by being a member of Mura's New Business team. But Cheryl seemed to know, having the natural sensitivity of a Japanese.

"You made them lose 'face'," Cheryl said. "Face, above everything else. Haven't I told you enough times?"

She did indeed. Smith was tired of hearing about all the nonsense about 'face'. Truth, honor and loyalty he could prescribe, but preservation of 'face'? That was a tough concept to grasp. He simply saw no point to it. At fifty-five years old, he could hardly afford to waste another day worrying about what other people thought of him. Moreover, who lost more 'face'? Him playing Pachinko after hours with money out of his own salary, or Mura, stuffing a bag of yen siphoned from God-knows-which project to Takeshita's greedy pocket?

"I will not do anything until I must."

"You must be first," Andy said. "It's like chess. You've gotta make the first move so they feel your sincerity. Fake it if you must. Offer to apologize in public at the same time they will give a corporate statement about Mura. This will divide the media's attention between your nighttime entertainment and the serious offense that Mura had got himself into. The executives will think you're a responsible guy, and the media are always more lenient with the white guy. It's a win-win."

"Don't you think the Head of Public Relations would be figuring all this out by herself?"

"The Head of Public Relations also put you on TV in the first place," Andy pointed out sarcastically. "She's a nitwit to use an actual employee for the commercial. Someone who actually works in Mura's team. That's just brilliant."

"That was a mere coincidence. She could hardly predict this..." Despite what he said, Smith could not help but be amazed at the coincidence himself.

"Darn. What a mess!" Andy remarked.

"You're the highest ranked executive on the floor, Mr. Smith," Chery said. "You must do something." She implored.

"Says who?" There were at least five other people on his level on this floor. The Director of Marketing, the Director of Finance, the Director of Core Business and the Director of Strategic Business Analysis.

"They all took sick leave today. Mr. Smith. They are not like you. *Japanese salarymen hide when they see danger.*"

"Jeez, then it's gotta be you, Cars."

"What?"

"Go talk to the big bosses," Andy said, "Figure out how to deal with the situation. We can ignore the scandal here in the office, but we cannot ignore our clients overseas, and don't forget our stockholders. They could send our stock to hell if they think we are operating on fairy dust. — I have Mr. Yamato's number on my cell phone. We played golf together once at the Yomiuri Golf Club. Let me send you his phone number." Yomiuri Golf Club was one of the most exclusive golf clubs in the Tokyo prefecture. It had been Andy's habit to sprinkle tidbits of his wide and deep spans of connections in the company into his conversations. He just did it again.

"The guy barely speaks English." Smith found the most convincing excuse he could come up with to avoid the responsibility. "Plus they probably already have a plan. Just be patient and wait for the orders."

"Since when did you start 'waiting for orders'? I'll go with you. If not, take Cheryl!"

"No! I am not going to sacrifice myself."

"Nobody is going to sacrifice you, babe. But just in case our Mr. American here made a social boo-boo, you can cover up for him with your charms and grace."

"You!" Cheryl pushed herself up with her elbows on the table and snapped at Andy. "Not every problem can be solved with feministic charms!"

"I never mentioned anything about your gender. Don't be so sensitive, feminist! Cars would have to be incarcerated already for what he did. He is just going to apologize, the Japanese way, and make his brilliant proposal, and you can translate for him."

"What nonsense are you two talking about?" Smith felt like he needed to stop this meaningless conversation. "Both of you are going with me. NOW."

The pair looked at each other like grumpy children who had just been reprimanded by their parents.

"I have received a text from Aileen. She needs our help."

"The press conference is at eleven!" Andy protested. "Should I be calling the Head of Public Relations directly instead? Damn, I wish I have gotten her phone number at the company Christmas dinner last year. I got her a martini and..."

"Who's Aileen?" Cheryl asked as her boss stormed out of the room towards the elevator, not even ten minutes in the office and now he was leaving again, with Andy trailing closely after him. She hated turbulence in her life.

48. The Protest

"Stay back! Everybody stand back!" The young police officer bellowed at the curious onlookers and aggressive journalists, piling over one another in a semi-circle to capture the protesting women with their cameras.

A dozens of other officers was trying to push the crowd back by cutting them off with the steel barricades in their hands. They formed jagged polygons around the group of women from InterHRLA, who were still screaming at the top of their lungs the same series of chants they had been saying since the morning. — *"Join us and fight! Don't let big pharmaceutical companies get away it!"*

One of the women took her trench coat off without warning. She was wearing nothing but a fuchsia bikini and stilettos. A few other protestors followed suit.

As soon as they took off their coats, the crowd gasps, for all of them had painted various designs of bruises, wounds, scars and scabs on their skins. Beautiful women in distressed physical state, that was the metaphor they were going for in today's protest against unethical clinical trials.

"Stop with your tests!"

"Barbaric practice treats human like lab rats!"

"Husband killed in clinical trial!"

"Humans are not your guinea pigs!"

The crowd pressed closer to the demonstration, straining the barricades.

There were camera flashes everywhere from female and male onlookers alike. People were trying to capture the spectacle.

Over on the far right, a man pushed through the gap between two barricades and reached his arms out to the women.

"I warned you! Stay back!" The officer grabbed the arm of the man and was about to twist it behind his back. But the man was stronger than him. Their tangled arms strained against each other and made them look like they were frozen there as if time had stood still for a moment.

A second police officer planted himself firmly behind a barricade and freed his right hand. From his belt, he produced a baton, which he bashed with no mercy towards the back of the intruder.

Suddenly, someone in the crowd said, *"Isn't she that girl in the DaiKe commercial?"*

"Yes, that's Misa Hayami!" Another person answered. *"I want to hear her speak!"*

Aileen knew Misa's recent appearance on the DaiKe commercial had made her a small internet celebrity due to the relating scandal, and that made her the main draw to today's event. She handed the wireless microphone to Misa.

"Tell the crowd what you are doing here today, Misa!" She urged.

"Hello, everyone, my name is Misa Hayami!" She screamed at the mic with all her mic over the racket of the pushing crowd hoping to see the TV-celebrity and other half-naked girls for all the wrong reasons. "We are the International Human Rights Lawyers Association, and we're here today together with victims of unethical clinical drug trials that are occurring every day in this country! Please sign our petition at the booth over there! I will be there waiting for you to join us in solidarity against the evil corporations!!"

There was a round of cheers from behind her, coming from the people who was representing today.

Misa passed the microphone back to Aileen as soon as she made her rally call. A mother of a child who lost her limb participating in what was supposed to be a harmless Hepatitis B vaccine study came up to the front with her daughter took the mic from Aileen.

Misa was about to move to the back when she caught sight of someone she least want to see today. It was Hisao Hasegawa. Misa was just there helping out with InterHRLA activities, and she couldn't care less if they were protesting about human rights or animal rights, but she could not possibly let Hasegawa see her.

As she expected, he was approaching the booth with simmering hostility. A man whose research was funded by big pharmaceutical companies himself, he would not approve of this protest, and most importantly, he would drag her off with him. She didn't want to have a public argument with the man. She needed to get out of this fast, but what could she possibly do?

***

Smith and his clique couldn't get pass the security to reach Misa. He was so far back he couldn't even identify who was who, except that she was one of the girls painted with Halloween-quality fake wounds all over their bodies in pink bikinis in the center of attention.

He thought he would stay back and just watch for a few moments to see how things develop, but when the smallest of the women in the middle of the group collapsed to the ground sobbing, he knew he had to go in.

Was that Misa who collapsed? — The pressure of being at the center of attention must have been too high for her. He had expected something like that to happen already as soon as he picked up Aileen's phone call asking them to join their demonstration. The crowd did not disperse despite what happened. But the more she could not remain calm, the more the crowd focused on her and wanted to look at her.

"Let me through! I know them!" Smith shouted, wriggling his arm out of a police officer's grip. Behind him the crowd had groped randomly at him as they tried to push through the barricade following his example, wishing to sneak through the barricade between them and the pretty demonstrators.

"He's my friend!" Aileen, who was leading the demonstration shouted at the officer. *"Watashitachi tomotachi desu! Tomotachi!"* She enunciated every word of the Japanese sentence she hacked together clearly above the noise of the crowd. "I know him!"

The police officer finally got the message and let the American through, but not without considerable annoyance.

"Them too! Please let them through!" Aileen pointed at Andy and the woman in a business suit that came up right behind Smith.

When Aileen turned back around to look, she saw Misa, in her fuchsia bikini, a team outfit for today's operation, squatted on the floor in agony. Her arms braced her head as if the noise around them were hurting her.

Smith took off his suit and lunged at Misa, wrapping her in a cocoon of fabric.

"What kind of nonsense is this?" He barked at Aileen as soon as she was in earshot, who was utterly shocked by his reaction, and carried Misa in his arms to a bench behind where the group of demonstrators stood. Misa did not stop sobbing, and knew she shouldn't.

Andy came up after him and handed Misa's trench coat to Smith. He had picked it up on the spot where Misa had dropped it just a moment ago.

"Shhh....shh..." Smith hushed the girl in his arms as if she was merely a child. His child. "Everything is going to be alright. Everything is going to be alright." He patted her back lightly and rocked her softly back and forth.

"What is going on?" Cheryl finally came through. Her hair was a mess as if a thousand hands had brushed through them at a random angle. In fact, that was what literally happened as she fumbled her way toward her boss. "Does she need medical attention?" she asked, commenting on Misa's condition.

"What happened? *Doushitano?* Misa?" Andy kneeled beside her and asked in Japanese.

Misa only shook her head and cried even more violently than before. Because she was faking it, she didn't really have anything to say to Andy's question.

"I know." Smith patted her lightly again, using the skills of an experienced father with a sobbing child. "I know. Shh....shh...We will take you home now. It's safe, and no one will be able to take pictures of you there, okay? Let's do that together, okay?"

She nodded.

"Can you walk?"

She nodded again, trying to wriggle her arms into the trench coat that Cheryl had held up behind her back for her. She buttoned the coat in one swift motion and begun to stand up, finding her balance on the pair of heels as she did it.

The crowd had begun to recognize who the oldest of the two white men that had burst through the police's blockade was. It was none other than the *Gaijin* in the trending forum post! They praised their good fortunes to see both of the internet celebrities firsthand. His picture at the Palatial had, by now, been viewed four million times. There were only twelve million Tokyians, which meant almost every four people had viewed the post. That was a good reason to be enthusiastic in the modern day society.

'Fans' of Smith drove themselves behind the group of protesters and surrounded him and Misa, and started fussing, snapping photographs or taking selfies with them!

For the second time in less than twenty-four hours, there were fresh materials sent all over Japan with him in it.

But this was the least of his concern.

***

"Look! I spotted the DaiKe pair!"

"What a heroic act! The American saved the girl in the commercial, in real life!"

"He's not too bad!"

"We should give them a break."

"Support DaiKe man!"

"Hey! It looks like the internet likes you even more than before," Andy rattled the comments off of the latest BBS post on 2Chan about Smith as Cheryl drove the corporate car back to the office. She now realized what her use was in all of this. The designated driver for her heroic boss, the poor girl, and an idiot.

They had dropped off Misa at her home, and Cheryl had seen to it that the girl went to bed to sleep after tiring herself out from tears as the men waited in the living room, discussing what had happened.

"Thanks, Cheryl," Smith turned to look at her from the front passenger seat. "I am so glad you're with us. It's always better to have a woman around in these kinds of situation."

Cheryl smiled. She had to do something that was completely outside of her realm of responsibility but being appreciated made it all worthwhile. If the department would still be there after the tumult of the bribery scandal, she would like to continue working there, for Smith, who had proven himself a real man today. As a matter of fact, she could not say she was not a little bit moved by what she saw. The old *Gaijin*, who had been abandoned by his wife and children in America, who spent his lonely hours in the pachinko parlor gambling away the sadness of his waking hours when he was not at work, had a good heart.

Nonetheless, she was curious. "Do you know why she reacted that way? It's a bit racy to protest in bikinis, but wouldn't her boss, this Aileen woman from Australia, have already warned her about it when they prepare for the day?" Cheryl asked curiously.

"Exactly my thought." Andy echoed from the back seat. "She had seen it all. She worked in an escort bar before, and as a waitress in entertainment centers. I couldn't believe that she was so timid."

Smith merely smiled back, not wanting to reveal the real reason behind her sudden onset of distress.

"Bullocks! We missed the press conference!" Cheryl checked the clock on her dashboard. It was a quarter past twelve.

"No, babe. We were in the center of it all. We missed nothing," Andy said, referring to the content pulled up on his cell phone.   "The media went crazy over what you just did."

Smith felt his cell vibrate incessantly in the pocket of his pants. He had felt it before and ignored it. Now he had settled down in the car back to the office, he fished it out to see who was looking so feverishly for him.

It was the Helen Choi, the Head of Public Relations. He rejected the call, and that revealed the two missed calls from Tanaka.

49. The Insider

"Yes, I knew about it. I saw the demonstration on the way to work. I have an inkling of what happened, but I didn't see everything with my own eyes because there were so many people. I saw them on the online newspaper afterward." Tanaka said, not telling the whole truth.

He and Arai had camped themselves on the best vantage point, a sloped outdoor terrace that belonged to a row of shops nearby, to watch the event unfold through the lens of his professional video camera since early in the morning. Arai had recorded everything under his supervision. He didn't know whether Misa realized it herself, but she had just created some of the best materials for his documentary. He still had the tapes in his leather laptop bag, perched by the leg of his swivel chair in the study. From where he sat in the living room, he could see it in the corner of his eyes through the gap between the half-shut door and its frame.

Ahhh...

Ahhhhhh....

Was it his hearing? Or was there really a soft moaning noise coming out of his room? No, he had flipped the power of the hub off. Nothing was powered up.

He shuddered.

"It's a disorder. It's what regular people called 'camera-shy' in English." Smith explained, which brought Tanaka's attention back to the discussion. "What Misa had yesterday was a manifestation of a kind of post-traumatic disorder. Have you ever seen or met anyone like this?"

"Why do you ask me?" Tanaka said. "Are you asking me if I knew anyone who became stressed in front of cameras after filming my movies?"

"You are the only person I know who had anything to do with the Adult Video industry." Smith opened the bottle of sherry sitting on the bar and poured himself a drink without so much as asking for permission from the owner. He took a swig of the sherry and waited for an answer.

"No, Smith, I am asking why did you ask me, and not someone else, like Misa's family doctor, or a psychiatrist. Did you ask me because you think it was always traumatic to have sex in front of the camera?"

"Well, these movies. How shall I put it? Some of these movies are quite obvious. If you see the faces of the victim in a forced intercourse..." He trailed off. "Not that I know anything about them. Andy likes to share his DVD collection with the other colleagues. I admit I glanced through the covers on various occasions." Smith cleared his throat. This was an uneasy topic for him.

Romans 13:13, Let us behave decently, as in the daytime, not in orgies and drunkenness, not in sexual immorality and debauchery, not in dissension and jealousy. In his faith, pornography was insidious and watching them destroy the purity of the mind, corrupted one's conscience and sent one straight to hell. He felt guilty.

"Smith, I know the industry inside out. It's all make-believe. If it was a film released by a proper, registered distributor, everything you see was make-believe. Doesn't matter what you think you are watching. It's all part of the script. Every actor and actress needs to sign a consent form and liability waiver before the filming can begin."

"Is that so?" Smith said, looking disappointed somehow for he might have made the wrong assumption starting out. He pressed on nonetheless. "But did you meet any?"

"No, not personally," Tanaka answered curtly. "What exactly are you looking for?"

"I need some information." Smith wiped his face with the palm of his hand and continued, "what I am about to tell you, you have to keep it a secret. Tell no one else about it. Not your assistant, not your wife, and not even Misa herself. Fine?"

Tanaka nodded. Neglecting to correct what Smith said about his wife.

"Misa had been raped," he paused. It was hard to talk about it even when it was in third-person perspective. Taking a deep breath, he continued. "And I was made aware by her brother that someone, I don't know whether that someone was the perpetrator himself or an accomplice, had filmed it and made it into a movie. An adult movie for sale. Possibly a hundred people could have watched it, possibly couple hundred thousand. We don't know. And because of that, my guess is Misa's problem with cameras came from her abuse. And this was more than just a regular post-traumatic disorder. This is a continuous mental assault. It's not something bad that just happened once and could be forgotten easily. It's something that she is confronted with over and over again by having people watching her suffer on this damned videotape as if it is just some mid-night entertainment for one. It has led her to fear cameras, to fear being recorded on tape."

"You're not a psychologist, Smith. She was fine when we filmed the TV commercial." Little did he know Smith had firsthand interest in his research. But before Tanaka could reveal it, he had to test him.

"It did happen a few years ago. There could be some adaptations of her behaviors along the way. Moreover, I have also seen her take pictures of herself. A selfie, as the lingo goes. The difference between then and now was she felt exposed in public at the ridiculous InterHRLA demonstration having been asked to wear a bikini to attract media attention. And when the attention comes, with flashes and all, that triggered her painful memories, and she broke down."

"Reasonable analysis," Tanaka rubbed the stubble on his chin. This conversation was getting interesting, but on the nape of his neck, he felt a cold chill, coming from his study. He scanned Smith's demeanor to see whether he had felt it too.

"If I can find this tape, its distributor would have been on it. I can have my lawyer send a temporary injunction as a first step to the distributor to stop them from further disseminating the materials. It will be a start. I want to help Misa."

"It depends on whether she signed a contract or not, or if she accepted money in return for being featured."

"...I cannot believe it if she did." Smith never considered these possibilities. He could of course just ask Misa, but if his conjecture turned out to be a mistake, it would just embarrass her further. And if it was correct, it would acerbate her pain, to be reminded that she had legally consented to whatever abuse she was subjected to. Anyhow, he had no way to know how to proceed without seeing what was on the tape. "We need to analyze the video."

In his mind, Smith had enlisted Aileen as his lawyer, making the natural assumption that Aileen would want to help him in his investigation. Being a human rights lawyer herself with a particular interest in Women's Rights in Japan, she had no reason to turn down the opportunity to work together. He had largely missed the fact that he had ignored Aileen at the square yesterday in the commotion and until now did not call her back to explain his absentmindedness. She was in fact quite offended at the moment by his behaviors.

Tanaka could see no sign of Smith's body reacting to the strange vibe that seemed to ooze out of his study, where he had in the previous months watched and re-watched the raw footage that was later compiled and edited into the tape in question. Smith's mind was busy coming up with a plan.

"So you want to know who did it?"

"Yes. Unfortunately, I only know that the director of that movie was a Frenchman, his surname 'Sergey'. I need all the information I can get my hands on about this. Names of people involved in the tape. From the names, I could track down the news report of Misa's rape and the guy's arrest. Can you help me?"

"What will you do when you have all of the information?"

"I will bring the perpetrator into justice," Smith said. "I have faith in the Japanese judiciary system."

"One of which you are not familiar with."

"I know what I am doing. Tell me, do you know this man? And if you don't you must have some acquaintance who might know or some database where you can search."

"Yes, of course, I can." Tanaka set down his glass of sherry, stood up and walked thoughtfully behind the couch on which Smith had sat himself. He glanced at this white-walled sun-lit study through the gap again. His table filled with equipment and documents were tempting his attention. His mind was ensnared by the monster that sat inside it, and he could hardly peel away. From the unattached earphone, he seemed to see puffs of dust swirling near the earpieces in shapes of a thrashing hand. The hand of Misa. It twirled in the air like it belonged to someone who was being strangled. In his ears, he heard Misa's low moan.

Should he tell Smith that Sergey is already dead?

And most importantly, should he tell him about his investigational documentary in which he hypothesis that the man didn't kill himself but was murdered, most possibly by Misa Hayami?

Tanaka had hoped to play the hero of the whole investigational adventure himself. He was not ready to share his part with someone else. On the other hand, with Smith in it, the storyline would become so much richer.

Was Smith the right character to cast? What would be more appealing to the critics?

He started to imagine the headlines of the news in the future when all was known from the release of his documentary. The possibility was endless. The combination of characters and outcome could make or break his work. He needed to make an intelligent decision about this. Pen and paper were what he needed at the moment, and they sat inside his haunted study.

Ohh....yahh...

He heard Misa again. For nights he had poured over every bit of detail of her case. It had to be just hallucinations he was having. Perhaps all he needed was a couple more drinks to shake off her voice.

Then his heart skipped a beat when he heard the jangle of keys outside his apartment door. A loud thump signaled that the neighbors were home.

Smith had cocked up his head to see Tanaka's troubled expression.

Something was amiss. Tanaka was apparently agitated by the news Smith had just shared.

"What do you have in the room?" He asked the man.

50. Magic Dragon

Smith chuckled.

"I cannot believe you," he said to Tanaka through the white, smoky haze they had created from smoking indoors, windows locked and the door of the study closed shut to keep the smoke from seeping out, thus alarming their neighbors. "What do you have to do to get these?" He held up the joint between his index and middle finger.

Tanaka took a drag of the fresh joint he just rolled up and exhaled. Beautiful trails of smoke danced in front of him.

Smith waved his arm in the air as if he could brush the white ribbons of smoke away like condensation on glass and said, "Incredible. This is the first joint I have ever smoked in Japan. Well, actually in years, even before Japan." He closed his eyes for a second for the setting sun coming through from the windows behind Tanaka hurt his eyes. Two long trails of smoke burst out of his nostrils.

To see Smith enjoyed his stash so much pleased Tanaka.

"I have my sources." He pointed the remote in his hand to the infra-red receiver of the air purifier. It was a high-end model. One could see its internal workings through the transparent outer case with metallic rims as decoration. The increased power of the filter machine zapped the air clean of white swirls in no time. "Are you surprised that the nation of stringent rules and regulations could produce such a malefactor like me?"

"There were more malefactors I have come in contact with around here than anywhere else I have been," Smith replied half-jokingly. "Our most respected leaders, Mura, Ogawa, Hirano, and Kojima were all excellent examples." Those were the latest list of executives from DaiKe arrested in the bribery probe.

"Money, money, money. And with money you can make *MORE* money. I supposed that's how the world has always worked. What does your God say about money?" Smith inquired.

"In Shintoism, there is not one God. Everything you could lay your eyes on can be a *kami (god)*. Generally, we thought them to be as much as eight million." He continued his explanation, spotting the surprise in Smith's countenance. "Our faith does not prescribe hard rules and our priests do not hand out moral judgments like those from the Western faith. Money, like everything else, could be created, obtained, exchanged, invested and divested so long as they were done with sincerity and honesty. These are the core values of Shintoism."

"Paying off a government official is definitely a form of public deception."

"Well, remorse usually comes too late. To live in an honored way, some of these men will die to atone."

Smith's forehead wrinkled in concern. He did not understand why Tanaka had made such a sudden introduction of death into what he thought was a lighthearted conversation between two men puffing away.

"I could see it on their faces," Tanaka smiled. He laid his half-smoked joint on the silver tray next to his computer and pulled up the latest news report on the DaiKe bribery scandal. A collage composed of the four men's headshots from their DaiKe website profiles had been uploaded online. Tanaka tapped the screen lightly with his fingers and picked up his cigarette again.

"Ogawa, Hirano," Tanaka told Smith. "Look at their eyes. The whites of their eyes above and under their irises were out of proportions. This is called *Sampuku*. They will die before they age. Ogawa has a wondering, shifty gaze in this picture. It is a sign of dishonest and opportunistic tendency. His lips curled down tells me he is always discontent."

"You're reading faces again." Smith connected the dots together. "And Hirano?"

"Hirano's chin is set too far back. The weak chin means a weak personality. This alone is sufficient to conclude he won't make it through the ordeal."

"If you can see it, wouldn't their families see it too?"

"If one has done something to tarnish the honor of himself and his family, I don't suppose they have much choice but to do what is left for them to correct their mistakes."

"And that would be to confess and go to jail for a very long time, or to hide forever behind a suicide."

"Thus saving the name of the family."

"It almost sounded like we are talking about The Hobbit. Here is Thorin Oakenshield and he must restore the kingdom of dwarfs and fight the five armies like men for the honor of his family name...." Smith's mind was getting more mixed up by the minute. The whitish wall was beginning to look like snows on Lonely Mountain.

"Yes, this is what I was getting at. I don't think Ogawa and Hirano will have much time left before we found them hanging by a rope somewhere."

"And their families would encourage it?" Smith exclaimed. "That's absurd..."

"The clues are all written on their faces. Face is born not made. Fate is not born but made. But Face wins most of the time, unfortunately. This has been my tragic observation."

"A major discovery. I feel like I had just landed on the moon and found out that it was the shittiest place, as the saying goes, on Earth."

"From an Earth where it was the place of desire for most men."

"Isn't it." Smith chuckled randomly. "'*Some of us are looking at the stars.*'"

"But *'we are all living in the gutter.'*"

The ventilated room had concentrated the effect of the joint on Smith. He pushed himself up from the swivel stool and said in a fussy haze that he had to leave and that Tanaka ought to take his barking dog out for a walk for the noise was bothering him. Both of them knew full well there was no dog. But Tanaka had become quite agreeing and imaginative himself when he was high. He fared Smith goodbye and slumped into a nap on the futon.

51. A Moment of Contemplation

What made me happy?

It was an extraordinarily difficult question to answer for Misa. She had very little memory of her own past, not just the distant past such as her childhood which most people had troubles recalling, but also the recent past. This was the reason for her reticence. Unbeknownst to her, she had become quieter and quieter after since she started assuming the life of her cousin Misaki. It was not her natural disposition to be reticent; she knew for a fact. However, she could not conjure up historical scenarios where she had behaved differently. Intellectually she knew any high school students would have gone through numerous classroom discussions, for example. However, she recalled none, let alone how she participated. Perhaps she did not participate, she explained to herself, which was why these memories did not exist.

For someone without memory of the past, it was hard to have very personal conversations with others where inevitably some tidbits of their lives were supposed to be exchanged as a sign of trust, of compassion. It was not to say that Misa had no compassion. Compassion she had a great deal of, for she had a good imagination. She could imagine herself being in the shoes of others, of their happiness, of their pain. She could say the most comforting phrases to others who need them, but it made her feel guilty sometimes. Sometimes she caught herself totally convinced of a reconstructed reality built from things other people had told her about herself, as Misaki. Other times she could not tell those were not her actual memories. Sooner or later she would forget even these fabricated memories. When she finally caught up with her problems, she decided the best thing was to keep her mouth shut so that no one would notice this girl, of no memory. A monster, among men.

This was the reason why she kept up Misaki's practice of writing diary in a small leather-bound book, now sitting inside a Ziploc evidence bag half a meter in front of her, on the desk in the interrogation room at the Harajuku police station.

She kept notes of everything in there. It was a practice exercise suggested from a self-help book she had read some time ago when she chanced upon it at the bookstore during some leisure time she had between her afternoon shift at the pachinko parlor and a meeting with one of her clients. The exercise was a simple one: jot down in a diary interesting events that happened each day and mark by the side of the entry one's mood with a happy, neutral or sad smiley. The aim was such that the person doing this exercise would, after a considerable amount of time, realized that there were wonders in everyday life and the total number of happy and neutral smileys often, in the unwavering optimism of the author, outnumber those of sad smileys. It had proven to be true by Misa's entry month after month. The tallying of smileys showed that she had a lot more to be happy about than to be sad about, despite the undying feeling of dread that constantly gnawed at her being despite the numerous moments of happiness, regardless of what was written down black and white in the boxes of her diary. Despite being none the happier, she now possessed the powerful knowledge that she could be, theoretically. Hence she kept the habit. She wrote entries religiously into the little black book every single day, goading herself into thinking that it would miraculously work one day. Perhaps when the numbers had finally reached a certain elusive threshold.

In front of the desk stood senior officer Miyazaki with his back to her. His stood looking at the invisible colleagues behind the one-way mirror, smoking the last bit of his cigarette. Another minute passed, and he turned around to stub it on the tray on the desk.

"Is it money?" He taunted, proposing a plausible answer to the question he posted to her earlier. "Easy money? Money from rich men like, let me see," he unzipped the evidence bag and pulled out Misa's diary. "Yoshiyuki Chino, Teuro Eiichi and, well, well, Toshiaki Ono. That's a big fish."

"I don't know what you are talking about."

"He gave you a diamond ring, remember?" He held up her own diary in front of her eyes and pointed at it. "You drew it out. Colored it and everything. Nice looking ring it must be in real life."

"The picture meant nothing. It's just some random scribbles."

"I wouldn't be wasting my time here if these were random scribbles of a school girl daydreaming about her wedding ring in History class. Guess whether we have found this in your house or not?" Miyazaki taunted.

"It was my birthday gift. Mr. Ono gave the ring to me as my birthday gift."

"What did you have to do in exchange?"

"Nothing. I said it was my birthday gift. I guess I turned a year older." Misa looked away from the diary and fixed her gaze on the cigarette dish. If she wanted, she could smash someone up badly with that metal dish.

The officer threw her diary on the desk surface. Before Misa could react, he grabbed her jaw and yanked it towards his direction with his right hand. "Don't look away when I am talking to you, Miss Hayami."

It did not scare Misa. Loud voices, threats, a bit of force. These she could handle. She had come under a lot of pressure in her life, conscious of them or not, they had fortified her with immunity to what others would find frightful, like lying to an officer who had just knocked some teeth out of her brother. Yet not a bit of fear could be seen from her steady stare back at Miyazaki.

"Now read to me this next one." He flipped the page to three days ago and pointed at the entry. "I want to know about this one."

She read the line she had written just a few days before.

"Oh, that was a lovely evening," She began.

52. Romance and Music

"What's this? Jazz festival at 8 PM?" Smith suspended all his manners momentarily when he discovered an unwanted agenda item.

Over the speakerphone, Cheryl answered unapologetically, "It's good for you to have something social once in a while in your calendar."

"Since when do you also schedule social appointments for me as well?"

"Well, since you're not so private 'private life' got on the internet." Cheryl, like everyone else, had been poking fun at him since his visit to Palatial had been photographed and put online to fuel a massive nation-wide mockery of DaiKe's management unscrupulous use of the company's finance. "You really ought to find a healthier interest."

"Like two million other salarymen who are addicted to the game of Pachinko." The number was probably slightly bloated. But if one were to visit them as often as Smith, one would probably agree.

"I know, I know." Cheryl hushed her kids in the background who was whining about the vegetables on their plates.

"You might as well pen me in on all the *Nomikai* drinking parties with all the dreadful people at work."

"I would have if you would not behave so sulkily. It ruins the mood. Mr. Mura said..."

"Forget what Mr. Mura said. He's probably not coming back, and neither are all of those ass-kissers that relish sucking his dick."

Cheryl frowned on hearing his comments. "Mr. Smith, I am not Andy. I am not accustomed to the way you speak about other colleagues."

"So what now?" Smith asked. "Do I really have to be in Shinjuku at eight?"

"Absolutely."

"How did she get you to do it? I am curious." Smith still could not believe his humorless secretary had booked him into a date with Aileen.

"She was persistent. She called the office five times. Well, you should know since you told me to tell her that you weren't around every time. There aren't that many women out there who are not put off by your charms, or the lack off, Mr. Smith. I suggest that you take this chance seriously because I don't know if you can find another one."

"Why do you have to say that, Cheryl?"

"I mean, you completely ignored her on the streets that day even though she was the one who summoned you there in the first place. She even had to fight with the police to get us in the demonstration area. I know because I was there, remember? You've probably forgotten about my presence, too."

"Well, I got there at her request, didn't I?" Smith retorted. "That sounded pretty responsible to me."

"And then you just up and left with the girl. You really should at least talk to her and explain the situation. She told me you did none of the above. You know how women are. We get a bit antsy, a bit jealous, even if the other woman is a young school girl...Hmm, maybe especially when the other woman is a young school girl."

"She's not a..." Smith wanted to explain, but he stopped himself. "That's really not the point. Cheryl, you are getting a bit chatty lately, aren't you? Talking on the company phone on company time with someone outside of your company contacts."

"Mr. Smith." Cheryl had this way of saying his name that made it sounded condescending even without seeing her facial expression. This reminded him of his mother every time, who would use this same tone of voice. "Trust me, you will like it. Just think that you're going there for the concert and see what happens. Your online dating profile says you are into Jazz music."

"Cheryl!" Smith couldn't believe his ears.

"Aileen reads it off of your profile, she told me," Cheryl said defensively, with a smile on her face. She did enjoy a bit of gossip about his boss with her future boss's wife, second wife, whom she liked a lot more than the first one since she had never had the chance to meet or talk to her even before their divorce. "A woman cares about you enough to get you concert tickets to music you like. That is unheard of for people our age. Stop whining." She seemed to have said the last thing to both her boss and her children at the same time.

Smith took a deep breath and said, "Yes, mam. I'll try to enjoy myself."

53. Run

Shinozaki had to run. He had seen what he should never have, and he was being hunted for it.

If St. Jude Hospital had reported the break-in of their research laboratory to the law enforcement, he would have been less scared. The worst thing that could happen to him was to be locked up temporarily until he would be redeem himself by explaining and putting his rash behavior in the right context. He would be seen as a martyr, someone who risked it all to expose the sinister work that was going on in that lab and be lauded forever by not only the medical community but society in general.

That visit to the animal testing lab had been a hollowing experience for him. Not because of the dozens upon dozens of poor animals — mice, hamsters, guinea pigs, rabbits, monkeys — thrashing about or whining in the dark corners of their cold, metal cage, making cacophonies of hair-raising noises in boredom, in hysteria or in pain. It was because of the data he saw in one of the computers that was left in Sleep Mode by a careless researcher who had forgotten to log out of the reporting system.

The lab was currently running a study for Doctor Hasegawa, his former roommate, concerning a sample with the serial number of H-51. Shinozaki knew instantly that his conjecture was correct and that Hasegawa had indeed never stopped working on the dangerous anti-depressant molecule despite the ban from the government on schedule I psychoactive drug research. Shinozaki had helped Hasegawa reviewed his paper on the HX molecule when they were both studying at the Tokyo Medical University twenty years ago, and the molecule was made into pill forms with filling agents for clinical trials. These pills would always be named with an H, followed by the version number. The last one he had heard was H-7, and now Hasegawa was already on version fifty-one. How did the bastard's research go undetected all these years?

The animal testing data did not look good. Looking at the average numbers of deaths across the animal species, the stuff was practically poison. But that was not what's worrying. The researcher conducting the test observed high rate of violent behaviors, nervous twitching, profuse salivation and sexual arousal in the short term, and severe losses nerve functions and mental capacity in the long term linked to signs of permanent brain damage.

Hasegawa's research was not only illegal, but also highly unethical. And to think that he might have tested them actually on humans…

It was then Shinozaki heard noises outside. When he looked up his eyes were blinded by flash lights. At that moment, he knew he had to go. There was no time to hesitate but to grab everything that was potentially useful within his reach and ran out the door. He didn't know what was in his hand but he needed something from the laboratory to at least let people believed that he had been in the lab and had not imagined the whole thing. With that folder he sprinted down the flights of stairs in the semi-darkness of the research wing of the hospital campus into the park lot, ignoring the shouts by the man with a familiar voice behind him telling him to stop.

"Shinozaki!" The voice called out in a patronizing voice. "*Yamero!*"

Stop? How could Shinozaki stop now? He had to tell the world about it. There was no other way. He had a moral obligation as a *Yi-sha*. — The word for doctor, *Yi-sha*, in Japanese meant a lot more than just a profession. It signified that one was a member of an ancient order of do-gooders for mankind that just happened to work with medical herbs and plants in the East, instead of the scalpels and sutures in the West. It was an honorable title, word for one's life's mission that was not to be toyed with and taken lightly.

As soon as he reached the car, Shinozaki threw the folders into the passenger seat, turned his key and tore out of the parking lot as fast as he could. The reflection of an exasperated Hasegawa, his hands on his hips and panting heavily, on his rear-view mirror made Shinozaki's heart pounded faster than it already did.

That man was a lunatic. He couldn't believe they used to occupy the different levels of one bunk bed together at the University dormitory. If his conjecture was correct, Hasegawa had been testing his HX molecule in illegal large scale studies for the past twenty years. Sergey Ribery, the subject of the case brought to his attention by an amateur film maker, along with countless others, were likely to have been the unwitting victims of his monstrous ambition to find the ultimate miracle drug.

54. Date Night

"I don't get it. He stood me up! Why did I fall for this guy? It's completely, utterly senseless!" Aileen moaned at the bartender, who lifted both of his eyebrows at the torrent of heavily Australian accented English words coming from the lone sitting guest at the bar. Everyone else was standing and chatting with their companions. The bartender did not speak much English, except for the names of all the cocktails and drinks from the menu. He supposed this foreign guest was just complaining about the quality of the jazz music behinds the curtain to the main hall of Cotton Club, of which he was forbidden to comment, so he went back to his work, wiping droplets of water from glasses piling by the sink.

"What's with the long face?"   Andy slid himself next to Aileen.

"OH-MY-GOD," Aileen said when she realized who appeared beside her. "He sent his friend. That's pathetic. No, I am pathetic."

"Wait, what are you talking about?" Andy asked, confused.

"Didn't Carson send you here?"

Andy started chuckling. "Don't tell me you're supposed to be on a date with Cars! Looks like he's not coming. What an asshole!"

Aileen took a gulp from her glass of wine. It was her fifth. Her wait had turned into binge drinking. Andy could tell from her demeanor that she was pissed and hell-bent on getting pissing drunk.

"Forget about him. We're here! The two of us, what a coincidence! I thought I would never see you again!"

"What do you mean?" Aileen gave him a light shove in the chest. "You knew it wouldn't work out between me and Carson?"

"You're too hot for him," Andy said as he gave her an appreciative once-over, which made Aileen blushed more than the wine she had already consumed made her. "He's asexual. I have never seen him get interested in women."

"Oh well, you could have warned me!" She replied. "Bastards. Both of you."

"Hey, lady, give me some credit for rescuing you from drowning in sorrows on your own at the bar."

That made Aileen smile. "Are you here for the concert?"

"I just escaped from the most boring evening of my life in there." Referring to the improvised music that came through the seam of the music hall entrance. "My date is still in there."

"Was it the music or the date you're referring to?"

"Both. I said 'Jazz music' when she asked me what music do I listened to. I mean what else do you say without sounding like a dumb-ass? Of course, you say 'Jazz music'. And the next thing I know she dragged me to this awful concert."

"You're exaggerating."

"No, I am not. They are trying to fuse Japanese Taiko drums with blues. It's not working, I am telling ya."

"So are you telling me all men just pretend to like jazz when they like something else?"

"Like sex," Andy said. "Yes, we are all after something else. You can trust me on this one."

Aileen crinkled her nose. "Carson is not that kind of guy."

"Which is precisely why he's not here today. I told you, he's not interested."

"Then why did he sign himself up for *Omiai*?   And attended the last two dates Miss Newton, who is probably no longer your girlfriend anymore by the looks of it? He bought me flowers. He was hinting to take me home the other day, and he even dropped everything at work for me when his company was in the middle of a crisis. Then he doesn't call anymore. I just can't figure him out."

"You're are a test case, lady, to prove a point."

"What?"

"To prove to himself that he was not an unattractive, undesirable middle-aged man with nothing going on for him. You came up, and he simply played along."

"Gosh, you have a way to make a woman feel bad about herself."

"Well, I once naively believe that Cars might get out of his shell with this one," he explained. "I helped Marie pick matching profiles from time to time."

"And all the while I thought she had some kind of secret algorithm."

"The secret algorithm used to be her mother. But she is getting old."

"And you guys decide to experiment with me."

"Based on your current emotional status, I declare the experiment a failure."

"So that's it?" Aileen asked, still hanging on to her bit of hope. "I don't believe it. We could have been together."

"Aren't you a little bit dramatic?" Andy teased. "You barely know each other."

"Which is why this whole affair is so...arousing." Then she sighed. "Your date...she might be looking for you." In the corner of her eyes, Aileen spotted a young woman in a black dress slipping out through the doors of the main hall and looking fervently to her left and right. "Shouldn't you be going back in there?"

"I told her I need a smoke," Andy said. "Give me two shots of those," Andy yelled over the counter to the bartender who at the time was pushing two red liquors in shot glasses over the bar top to another customer. The man managed to not show his annoyance. Professionalism.

When the alcohol came, Aileen picked it up and feigned disbelief. "What are these? And I thought we are in a Jazz festival. Show some class!" she jested.

"They are called Red Haired Slut. Drink up!"

Aileen pushed the vicious, lumpy drink down her throat. The drink was not made out of tomato juice but had the same texture which threw her off a little when she tasted something and expected another.

"Yuck! That was disgusting." Aileen wiped the dripping red juice from the corner of her mouth.

"You're funny," Andy said.

"Are Japanese girls not funny?" Aileen probed, seeing how his date might be the poor girl who was standing helplessly on her own at the entrance, dialing and redialing some numbers to no avail.

"Too much politeness. Too much pretension. I can't breathe anymore." He pulled his tie loose and elaborated. "They smiled at everything I said even when they didn't have a clue about what I was saying. Just tell me, you know? I don't give a fuck if they don't understand my English, I can explain myself in Japanese. I mean I learnt to speak fluent Japanese for a reason. But no, they all want to practice their English, they all want to listen to Western music, eat Western food, live a Western life, be a foreigner's wife. I don't get the appeal. They come in droves like bees over honey on everything Western."

Aileen laughed and stroked his back as if he was a child. "Oh, come here. Poor soul. You're so popular."

"It really gets on my nerves sometimes that no matter how many times I told them to speak up when something's wrong, they never do. They just accept whatever I impose on them, like gospel."

"I thought men liked to have women who worship them like Gods."

"It was fun at the beginning. Now I can't stand it anymore. I don't like to think that their panties get all wet as soon as they see another one of me."

"You mean some other white guy?"

"Yes! I mean, how do you tell when someone sees you not as yourself but as a shining trophy. When some other men come along, they would not give two sheeps about me."

"Is that why you're never serious?"

"I don't know why you'd think that. I am a hundred percent into it every time."

Aileen snorted.

"What was that?" Andy smiled. "Don't tell me you haven't had a fling or two in Japan, huh?"

"I was hoping to get off with Smith."

"And Smith is probably trying to get you off of him." Andy looked down at his phone. He had texted 'Where are you?' to Smith and the answer he got back was 'at a concert'. He held it up unceremoniously for Aileen to read, who rolled her eyes.

"When am I ever gonna get laid?" She bellowed, ignoring curious glances from people around her. The pair chuckled.

"There is always someone who thinks you are smart, funny and gorgeous, and thinks whoever stood you up tonight is an absolute idiot."

Aileen could not stop herself from smiling.

"Hey, I think your girlfriend is looking for you." She pointed to the direction of the girl who had her arms now crossed still standing in front of the entrance, in a stance that showed anger.

"Let's dash out of here!" Andy slammed two thousand yen on the bar and pulled Aileen out of the Cotton Club into the dazzling city streets.

55. Unforgettable Past

"Unforgettable...that's what you are. Unforgettable..."

Smith found himself singing the lyrics to the tunes he heard over the street noise of the relentless part of Shinjuku. The outdoor stage of the Tokyo Jazz Festival was currently occupied by the Tokyo Jazz Orchestra. Nat King Cole's *Unforgettable*, their current piece, plucked at Smith's memory. A bygone time when he was still young enough to be romantic.

He walked towards the stage while humming, wanting to take a better look at the talented Japanese musician who was working his magic on the saxophone. The instrument was as big as his upper torso. How he longed to switch places with him.

"Unforgettable, though near or far."

"Oh! *Sumimasen!*" Entranced by the music, he had bumped into someone accidentally. *"Daijoubu deska? Are you alright?"*

"Sumizu-san!" It was Misa, as chance would have it. "Pleasure seeing you here!"

"The pleasure is all mine." Smith instinctively leaned over to give her a hug as greetings the American way but retracted as soon as he remembered where he was.

Misa smiled and went for it. The embrace was sweet and warm, like between long lost friends. Smith was smiling profusely as he could hardly contain how glad he felt to see her again.

"Come sit down with me," Misa suggested.

It had been a while since he had found the time to enjoy an outdoor concert. He was a bit out of practice for such carefree evenings. He crossed his legs on the grass lawn in front of the stage next to Misa and took off his suit jacket.

As with everything in Japan, there was nothing accidental about this piece of lawn in the middle of the city. It belonged to a cafe. A waitress came over to take their drink orders.

"Did you come here just for the concert?" Smith asked.

"I went to an interview at a Pachinko parlor around here. The Neverlands. When I stepped out, I heard this beautiful music, and it was like a hand that pulled on my heartstrings. Before I knew it, I had been here for an hour already." She shrugged.

"You are quitting InterHRLA?"

"Oh, I am sorry. I know I should have stayed longer but I can't...I am afraid. Not after what happened the other day..." She tilted her head down, seemingly still embarrassed for what happened to her at the demonstration.

"That was probably a one-off," Smith said. "Let me talk to Aileen. I will tell her to back off. You are a researcher, not a, not a billboard. If you're a bit sensitive to the limelight, who could blame you? I have those moments myself. Everyone has them. Don't worry about it, especially not if I am going to tell Aileen to let you stick to your desk job."

"It's not that. You still don't read Japanese newspapers, do you?" Misa bit her fingernails.

"That's a nasty habit." Smith pried her fingers from her locked teeth. "You would ruin your nails like this." He had made it a habit to stop his kids from biting their nails as soon as he saw it. Misa was taken aback by his direct approach, and she gawked at him. Smith regretted soon after for the blurring of boundaries between friends and family. "Sorry, I shouldn't have done that. And no, I don't read Japanese newspaper if I can avoid it."

Misa smiled. She fished her flip phone from her pink striped Burberry handbag. Its myriads of decorative chains jingled as she did it. With swift fingers, she typed her own name in Kanji into the internet browser on her phone and clicked a few times that led her deeper into one of the entries. A tabloid article appeared. She presented it to Smith, who read words out loud habitually whenever he encountered difficult Japanese writings. Seeing his difficulty, Misa loaded the website once more through Google translate.

"Feminist from InterHRLA an ex-porn star and escort. Double standard harms organization's reputation." Below the headline was a photograph of Misa in the midst of her breakdown on the streets during the last InterHRLA demonstration. Smith grabbed the phone with two hands, unable to contain his shock.

"I have been kicked out," she said with a reassuring smile as if she knew Smith would feel more hurt about the news than she was. "I knew it would happen."

"How did they find out?"

"You can find everything online these days," Misa replied dryly. "I just didn't expect someone to find out so soon. If I hadn't suffered a breakdown in public, perhaps it could only come out much later. Maybe years later."

It was hard on her, because she hadn't actually been the girl in the porn tape. It was Misaki. But Misa had taken over her life now, and she would have to take all the consequences with it.

"That's..." Smith could not find the right words to describe how he felt at the moment. It was a mixture of blatant betrayal and sharp guilt. If some journalists could find it online, there was no way that Tanaka had not known of it. It was at that moment that Smith realized Tanaka was withholding information from him. But to what end? It bothered him immensely that he, who had resolved to call himself Misa's guardian angel, did not spot the coy and did nothing to protect her since he made his resolution, which now felt completely irrelevant. "That's...I am speechless. I'm sorry."

There was no safe place for anyone on the web. The two of them, victims of the brutally unforgiving internet. He let out a deep sigh.

"You knew it already, didn't you? You don't have to pretend to be surprised for my sake. If not from Tatsu, you probably would have heard from Andy."

"What about Andy?"   Now he felt totally powerless. Even Andy knew more than him.

Misa laughed. "You didn't know? Andy...he is a fan."

"A fan of what?"

"A fan of my movies."

That made blood left his limbs and shot up his head at what felt like a hundred miles per hours. His face was immediately red with anger and embarrassment. It was as uncomfortable for him to think about these unseemly tapes which Misa was in, as knowing his good friends knew about them all along but did not find it necessary to disclose when he inquired.

"A cappuccino and a green tea latte macchiato." The waitress laid their drinks out in front of them. "Enjoy!"

"The piano improv is incredible. Sometimes I wish I have a piano so I could learn to play like that." Misa stared at longingly at the musician behind the piano, swaying her body from side to side, humming along.

Smith could not help but notice how his entire being was captivated by the girl in front of him, and not the music. His temper died a little bit at Misa's every sway to the music.

"You're not sad?" He knew he should have shut up, but his curiosity won the wrestle. What kind of superhuman mental strength did Misa possess that enable her to live so carefree, despite everything that should not have to happen to a girl like her had happened? He would have thought it impossible if he hadn't known her personally.

"These things happened a long time ago. I am now like a lotus leaf on a rippling pond. I will float regardless of the waves."

"Nice analogy."

"Besides, I will have my revenge." She smiled again. This time a bit more genuine than the last.

"That's why darling it's incredible, that someone so unforgettable thinks that I am unforgettable too."

56. An Interrogation

"Get to the point." Miyazaki snapped, after hearing Misa's idle recollection of some Jazz festival he had no interest in. "What did you do with this person, *Sumisu*? He is the same *Sumisu* who was in the TV commercial with you, isn't it?"

"You seem to have the answer already. Why do you ask me?" Misa said.

"Don't get cheeky!" The officer slammed his palm on the desk. Ashes in the cigarette dish tumbled to one side. "Did he pay you money to sleep with him?"

"No."

"Someone caught you guys on photograph three days ago. You spent the night in his apartment."

"Says who?"

"Says this photograph." He pulled a photograph up on the display of his phone. It was dark and grainy, but Misa could tell it was she and Smith-san, posted on the forum now Misa would never visit again.

"Yes, that was us, so?"

"So you will be charged with prostitution. Do you admit to the crime?"

"We love each other. There was no money involved."

"What about these ten dollars he gave you? They are tips aren't they?"

"They are in American dollars, as a keepsake, memorabilia from a faraway place. What could I possibly do with them in Japan? Besides they are tokens of his appreciation for the times, I taught him Japanese, in public. The security cameras in the museum cafe would have footages of it."

"What about the 1.4 million yen in the visa debit card he owns we found in your house?" Miyazaki dealt his trump card. It rendered Misa speechless.

The police had raid Misa and Tatsu's apartment on grounds of suspicion over drug possessions. Revenge or prank, their house was turned upside down by an anonymous call made to the police, pointing at Tatsu for being in possessions of a large quantity of marijuana. The source had indicated that he was a leg in the intricate drug smuggling route around inner Tokyo high schools. Unfortunate for Tatsu, he fit the profile for the runner. A young, unemployed nobody who happened to have lots of friends still in school, who could, in turn, disseminate the product to a large number of fellow students quickly for profits. The police decided to pursue this tip and busted their apartment late this evening, with both of them in the house.

While they could not find the large quantity of weed they were hoping to bag, they did find a few ounces fit for personal consumption and a leather-bound diary full of recognizable names and numbers that were, to Miyazaki, a bigger treasure trove.

57. Lunch

"Don't be a child, Aily," Andy whispered to Aileen, squeezing her hand under the table. "They are our friends."

Despite the lack of sleep and overwhelming of senses by the twinkles of lights reflected by the restaurant's impressive ornamental gemstones murals of samurais on its four walls, Smith could tell that he was no longer the object of desire for Aileen. Not only that, but there was an air of hostility between them which he could not explain.

It was not too much to ask for, he thought. He was handing her a case the entire Japan had their eyes on. Any lawyer who wanted to make a name for him or herself would covet a case like this to land in their lap once in their lifetime. Cheryl had been contacted by a few solicitors, whom he asked her to turn away for want of someone he knew he could trust, that being Aileen. She was to represent all three of them, Tatsu, Misa and himself, as their lawyers. Or at least that was the idea Smith had when he had made the tea appointment at one of the most extravagant locations for a few pieces of sandwiches served on three-tier display on Andy's suggestion.

"I managed to bail him out by invoking international human rights laws. That's virtually unheard of for foreigners in Japan. Nobody gets bail under normal circumstances," Aileen said. "I think I have done enough for..."

"A pedophile," Andy finished her sentence.

"That's not what I was trying to say!" Aileen frowned and pulled her hand free from Andy's under the table. Its abruptness knocked the orange juice over. Smith caught it in time.

"I was just trying to lighten up the mood." Andy gave everyone his signature smile of innocence.

"I know you will say something like that just to get it out of your system," Smith said knowingly. After all, they had spent years together as pals and colleagues.

"This is not an InterHRLA case. You know I work for an organization, and not for clients who are not part of an InterHRLA case."

"Then make a case file for us."

"'No' is 'no', Smith," Aileen repeated her stand. "As a friend, I do wish that you understand the gravity of the situation. They have found two and a half ounces of cannabis in the boy's room marked for three. It was opened and partly consumed, with stubs stained with his saliva found in his garbage can. The boy is done. Possession and usage of cannabis in this country is punishable up to five years in prison. It's only a matter of how long the judge will put him behind bars. For that, his family better start rounding up some character-witnesses and testimonials in his favors to put him in a better light, make it look like it was a momentary lapse of judgment. And not to mention they had better find him a native speaking lawyer who can deliver a plea so good the Gods tear up."

She took a sip of her coffee and continued.

"As for you and Misa...." she paused to let out a withheld breath. "Did you two do it?"

"No! No, no, no." Smith said, adamantly denying any wrongdoing. "How many times do I have to tell you guys? I let her sleep in my place because she was too drunk. I did not touch her."

"Then why did Misa admit it?" Andy interrupted.

Aileen held up a hand to hush him up. "Her exact words were 'We love each other. There was no money involved.' That is technically slightly different from admitting to having intercourse with a man."

"Is that what she said?" Smith questioned, not entirely trusting his ears.

"We had a few too many wines, and she was getting drunk. Instead of going home, she proposed to stay at my place that evening. I thought it was understandable, given how her relationship with Tatsu had worsened over the last couple of weeks. They had a row when she found him smoking."

"Jeeze, Smith, save your explanation for the federal prosecutor," Andy said, twisting his mouth in disapproval. "That is one of the worse alibis I have heard. Have years of Detective Conan taught you nothing?"

"Detective Conan?" Aileen repeated, puzzled.

"The anime," Smith answered for Andy. "Andy is reliving his childhood in Japan."

"Come on people. There is a grainy photograph of you two going home together at three AM in the morning. Then there is a bunch of records for your rendezvous in her diary, as well as a debit card with a large sum of money that belongs to you in her house. Put two and two together and voilà, you're a paying customer."

"Don't get yourself excited," Aileen said. "Under Japanese law, the definition of prostitution is strictly limited to coitus. Any non-coital sexual acts do not fall within the scope of the regulation. They have no case unless you were arrested in the act or the prosecutor has managed to get clear evidence, like a videotape, of it in progress."

"There was no case, yet they invite you for a day at the detention center..." Andy said.

"They have something in hand that we don't know," Aileen said thoughtfully.

"We did nothing," Smith grunted. "Absolutely nothing. I am so glad my wife is not here to witness this."

"You're divorced," Andy said sarcastically. "Show me the photograph," He asked Aileen, who had the case files in her lap. They looked at it together. In the shadow of the street lamps, Smith was seen hugging with one arm an almost unconscious Misa from behind while he entered the passcode to his apartment building with another hand.

"Misa is a good drinker. She can easily out drink you and I, Cars."

"You mean she was pretending to be drunk?"

"What's so surprising about it? That's straight out of Japanese television. Ninety-nine percent of television sex occurs in this scenario. Japanese women are too shy to ask for it."

"Yet there was no sex." Smith rebuffed his claim.

"Who can testify to it? Your neighbors who were deeply engrossed in their sleep cycles that were not awakened by your lack of noise? Too absurd."

"My faith, my principles. They are the best witnesses to my soul."

"I told you he was asexual," Andy said to Aileen, who could not help but chuckle. She put her arm under the table on his leg and gave it a squeeze. Smith chose to ignore it.

"Then there was the anonymous call. The photograph and the call, these were both external evidence, collected almost as if intentionally to frame you and her."

"The two of them are the hottest items on the internet. The photographer and the caller might just be one of their fans."

"Yes, Misa had fans." Smith glared at Andy, who looked away as if he was caught stealing.

"Given Misa's track record, nobody will believe Misa is innocent. The only point of contention is, are you a paying customer, or are you her boyfriend," said Aileen.

"I am not her boyfriend."

"Well, friends with benefit?" said Andy.

"You're not helping." Smith glared at Andy.

"You did give her the money."

"Her brother. For his medical bills," Smith said. "That was also ages ago."

"The siblings share their expenses. We could argue this point, but this is not the weakest point in the chain of events."

"What is in your opinion, Detective Conan?" Smith asked.

"Are you not curious why of all the names in her diary, you were the only one who was arrested?" he said.

"Well, that's what I was saying. The police probably got something on them." Aileen said.

"Even if someone had installed a night vision video camera inside my apartment, there would be nothing to see," Smith said with conviction. I made some hot tea and put Misa to bed. I went to take a shower and slept on the couch by myself. As simple as that."

"What about body fluids?" Andy suggested.

"...in a used condom, for example." Aileen finished his sentence. "They could have found it in the garbage."

"Garbage sweep. That would be saying that the police know what they were looking for and where they could find it."

"Well, looking in someone's garbage for clues is detective work 101."

"They wouldn't have let me have bail if they have confirmatory evidence," Smith interjected on their preposterous speculations.

Andy's face turned blue.

"What's the matter?" Aileen asked.

"Someone wants you to stay away from Misa," Andy said to Smith, his eyes brighten with enlightenment.

"What do you mean?" Aileen asked again, baffled.

"That's it!" Andy slammed his palm on the table. "It's a warning! It's a warning to you to keep you away from Misa." He turned to Aileen and said, "You said it yourself. There is no case unless they have some fairly strong evidence which we would have heard of it already. The police are bluffing."

"Why would anyone spend such a huge effort to keep me away from Misa?"

"You're a public figure now, Smith," Andy said. "You're dragging Misa into the spotlight by your association with her. Someone wants to keep her out of it, desperately."

"The anonymous tip," Aileen said thoughtfully.

"And the photograph. They were planted to give the police enough clues to go on, but nothing to get both of you into serious trouble."

"Do you mean someone wants to protect Misa?" Smith asked. "That made no sense. How's getting her arrested protecting her? How's that keeping her from the limelight?"

"No, you still don't get it?" Andy sighed deeply. "It's not her that someone wants to protect. It was himself. There were all distractions from something that really concerned this person. Something must have happened in the last few days. We need to search the web."

58. The Jail Cell

Misa heard muffled voices outside her cell. Her ears twitched, but she did not move.

The cell room was made for isolation. For someone with less mental strength, she would have already admitted to whatever crimes they pinned on her. Misa could, however, focused her mind on something other than her present circumstances, which other would consider as plight, on the passing of the time. An excellent distraction for someone with ample of it on hand. Still fourteen more hours to go till the end of her forty-eight hours' detention.

Being locked in a jail cell was the perfect moment for meditation. Meditation did not require physical comfort. It did not require any more physical space than a body took. It did not require external resource. Everything needed was vested already in her mind. She could practically bend walls with her mind, or pierce through them with the fire that spits out of her eyes. They felt sore from staring at the wall through the semi-darkness. The weak lamp shone only to one corner of the cell. Casually, Misa rubbed her eyes.

Outside, the row between a disgruntled fellow detainee and an annoyed jailer could be heard. Futile display of resistance, Misa thought to herself.

She exhaled.

Her energy pushed the whisk of sound out at once, and the noise whizzed out of her cell as if it had been pressurized from the inside.

Peace, finally. This act required a certain level of mental concentration. What a beautiful feat she had achieved. She lauded herself on the inside.

It took about five seconds. Then she immediately got attuned to the room's lighting and its interior. The strangeness of the place no longer seemed strange. This was her stage today, she noted mentally. A quick scan proved that this would be an easy show to do.

As a priced skill that came from years of practice, she was always able to feel comfortable in the unknown. Much like a door-to-door salesman, it was essential to her to be able to perform at her best regardless of where and whom she met. What she had witnessed as a working girl would likely set off days of nightmares for someone else. Misa, not, not her. And because even feelings were relative, in the absence of any immediate audience, she felt almost relaxed. She might even be able to enjoy herself a little bit in the solitude. No one to watch her except the cursory glance of the video feed from the security guards who kept an eye on hers and many other's security cameras, she could be said to be having some near-privacy. A luxury.

The hardness of the block she was sitting on, the stiff muscle on her back from sitting in the same posture for way too long, the twitch in her toes from being cramped in the same shoes she had since yesterday, none of those bothered her. She could carry on with not a care in the world.

That was the trick that her mind and body knew well. She had acquired it without instruction from her brief entrapment by the dead man. That was years ago. She could barely remember it. The story that her reaction, or lack of, at the present moment told was one that Tanaka and Smith wanted desperately to uncover. Had they asked Misa directly, she would not be able to answer questions about what really transpired. Was she even there? The only thing that mattered to her was that no one should ever make her feel bad again. Everything else was better forgotten. And forget she did.

That was a couple of years ago. It was now nothing but a few flickers...

Entrapped, helpless, she was fatigued from resistance. Her mind finally tricked her into believing that she enjoyed her present status. Were there other sources of solace if not one that came from within her? Her brain had saved her from desperation, from dementia, from hurting herself. Instead of fighting her way out, she had suppressed the wish to escape. It had persuaded her whole being to live the moment, to relish the extraordinary of circumstances, the suspense, the surprise, the climax, the mess afterward, the cleansing. The cycles she had become expectant of during those times. And then suddenly they were over. That left her hollow when she was let out.

She wanted more.

No, she did not enjoy it. She could not have been. That was what she kept telling herself so she could behave normally like other people. Deep down she knew she was a different person. There was no way she could keep herself away from temptation. The dead man had poisoned her soul with a craving she could not suppress. Worse than drugs, worse than a curse. It was the moment when Eve tasted the forbidden fruit. What she bit was not just an apple, but an apple dipped in golden caramel. It rotted her soul like unbrushed teeth. Bacteria grew all over it. The bacteria grew and grew into a colony until it was too thick to get rid of. She was one with sin.

Sin reeked from her. She reeked of sin.

Wait. — That was not her own memory. They belonged to another Misa. Misaki, to be precise. It was her cousin's memory. She not only recreated it in her head but she also believed that she was her, so she could walk and talk and live like her, and find out what really truly happened to her three years ago, what killed her, and why.

Of course, there were times that she could hardly tell whether the thoughts in her head was hers or Misaki's anymore. And what if she made a wrong conjecture about one piece of information she collected about

Misaki? Then her whole memory would be faulty. Certainly at some point it would be impossible to correct it anymore.

Never did she speak of any of this to anyone, for fear that they would take her as mentally ill. It did occur to her that her denial likely signified that she was ill, theoretically speaking. Knowing about your own mental illness, having deduced it with your sick mind was about as senseless as a blind man reading out loud text he read on a printed book he could not read. A conundrum Misa assigned as trivial incongruence of a self-aware life.

Since then she irked out an existence that suited Misa's true colors. One that led her from one arm of a stranger to another. From one violent thrashing to another bodily torture. It suited her. She came alive in those moments. The thrills sent her off to seven heavens. Everything else was just distraction, putting up appearance, keeping her body healthy enough to do it again.

Recalling all these made her underwear damp. She squirmed.

Was it she or was it Misaki who was arouse? It was hard to tell.

59. Warning

Hasegawa did not wait for Misa to get into his car before he started giving her the 'I told you so' speech. Despite him being the only person she could ask to come pick her up from the detention center, she was not intending to give the man his satisfaction that he had been right all along.

"Would you shut up? I'm released, ain't I?" Misa snapped at Hasegawa, who was lecturing her about how she ought to live her life. "The police can't do anything to me."

"Not this time, but what about next time?" Hasegawa use of the two words 'next time' left a distaste in his mouth. There should not be a 'next time' at all.

"Look, I know some people from my job at St. Jude. People from the inside." He didn't explain where, but Misa understood it to be the police force. "I could pull some strings and try to get the info you want on Misaki's case. There's really no need for you to get yourself knee-deep into her mess. There are people of high stature in her list. You're just playing with fire. Who knows what excuse they would make up to get your out of the way next time?!"

"Well, if you truly want to help me and Misaki, you would have done it a long time ago, wouldn't you?!" Misa bellowed at him.

"In all fairness, I wasn't expecting you to play Russian spy and mingle yourself all the way into their corrupted political circle! The guy you were telling me about, this Mura guy, he was arrested for bribing a congressman in order to get some legislative work done in his benefit just a few days ago. This is serious business. I don't know whether Misaki knew who she was dealing with, but you are an innocent young woman with a bright future ahead of you. You should not throw everything away just because you're *curious.*"

"I'm *curious*?!" Misa laughed sarcastically. "That is maybe the biggest understatement I have ever heard."

"These people on the list whose lives you're probing into could get you and Tatsu's house raided and have you two detained just like that. They are not ordinary people. You should take the warning very seriously."

"Tatsu will be fine, right?" Misa asked. Her brother was the only person she had left that she really cared about. "He's not a marijuana addict. I have never seen him smokes!"

"I'll ask someone to take care of him," the doctor said assuringly.

"Thank you…" Misa said weakly. It had been a long time ago since the doctor had heard her say thanks.

"Well, you know I'm always on your side. I hope you've learnt your lesson."

60. The Fall Guy

Hasegawa knelt next to the dead body of Shinozaki. His arms to the side, his mouth agape, the dead man's awkward position on the floor reminded him of the way he used to sleep on the bunk bed below his in the university dormitory many years ago.

It was a pity that Shinozaki had such a low opinion of his work. It was honorable scientific work combined with diligent system of validating a hypothesis. He was not afraid to test and fail, at least, because without failure, one would never succeed. He had as much regard for himself as Koch, Fleming and Pasteur, but Shinozaki thought him the likes of Nazi Doctor Mengele. Every empirical data had value, even if it deviated from the scientist's expectations, as it did at the beginning of research. Shinozaki was too tied up with the moral aspect of things, and worse yet, his sense of morality was biased. Why thought of humans different from the guinea pig they raised, probed and killed by laboratories all over Japan differently? Hasegawa, unlike Shinozaki, he was an *equalist*. All lives mattered equally, and equally little to him except as vessels of a greater purpose. As a scientist, he had the divined right to use them to figure out what that is.

"Doctor, should we get rid of the body the old fashion way?" The man in hoodie asked him. He was a hitman Fat Gado had sent over to hunt down Shinozaki. Hasegawa had requested the pleasure of sending his friend off personally.

Hasegawa stared vacantly at his ex-roommate's body.

"No, I want something special for him. He's not just anybody," Hasegawa replied, and he meant it. Shinozaki was not a petty theft caught stealing from the Yakuza. He was a renowned doctor in his field, and he deserved more than just a hasty burial in the woods or being dump in the sea only to be washed up the shore a few days later with his body all bloated and mangled.

Hasegawa wasn't keeping track like he used to anymore, but it didn't mean he was becoming sloppy. Every new death required careful planning, every kill was a milestone in the grand scheme. There would not be a boring kill for him, not in a lifetime. What everyone wanted at the end of their lives was different, but what he should do with the dead, there were not so many choices, and yet he always had new ideas.

To throw off the crime scene investigators, he needed to avoid dealing with the body himself, because whatever he would do came from ideas in his own mind, and his own mind had been wired to work in a certain way, with certain habits and preferences. The same was true for the hitman. The signatures of their behaviors would manifest themselves over and over again, and eventually the investigators would see a pattern. And that pattern would sell them out.

He needed someone random. Someone different every time, so that serial kills would become isolated incidents, and planned executions would become acts of passions, or even accidents.

"You should go," Hasegawa said to the man.

"Really, doctor? Are you sure you could handle this all by yourself?" The man was skeptical, but he had never met any other doctor that was as unscrupulous as he was for science.

"Yes, trust me," Hasegawa gave him a cold smile, and added, "Tell Fat Gado I said thanks."

The hitman left the washroom at the hospital where Shinozaki worked with a quick affirmative nod.

In five minutes, the janitor would come in to clean according to the schedule. Once in here, she would find the doctor lying unconsciously on the floor, his head bloodied from the shards of glasses scattered everywhere and assumed that he had a fight with someone who worked in the department. Now all the story needed was just the 'someone'. And in came one of the poor fellows in whose late-night coffee he had put half a crushed pink pill.

Hasegawa stood up and smiled at the guy as he passed him in the hallway.

61. The Imposter

The imposter adjusted the tails of his lab coat once more. — While he was normally not a man to fuzz over the tails of his lab coat, he was deciding between leaving the tails hanging on the side of the chair, or tucked neatly under him. He squinted annoyingly at Tanaka, who had asked him to wear the coat. There was no practical reason for a psychologist to wear the uniform over his suit, but the whiteness and the rigid shape of the garment were conventional signs of authority in the medical field. It worked much like a suit in business settings. Most people would automatically associate positive attributes to a person if he or she was in a uniform, and would only reverse their opinions when signs of his or her inability were displayed clearly. Being fully aware of the influence the subtlety affects people around him, however, was not the same thing as allowing it to persist.

Directly in front of him stood the director himself, adjusting his filming equipment. The easily guiled man had picked a silver and blue striped silk tie and a white shirt — the by-the-book look that spelled trust and elicited confidence, for a plebeian. It would not work on him, the imposter smirked.

Tanaka winded the knob of his tripod and looked into the eyepiece of his video camera. He considered the view for a moment, then he pulled the chair facing the doctor an inch to the right.

"*Kyouju* (Professor), could you sit over here in this chair while I adjust the angle?" he asked the doctor, who appeared not to have heard him. He blinked steadily at him, yet not moving an inch of his body. — Tanaka recognized that look. He had worked with many self-important actors and actresses in his career and if he gained anything from those experience, was learning to be immune to such behaviors. After all, they were co-dependent in every film he made. He knew it, and they knew it, too. Nothing good ever came out of animosity.

What bothered Tanaka was the fact that because this documentary involved a very sensitive topic, the only people who knew about it was Doctor Shinozaki, who would provide his professional analyses on film today, and his boyfriend Damien. He did not have an assistant to do angle confirmation, lighting and sound checks for him. Given the lack of a crew, he would have to rely on his instinct and experience to compensate it.

Tanaka decided to shift his own chair another inch to the right, making sure that the camera had a full view of the doctor. The original idea was to show a side view of himself, out of focus but still recognizable, interviewing Tanaka, who would be in focus, to create a sense of conversation, emphasizing the project as a result of thorough investigation and research on his part. Sort of like in 20/20. He had run through how it should go in his head multiple times already and yet things still go wrong. Things always do. For one, the doctor seemed to be a bit taller than he expected. — Certainly, if the positioning was wrong, he could always edit the film and add a shadow on the side to highlight his presence.

Having thought it through, Tanaka emerged from behind the eyepiece once again, convincing himself that his request for Doctor Shinozaki to help was so out of line it ought to be ignored. After all, Dr. Shinozaki was one of the most famous psychologists in the world on Abuse Psychology. Many Japanese television stations pay him hefty sums to appear on their programs. His willingness to participate in Tanaka's low-budget documentary that might never make it out of the projector in his apartment was more than condescending to him. Renewed with a sense of gratefulness, Tanaka reminded himself to behave.

"*Kyouju*, when I press the button, the machine will start recording. This light over here will turn red, and I will start asking you the list of questions. You can deliver your response as naturally as possible. And I would like to see a little bit of compassion from you to the girl..."

"Do you think that this is the first time I've recorded anything?" Doctor Shinozaki snapped, he grabbed the script off Tanaka's hand and threw it on the desk behind him. The papers had cut into Tanaka's thumb and made him bleed, but he decided to hide it. He would tolerate anything as long as Doctor Shinozaki deliver up to standard.

62. Waterfall

Tanaka was meditating with his legs crossed on a bamboo mat he had placed on the floor of the empty flat.

Outside, the slow hum of the train passing filtered through the cracks of the dusty window. The flat had been unused now for a few years. It was the property of a now defunct adult movie production company. The flat was seized by the bank, but it had a lot of trouble selling it, given its history. Japanese is a superstitious nation after all. A place where a man had died was bad luck. Everyone with sense would avoid it.

Out of negligence or intentional abandonment, the place was still kept in the same state the day it stopped being used as a filming studio. Everything in this place was etched with invisible marks of its former cruelness.

In this studio, Sergey Ribery edited the last scene of his last remaining work with his favorite actress, Misa Hayami, who was only fifteen at the time.

The scene was simple. The naked girl stood in the middle of the shallow part of the river. Not too far behind her, a waterfall was splashing noisily behind. The camera swung to her muddled reflection on the slipping water gushing from the gap between a fallen tree trunk and the river bed.

Suddenly a man appeared beside her. It was the same man who had sexually abused her all along. The man hooked a loop of rope he had in his hand around her neck. She slipped motionlessly, without any resistance, into it, her hands grabbing the side of the rope as the man pulled the knot tighter, and tighter, and tighter until her facial expression was one of shock, which quickly warped into one of fear, of being betrayed.

A ritual murder scene laid out in superbly poetic surroundings. One that was designed so well the audience believed a hundred percent she was going to die. And die she did.

It was a mistake, the movie continued, showing the flustered male actor crying for help, pulling at the unyielding knot that had wrung the neck of his fellow actress. Panic rose inside him, he slipped on the wet, round stones and fell on his back, the power of the gushing river water was so strong he could not remain in his spot.

The girl had died, but he did not have to, he thought to himself.

He held the rope that was still tied to the girl's body as tight as he could, hoping that the weight of her body would impede the force of the gushing water. Thrashing helplessly in the shallow water, he dragged the lifeless body of Misa Hayami behind him down river until he was washed up the bank and rescued.

Her face was mangled unrecognizable.

Two days after the real Misa Hayami's death, Sergey sat at the table across the room from where Tanaka was now meditating, edited that part out without wincing. His steady hands had taken over the camera from the videographer when his knees buckled and captured the incident till the very end.

It was then, someone had stabbed him from behind. His dead body was found without a single piece of his clothing, and all of his hair was shaved before he died. The murderer had wanted him to get a taste of his own medicine.

Tanaka let out a deep sigh.

Twenty minutes of total focus without interruption.

Not bad in a place so full of secrets.

He stretched out his legs and put his arms behind him. Clearing his mind helped him become more observant normally. Once again he scanned centimeter by centimeter around the room.

"What did I miss?"

Tanaka couldn't see it, but the whole place was in fact full of clues. They were in every particle of dust that was either swirling in the room or lying in wait on top of every furniture in the room. They were the flakes of skins, locks of hair and drops of dried blood that had been left by the studio's former occupants.

If he could find the clues he needed and recognize the incongruences of the DNA evidences, he would know who Sergey was filming that day. He would know the true identity of the girl who was now called Misa Hayami.

End of Book I

BUT...

here is a preview of the next book.

The Kiss of the Pachinko Girl

by Vann Chow

Prologue

Rows and rows of Pachinkos raised into view when Smith entered *The Palatial*. The talking devices of chance emitted a purplish pink halo above the horde of adrenalin-pumped, highly concentrated customers in the dim-lit library of gambling in the middle of Shinjuku in the wee morning hours.

Smith felt no qualm about his presence in *The Palatial* despite everything that happened because of his visit to the Pachinko parlor. ---- He had gotten *The Palatial* a lot of free publicity in the last couple of weeks when the DiaKe corruption scandal broke. Although he was not personally involved in it, due to his appearance on the company's television commercial, he was the publicly acknowledged *Face of DaiKe*. His every move was watched. His patronizing of *The Palatial* were photographed and put on the internet forums. At the hike of public interests in the corruption case, the photo of him feeding money eagerly to the hungry machine was shared like a spreading wildfire online for the symbolism behind his action.

The Palatial, a member of the NABUO group that owned a large chunk of the Pachinko business in Tokyo and beyond took the opportunity to advertise themselves by sharing the news that Smith had once won a jackpot worth 1.4 million yen at one of their other Pachinko parlors, the *Passage* in Ikebukuro on the internet. It was quickly assimilated into mainstream media. Soon after, the police came knocking. They had found the visa debit card with his winnings at the *Passage* in Misa and Tatsu's shared apartment when it was being swept for drug possession based on an anonymous tip and a diary that Misa had kept in which his name and those of other men Misa were involved with were found in the apartment.

At that inopportune time, a photograph surfaced on the internet of Misa and himself entering his Tokyo apartment. A man called Miyazaki, the detective heading the investigation of what was originally a simple case of illegal marijuana possession, put two and two together and decided that there was enough evidence for him to open a possible sex trade investigation between Misa and Smith.

"Here!" A young Japanese man in a baseball cap and black sports coats called him over.

"What's with the outfit? I hope you're not planning anything foolish. You know everything here is being recorded anyway."

"What are you talking about?"

"Take off that ridiculous cap and stop looking so suspicious. I don't know if you've noticed, but the security guard over there has been watching you the whole time."

"I'm not worried about him. It's just," the boy broke off and looked around nervously. "Tanaka-san can absolutely not see me with you."

"So you're here to rant about the boss." Smith sat down. "What's the matter, Arai?"

"Shh..." the agitated young man, who was the assistant of Ryuuji Tanaka, said. "Don't say my name out loud!"

"Nobody's gonna hear it over the noise." Smith load a bucket of steel balls into the tray of the Pachinko machine in front of him, and he turned the lever. It sprung to life. "Tell me, why did you ask me to come here. What is it that we cannot talk about at the office?"

"I've been following you for days." The boy said, his eyes drooping in remorse. "I was the one who photographed the pictures of you online. *Hondoni gomenasai.* I'm really, really sorry. *Watashi ga shita koto wo yurushite kudasai*, please forgive me for what I've done, *Sumisu-san.*"

Smith had a lot of guesses who the culprit might be. The confession of Arai, however, he did not see coming. "Why did you do that?" he asked.

"Tanaka-san..." Arai stuttered at the sound of his superior's name. "He had asked me to stalk you. I had no idea he was going to put them online and use them against you. When I found out that you have been taken into detention by the police, I was shocked. *Watashi wa bikkuri shita.* I had no idea what I was doing would become something like this."

"Good evening our esteemed guests! Would you like something to drink, sir?" A waitress poked her head between the two conversing men and offered to take their drinks order. Like many others, she recognized the blonde hair *Gaijin* from the news.

At the moment, however, the new information Arai gave Smith clouded his mind. He had thought Tanaka an ally, not an enemy. Albeit being slightly eccentric, as an artist usually was, he had not read any sign of betrayal from Tanaka's demeanor the last he saw him in his study. The fact that they spent a whole afternoon smoking together as if they were best pals bothered him.

"Nothing for us. Please leave us alone." Annoyed at the interruption, Arai shooed the girl off.

Smith watched the girl walk away disappointed that she could not entertain her guests with some beverages. The girl reminded him of Misa, a waiting girl working in a gambling establishment with no real career prospect.

"Why did he ask you to stalk me?"

"You'll have to excuse my foolishness. I am but a lowly salary-receiving employee, an assistant to Tanaka-san. I did his bidding without question."

"Even when you could not justify it?"

"This is not uncommon in Japan, *Sumisu-san.* I think you know what I mean."

"Do you not have a guess of your own why he asked that of you?"

"I truly do not know, *Sumisu-san,*"   Arai said. "This has vexed me ever since I knew my photos got you into trouble. I have thought about it long and hard, but I couldn't come up with a good reason why Tanaka-san wanted me to stalk you. Obviously, he's interested in what you are doing with Hayami-san."

"With Misa?"

"Yes. He wanted me to follow you, but I can tell he was most intrigued by the materials I gathered when you were with her. In the beginning, I thought he wanted some extra footage for certain company communications he was planning. When you were arrested by the police, I could not help but wonder what I was doing for the whole time..."

Smith ruffled through his hair with his fingers. This was a puzzle. What was Tanaka hiding from him? Why had he come under his surveillance? Was it his idea? Or was he employed by someone else? There were so many questions flooding his head that it hurt. "Thanks for telling me all this," he said, managing to stay civilized despite the news of betrayal.

"I have to apologize. I cannot say more, and I cannot stay any longer," he said. "Please be careful from now on. Happy holidays." Arai fixed his hat once more and skipped out of the Pachinko parlor as soon as he had left the holiday greetings.

1. The Doctor's Analysis

Dr. Shinozaki coughed to clear his throat. He laid his left hand over his right resting on his lap and sat himself upright. Then he began by looking at the camera.

"The Étourdir is a very complex work of art. It cannot be explained in a few words."

"Can you try to tell us what is so complex about it?" The interviewer sitting in front of him with his back to the camera asked. "Perhaps as a start, why did you frame it as an art? To a layman's eyes, it's not more than a pornographic work of eccentric storylines."

"This is a good place to start." The doctor seemed pleased by his interviewer's question. "The distinction between art and pornography has long been debated by the philosophical society at large. Pornography and art may seem similar, but they are representations of very different ideas. Pornography is a degradation of human bodies whilst artistically graphical nudity is accepted and admired. Take the example of the celebrated work of art, the Birth of Venus by Titian, the painting depicted a nude woman in a serene nature scene surrounded by angels. The nude body of Venus was a mere tool to reflect the innocence and the purity of the Goddess. The same work would be less sensual and less powerful when Venus, a Goddess, someone whose beauty transcends that of a human, would be sporting human attires. Meanwhile, in a pornographic work, the exposition of bodies, often engaging in sexual acts as well, are the sole subject of it. There is no more depth than what was revealed."

"When you said that Étourdir was a work of art? What artistic qualities did you see from it? How is it different from regular pornography?"

"I would not say Sergey's work is not pornography. It is a hybrid of the two worlds. Pornography focused on creating sexual arousal from its audience. Nude art is mystical, it keeps you guessing. Its theme is often suggestive. It doesn't reveal its purpose through the revelation of sexual content. It doesn't endorse or consent to actions depicted in it. Pornography makes no moral judgment. Art often has one, however, what it is, is not always obvious." The doctor picked up the glass of water on the coffee table before him and took a sip. "Étourdir is a collage of both. This was why it was regarded as the best work of Sergey. He tried to do the impossible, and through it exposed the irony of the intellectual world which decides if one's work is a success or failure, vulgar or transcendental by putting them in strict brackets. Vulgar works can be full of emotions, emotionless acts can be full of meaning, meaningless actions can be full of purpose. This was the way he thought.   He wanted the world to understand that sexual experience is not a marginal aspect of human life, that it deserved critical appreciation and exploration, both physically and emotionally. In fact, his work runs like a sensory experiment. His audience is in on it together."

"Can you give us an example?"

"Sure. The first person perspective of many scenes is pivotal to the conveyance of this empiricism he promoted. It brings the experience to life such that a viewer believes he is right then and there, experiencing the increased heart rate, the awkwardness of the confrontation of one's darkest desires, the fear of being caught, the regret from committing the unthinkable, the confusion of the urge of the sums of all emotions. Any nudity or graphic scenes are of supportive function to him and no less important than the string of the sophisticated and unfathomable study of the human psychology behind it."

"Some critics said that Étourdir is the pioneering work in the category of fetish for absurdity. Do you think that someone can be fetish over absurdity? It seemed to defy the general regards that humans are the most logical and rational beings in the animal kingdom."

"Absurdity is a conclusion from the rational mind when it could not draw patterns or meanings from truly random events. Absurdity is, in fact, a way for human beings to accept things as they are and not try to attribute an attitude toward it. An absurd scene in a movie would be a scene that has no added value to the story, and it would never appear in a mainstream Hollywood movie, for example, except that of a famous director such as that of Quentin Tarantino."

"Absurdity can then be understood as something that is random, has no meaning and cannot be understood?"

"Yes. The fetish, or in a better word, the admiration for absurdity is in fact very close to the idea of respecting nature in Taoism. In fact, a large number of Japanese creative works have a certain level of absurdity to them. Japanese is one of the few nations in the world that adores absurdity as much as they adore science and reasons."

"You mentioned Taoism. Do you believe that Étourdir is representing ideas of Taoism?"

"Absolutely. Étourdir means to be stunned, to be surprised, to be left astonished. Nature's way, or Tao, is without form, without sound, without weight. It goes with the flow, yet something was achieved with it. This is the philosophy hidden in Étourdir."

"Fascinating."

Dr. Shinozaki nodded to his interviewer and said, "Very."

2. Christmas Dinner

Smith went to the kitchen of his Cincinnati home to fetch a glass of water for himself.

"What did you say he did?"

He heard Debra question her older brother in an accusing tone. "He told me about the girl some time ago, and I didn't connect the dots. I knew he would get into trouble by himself in Japan."

It has been a rather rough year. He decided it was best for him to return to his home country and spend a quiet Christmas with his family the traditional way. Of course, there was nothing traditional about it. His wife, ex-wife, actually, was missing. His children had grown customary to spending their Christmas either with their partners' side of the family or flying out of the state for holiday to avoid being confronted with time at home that would remind them of the bitter separation between their father and mother.

There was, of course, a way to get them together. Cheryl, his rather nosy but indispensable secretary who followed him all these years from America to Japan had told them of their father's brief brush with the law when she called them to invite them to Christmas dinner back at the Rose Hill residence, and the fact that she had reserved two grilled duck from a neighborhood butcher that needed to be picked up on Christmas Eve since her boss, the way she knew him, was very likely not to remember this kind of holiday triviality when left to his own accord.

"Madness! You can't be serious." He heard Debra's voice again, reacting to the story that Ethan was relating to her. Ethan had apparently tried to verify Cheryl's story himself, and with a few keystrokes, he found his father's rather embarrassing records of his lonely life in Japan everywhere on Google. *Damn these translating technologies*, Smith thought.

"You must say he looked rather dashing in the commercial," Ethan said. It made Smith chuckle. His son had a sense of humor that was definitely not from him.

Debra snorted at Ethan's joke. Baby Nathan, Smith's grandson, started to cry, perhaps unused to the dismissive vibe emitting from his usually loving mother. The conversation about Smith's Japanese adventure was thus paused temporarily. Smith thought it was time to come back out from hiding.

"Try this Japanese tea. They are wrapped in fancy diamond-shaped tea bags nowadays." He lifted four Sencha tea bags from the box in the shelf where he dumped all his supplies of Japanese souvenirs Cheryl purchased   for his family. Knowing that he would be the only one who would truly appreciate these Asian gourmet foods and drinks, he put the majority away for himself.

"No, thank you," Debra said curtly.   She had never been an adventurous one. Her husband was about to grab one of them but retracted his hand embarrassingly as soon as he heard his wife's rejection of the offer.

"Why not?" Ethan took one and offered another to his wife, who wrinkled her nose as usual towards anything he ever offered to her as if she thought her in-law was out to get her with spoiled, if not poisonous food items.

Smith wanted to test a theory, so he asked further, "How about a couple of those Mochi candies." He pointed at the opened box on the coffee table.

"I'm on a diet," Debra said curtly. "We all are." She corrected herself to indicate that no one from her family was going to eat or drink anything strange his father brought over from Japan. Exotic items from foreign countries were generally appreciated, except when they were from your tasteless, aging father who could do nothing right anymore, Smith ruminated about that thought with familiarity. He used to think that about his own father as well.

"Those things kill a couple of Japanese every year I heard," Ethan said. "They can stick to your throat and make you choke if you're not careful." He had a strange interest in Japanese news. *At least he is interested*, Smith thought.

"All the more reason to skip it," Debra said.

"You should be careful, Grandpa!" May, his oldest granddaughter cautioned, taking after her mother's cautiousness for food from strange origins.

Everybody in the room laughed.

3. New Year's Fireworks

The loud bang of fireworks filled her ears. Misa raised her hands to cover her ears.

"It's beautiful, isn't it?" Kyoko, a girl who lived at the InterHRLA dormitory with Misa, came over from the steps behind her and said.

Misa, deep in thought in her own world, stared blankly at the showering golden sparkles that fluttered in the cold wind, disappearing into the night, and coming back to life again in a light pink frenzy. Another one of the same kind was shot to the sky, lighting up the skyline of Tokyo Bay.

Her thoughts were with her brother, Tatsu. She wondered if he could see or hear the New Year fireworks from his jail cell. How she missed him. If it were not for her, he would never have moved to Tokyo from the countryside. He would still be studying high school, hanging out with friends on New Year's Eve, having fun like any normal youth his age, instead of spending tonight, and the next nine months in the Tokyo Juvenile Correction Center.

Everybody had told her he was lucky to get just nine months.

What nonsense.

A day would be too long. She should never have convinced him to come to Tokyo with her. A tear beaded up in her eye, threatening to fall off the edge of her lower eyelid.

"*Kore, douzo*. Have one!" Kyoko offered her a *Ringoame*, caramel apple on a stick. Misa took one and unwrapped it mindlessly. The kind girl understood her body language. She did not want to talk. That was fine by her. A lot of girls who were living in the InterHRLA dormitory had lived a tough life before arriving here. Eccentricity among some of the girls could be expected. Kyoko bit into her apple candy and moved away to talk to the other girls.

"I don't need any friends," Misa said to herself. Despite what she believed, she did need friends.

When Misa was fifteen, she was transposed by circumstance to Tokyo from Chitose, a small village in Central Hokkaido by the famous lake. Misa didn't have many friends in Tokyo. Most of her friends from childhood had never ventured as far into the country as she did.

That was the only reason why Misa had no choice but to go to Aileen for help about her housing situation. Aileen was the senior legal adviser of InterHRLA, an acquaintance of Smith. Being an active case at the InterHRLA, Misa was quickly given a spot at the temporary dormitory for girls and women in difficult times of their lives.

After Tatsu had been sentenced to the Juvenile Correction Center, Misa found their apartment unlivable. Being alone was not a problem for her, especially because she worked so much, at almost all hours of the day and was barely home. There had been, however, several incidences since that worried her.

At the oddest hours, she would receive phone calls, and when she picked up, the other end was dead silent. After a few times, she simply disconnected her landline from the wall connector.

Then there had been noises of people conversing right outside of her front door, and their voices lingered long after it was usual as if they were waiting to catch her as soon as she would step out. In those instances, she would hide under the thick duvet comforter and curl up inside the huge sliding wardrobe where the bedding was usually stored and waited until the noises died away.

One evening when she was at work, her apartment had been broken into. She lived in a part of the neighborhood where its residents did not want to attract attention to themselves, and therefore even when her front door was busted opened and stayed ajar for several hours of that day, no one had found it important enough to contact her nor the police.

As unpleasant as it was, the break-in provided important clues as to the reasons behind all the disturbance, though, because while her place had been ransacked, nothing valuable was missing. Misa immediately understood the burglar or the burglars were searching for information. They were searching for her diary, or what was in effect the transaction log with all her clients. The who, what, when, where. Everything from the beginning of last year was recorded in it, its content mostly in shorthand to avoid scrutiny in case someone accidentally read it. This precaution had saved her from being indicted for the crime of *fuzoku,* even the terrifying detective Miyazaki, who was not able to get a word out of her, had to let her go, and returned the diary to her together with other items they took with them when they raided the house previously.

But now the word was out on her. Being a one-time adult movie star, the public had made up their minds about her relationship with Carson Smith even when the police couldn't convict her based on the lack of evidence. The media and the forums were referring to her as an escort at best and a prostitute at worst, and there were wild speculations of who her other clients would be. Given the high social status of Carson Smith, everyone assumed that there must be some more big names to be associated with her, and Misa knew full well they were not wrong.

And the witch hunt began.

Every one of those names inside her diary could be looking for it because even when the nature of their appointments was masked in the facade of language lessons, just being on that book alone was enough to make their public images nosedive. *Face* was an important thing in Japanese society, unlike in the West, where men of importance could navigate shamelessly from one scandal to the next and still managed to stay in office.

But they wouldn't find the diary anywhere in her apartment. She was smarter than that. She had it hidden in a place nobody would look.

Find Vann Chow on Social Media

Thank you for reading Book I, The Pachinko Girl of the Tokyo Faces series and the preview for Book II, The Kiss of the Pachinko Girl. You may find a copy of Book II on Amazon.

Do share with Vann your thoughts about The Pachinko Girl via the social media, and last but not least, the author would appreciate it very much if you can write a review for the book on its Amazon page to help others discover it.

33567088R00205

Made in the USA
San Bernardino, CA
24 April 2019